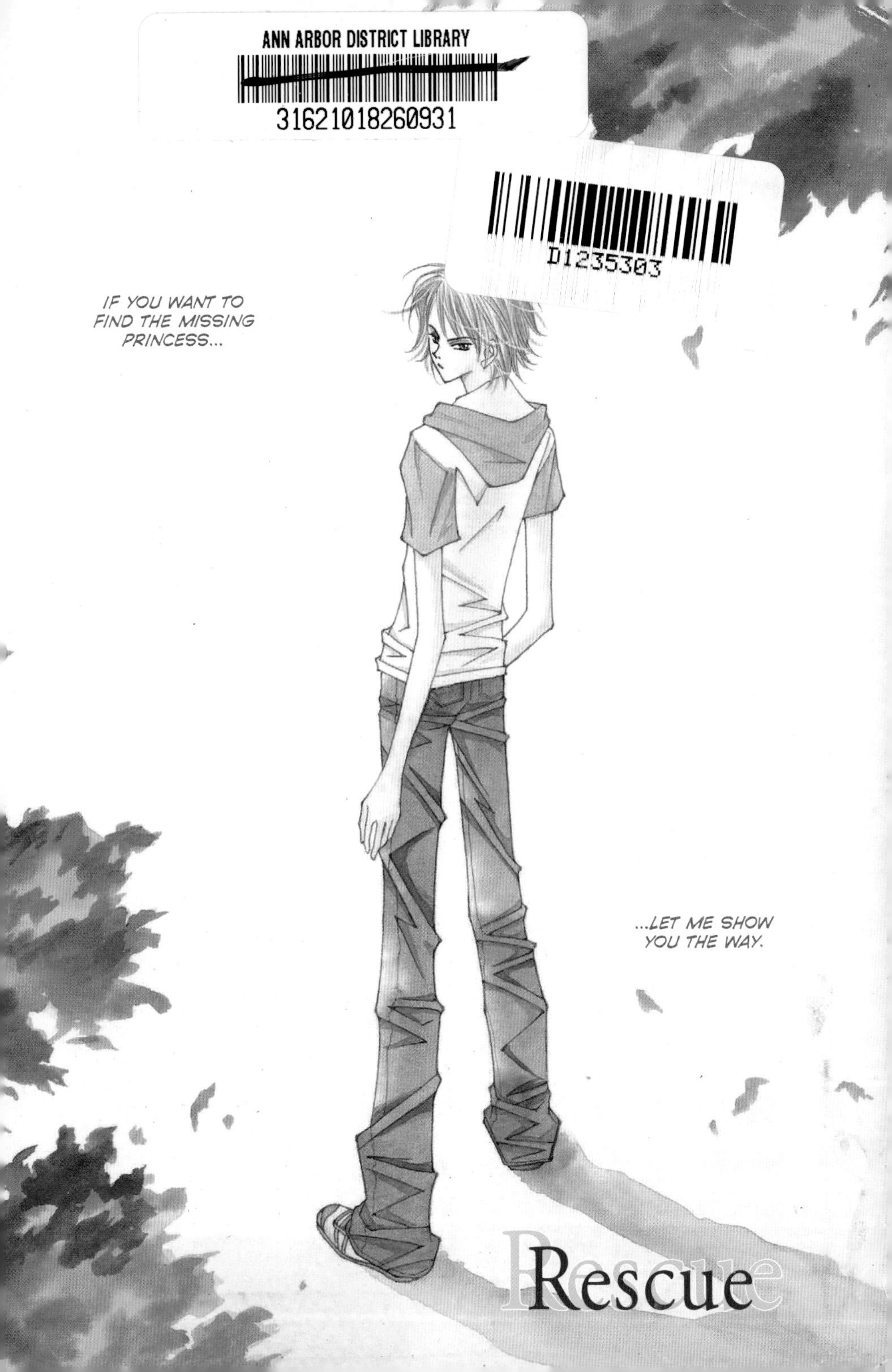
IF YOU WANT TO FIND THE MISSING PRINCESS...
...LET ME SHOW YOU THE WAY.
Rescue

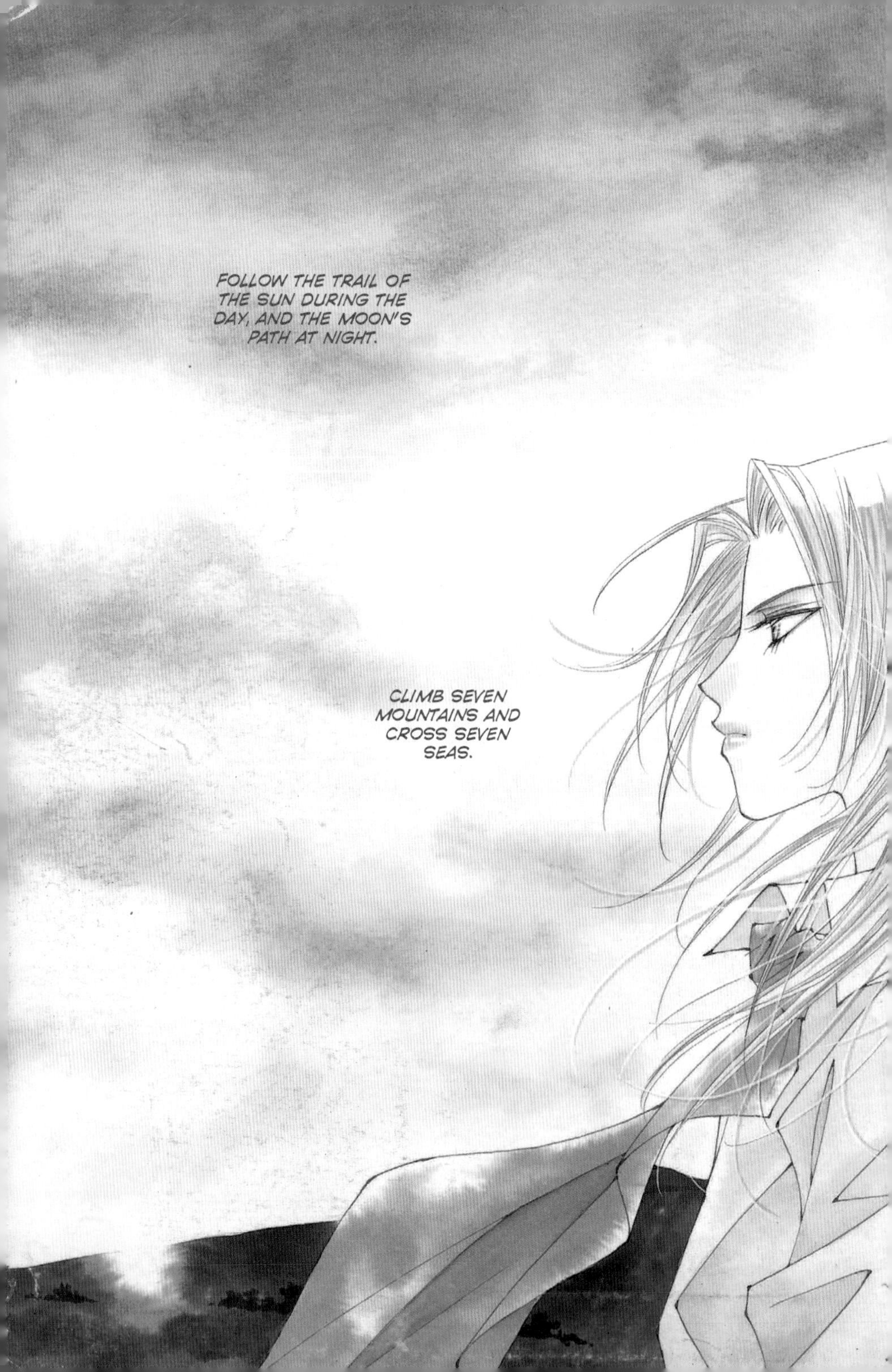

FOLLOW THE TRAIL OF THE SUN DURING THE DAY, AND THE MOON'S PATH AT NIGHT.
CLIMB SEVEN MOUNTAINS AND CROSS SEVEN SEAS.

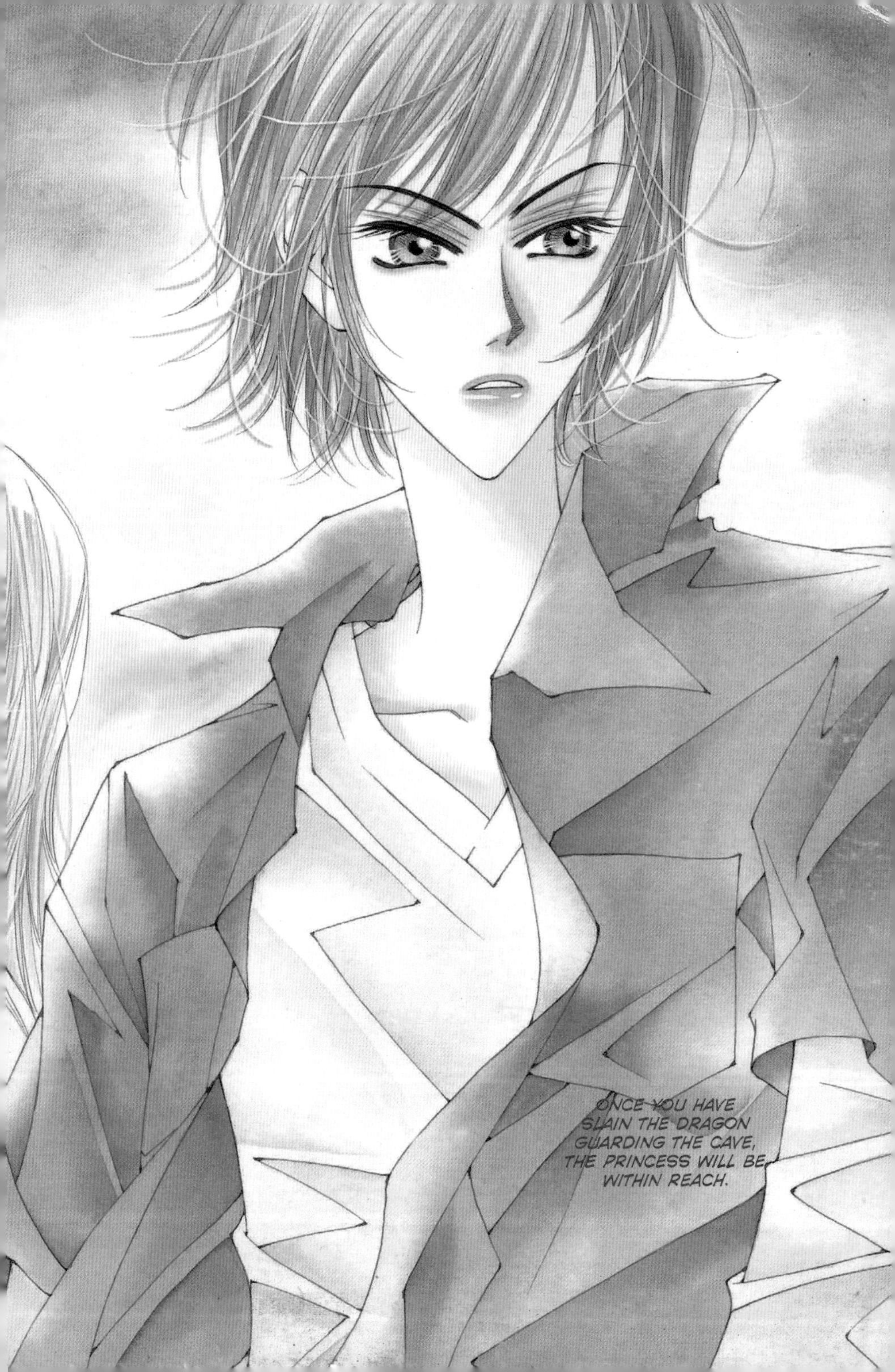
ONCE YOU HAVE SLAIN THE DRAGON GUARDING THE CAVE, THE PRINCESS WILL BE WITHIN REACH.

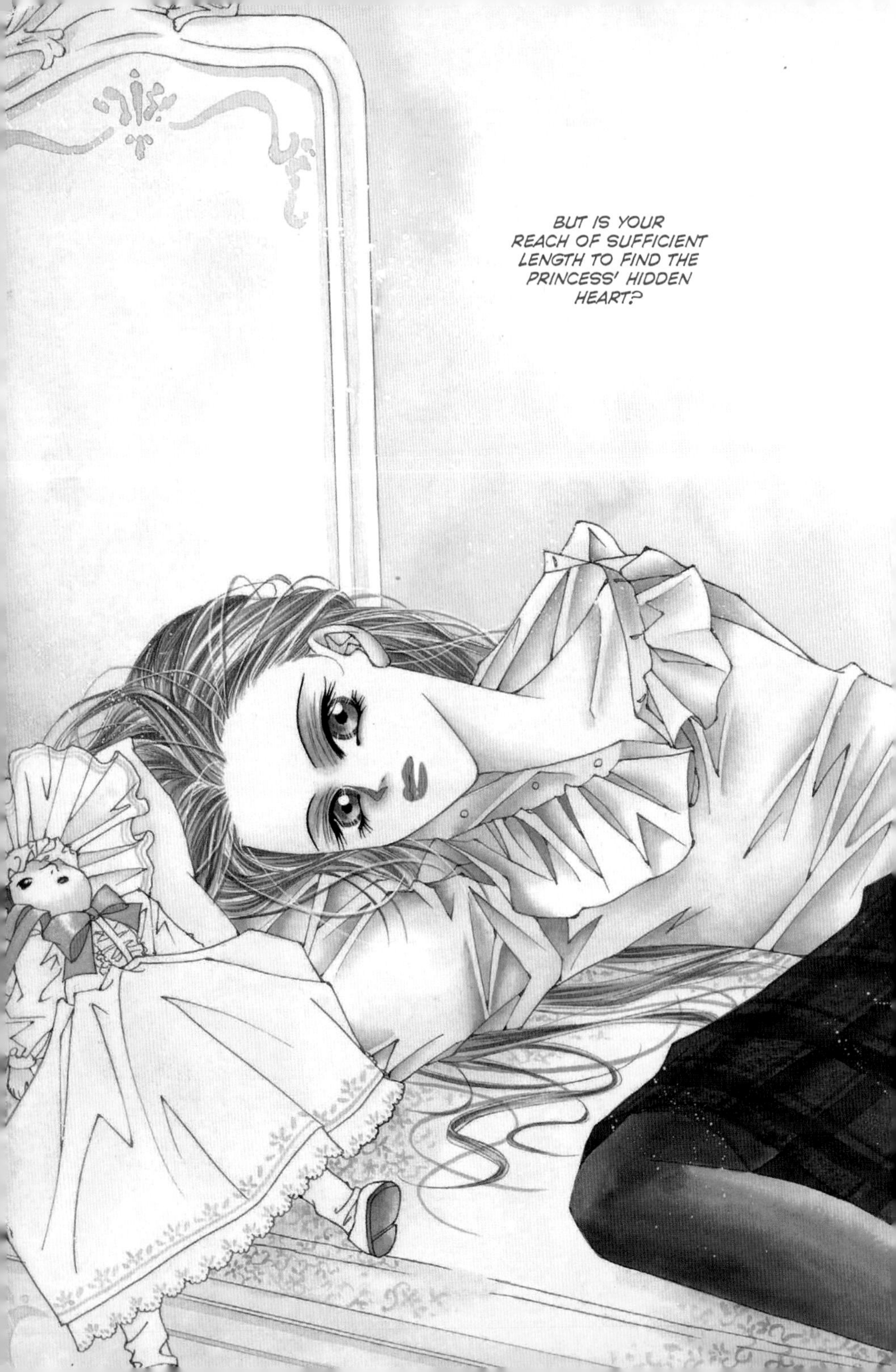
BUT IS YOUR REACH OF SUFFICIENT LENGTH TO FIND THE PRINCESS' HIDDEN HEART?

ginal · Danbi Original · Danbi Original · Danbi Original · Danbi Original · Danbi Original ·

Cynical Orange

vol.2

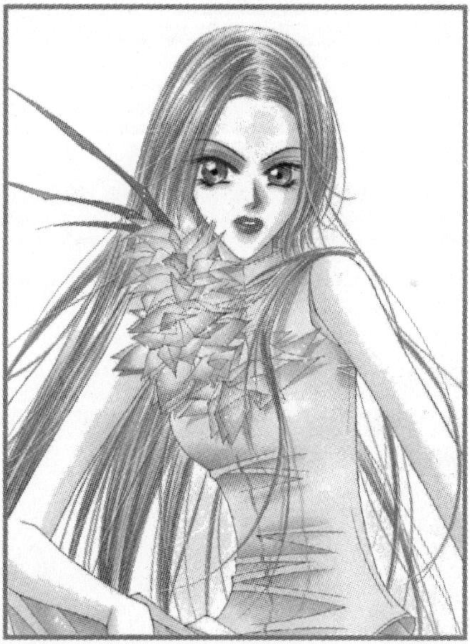

Yun JiUn

ice Kunion

About the Creator

Cynical Orange

Ji-Un Yun

Ji-Un Yun made her professional debut in 2000 by placing second in a Manhwa competition with her short story <Are you? I am!>. However, she was already famous among the amateur Manhwa clubs in Korea for her delicate drawings, unique heroines, and distinctive plots. Her special style of combining artistic creativity with beautiful composition has led to an enormous fan base in Asia.

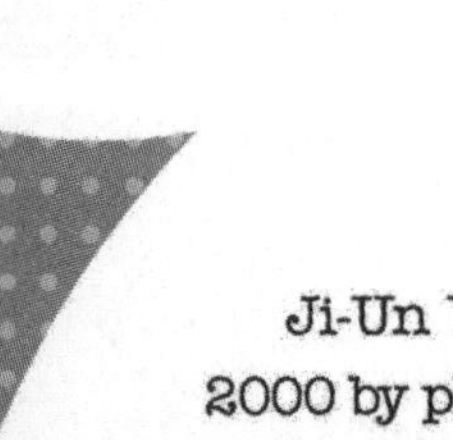

Other major works
<Are you? I am!>, <The Doll's Request>, <Happy End>, <Hush>, <Excel>

Words from the Creator

My mother bought me lots of story
books when I was little. Sometimes my
friends are shocked by all the strange and
obscure tales I seem to know (As you know,
children's stories are usually very bizarre...). The
strangest story I've ever read is Lewis Carroll's <Alice in
Wonderland>, and my favorite story of all time is Hoffman's
<Nutcracker>. Among the novels I read in my teens,
Bronte's <Wuthering Heights> stands out as the most
memorable and touching. These books shaped and defined
my mental and emotional world, they are my own
Zaubergarten--my secret, magical garden...

Don't ask me how those wonderful stories merged
together to form such a pathetic brain pattern
as mine, though. That's a mystery.

- Ji-Un Yun

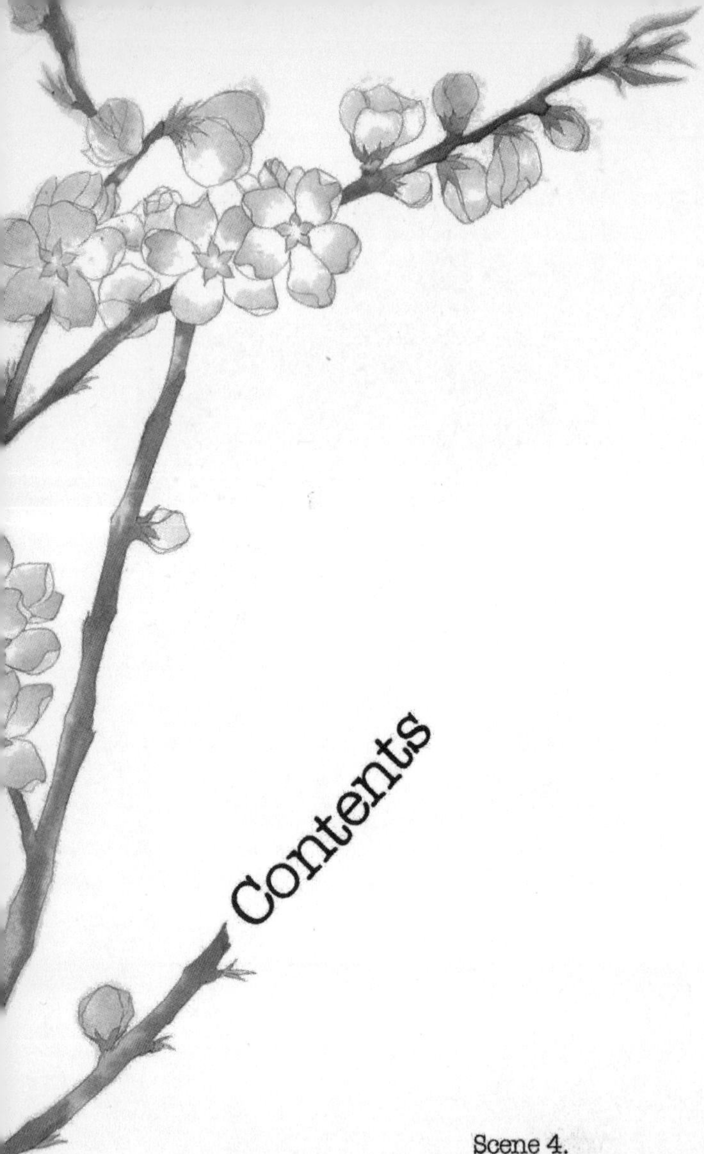

Contents

DEALING WITH PEOPLE CAN REALLY TIRE A PERSON OUT.

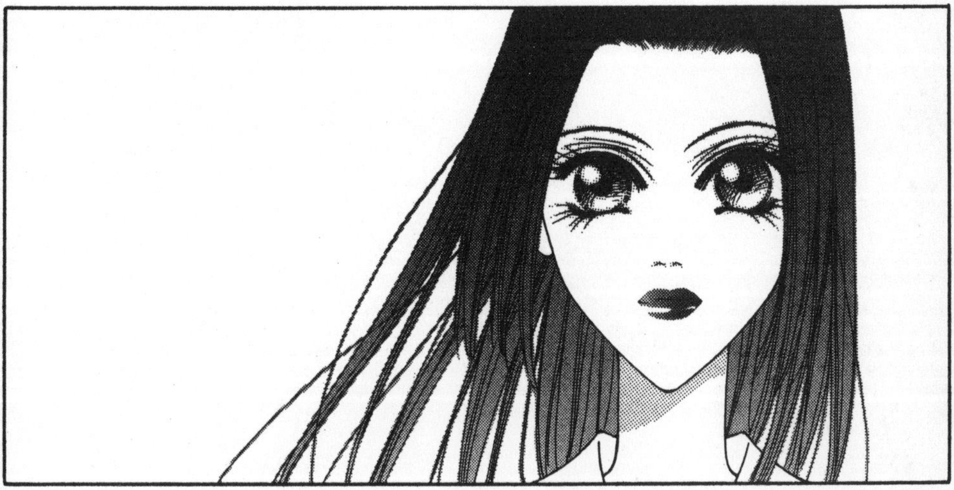

ESPECIALLY WHEN YOU HAVE NO DESIRE TO FORGE A REAL RELATIONSHIP WITH ANYONE.

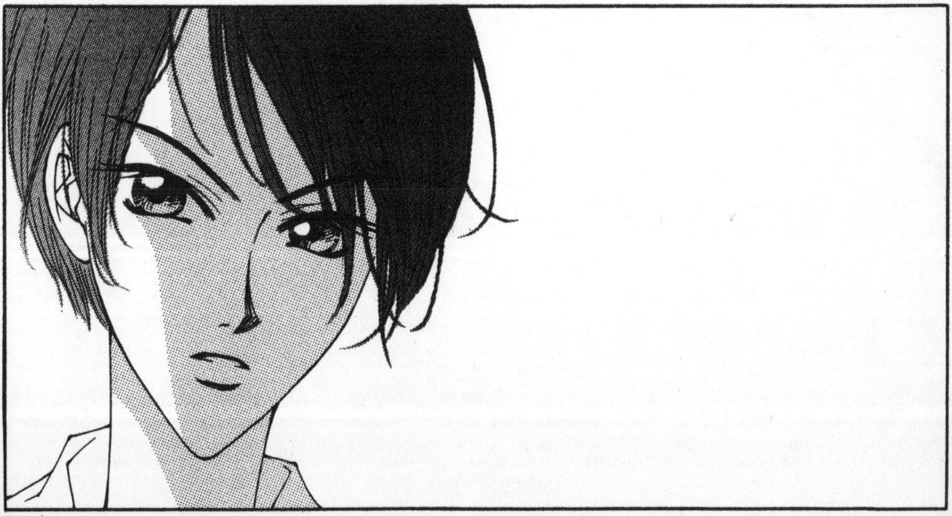

NOT EVEN
WITH...

Scene. 4
Kindly Curses and A
Wandering Heart

...JUNG-YUN.

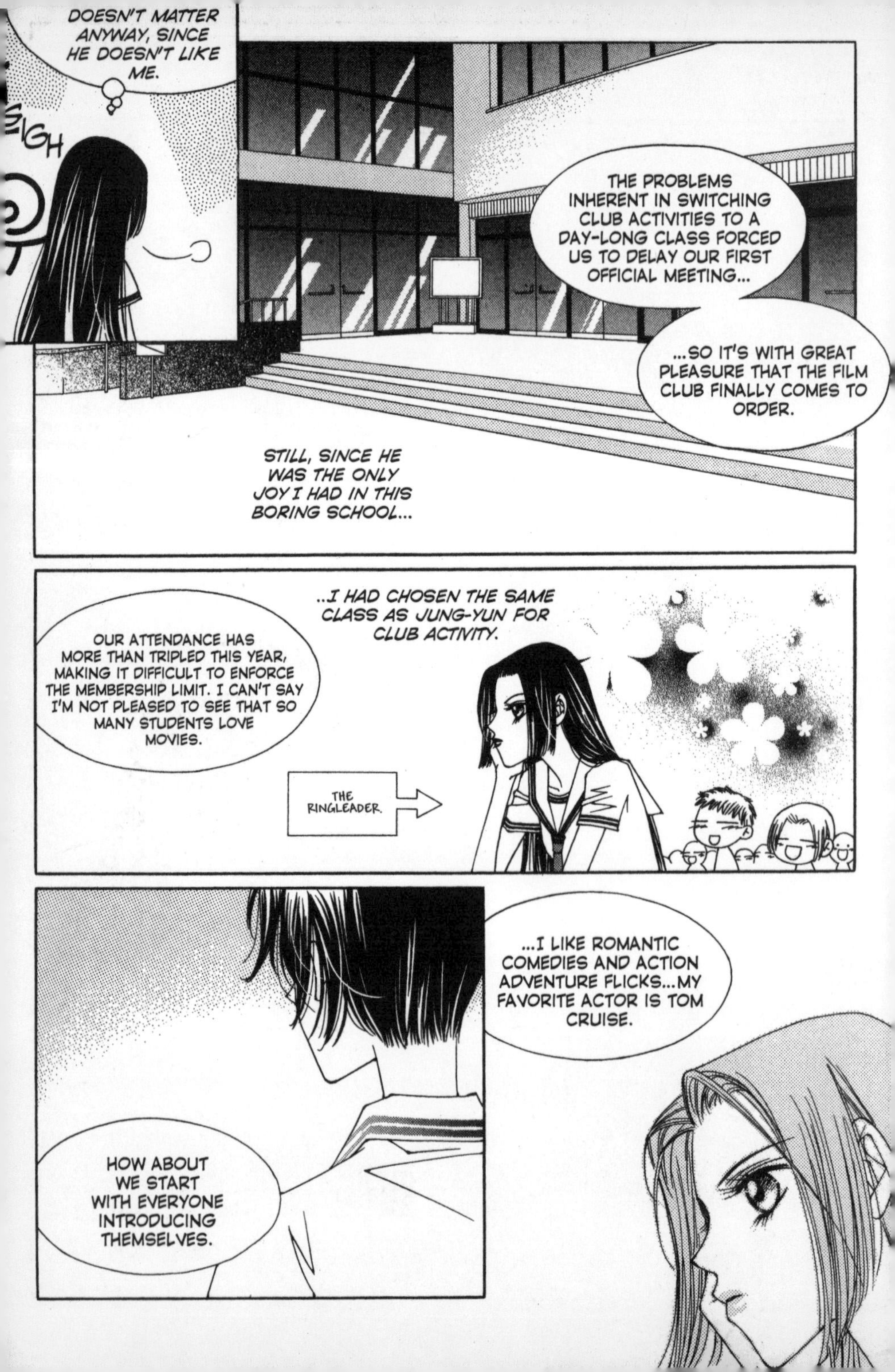
DOESN'T MATTER ANYWAY, SINCE HE DOESN'T LIKE ME.
SIGH
THE PROBLEMS INHERENT IN SWITCHING CLUB ACTIVITIES TO A DAY-LONG CLASS FORCED US TO DELAY OUR FIRST OFFICIAL MEETING...
...SO IT'S WITH GREAT PLEASURE THAT THE FILM CLUB FINALLY COMES TO ORDER.
STILL, SINCE HE WAS THE ONLY JOY I HAD IN THIS BORING SCHOOL...
OUR ATTENDANCE HAS MORE THAN TRIPLED THIS YEAR, MAKING IT DIFFICULT TO ENFORCE THE MEMBERSHIP LIMIT. I CAN'T SAY I'M NOT PLEASED TO SEE THAT SO MANY STUDENTS LOVE MOVIES.
...I HAD CHOSEN THE SAME CLASS AS JUNG-YUN FOR CLUB ACTIVITY.
THE RINGLEADER.
HOW ABOUT WE START WITH EVERYONE INTRODUCING THEMSELVES.
...I LIKE ROMANTIC COMEDIES AND ACTION ADVENTURE FLICKS...MY FAVORITE ACTOR IS TOM CRUISE.

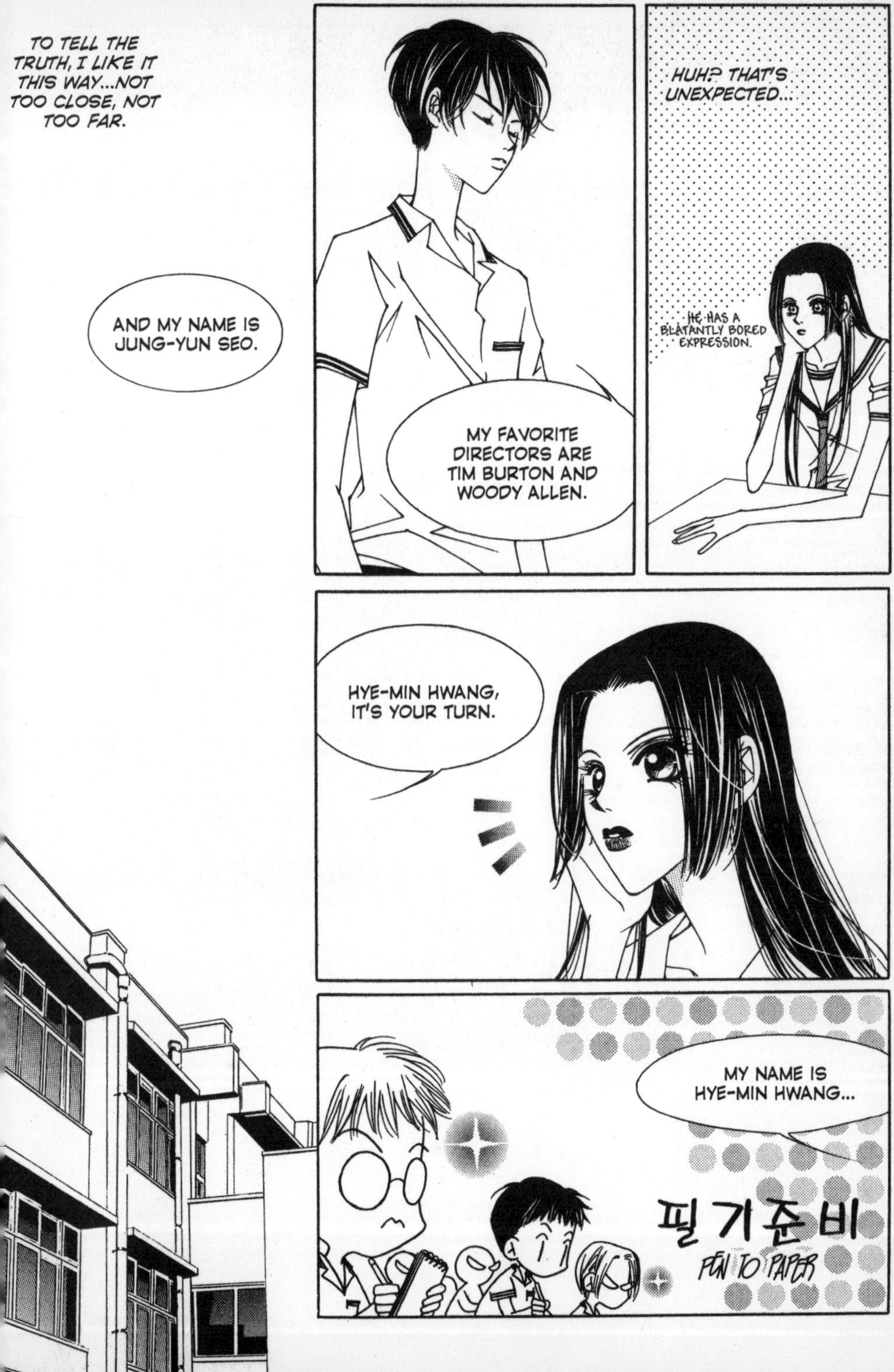
TO TELL THE TRUTH, I LIKE IT THIS WAY...NOT TOO CLOSE, NOT TOO FAR.
AND MY NAME IS JUNG-YUN SEO.
MY FAVORITE DIRECTORS ARE TIM BURTON AND WOODY ALLEN.
HUH? THAT'S UNEXPECTED...
HE HAS A BLATANTLY BORED EXPRESSION.
HYE-MIN HWANG, IT'S YOUR TURN.
MY NAME IS HYE-MIN HWANG...
필기준비
PEN TO PAPER

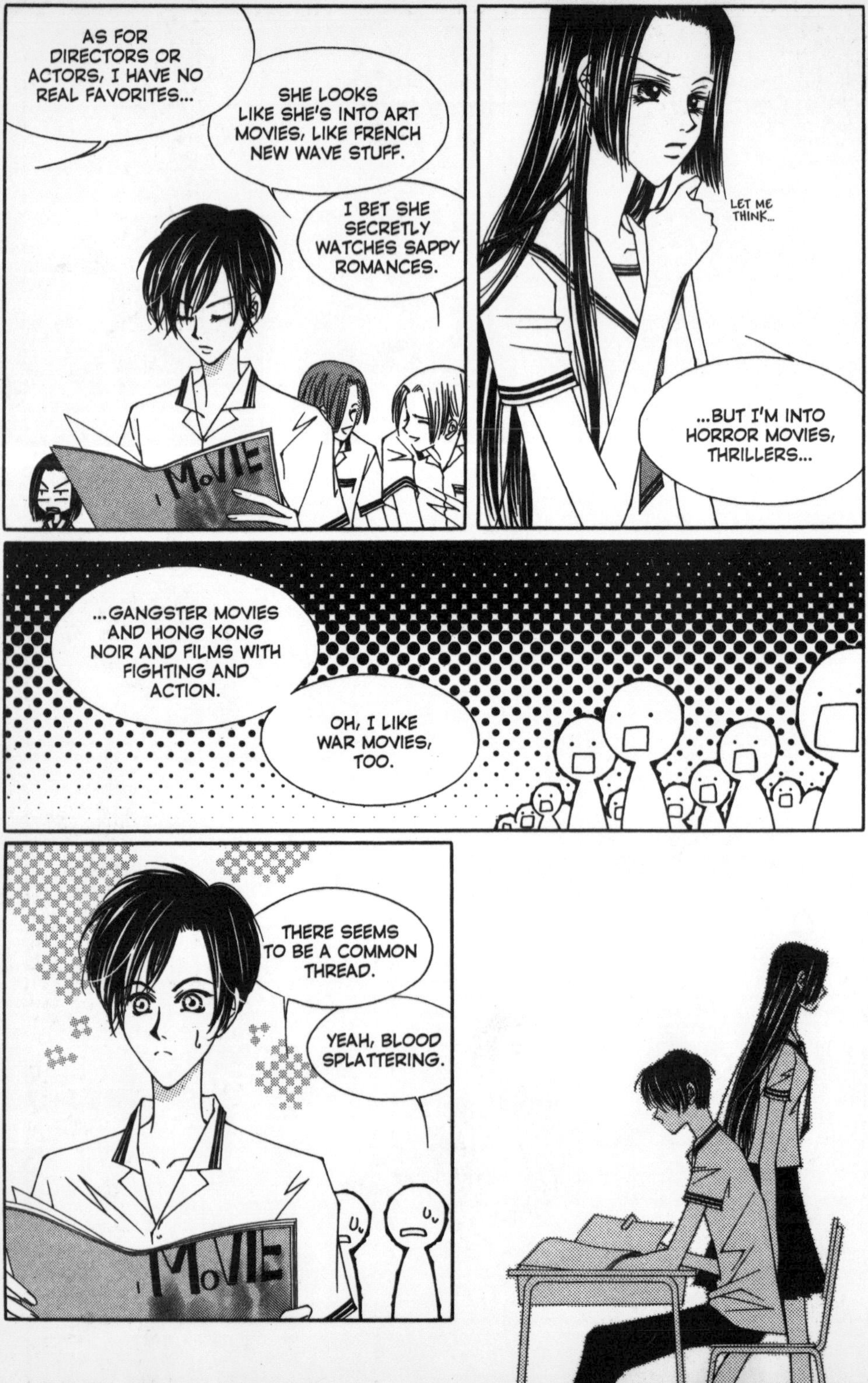
AS FOR DIRECTORS OR ACTORS, I HAVE NO REAL FAVORITES...
SHE LOOKS LIKE SHE'S INTO ART MOVIES, LIKE FRENCH NEW WAVE STUFF.
I BET SHE SECRETLY WATCHES SAPPY ROMANCES.
MOVIE
LET ME THINK...
...BUT I'M INTO HORROR MOVIES, THRILLERS...
...GANGSTER MOVIES AND HONG KONG NOIR AND FILMS WITH FIGHTING AND ACTION.
OH, I LIKE WAR MOVIES, TOO.
THERE SEEMS TO BE A COMMON THREAD.
YEAH, BLOOD SPLATTERING.
MOVIE

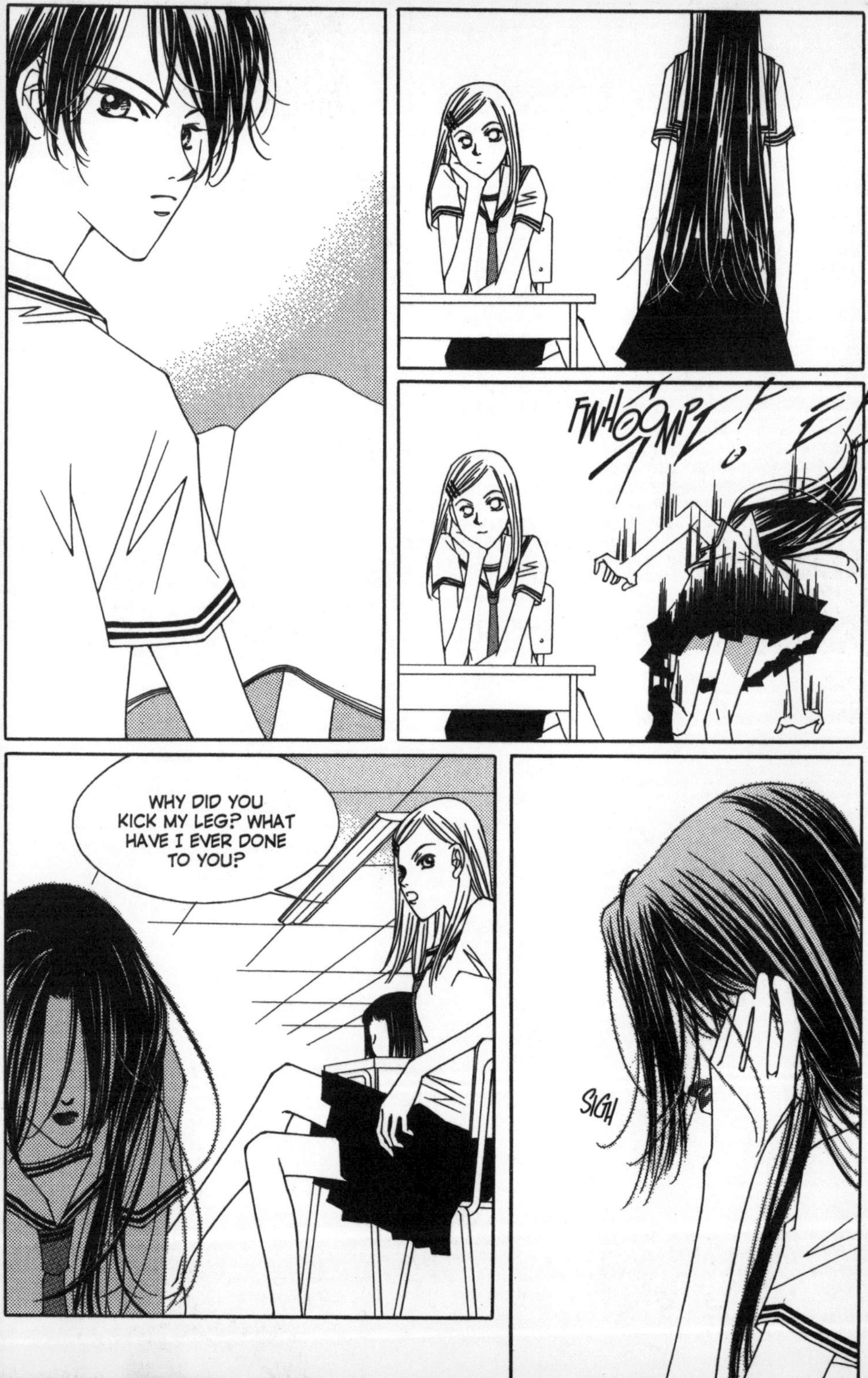
FWHOOMP
WHY DID YOU KICK MY LEG? WHAT HAVE I EVER DONE TO YOU?
SIGH

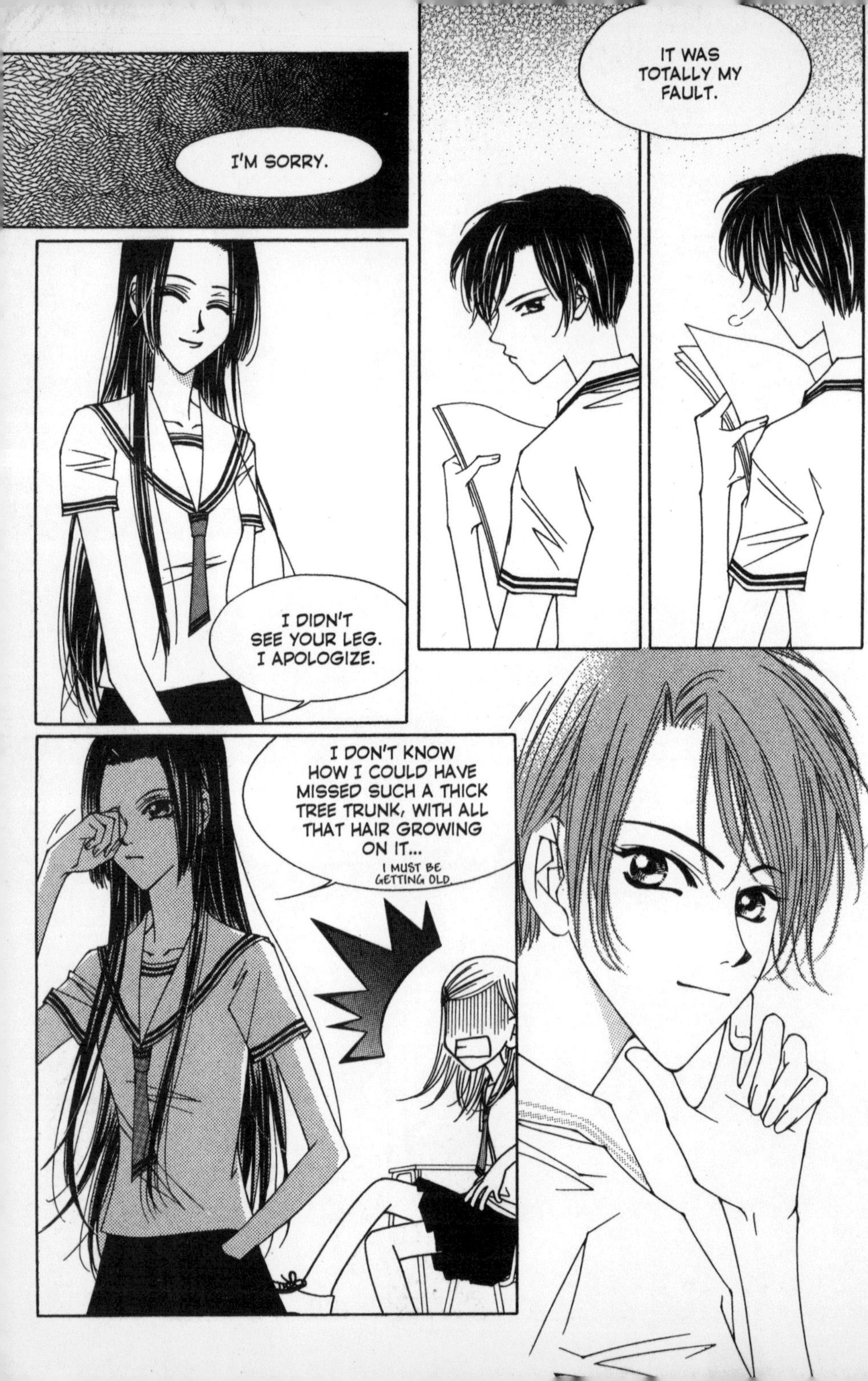
I'M SORRY.
I DIDN'T SEE YOUR LEG. I APOLOGIZE.
IT WAS TOTALLY MY FAULT.
I DON'T KNOW HOW I COULD HAVE MISSED SUCH A THICK TREE TRUNK, WITH ALL THAT HAIR GROWING ON IT...
I MUST BE GETTING OLD.

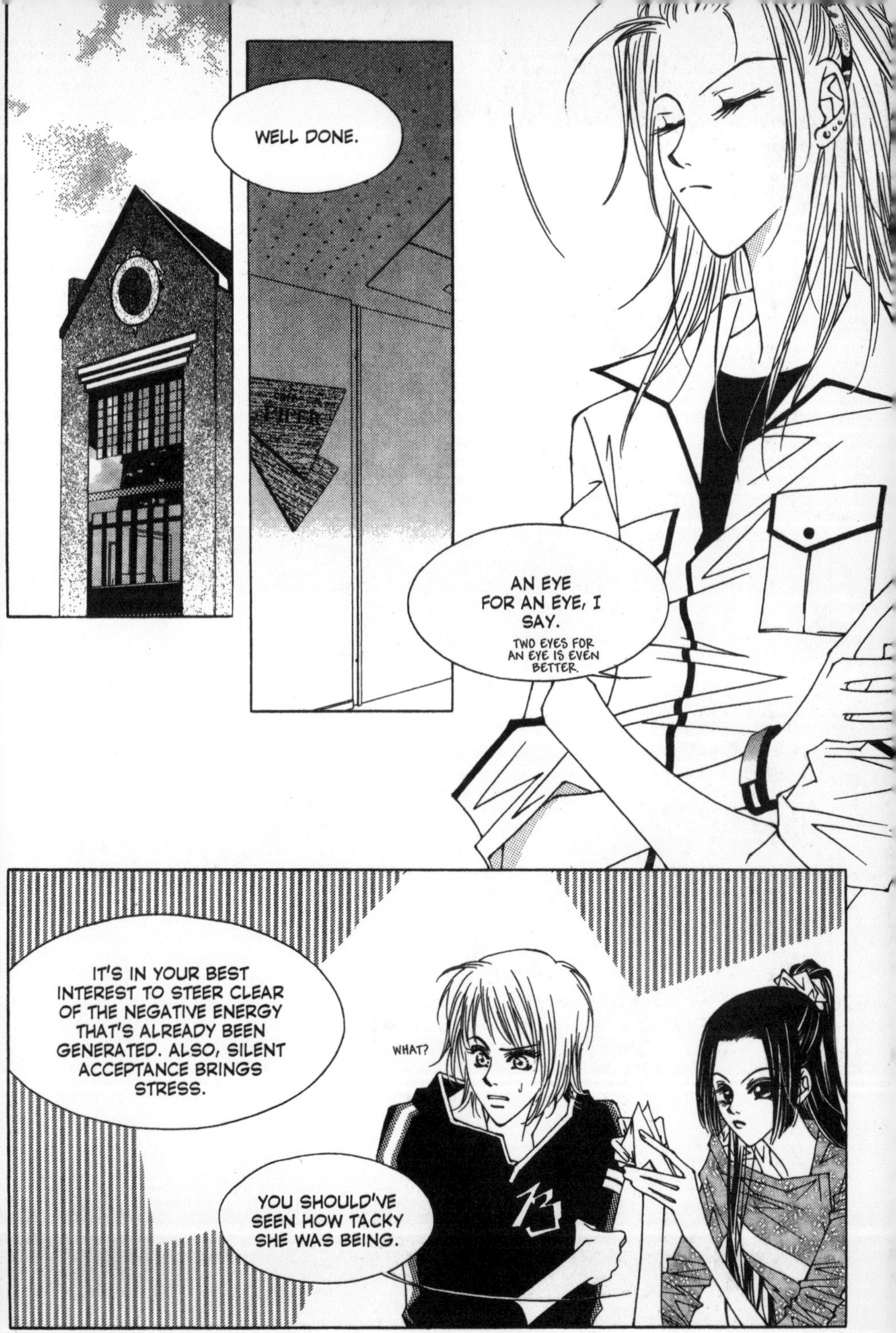
WELL DONE.
PIPER
AN EYE FOR AN EYE, I SAY.
TWO EYES FOR AN EYE IS EVEN BETTER.
IT'S IN YOUR BEST INTEREST TO STEER CLEAR OF THE NEGATIVE ENERGY THAT'S ALREADY BEEN GENERATED. ALSO, SILENT ACCEPTANCE BRINGS STRESS.
WHAT?
YOU SHOULD'VE SEEN HOW TACKY SHE WAS BEING.

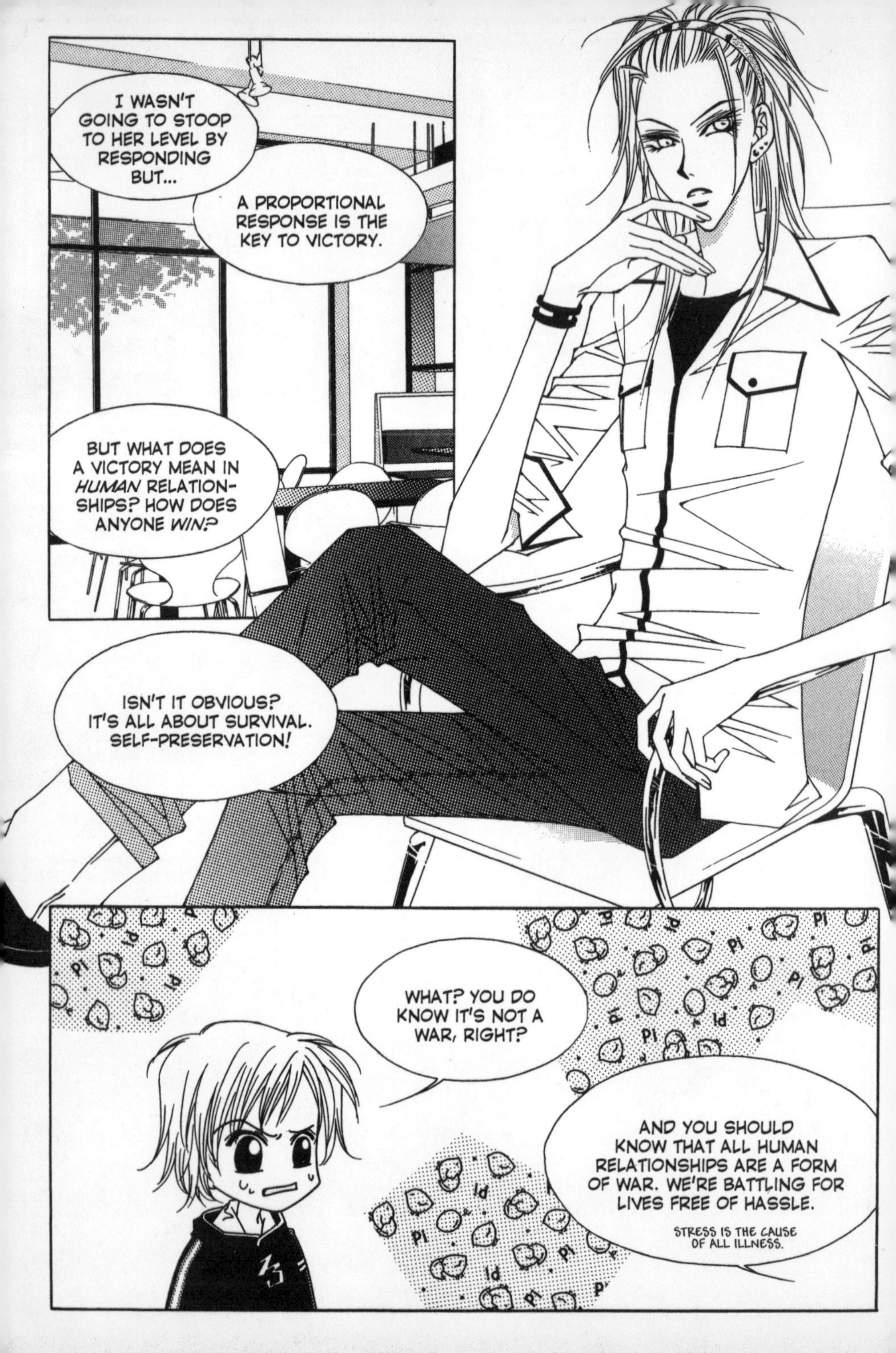
I WASN'T GOING TO STOOP TO HER LEVEL BY RESPONDING BUT...
A PROPORTIONAL RESPONSE IS THE KEY TO VICTORY.
BUT WHAT DOES A VICTORY MEAN IN *HUMAN* RELATION-SHIPS? HOW DOES ANYONE *WIN*?
ISN'T IT OBVIOUS? IT'S ALL ABOUT SURVIVAL. SELF-PRESERVATION!
WHAT? YOU DO KNOW IT'S NOT A WAR, RIGHT?
AND YOU SHOULD KNOW THAT ALL HUMAN RELATIONSHIPS ARE A FORM OF WAR. WE'RE BATTLING FOR LIVES FREE OF HASSLE.
STRESS IS THE CAUSE OF ALL ILLNESS.

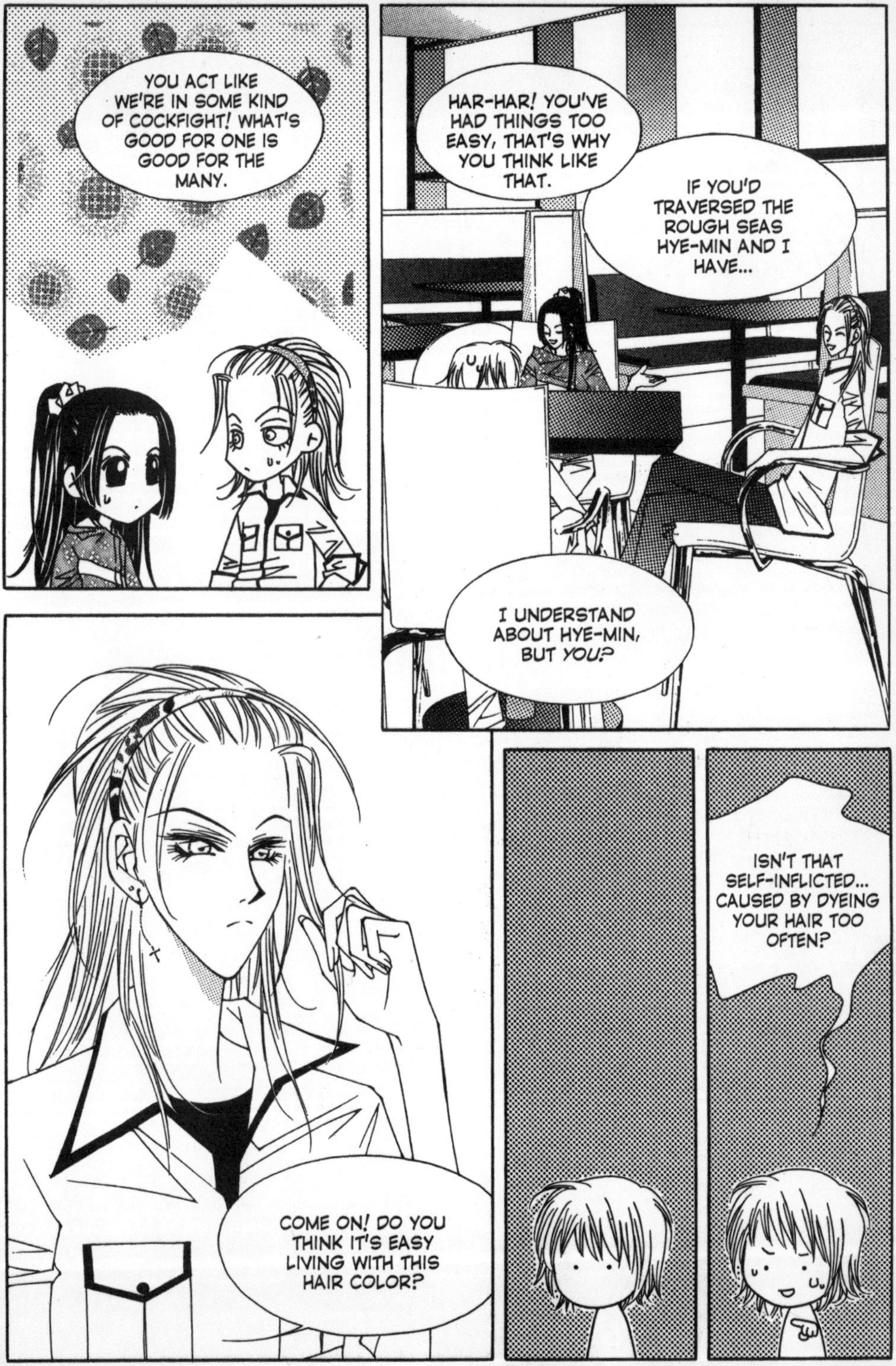
YOU ACT LIKE WE'RE IN SOME KIND OF COCKFIGHT! WHAT'S GOOD FOR ONE IS GOOD FOR THE MANY.
HAR-HAR! YOU'VE HAD THINGS TOO EASY, THAT'S WHY YOU THINK LIKE THAT.
IF YOU'D TRAVERSED THE ROUGH SEAS HYE-MIN AND I HAVE...
I UNDERSTAND ABOUT HYE-MIN, BUT *YOU?*
COME ON! DO YOU THINK IT'S EASY LIVING WITH THIS HAIR COLOR?
ISN'T THAT SELF-INFLICTED... CAUSED BY DYEING YOUR HAIR TOO OFTEN?

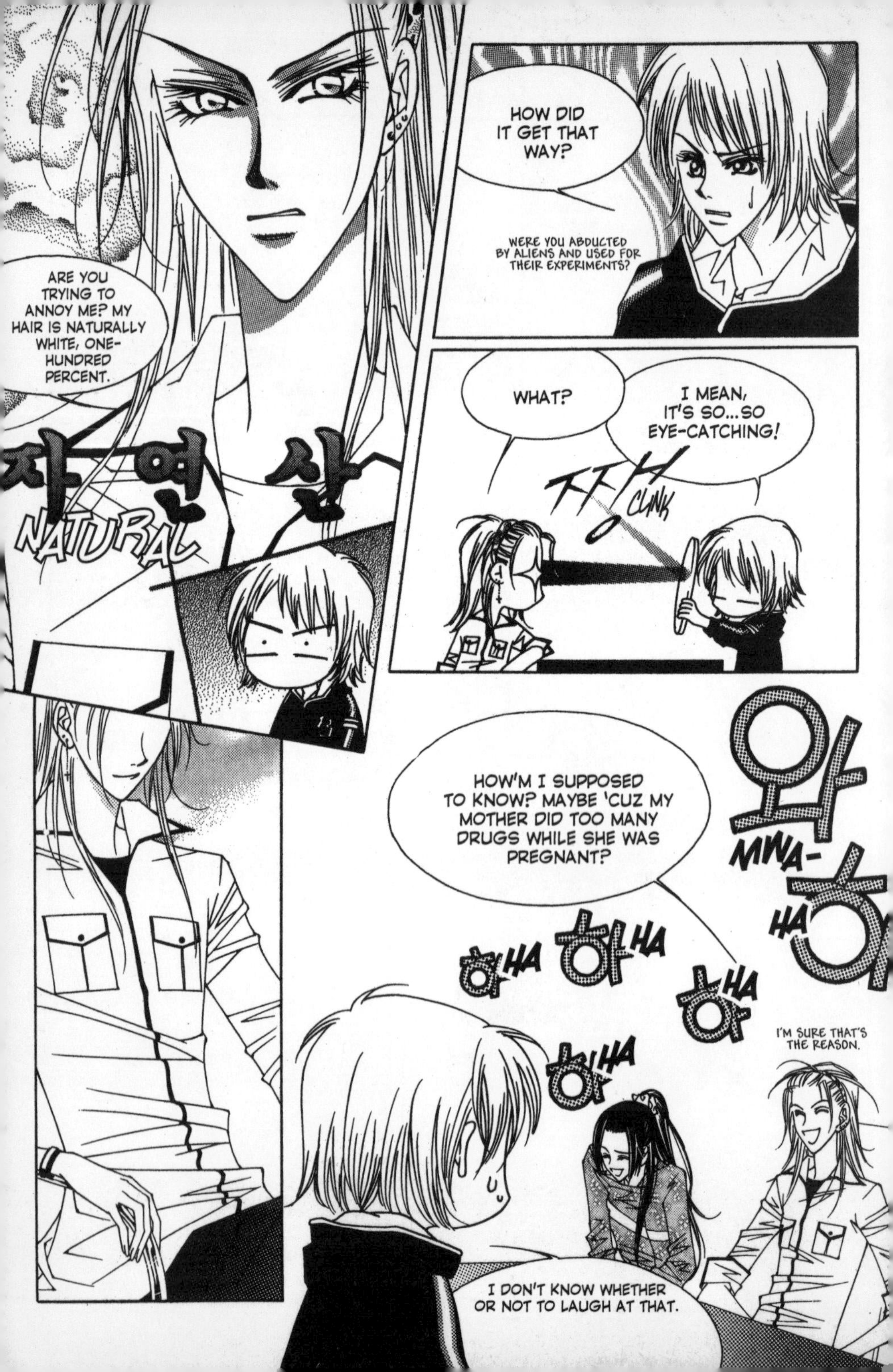
ARE YOU TRYING TO ANNOY ME? MY HAIR IS NATURALLY WHITE, ONE-HUNDRED PERCENT.
자연산
NATURAL
HOW DID IT GET THAT WAY?
WERE YOU ABDUCTED BY ALIENS AND USED FOR THEIR EXPERIMENTS?
WHAT?
I MEAN, IT'S SO...SO EYE-CATCHING!
CLINK
HOW'M I SUPPOSED TO KNOW? MAYBE 'CUZ MY MOTHER DID TOO MANY DRUGS WHILE SHE WAS PREGNANT?
와 MWA-
하 HA
하 HA
하 HA
하 HA
하 HA
I'M SURE THAT'S THE REASON.
I DON'T KNOW WHETHER OR NOT TO LAUGH AT THAT.

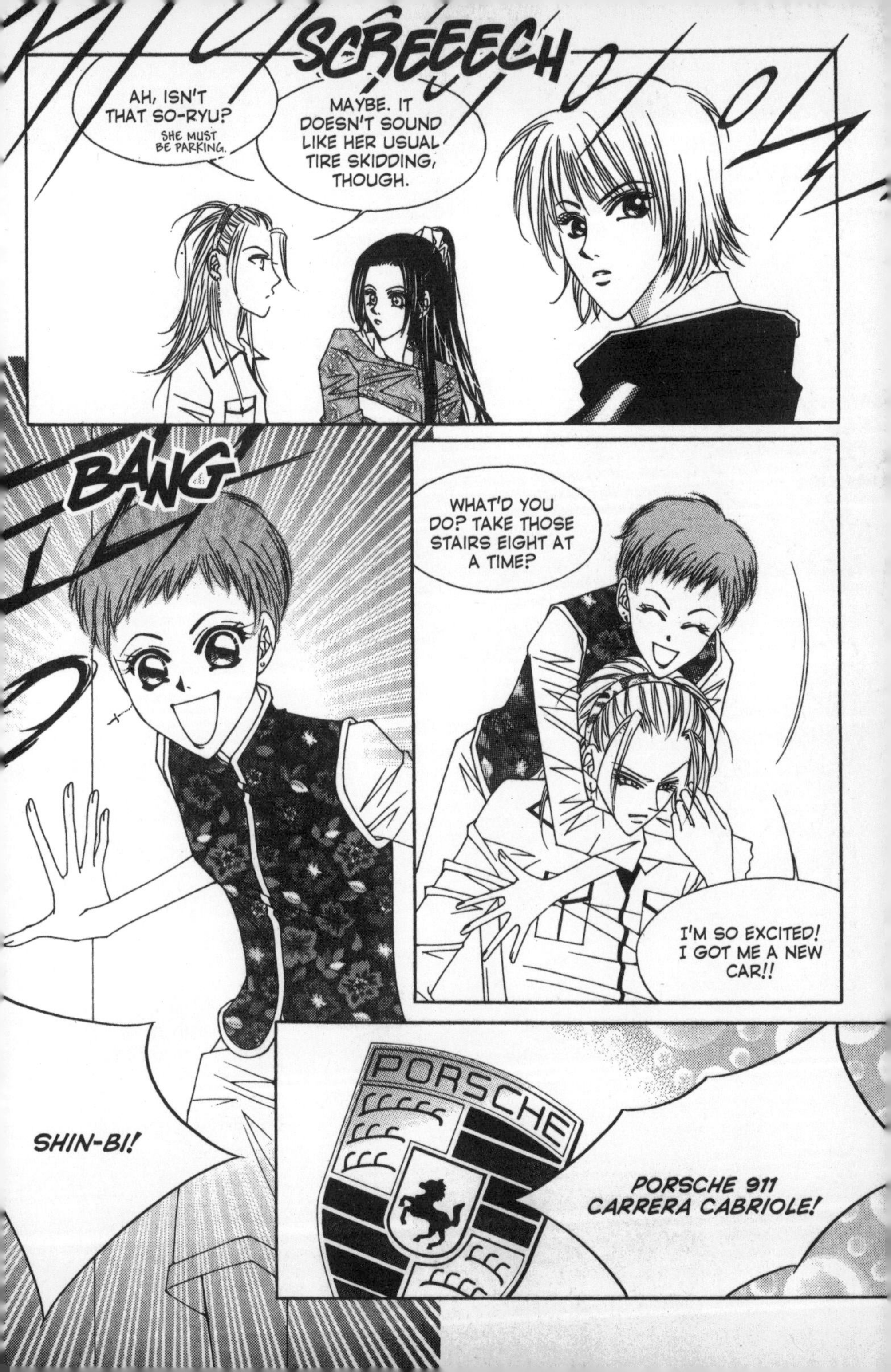
SCREEECH
AH, ISN'T THAT SO-RYU?
SHE MUST BE PARKING.
MAYBE. IT DOESN'T SOUND LIKE HER USUAL TIRE SKIDDING, THOUGH.
BANG
SHIN-BI!
WHAT'D YOU DO? TAKE THOSE STAIRS EIGHT AT A TIME?
I'M SO EXCITED! I GOT ME A NEW CAR!!
PORSCHE
PORSCHE 911 CARRERA CABRIOLE!

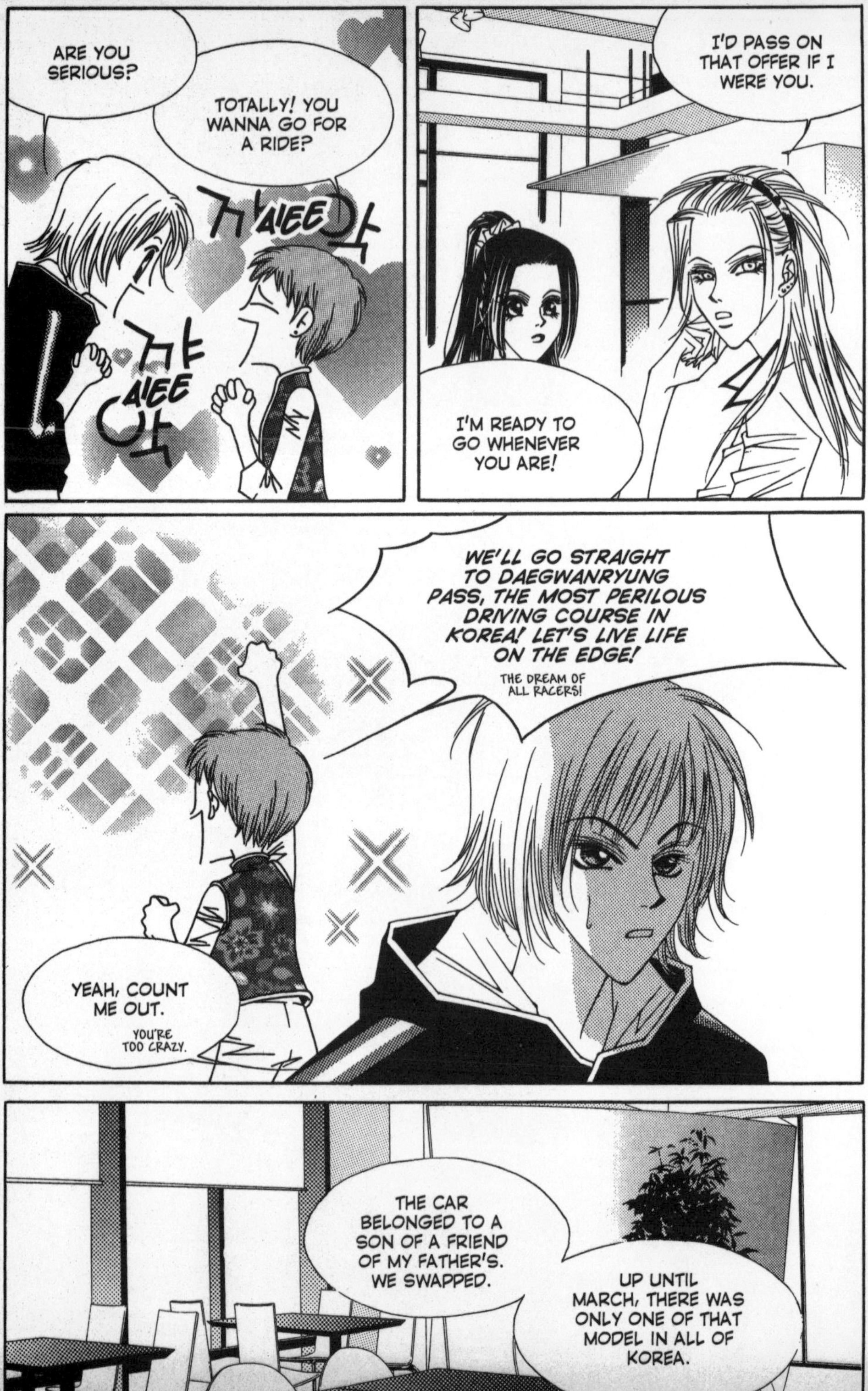
ARE YOU SERIOUS?
TOTALLY! YOU WANNA GO FOR A RIDE?
AIEE
AIEE
I'D PASS ON THAT OFFER IF I WERE YOU.
I'M READY TO GO WHENEVER YOU ARE!
WE'LL GO STRAIGHT TO DAEGWANRYUNG PASS, THE MOST PERILOUS DRIVING COURSE IN KOREA! LET'S LIVE LIFE ON THE EDGE!
THE DREAM OF ALL RACERS!
YEAH, COUNT ME OUT.
YOU'RE TOO CRAZY.
THE CAR BELONGED TO A SON OF A FRIEND OF MY FATHER'S. WE SWAPPED.
UP UNTIL MARCH, THERE WAS ONLY ONE OF THAT MODEL IN ALL OF KOREA.

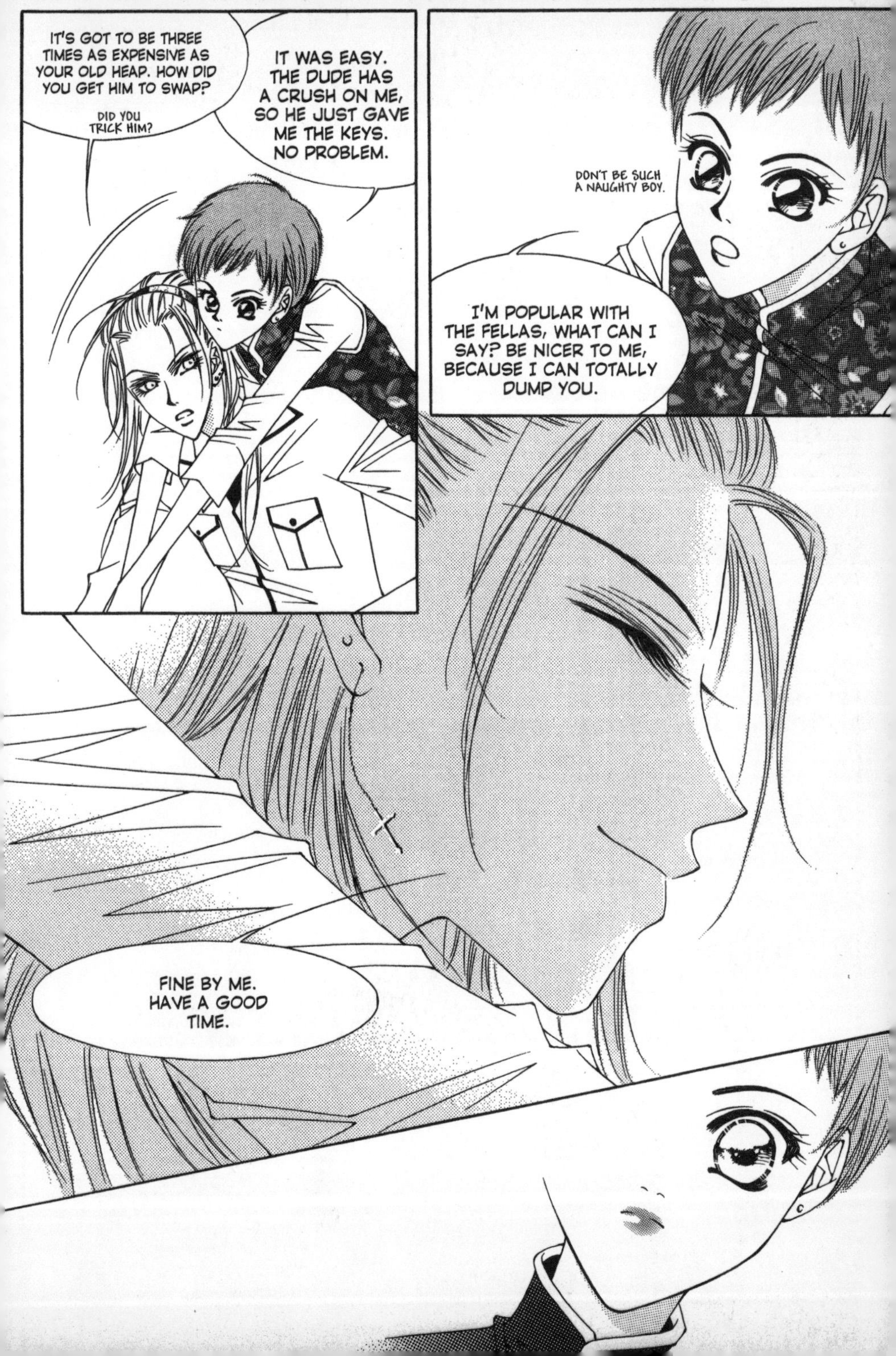

IT'S GOT TO BE THREE TIMES AS EXPENSIVE AS YOUR OLD HEAP. HOW DID YOU GET HIM TO SWAP?
DID YOU TRICK HIM?
IT WAS EASY. THE DUDE HAS A CRUSH ON ME, SO HE JUST GAVE ME THE KEYS. NO PROBLEM.
DON'T BE SUCH A NAUGHTY BOY.
I'M POPULAR WITH THE FELLAS, WHAT CAN I SAY? BE NICER TO ME, BECAUSE I CAN TOTALLY DUMP YOU.
FINE BY ME. HAVE A GOOD TIME.

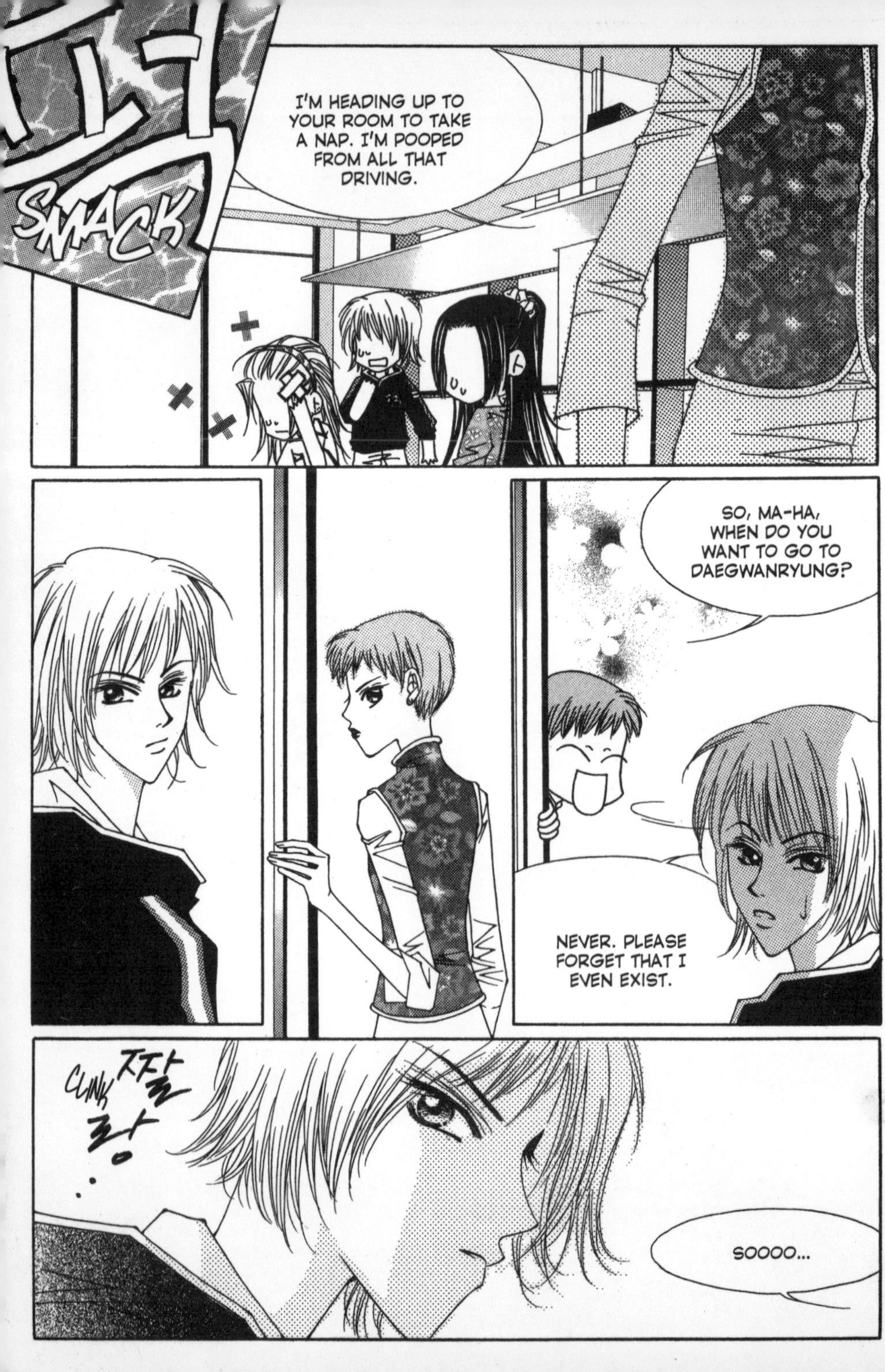
SMACK
I'M HEADING UP TO YOUR ROOM TO TAKE A NAP. I'M POOPED FROM ALL THAT DRIVING.
SO, MA-HA, WHEN DO YOU WANT TO GO TO DAEGWANRYUNG?
NEVER. PLEASE FORGET THAT I EVEN EXIST.
CLINK
SOOOO...

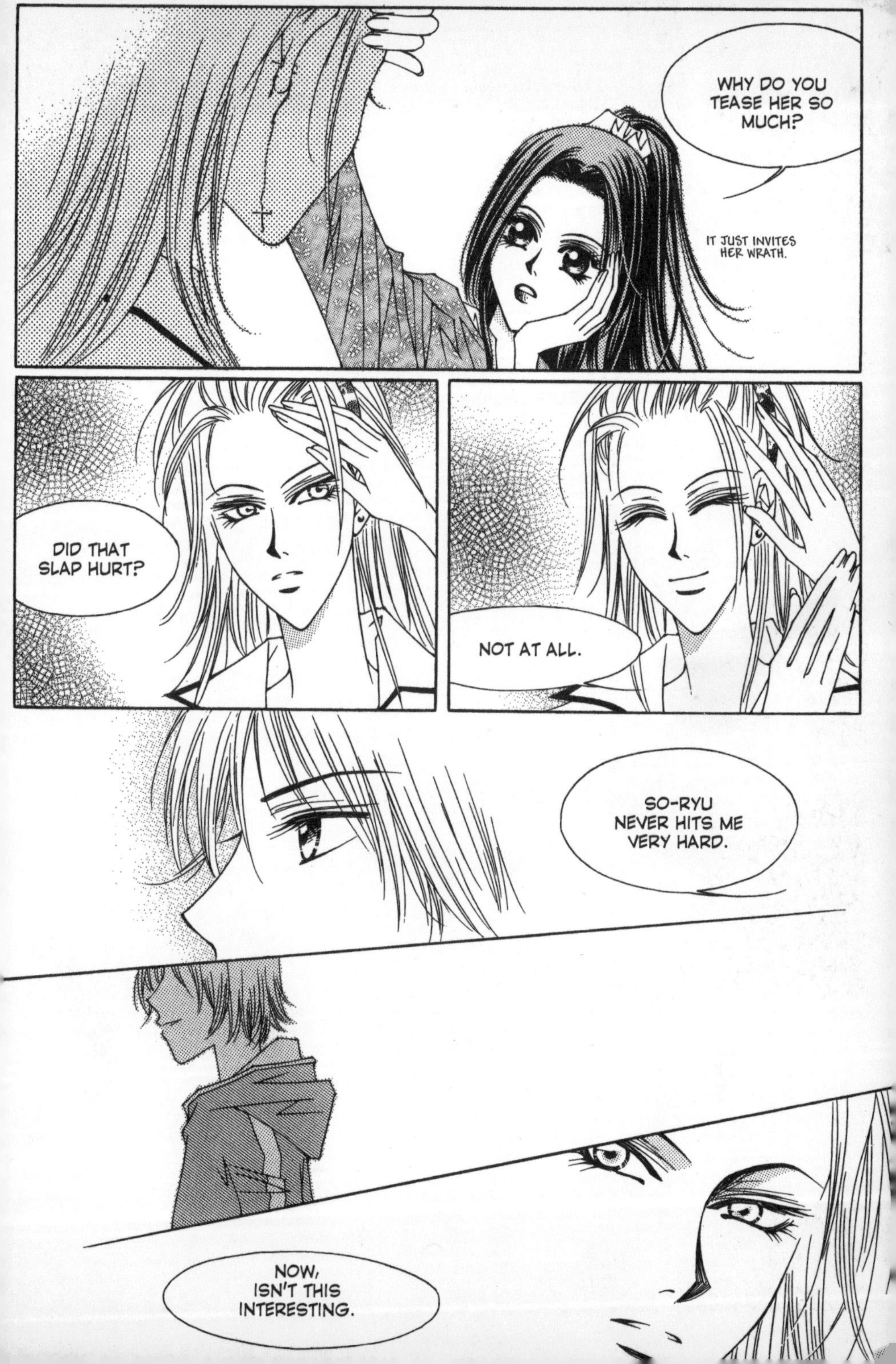
WHY DO YOU TEASE HER SO MUCH?
IT JUST INVITES HER WRATH.
DID THAT SLAP HURT?
NOT AT ALL.
SO-RYU NEVER HITS ME VERY HARD.
NOW, ISN'T THIS INTERESTING.

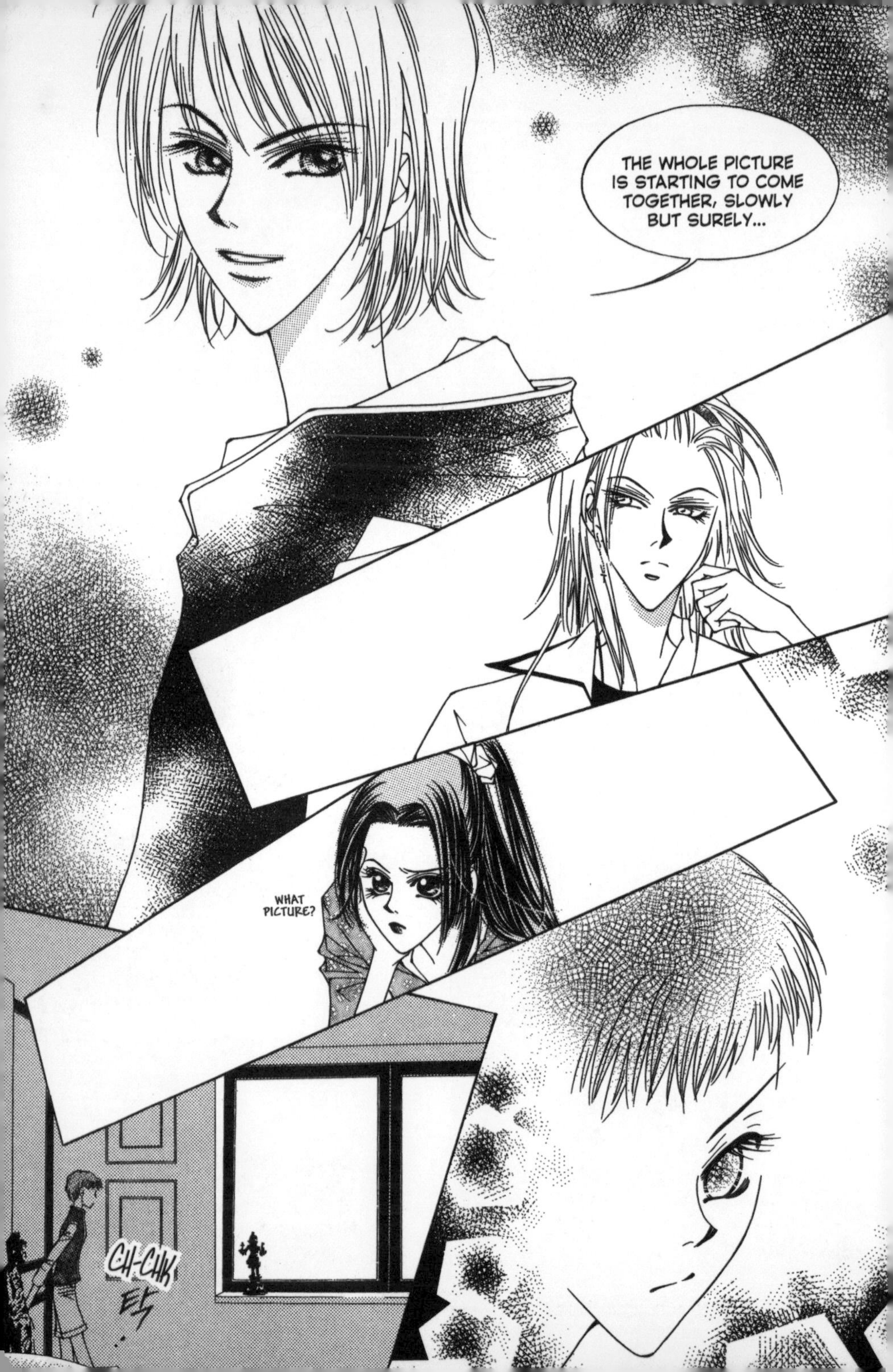
THE WHOLE PICTURE IS STARTING TO COME TOGETHER, SLOWLY BUT SURELY...
WHAT PICTURE?
CH-CHK

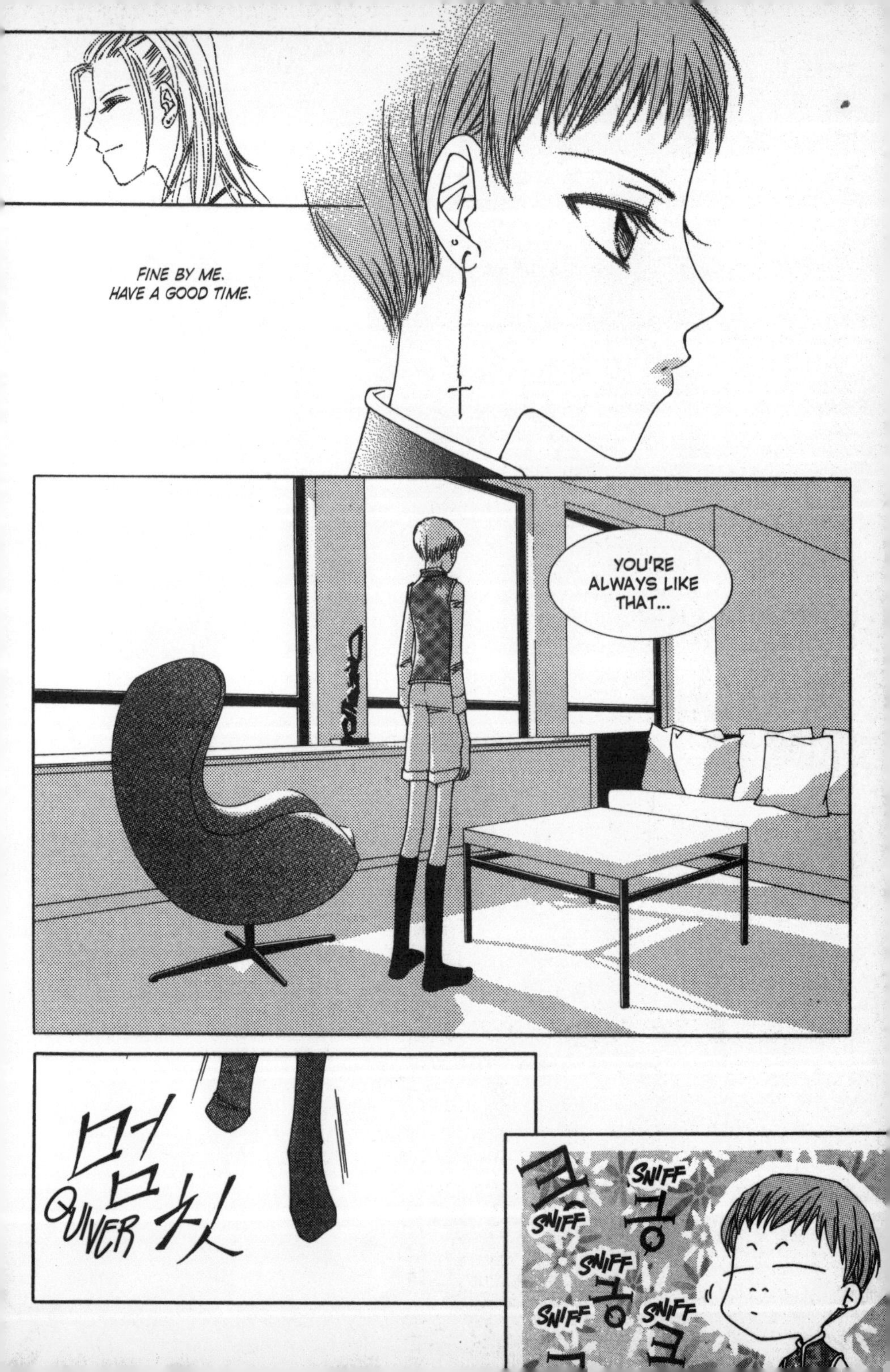
FINE BY ME.
HAVE A GOOD TIME.
YOU'RE ALWAYS LIKE THAT...
멈칫
QUIVER
SNIFF
SNIFF
SNIFF
SNIFF
SNIFF

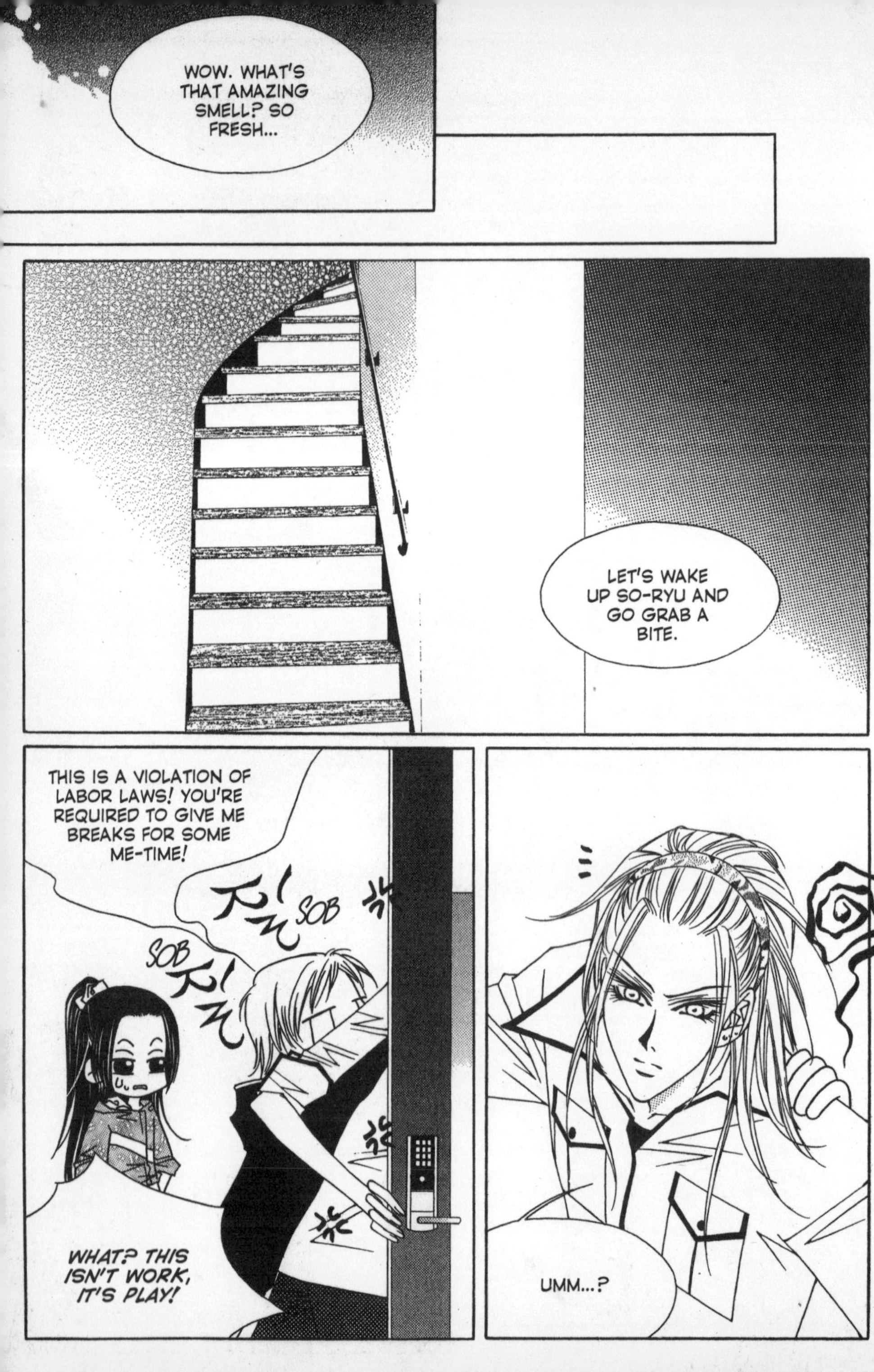
WOW. WHAT'S THAT AMAZING SMELL? SO FRESH...
LET'S WAKE UP SO-RYU AND GO GRAB A BITE.
THIS IS A VIOLATION OF LABOR LAWS! YOU'RE REQUIRED TO GIVE ME BREAKS FOR SOME ME-TIME!
SOB
SOB
WHAT? THIS ISN'T WORK, IT'S PLAY!
UMM...?

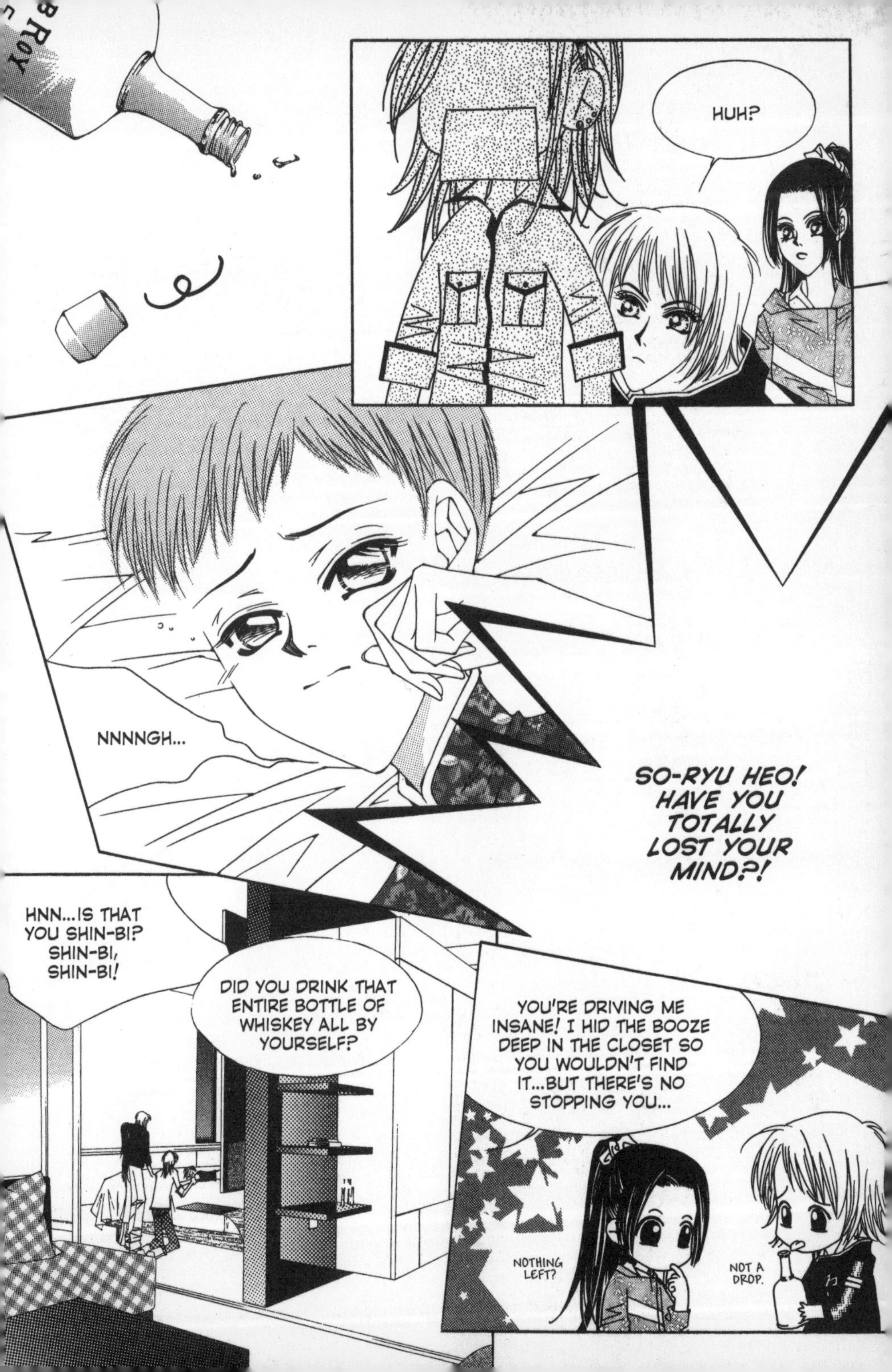
HUH?
NNNNGH...
SO-RYU HEO! HAVE YOU TOTALLY LOST YOUR MIND?!
HNN...IS THAT YOU SHIN-BI? SHIN-BI, SHIN-BI!
DID YOU DRINK THAT ENTIRE BOTTLE OF WHISKEY ALL BY YOURSELF?
YOU'RE DRIVING ME INSANE! I HID THE BOOZE DEEP IN THE CLOSET SO YOU WOULDN'T FIND IT...BUT THERE'S NO STOPPING YOU...
NOTHING LEFT?
NOT A DROP.

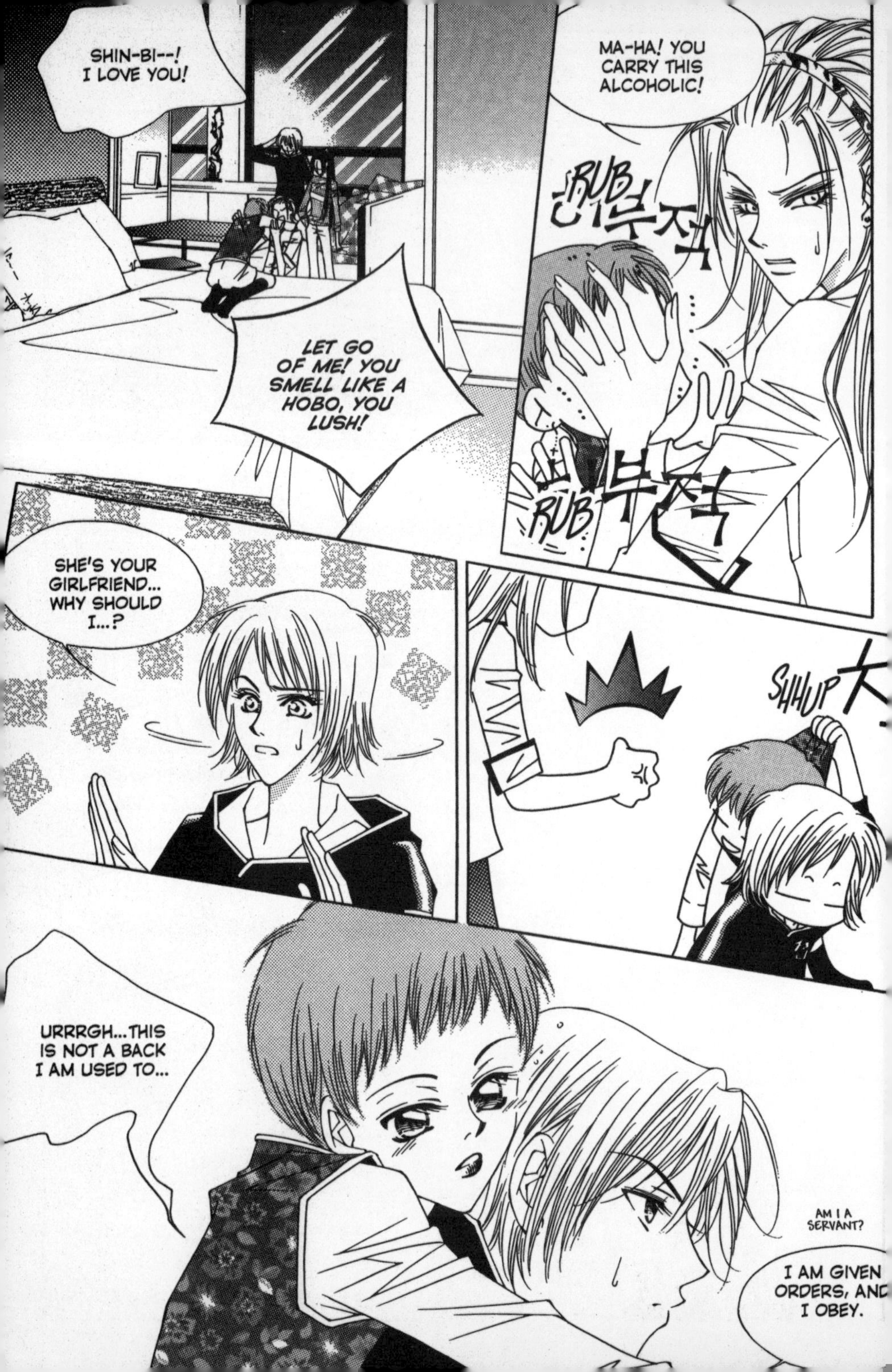
SHIN-BI--! I LOVE YOU!
LET GO OF ME! YOU SMELL LIKE A HOBO, YOU LUSH!
MA-HA! YOU CARRY THIS ALCOHOLIC!
RUB
RUB
SHE'S YOUR GIRLFRIEND... WHY SHOULD I...?
SHHUP
URRRGH...THIS IS NOT A BACK I AM USED TO...
AM I A SERVANT?
I AM GIVEN ORDERS, AND I OBEY.

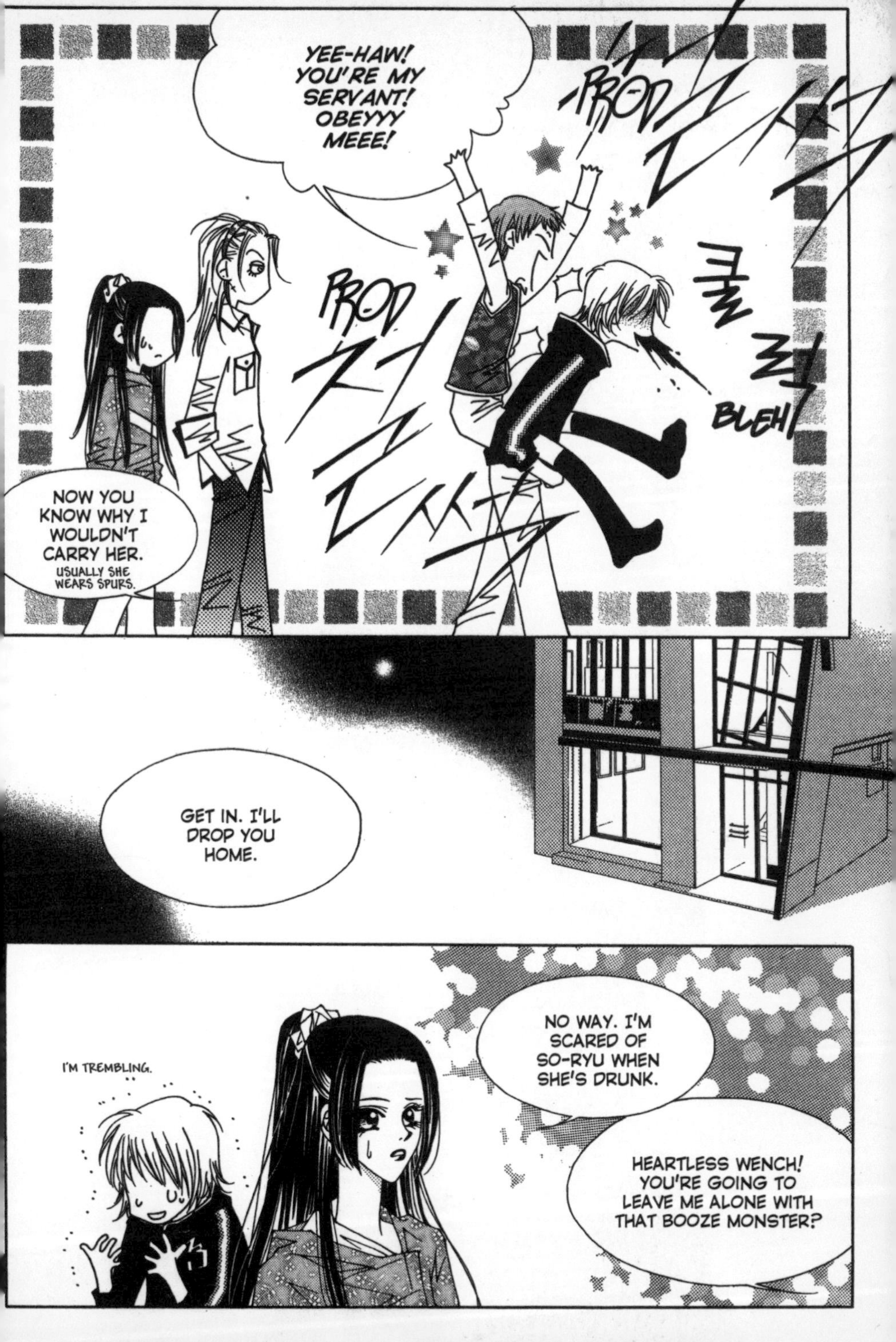
YEE-HAW! YOU'RE MY SERVANT! OBEYYY MEEE!
PROD
PROD
BLEH
NOW YOU KNOW WHY I WOULDN'T CARRY HER.
USUALLY SHE WEARS SPURS.
GET IN. I'LL DROP YOU HOME.
I'M TREMBLING.
NO WAY. I'M SCARED OF SO-RYU WHEN SHE'S DRUNK.
HEARTLESS WENCH! YOU'RE GOING TO LEAVE ME ALONE WITH THAT BOOZE MONSTER?

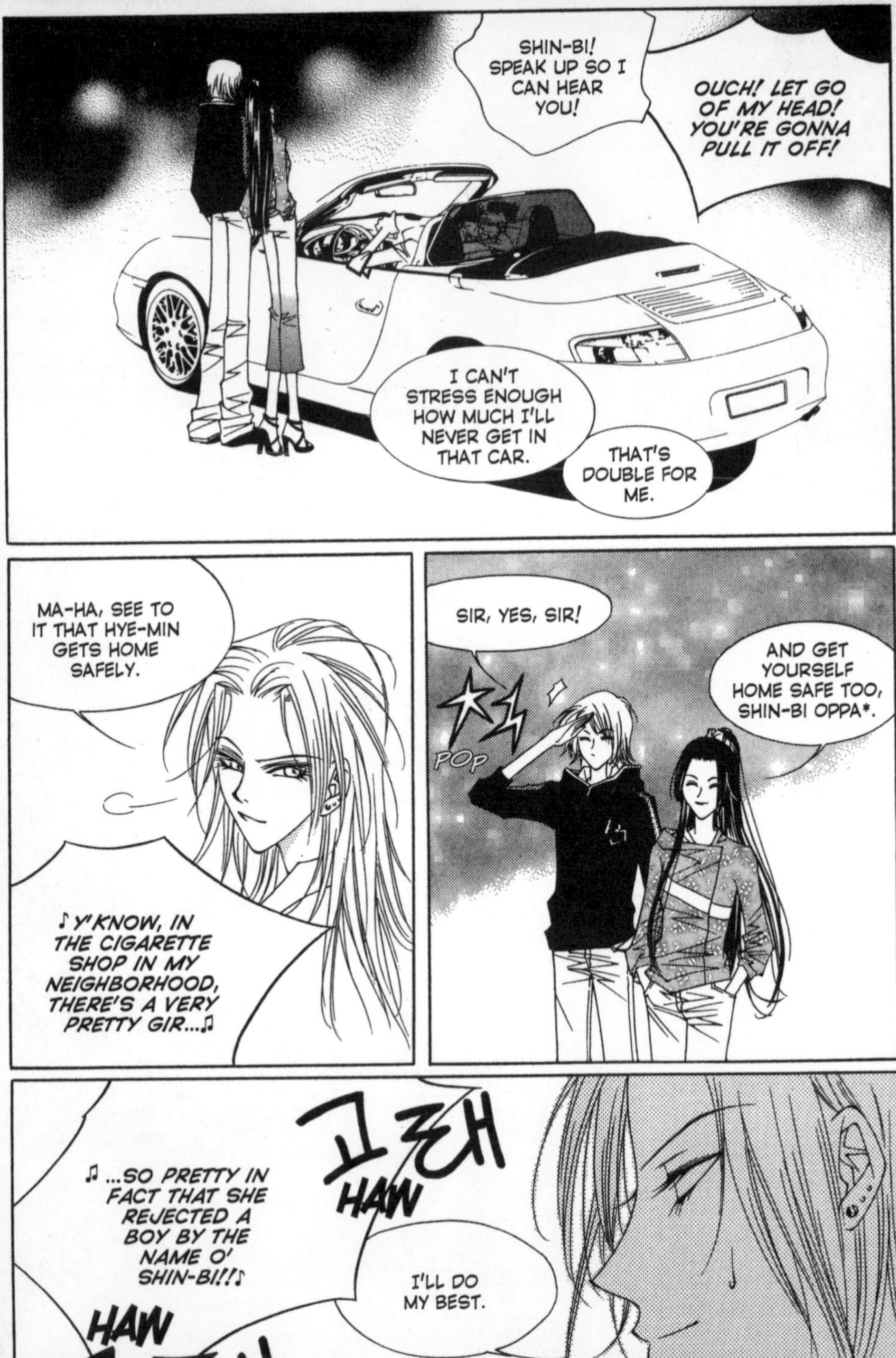
SHIN-BI! SPEAK UP SO I CAN HEAR YOU!
OUCH! LET GO OF MY HEAD! YOU'RE GONNA PULL IT OFF!
I CAN'T STRESS ENOUGH HOW MUCH I'LL NEVER GET IN THAT CAR.
THAT'S DOUBLE FOR ME.
MA-HA, SEE TO IT THAT HYE-MIN GETS HOME SAFELY.
♪ Y'KNOW, IN THE CIGARETTE SHOP IN MY NEIGHBORHOOD, THERE'S A VERY PRETTY GIR...♫
SIR, YES, SIR!
POP
AND GET YOURSELF HOME SAFE TOO, SHIN-BI OPPA*.
♫ ...SO PRETTY IN FACT THAT SHE REJECTED A BOY BY THE NAME O' SHIN-BI!!♪
HAW
I'LL DO MY BEST.
HAW

* OPPA: TERM KOREAN GIRLS USE FOR OLDER BOYS. LITERALLY MEANS "OLDER BROTHER".

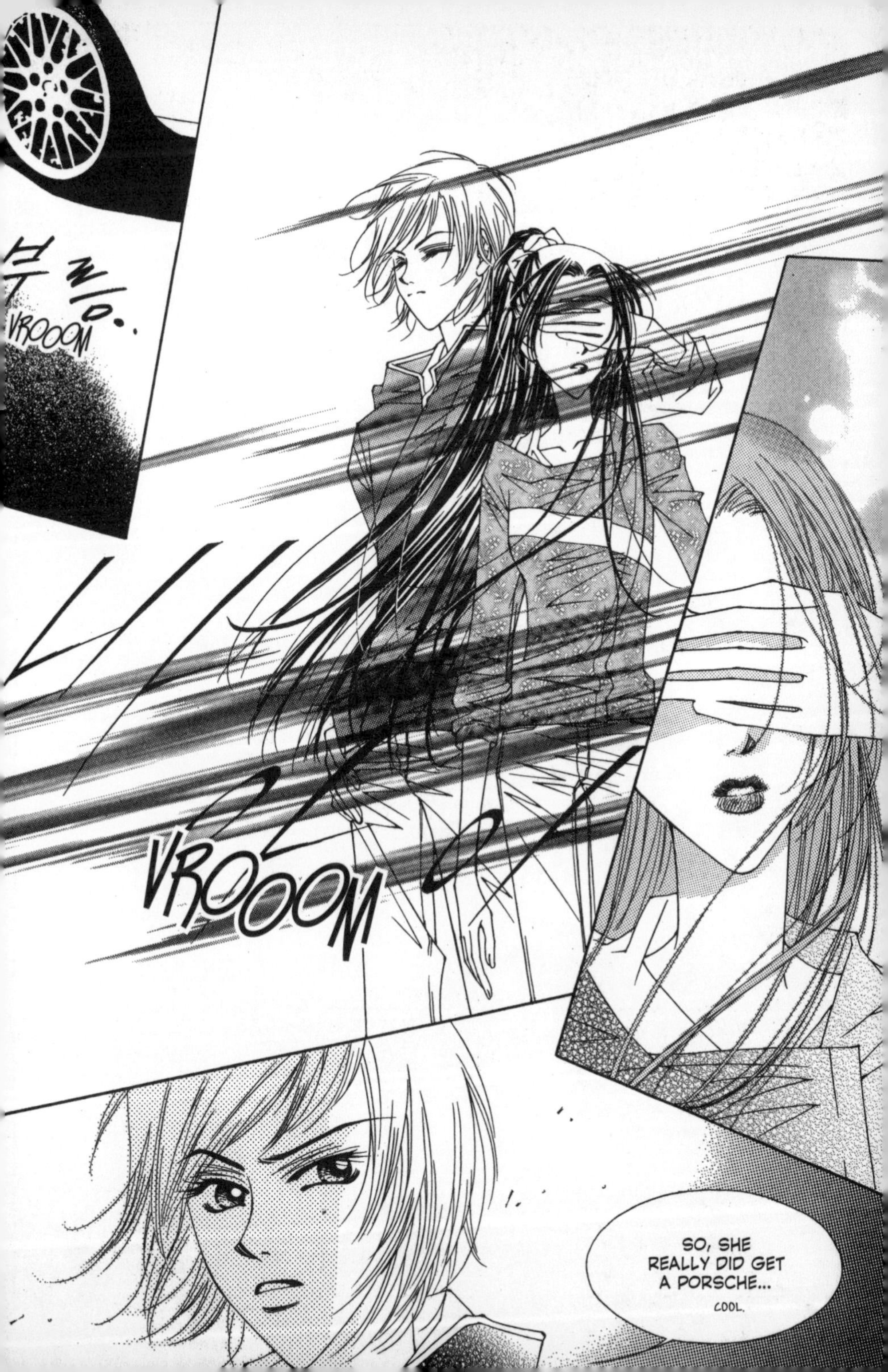
VROOOM
VROOOM
SO, SHE REALLY DID GET A PORSCHE...
COOL.

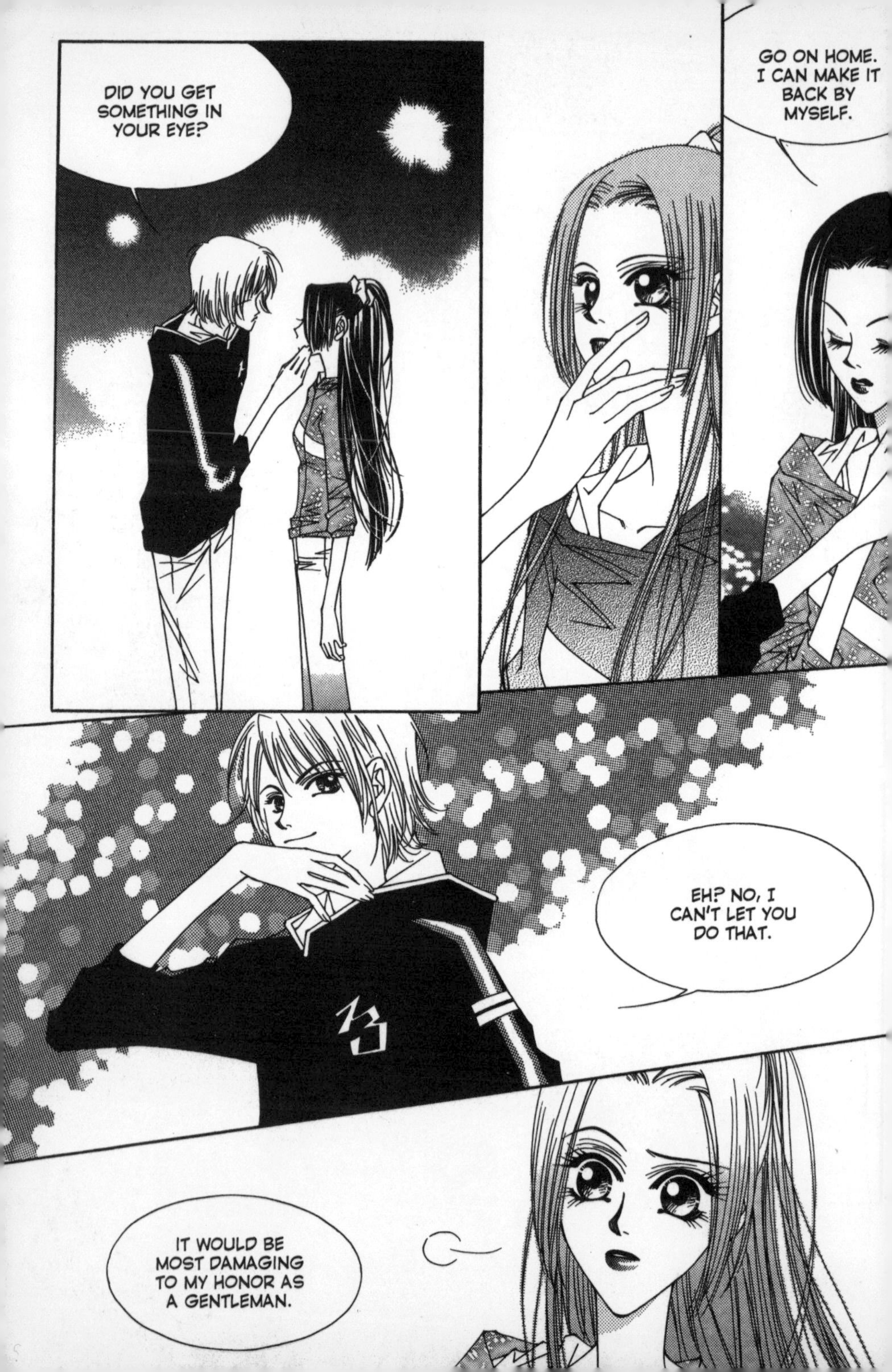
DID YOU GET SOMETHING IN YOUR EYE?
GO ON HOME. I CAN MAKE IT BACK BY MYSELF.
EH? NO, I CAN'T LET YOU DO THAT.
IT WOULD BE MOST DAMAGING TO MY HONOR AS A GENTLEMAN.

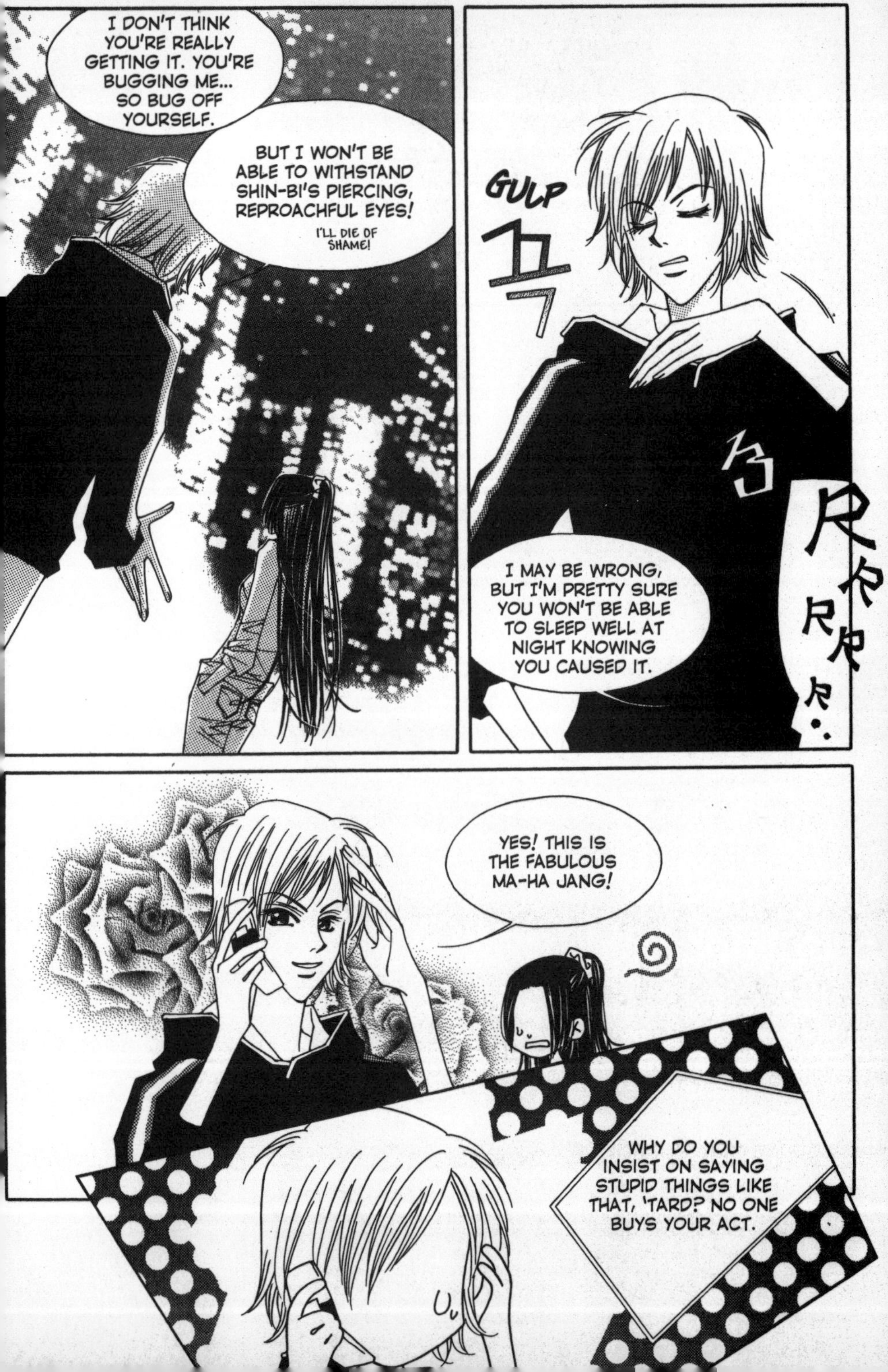
I DON'T THINK YOU'RE REALLY GETTING IT. YOU'RE BUGGING ME... SO BUG OFF YOURSELF.
BUT I WON'T BE ABLE TO WITHSTAND SHIN-BI'S PIERCING, REPROACHFUL EYES!
I'LL DIE OF SHAME!
GULP
I MAY BE WRONG, BUT I'M PRETTY SURE YOU WON'T BE ABLE TO SLEEP WELL AT NIGHT KNOWING YOU CAUSED IT.
YES! THIS IS THE FABULOUS MA-HA JANG!
WHY DO YOU INSIST ON SAYING STUPID THINGS LIKE THAT, 'TARD? NO ONE BUYS YOUR ACT.

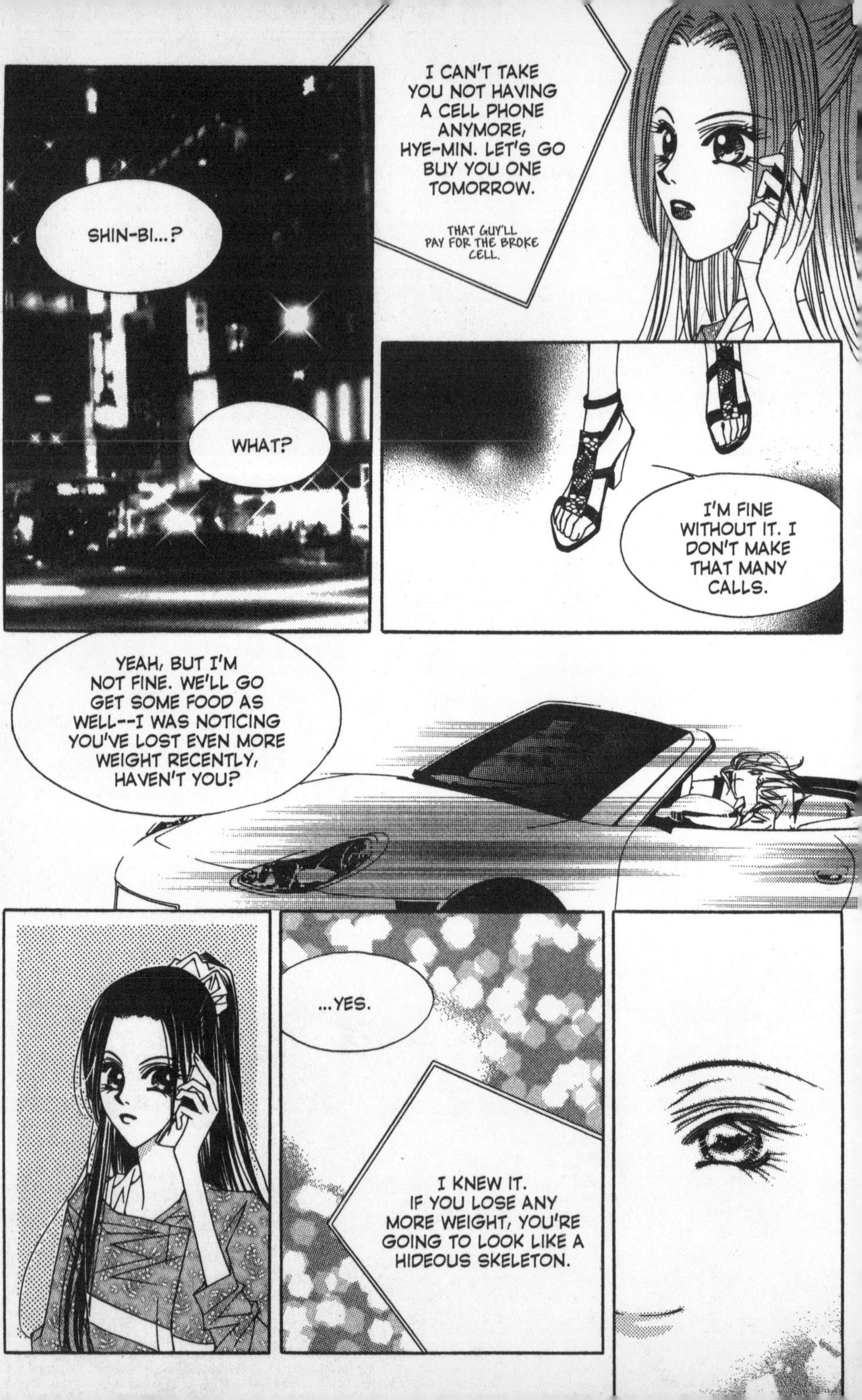
SHIN-BI...?
WHAT?
I CAN'T TAKE YOU NOT HAVING A CELL PHONE ANYMORE, HYE-MIN. LET'S GO BUY YOU ONE TOMORROW.
THAT GUY'LL PAY FOR THE BROKE CELL.
I'M FINE WITHOUT IT. I DON'T MAKE THAT MANY CALLS.
YEAH, BUT I'M NOT FINE. WE'LL GO GET SOME FOOD AS WELL--I WAS NOTICING YOU'VE LOST EVEN MORE WEIGHT RECENTLY, HAVEN'T YOU?
...YES.
I KNEW IT. IF YOU LOSE ANY MORE WEIGHT, YOU'RE GOING TO LOOK LIKE A HIDEOUS SKELETON.

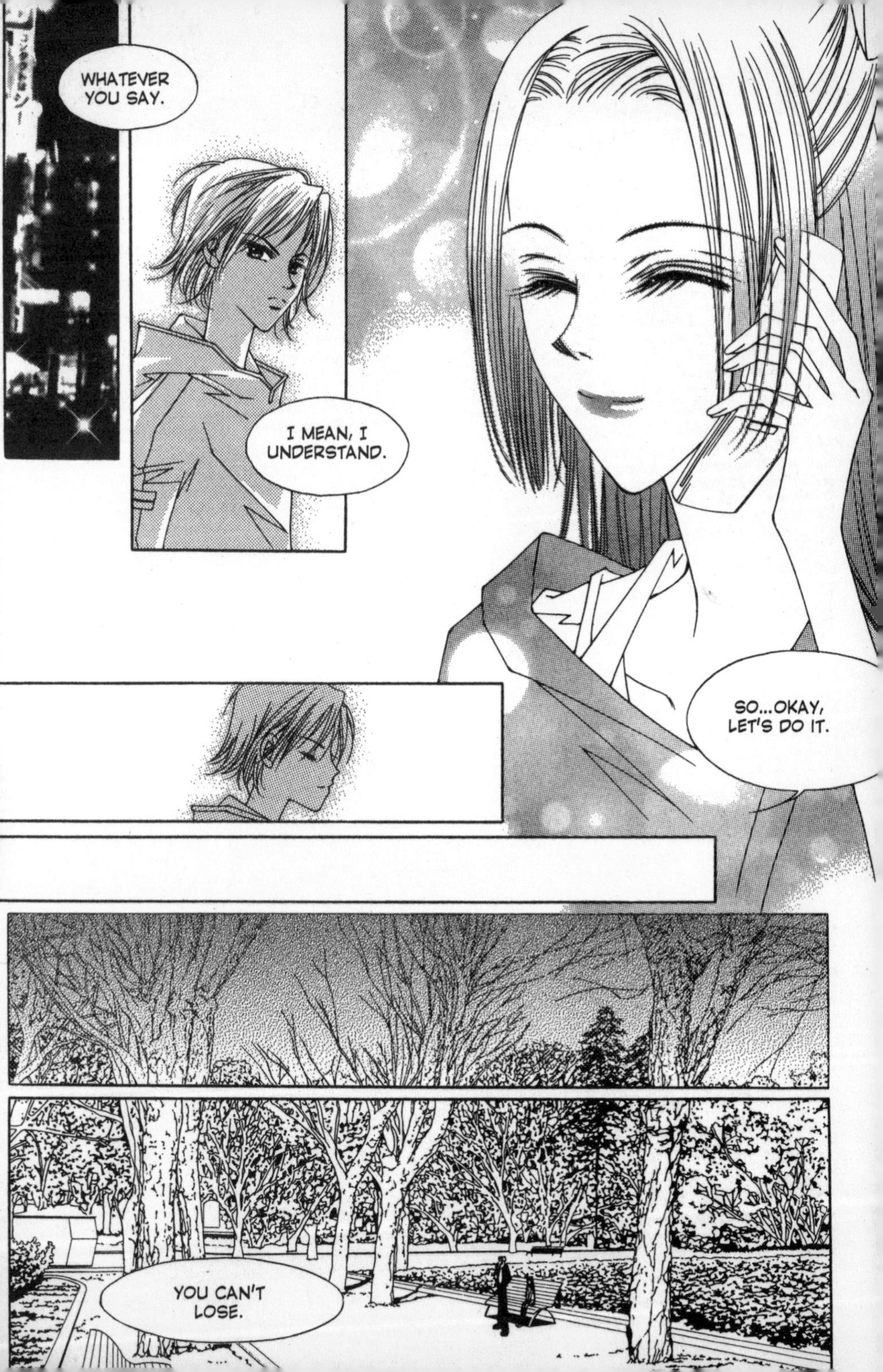
WHATEVER YOU SAY.
I MEAN, I UNDERSTAND.
SO...OKAY, LET'S DO IT.
YOU CAN'T LOSE.

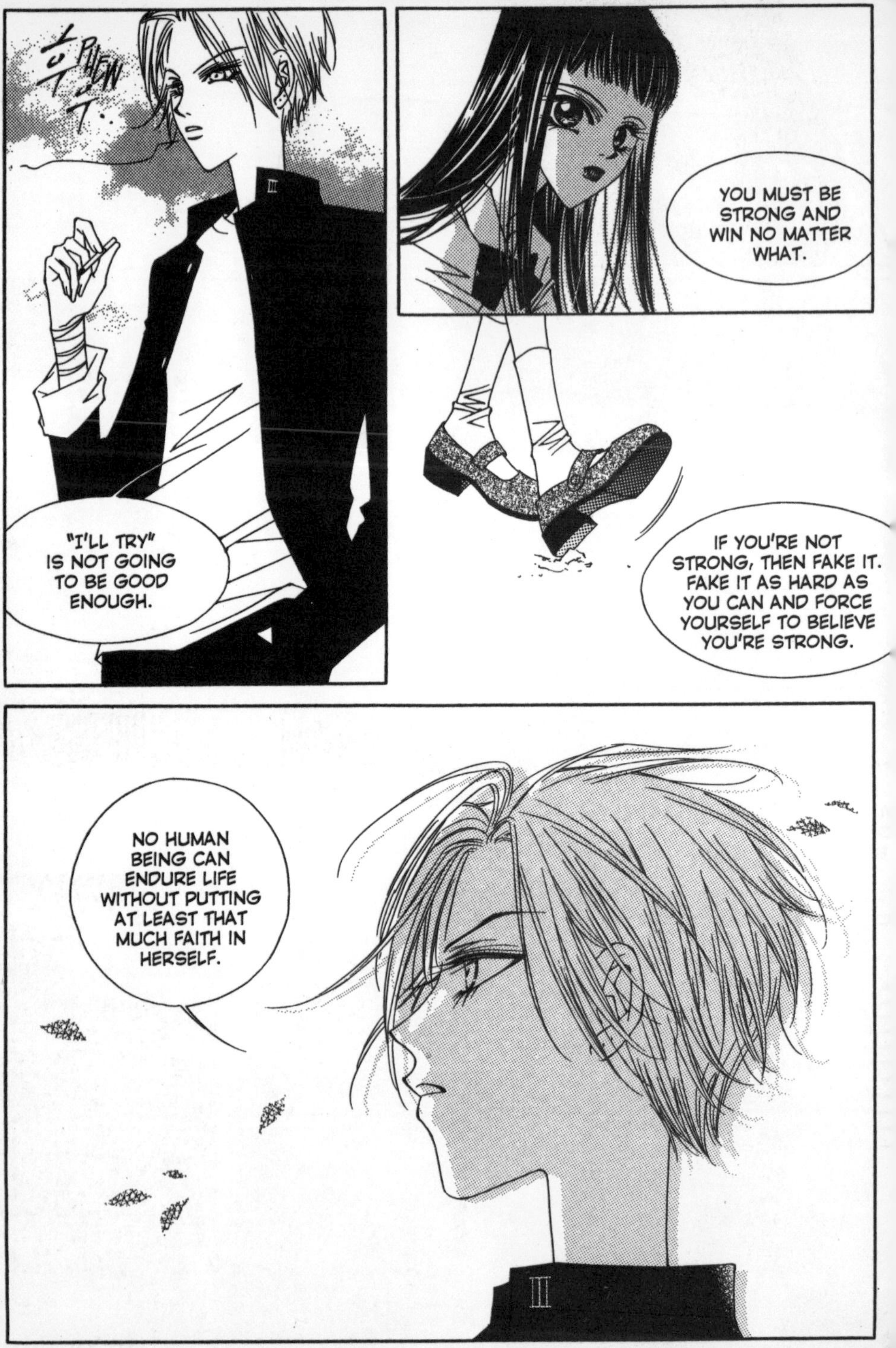
PHEW
"I'LL TRY" IS NOT GOING TO BE GOOD ENOUGH.
YOU MUST BE STRONG AND WIN NO MATTER WHAT.
IF YOU'RE NOT STRONG, THEN FAKE IT. FAKE IT AS HARD AS YOU CAN AND FORCE YOURSELF TO BELIEVE YOU'RE STRONG.
NO HUMAN BEING CAN ENDURE LIFE WITHOUT PUTTING AT LEAST THAT MUCH FAITH IN HERSELF.

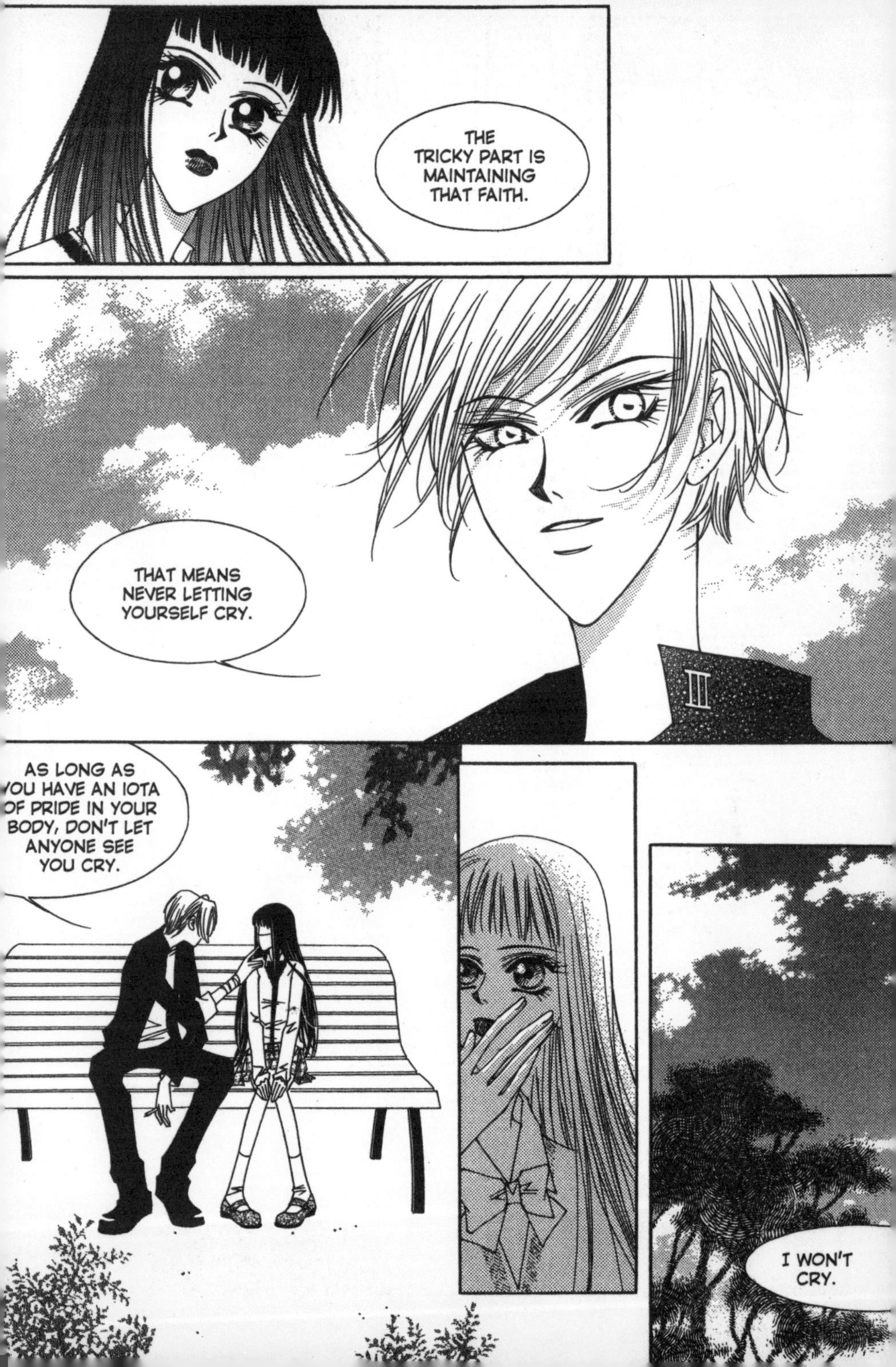
THE TRICKY PART IS MAINTAINING THAT FAITH.
THAT MEANS NEVER LETTING YOURSELF CRY.
AS LONG AS YOU HAVE AN IOTA OF PRIDE IN YOUR BODY, DON'T LET ANYONE SEE YOU CRY.
I WON'T CRY.

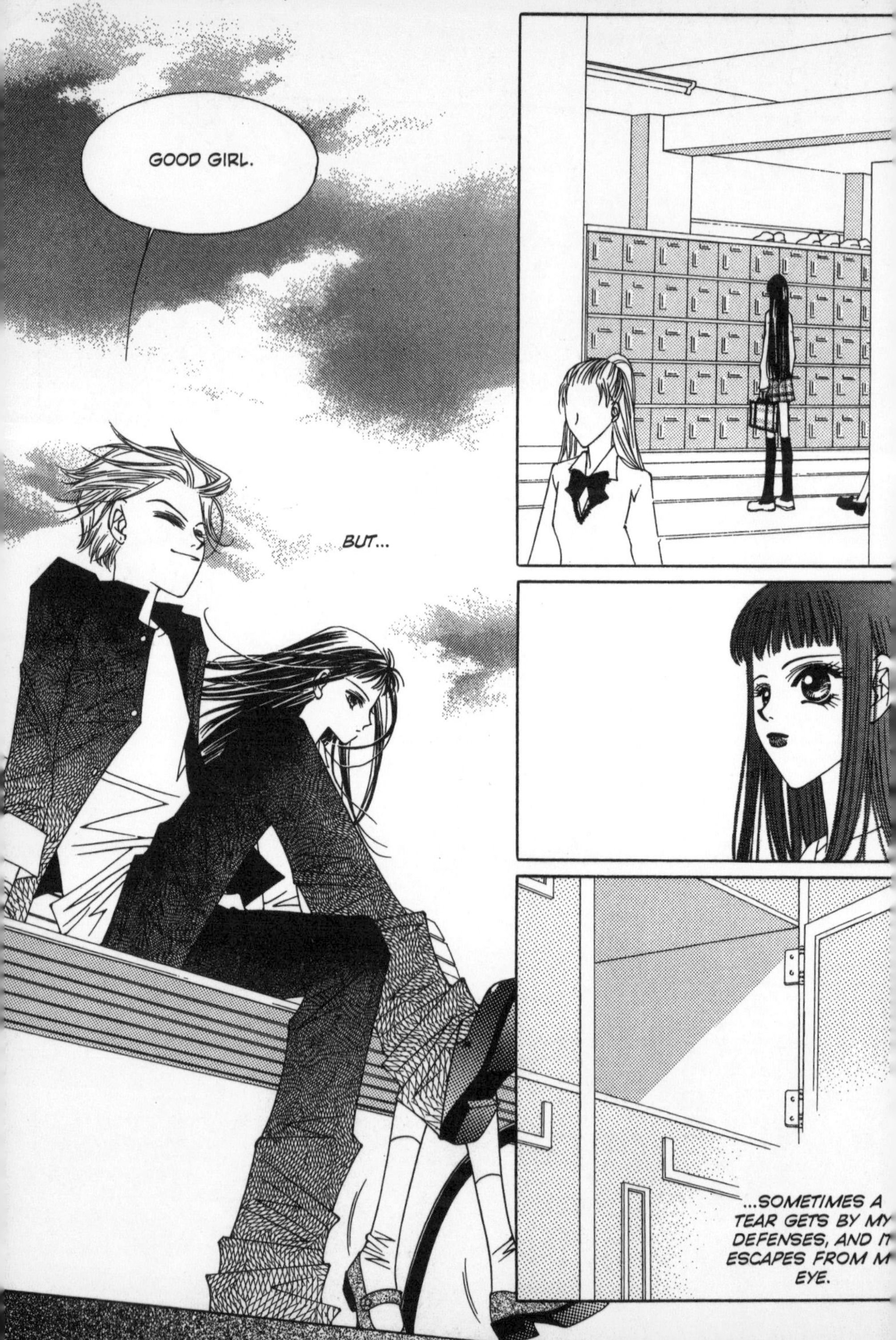
GOOD GIRL.
BUT...
...SOMETIMES A TEAR GETS BY MY DEFENSES, AND IT ESCAPES FROM M EYE.

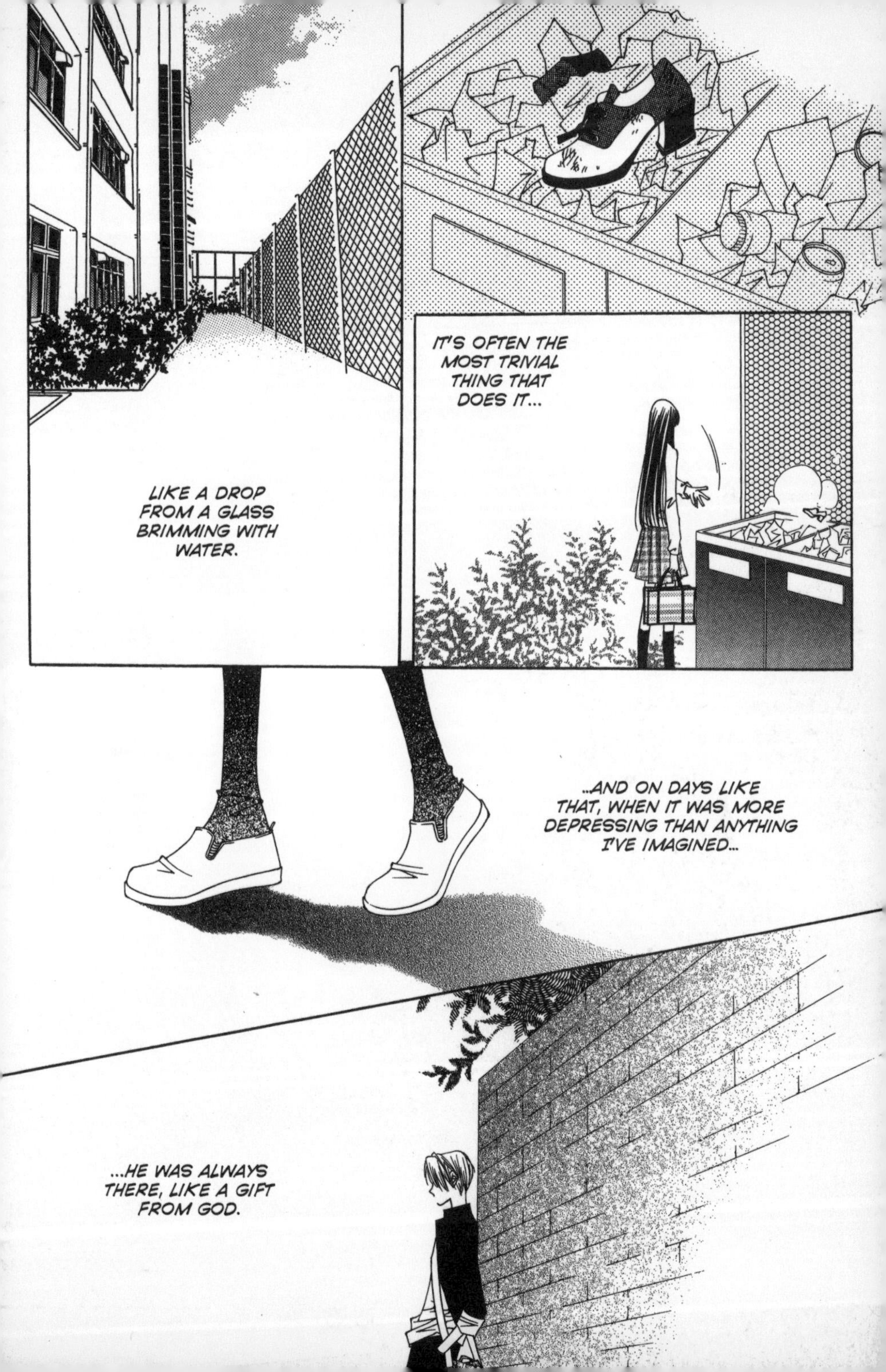
LIKE A DROP FROM A GLASS BRIMMING WITH WATER.
IT'S OFTEN THE MOST TRIVIAL THING THAT DOES IT...
...AND ON DAYS LIKE THAT, WHEN IT WAS MORE DEPRESSING THAN ANYTHING I'VE IMAGINED...
...HE WAS ALWAYS THERE, LIKE A GIFT FROM GOD.

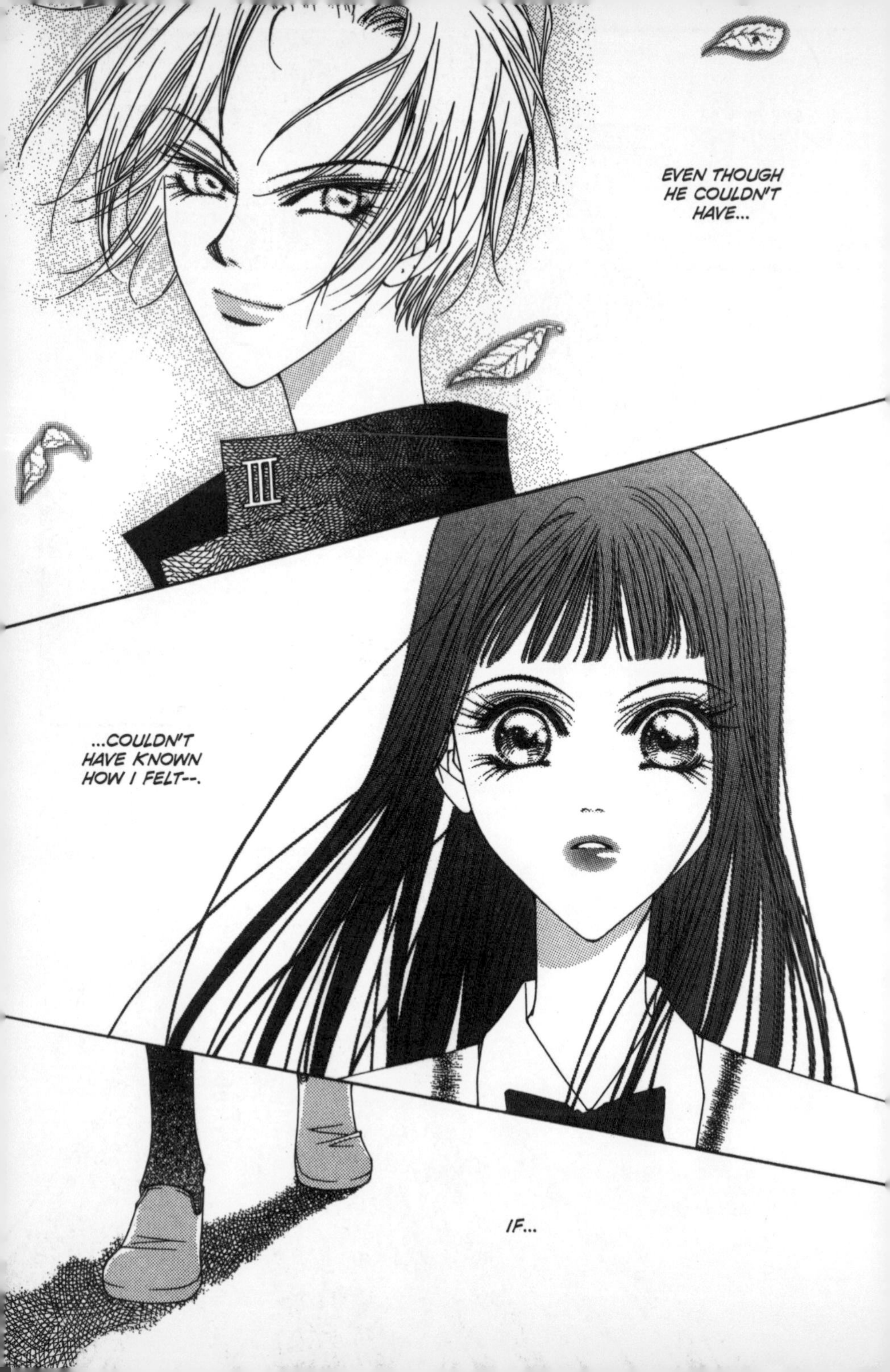
EVEN THOUGH HE COULDN'T HAVE...
...COULDN'T HAVE KNOWN HOW I FELT--.
IF...

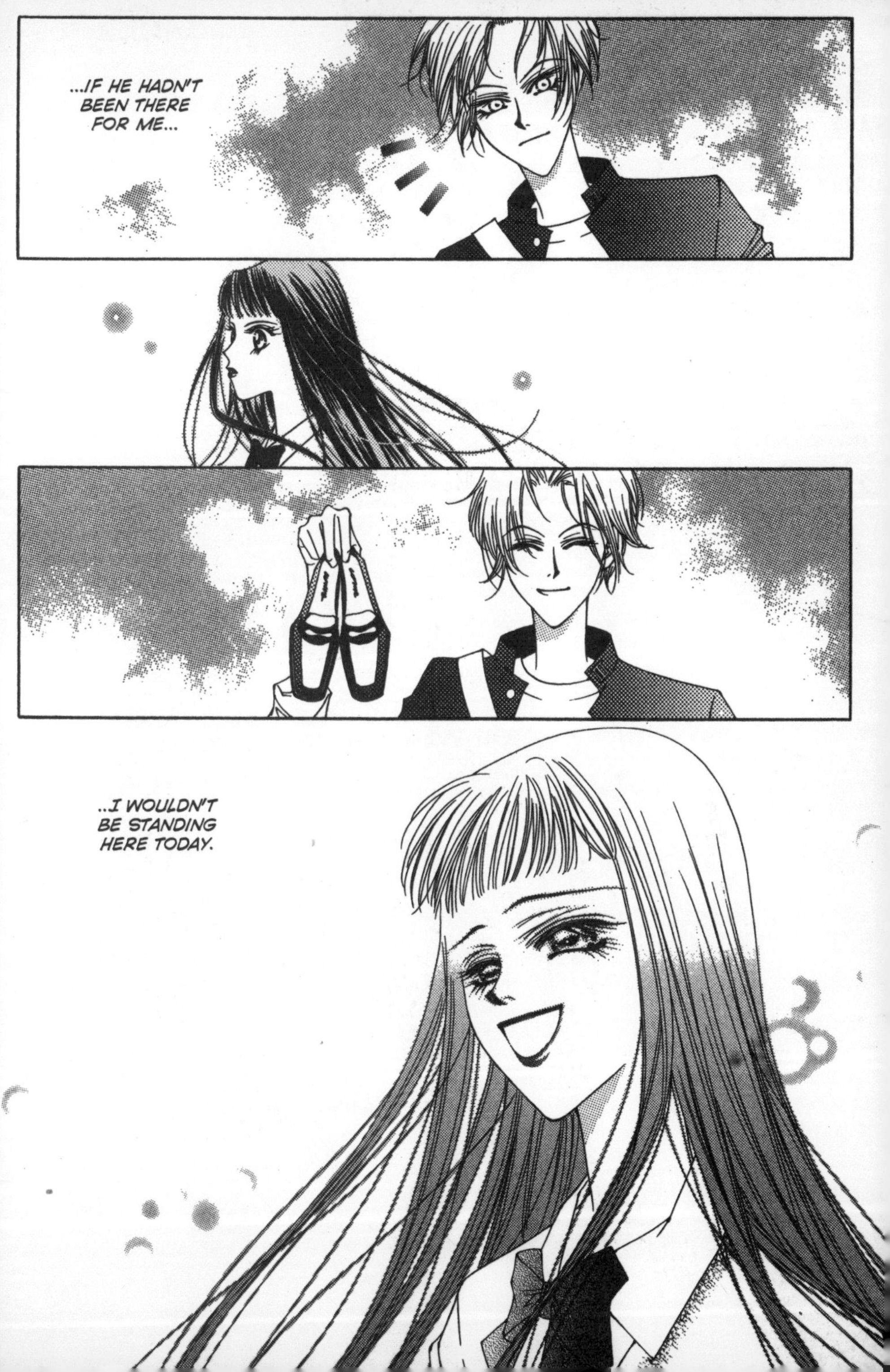
...IF HE HADN'T BEEN THERE FOR ME...
..I WOULDN'T BE STANDING HERE TODAY.

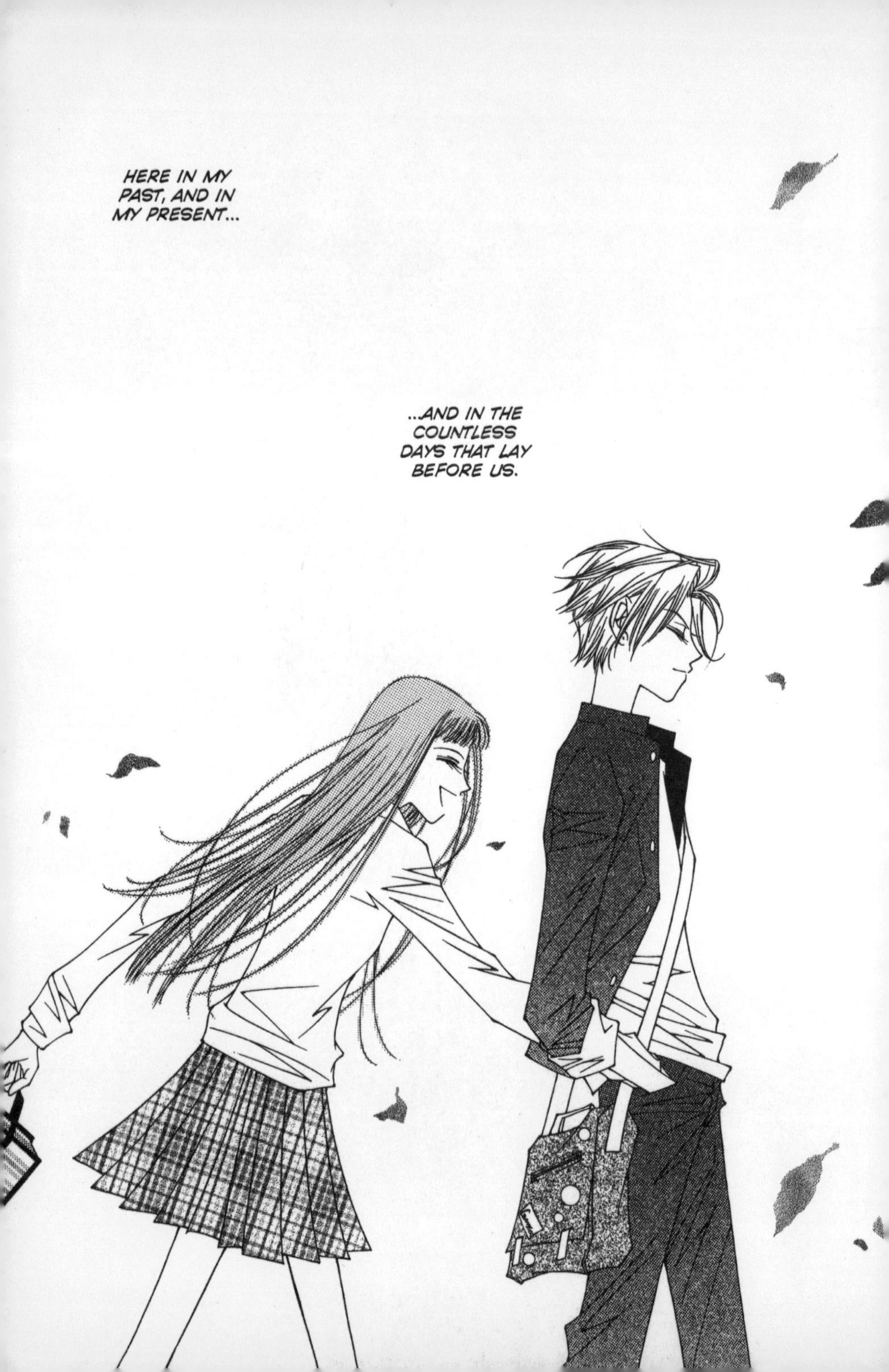
HERE IN MY
PAST, AND IN
MY PRESENT...
...AND IN THE
COUNTLESS
DAYS THAT LAY
BEFORE US.

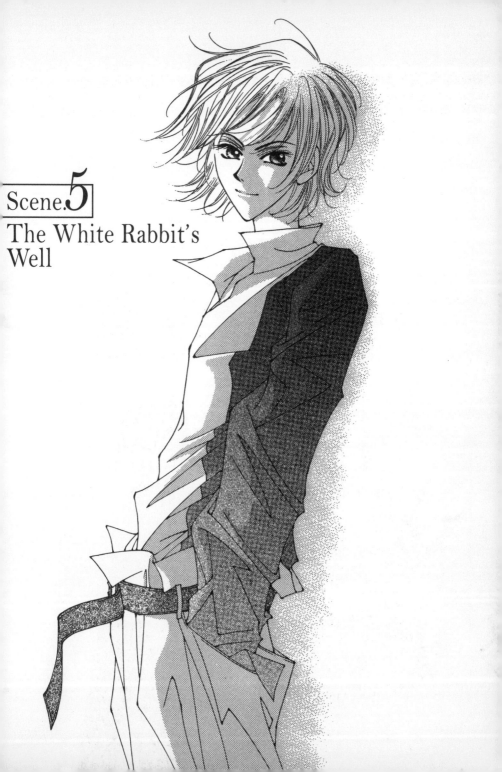

Scene.5
The White Rabbit's Well

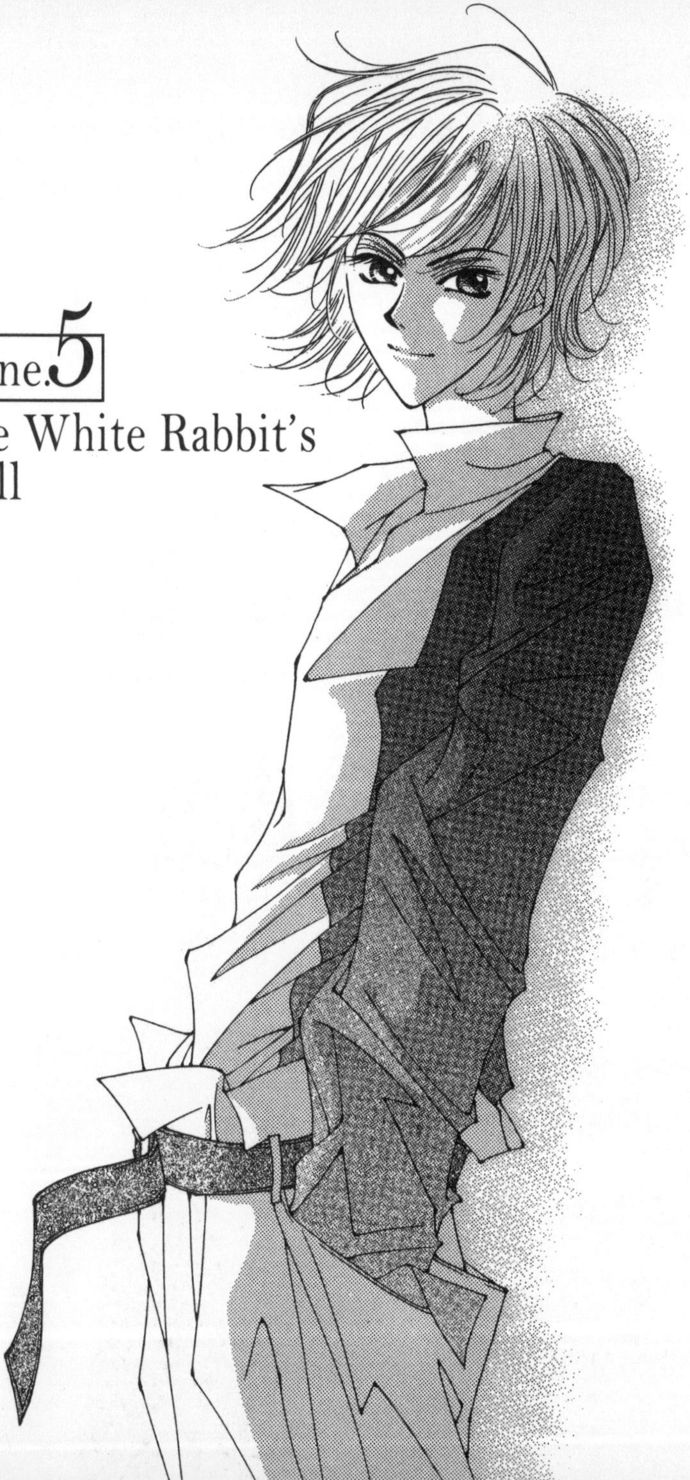

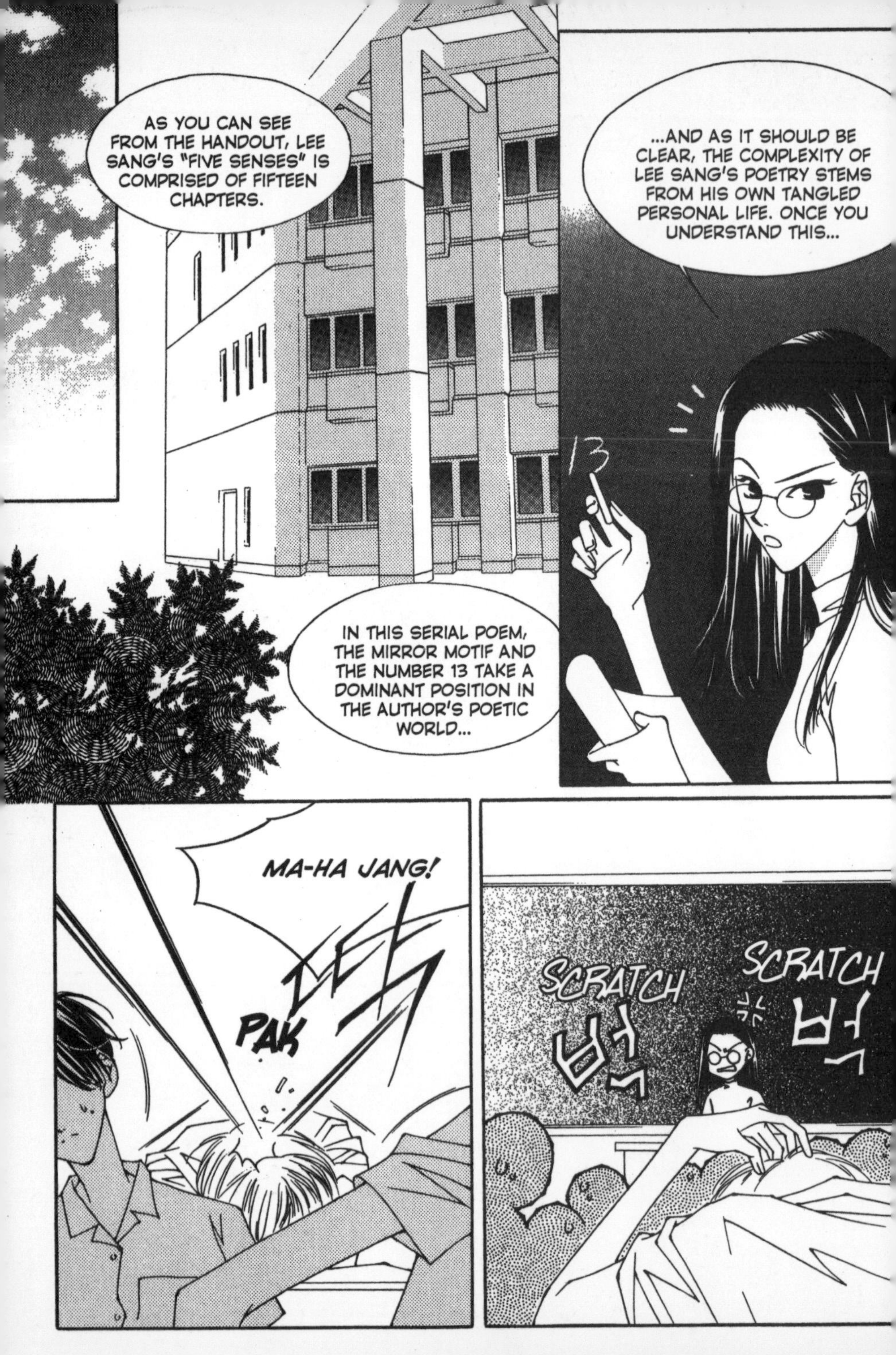
AS YOU CAN SEE FROM THE HANDOUT, LEE SANG'S "FIVE SENSES" IS COMPRISED OF FIFTEEN CHAPTERS.
IN THIS SERIAL POEM, THE MIRROR MOTIF AND THE NUMBER 13 TAKE A DOMINANT POSITION IN THE AUTHOR'S POETIC WORLD...
...AND AS IT SHOULD BE CLEAR, THE COMPLEXITY OF LEE SANG'S POETRY STEMS FROM HIS OWN TANGLED PERSONAL LIFE. ONCE YOU UNDERSTAND THIS...
13
MA-HA JANG!
PAK
SCRATCH
SCRATCH

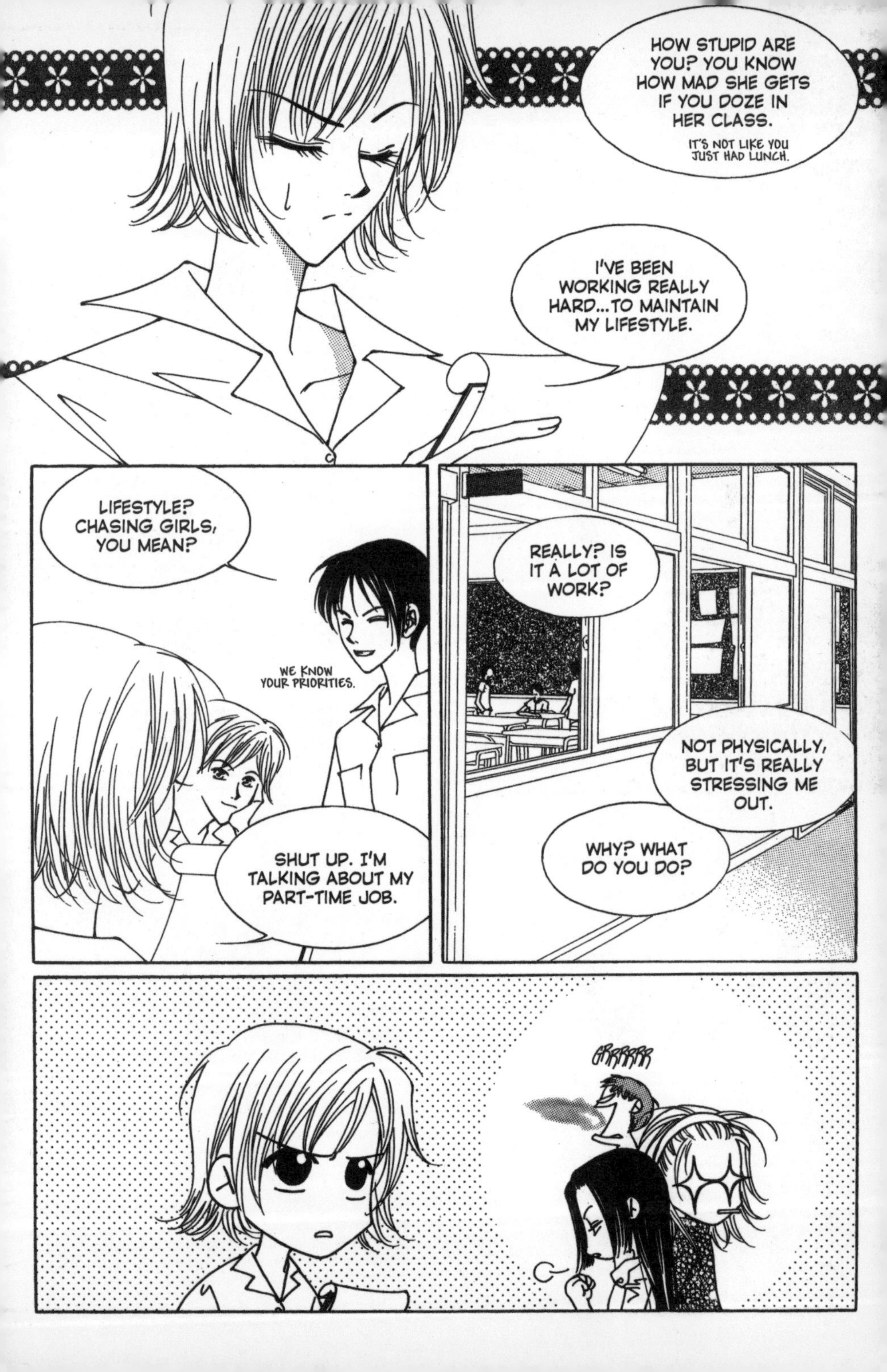
HOW STUPID ARE YOU? YOU KNOW HOW MAD SHE GETS IF YOU DOZE IN HER CLASS.
IT'S NOT LIKE YOU JUST HAD LUNCH.
I'VE BEEN WORKING REALLY HARD...TO MAINTAIN MY LIFESTYLE.
LIFESTYLE? CHASING GIRLS, YOU MEAN?
WE KNOW YOUR PRIORITIES.
SHUT UP. I'M TALKING ABOUT MY PART-TIME JOB.
REALLY? IS IT A LOT OF WORK?
NOT PHYSICALLY, BUT IT'S REALLY STRESSING ME OUT.
WHY? WHAT DO YOU DO?
GRRRRRR

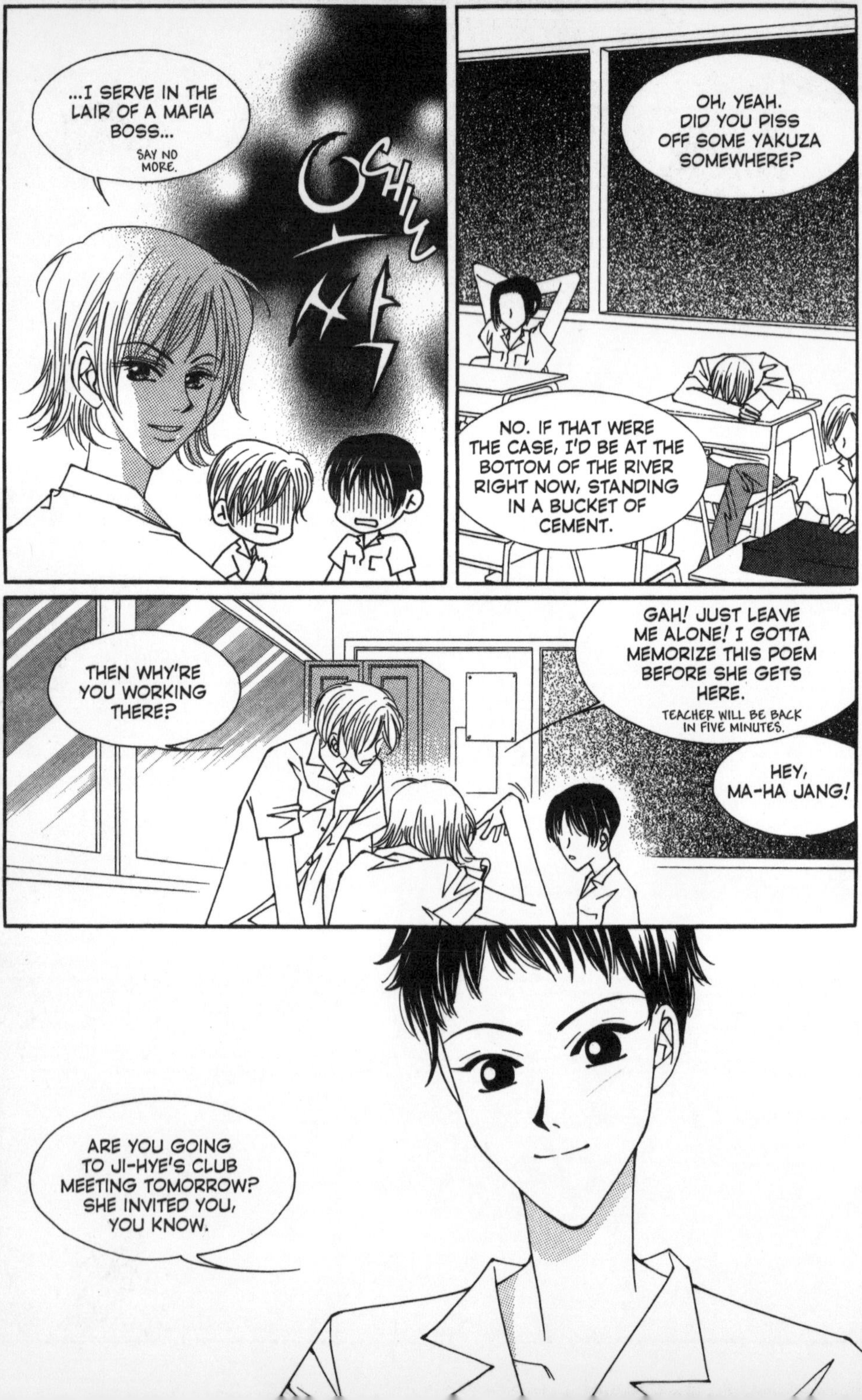
...I SERVE IN THE LAIR OF A MAFIA BOSS...
SAY NO MORE.
CHIW
OH, YEAH. DID YOU PISS OFF SOME YAKUZA SOMEWHERE?
NO. IF THAT WERE THE CASE, I'D BE AT THE BOTTOM OF THE RIVER RIGHT NOW, STANDING IN A BUCKET OF CEMENT.
THEN WHY'RE YOU WORKING THERE?
GAH! JUST LEAVE ME ALONE! I GOTTA MEMORIZE THIS POEM BEFORE SHE GETS HERE.
TEACHER WILL BE BACK IN FIVE MINUTES.
HEY, MA-HA JANG!
ARE YOU GOING TO JI-HYE'S CLUB MEETING TOMORROW? SHE INVITED YOU, YOU KNOW.

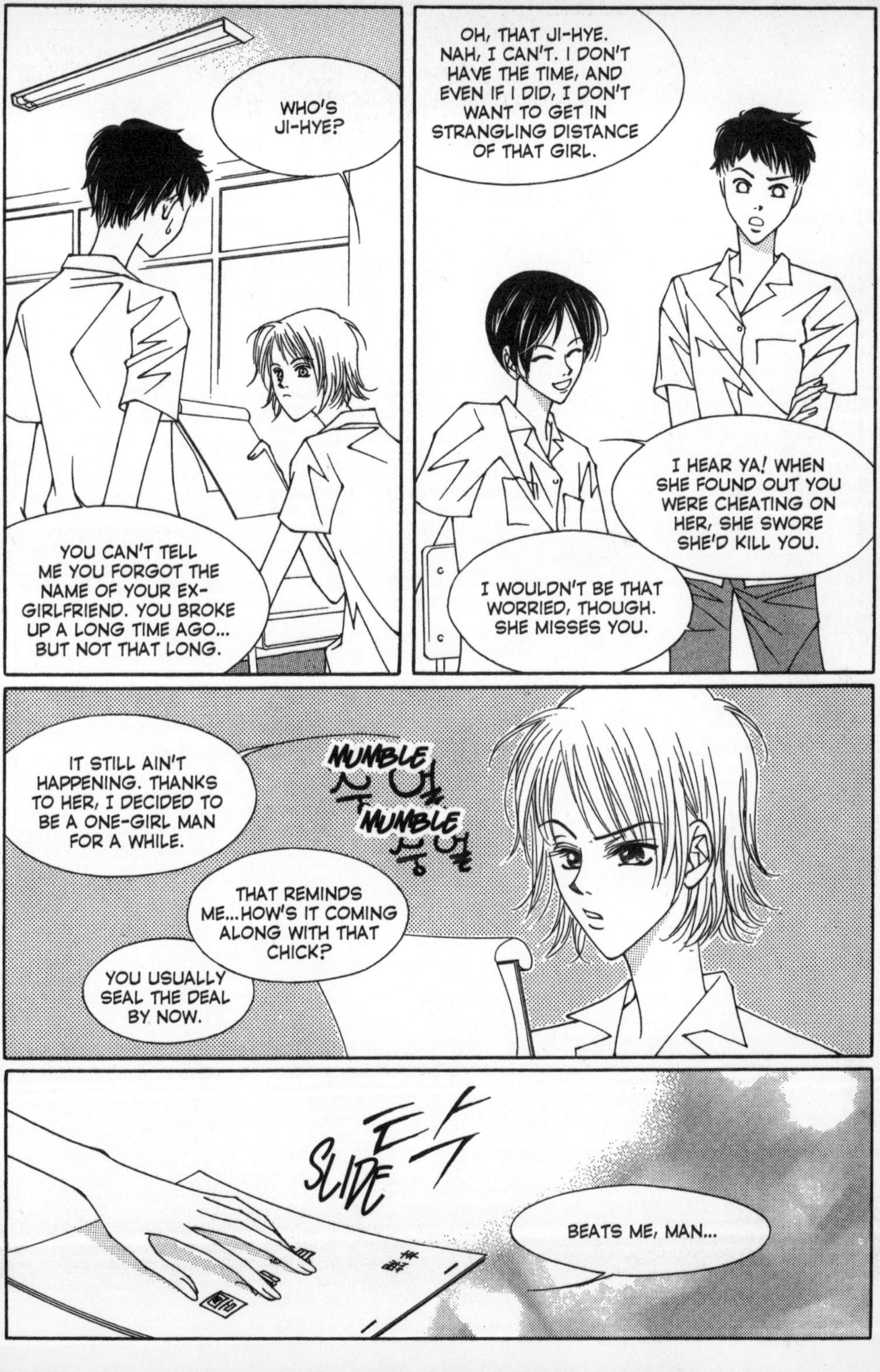
WHO'S JI-HYE?
YOU CAN'T TELL ME YOU FORGOT THE NAME OF YOUR EX-GIRLFRIEND. YOU BROKE UP A LONG TIME AGO... BUT NOT THAT LONG.
OH, THAT JI-HYE. NAH, I CAN'T. I DON'T HAVE THE TIME, AND EVEN IF I DID, I DON'T WANT TO GET IN STRANGLING DISTANCE OF THAT GIRL.
I HEAR YA! WHEN SHE FOUND OUT YOU WERE CHEATING ON HER, SHE SWORE SHE'D KILL YOU.
I WOULDN'T BE THAT WORRIED, THOUGH. SHE MISSES YOU.
IT STILL AIN'T HAPPENING. THANKS TO HER, I DECIDED TO BE A ONE-GIRL MAN FOR A WHILE.
MUMBLE
MUMBLE
THAT REMINDS ME...HOW'S IT COMING ALONG WITH THAT CHICK?
YOU USUALLY SEAL THE DEAL BY NOW.
SLIDE
BEATS ME, MAN...

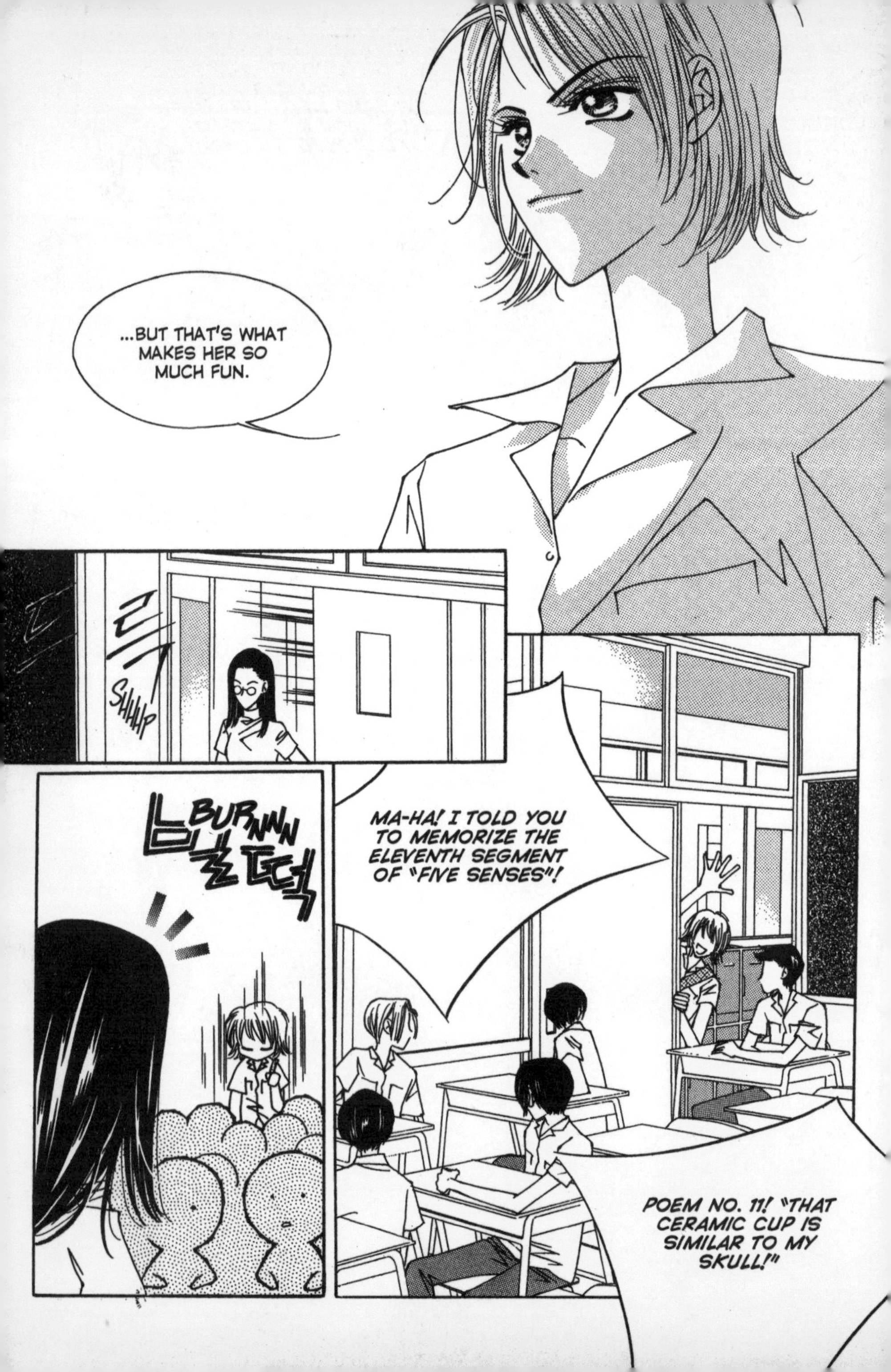
...BUT THAT'S WHAT MAKES HER SO MUCH FUN.
SHUUP
BURNNN
MA-HA! I TOLD YOU TO MEMORIZE THE ELEVENTH SEGMENT OF "FIVE SENSES"!
POEM NO. 11! "THAT CERAMIC CUP IS SIMILAR TO MY SKULL!"

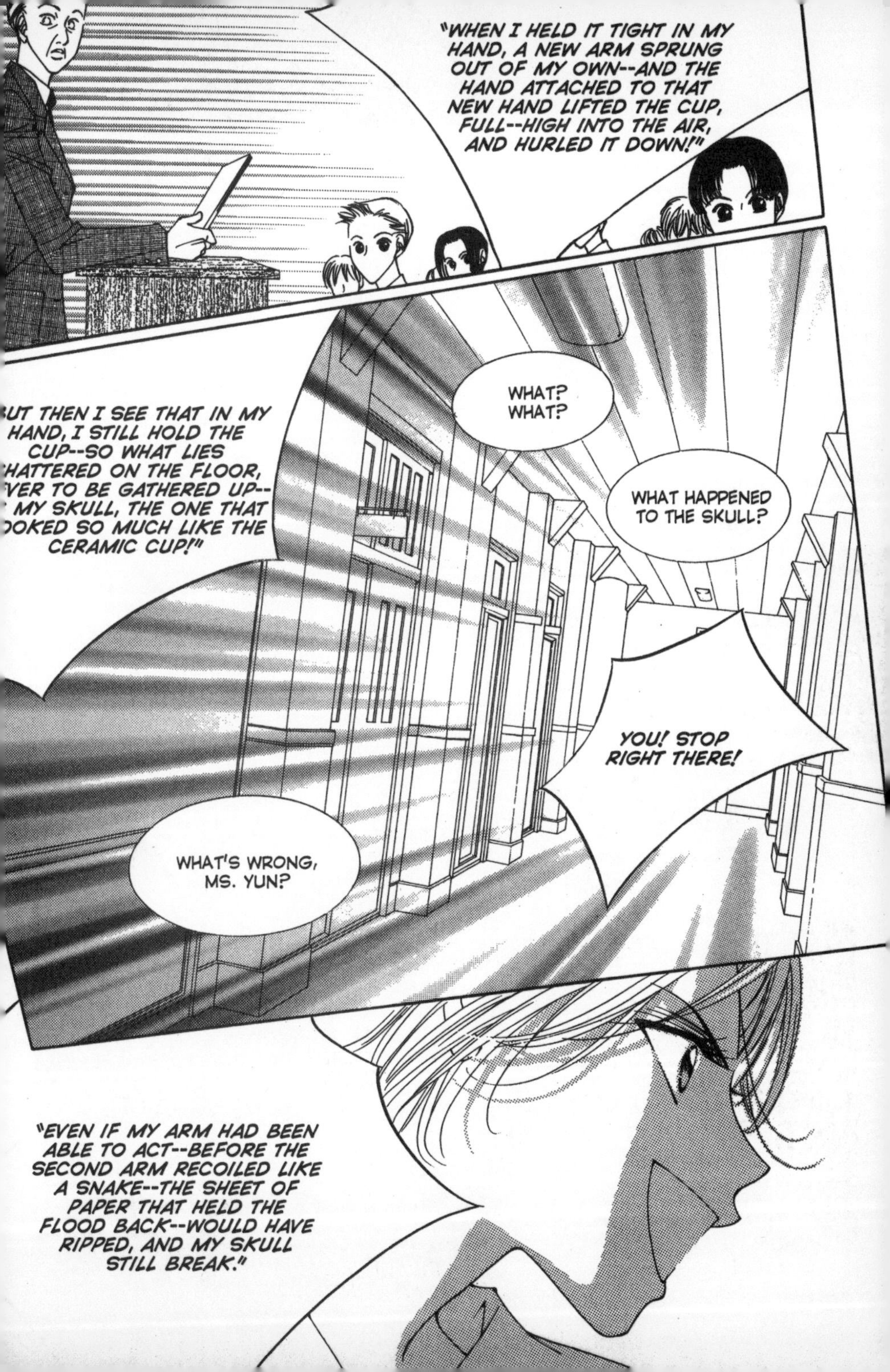
"WHEN I HELD IT TIGHT IN MY HAND, A NEW ARM SPRUNG OUT OF MY OWN--AND THE HAND ATTACHED TO THAT NEW HAND LIFTED THE CUP, FULL--HIGH INTO THE AIR, AND HURLED IT DOWN!"
UT THEN I SEE THAT IN MY HAND, I STILL HOLD THE CUP--SO WHAT LIES HATTERED ON THE FLOOR, VER TO BE GATHERED UP-- MY SKULL, THE ONE THAT OOKED SO MUCH LIKE THE CERAMIC CUP!"
WHAT? WHAT?
WHAT HAPPENED TO THE SKULL?
YOU! STOP RIGHT THERE!
WHAT'S WRONG, MS. YUN?
"EVEN IF MY ARM HAD BEEN ABLE TO ACT--BEFORE THE SECOND ARM RECOILED LIKE A SNAKE--THE SHEET OF PAPER THAT HELD THE FLOOD BACK--WOULD HAVE RIPPED, AND MY SKULL STILL BREAK."

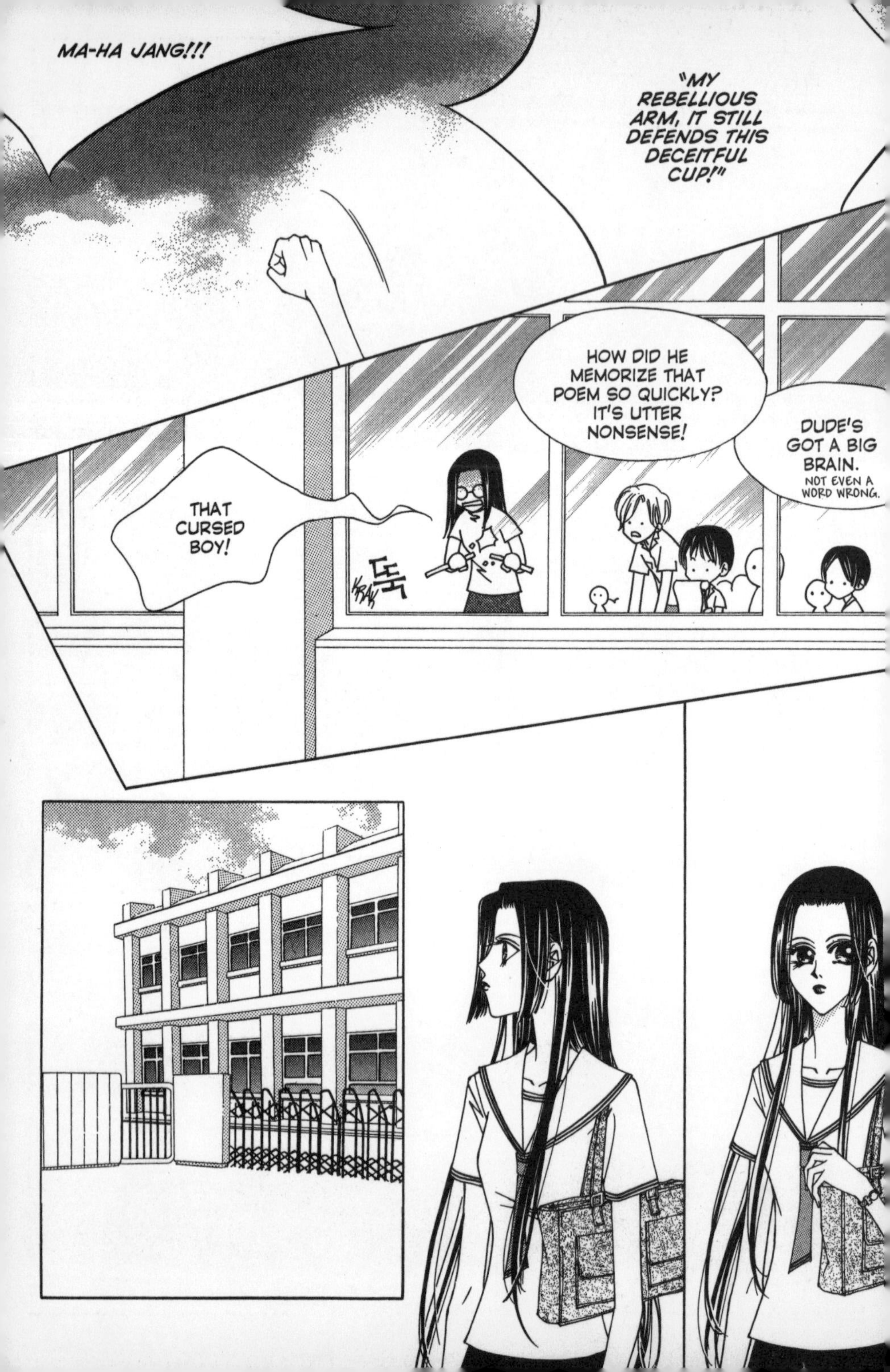
MA-HA JANG!!!
"MY REBELLIOUS ARM, IT STILL DEFENDS THIS DECEITFUL CUP!"
THAT CURSED BOY!
KRAK
HOW DID HE MEMORIZE THAT POEM SO QUICKLY? IT'S UTTER NONSENSE!
DUDE'S GOT A BIG BRAIN.
NOT EVEN A WORD WRONG.

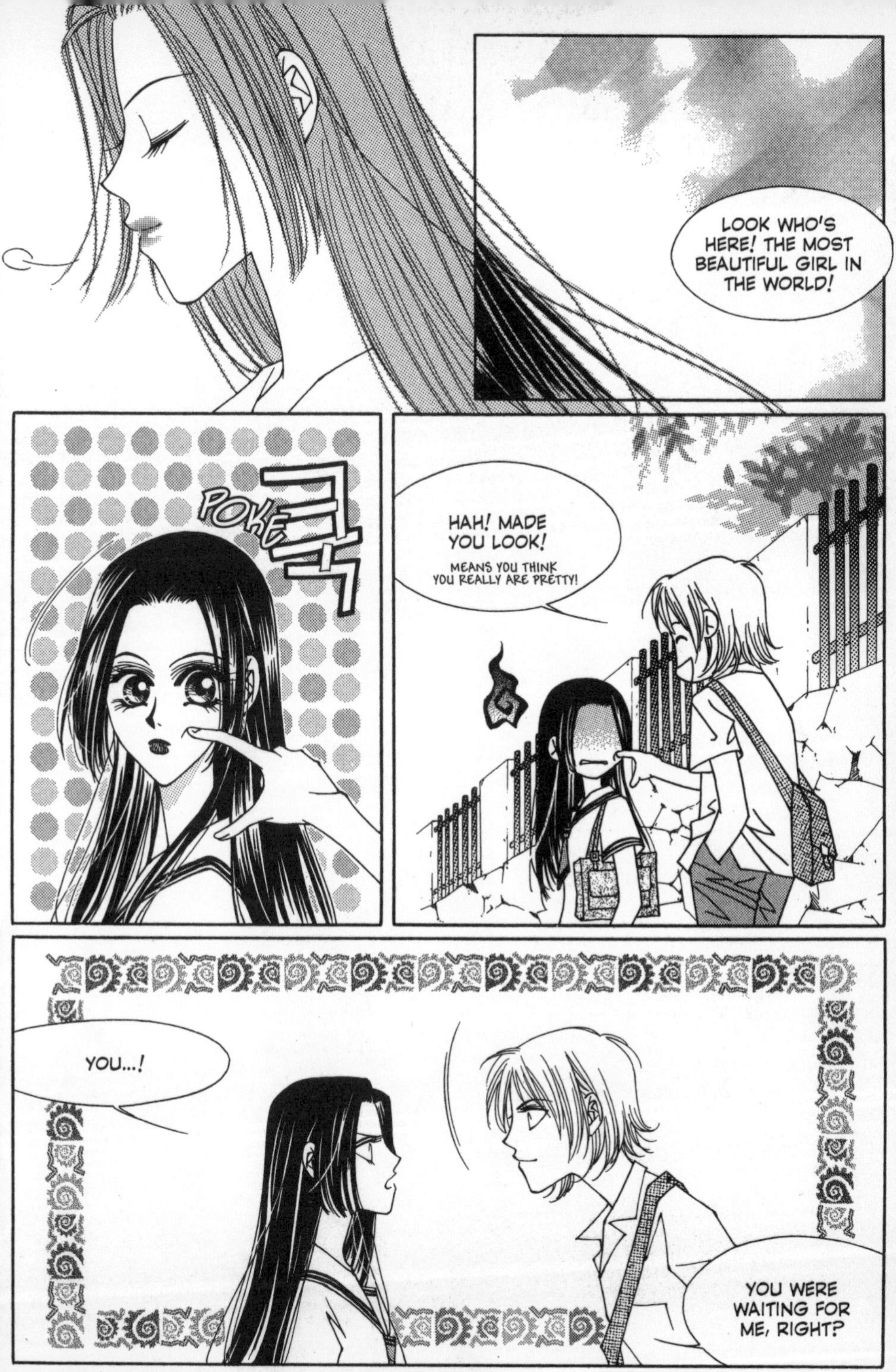
LOOK WHO'S HERE! THE MOST BEAUTIFUL GIRL IN THE WORLD!
POKE
HAH! MADE YOU LOOK!
MEANS YOU THINK YOU REALLY ARE PRETTY!
YOU...!
YOU WERE WAITING FOR ME, RIGHT?

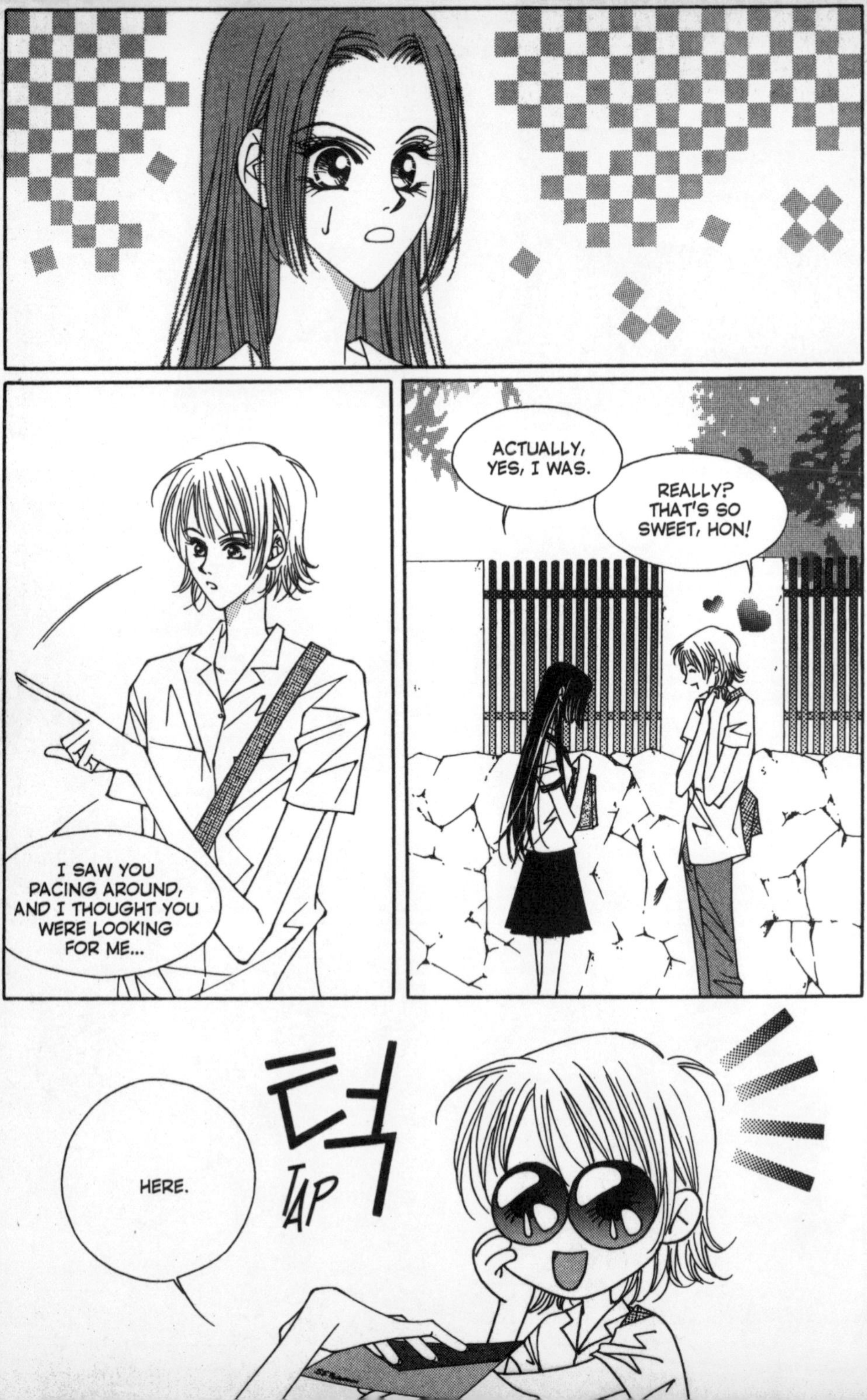
I SAW YOU PACING AROUND, AND I THOUGHT YOU WERE LOOKING FOR ME...
ACTUALLY, YES, I WAS.
REALLY? THAT'S SO SWEET, HON!
HERE.
턱
TAP

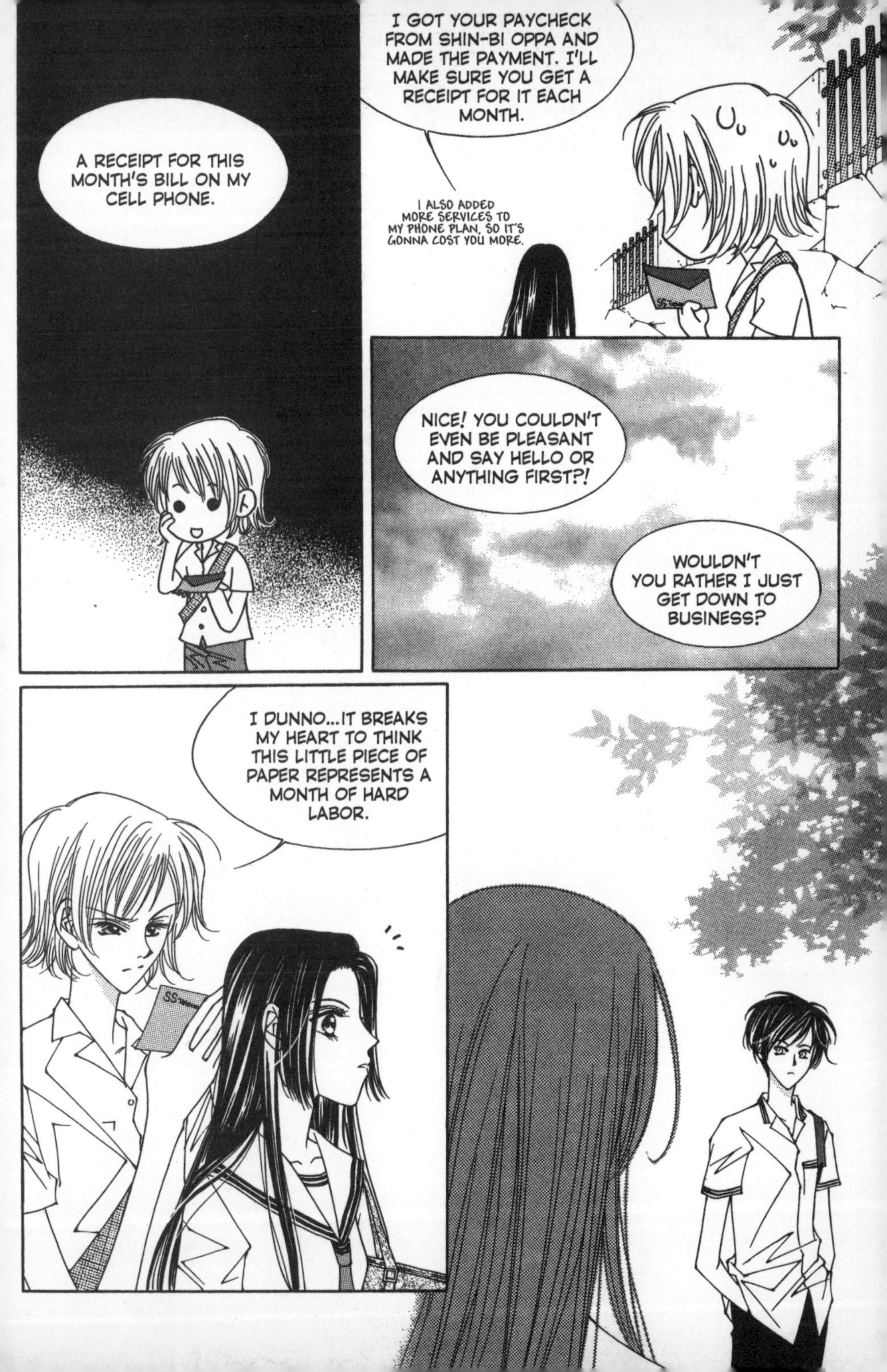
A RECEIPT FOR THIS MONTH'S BILL ON MY CELL PHONE.
I GOT YOUR PAYCHECK FROM SHIN-BI OPPA AND MADE THE PAYMENT. I'LL MAKE SURE YOU GET A RECEIPT FOR IT EACH MONTH.
I ALSO ADDED MORE SERVICES TO MY PHONE PLAN, SO IT'S GONNA COST YOU MORE.
NICE! YOU COULDN'T EVEN BE PLEASANT AND SAY HELLO OR ANYTHING FIRST?!
WOULDN'T YOU RATHER I JUST GET DOWN TO BUSINESS?
I DUNNO...IT BREAKS MY HEART TO THINK THIS LITTLE PIECE OF PAPER REPRESENTS A MONTH OF HARD LABOR.

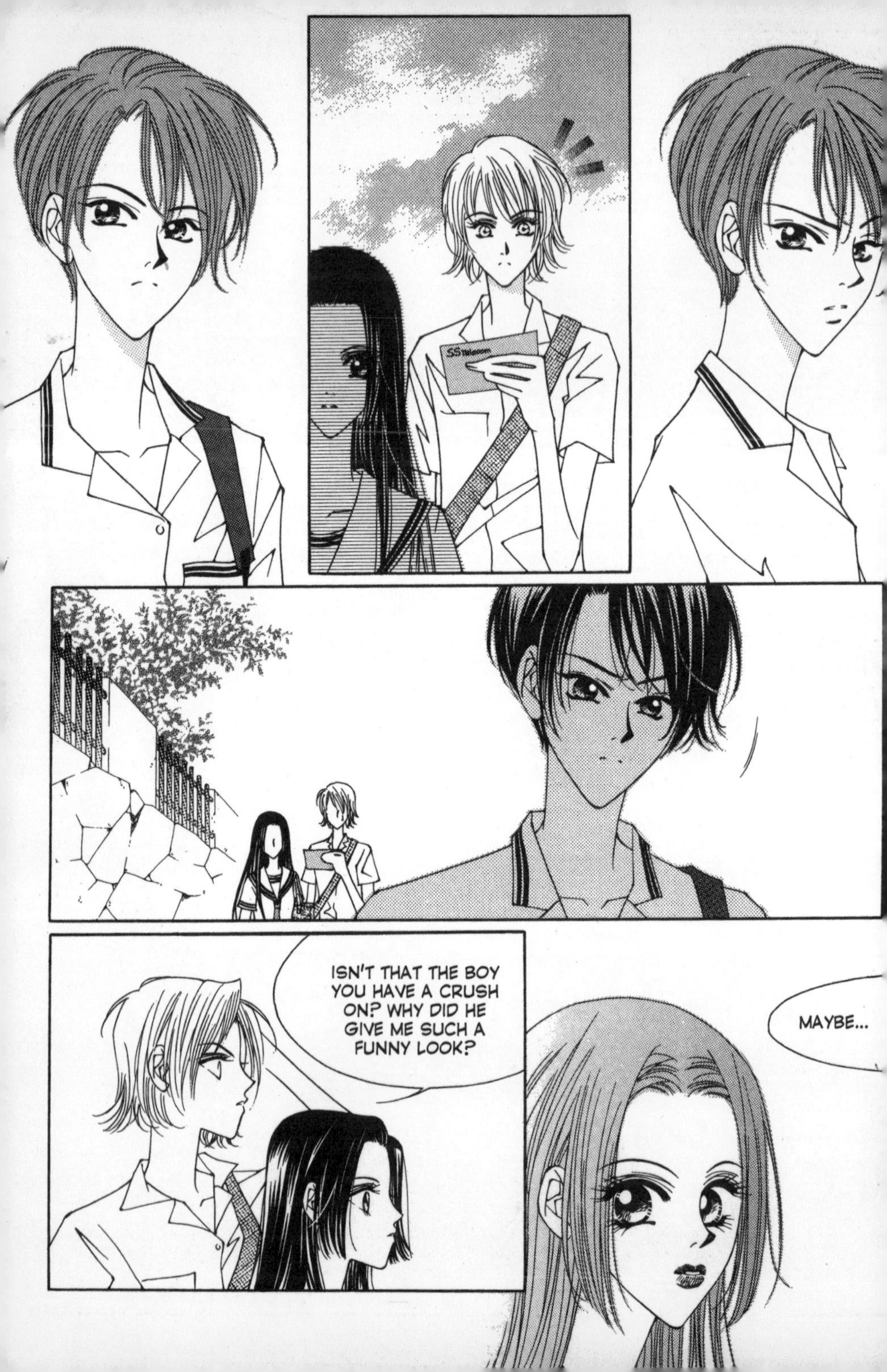
SSTelecom
ISN'T THAT THE BOY YOU HAVE A CRUSH ON? WHY DID HE GIVE ME SUCH A FUNNY LOOK?
MAYBE...

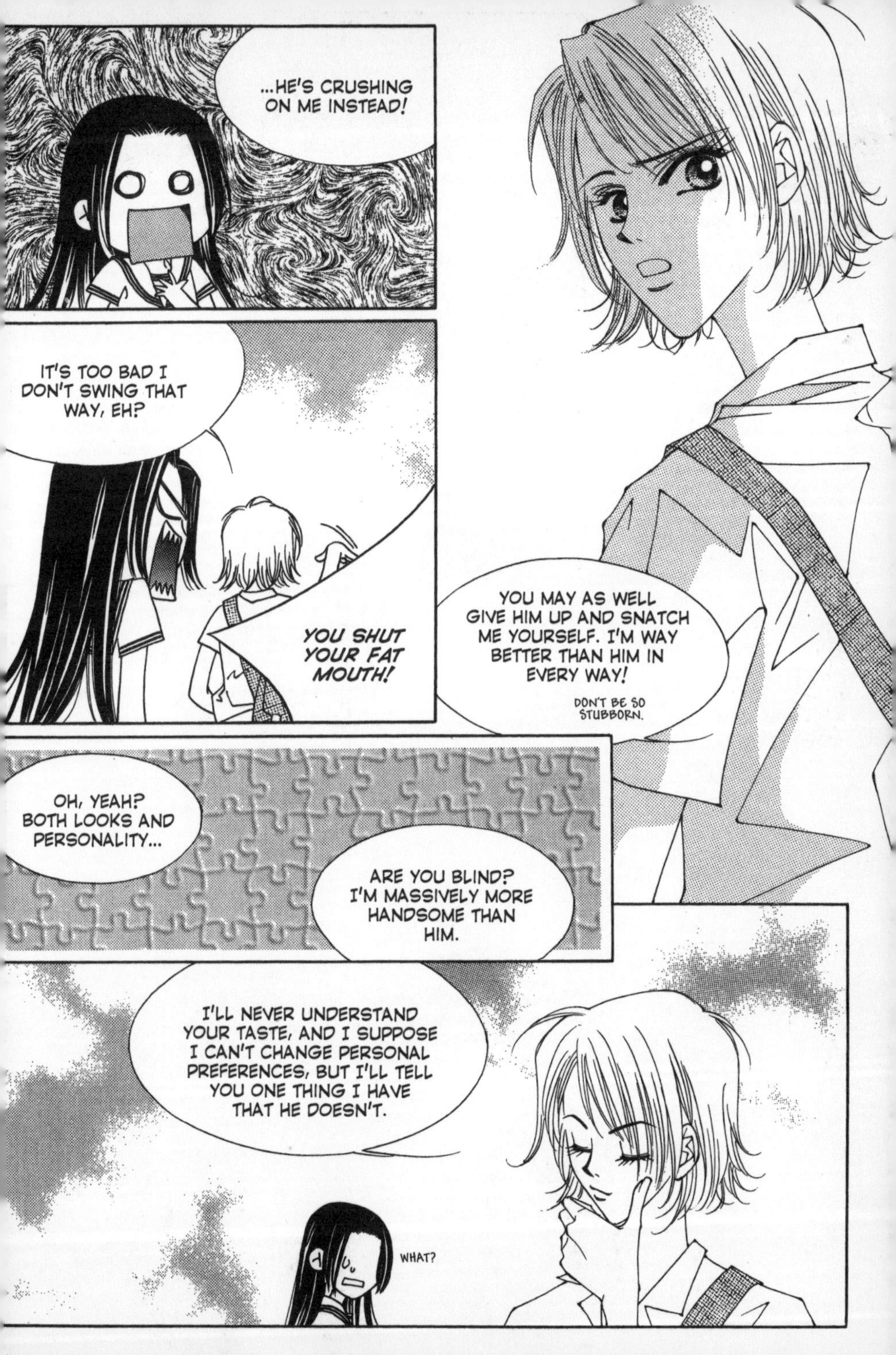
...HE'S CRUSHING ON ME INSTEAD!
IT'S TOO BAD I DON'T SWING THAT WAY, EH?
YOU SHUT YOUR FAT MOUTH!
OH, YEAH? BOTH LOOKS AND PERSONALITY...
ARE YOU BLIND? I'M MASSIVELY MORE HANDSOME THAN HIM.
YOU MAY AS WELL GIVE HIM UP AND SNATCH ME YOURSELF. I'M WAY BETTER THAN HIM IN EVERY WAY!
DON'T BE SO STUBBORN.
I'LL NEVER UNDERSTAND YOUR TASTE, AND I SUPPOSE I CAN'T CHANGE PERSONAL PREFERENCES, BUT I'LL TELL YOU ONE THING I HAVE THAT HE DOESN'T.
WHAT?

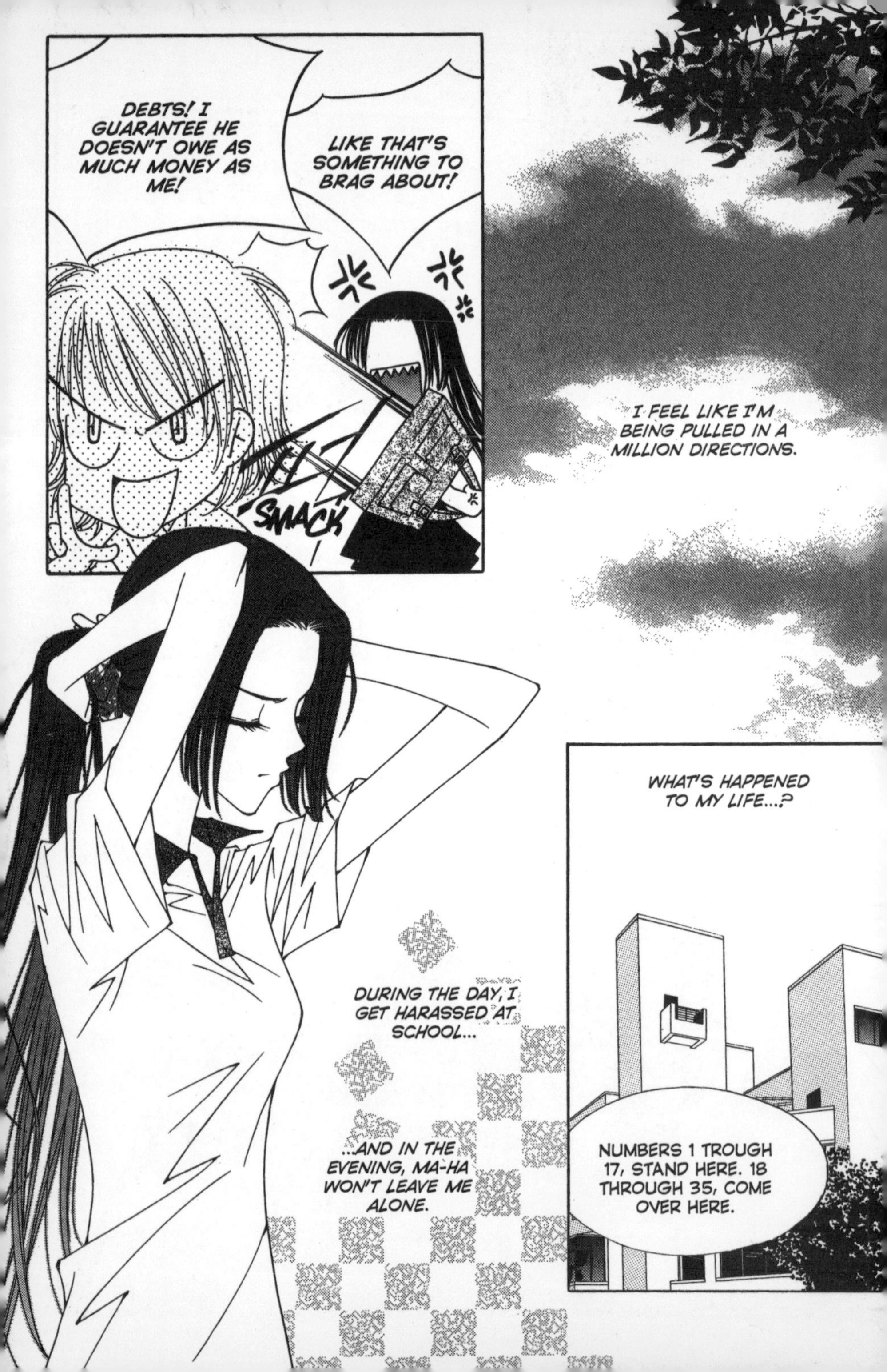
DEBTS! I GUARANTEE HE DOESN'T OWE AS MUCH MONEY AS ME!
LIKE THAT'S SOMETHING TO BRAG ABOUT!
SMACK
I FEEL LIKE I'M BEING PULLED IN A MILLION DIRECTIONS.
DURING THE DAY, I GET HARASSED AT SCHOOL...
...AND IN THE EVENING, MA-HA WON'T LEAVE ME ALONE.
WHAT'S HAPPENED TO MY LIFE...?
NUMBERS 1 TROUGH 17, STAND HERE. 18 THROUGH 35, COME OVER HERE.

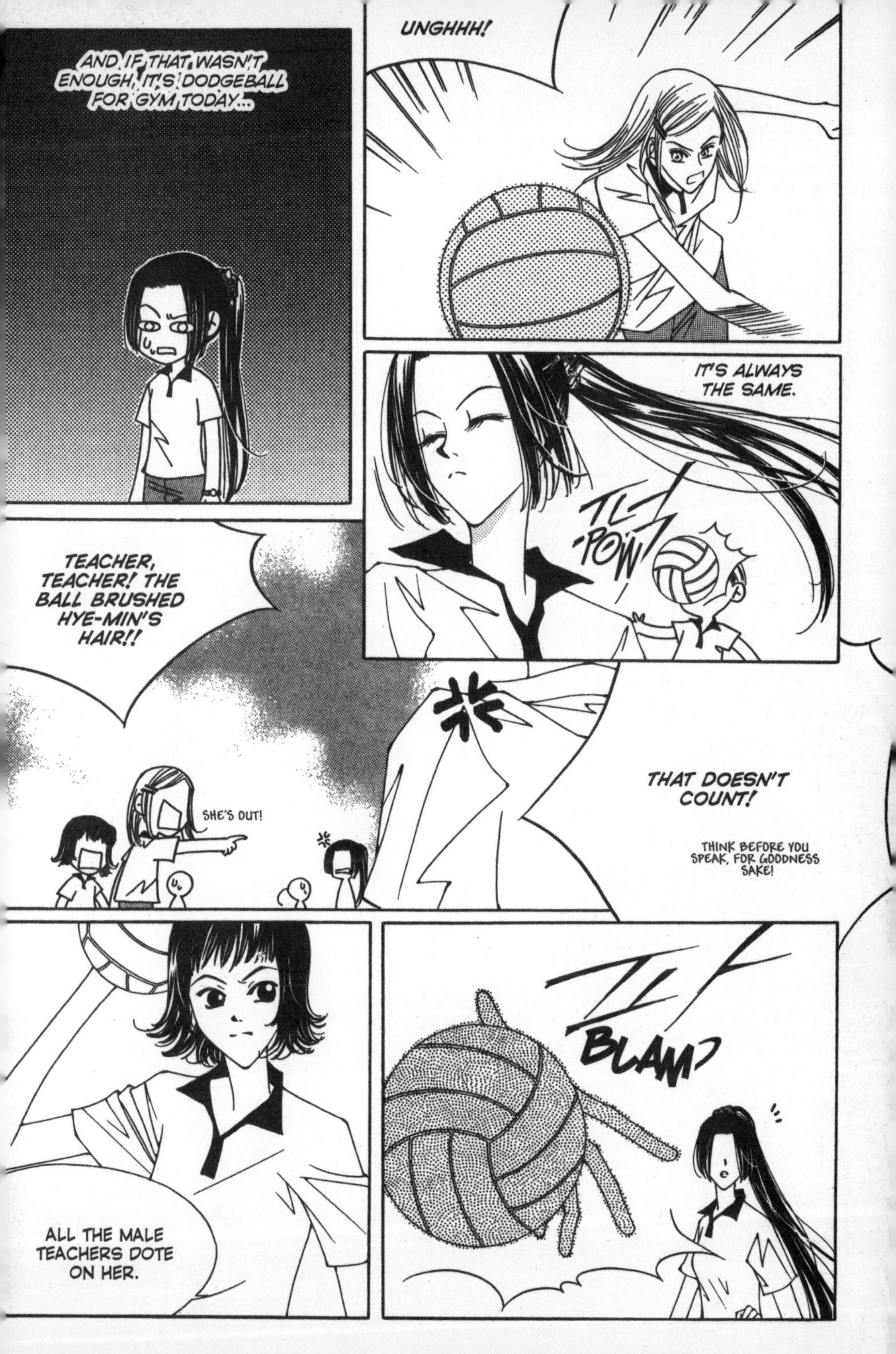
AND IF THAT WASN'T ENOUGH, IT'S DODGEBALL FOR GYM TODAY...
UNGHHH!
IT'S ALWAYS THE SAME.
TL-POW
TEACHER, TEACHER! THE BALL BRUSHED HYE-MIN'S HAIR!!
SHE'S OUT!
THAT DOESN'T COUNT!
THINK BEFORE YOU SPEAK, FOR GOODNESS SAKE!
ALL THE MALE TEACHERS DOTE ON HER.
BLAM

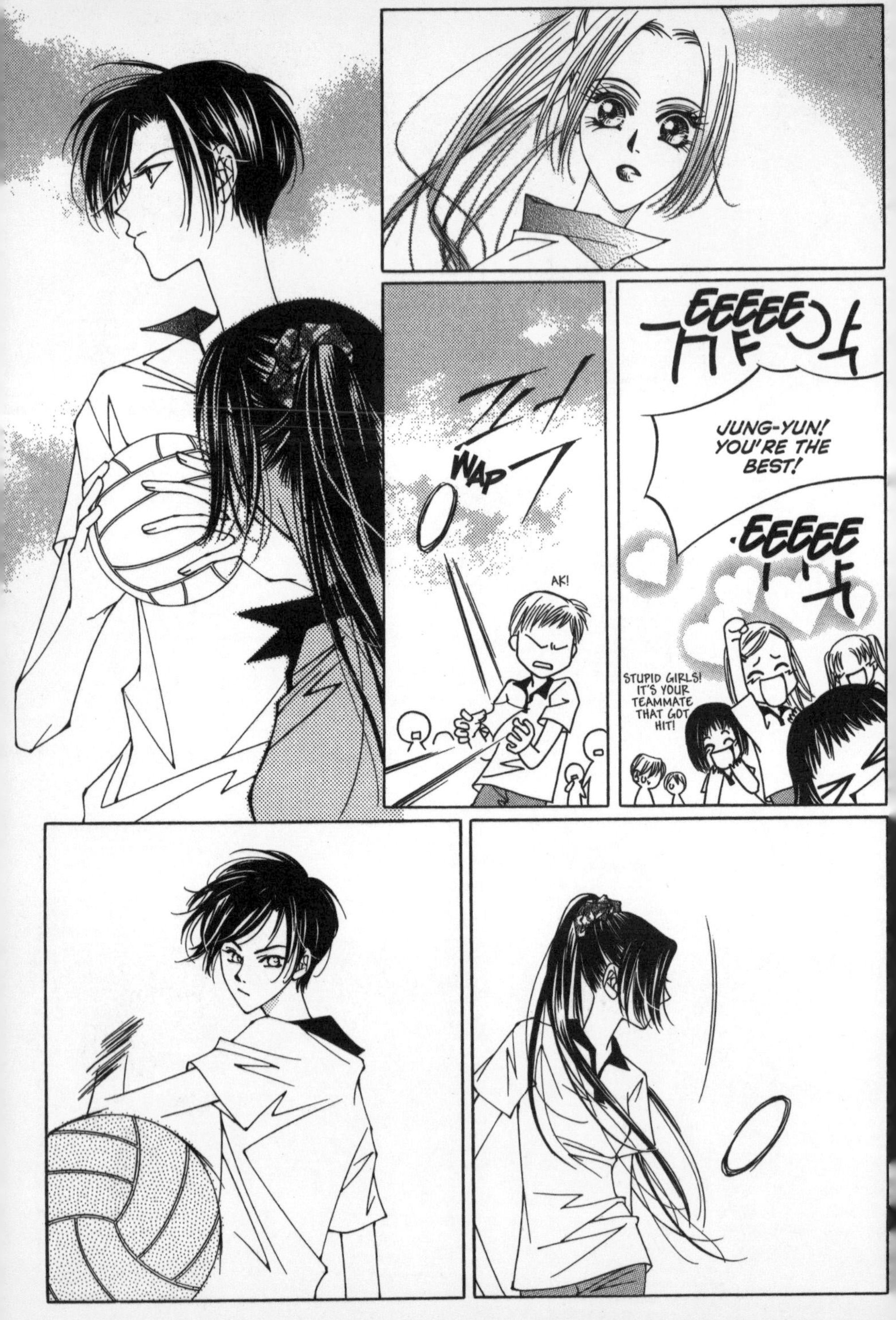
WAP
AK!
EEEEE
JUNG-YUN! YOU'RE THE BEST!
EEEEE
STUPID GIRLS! IT'S YOUR TEAMMATE THAT GOT HIT!

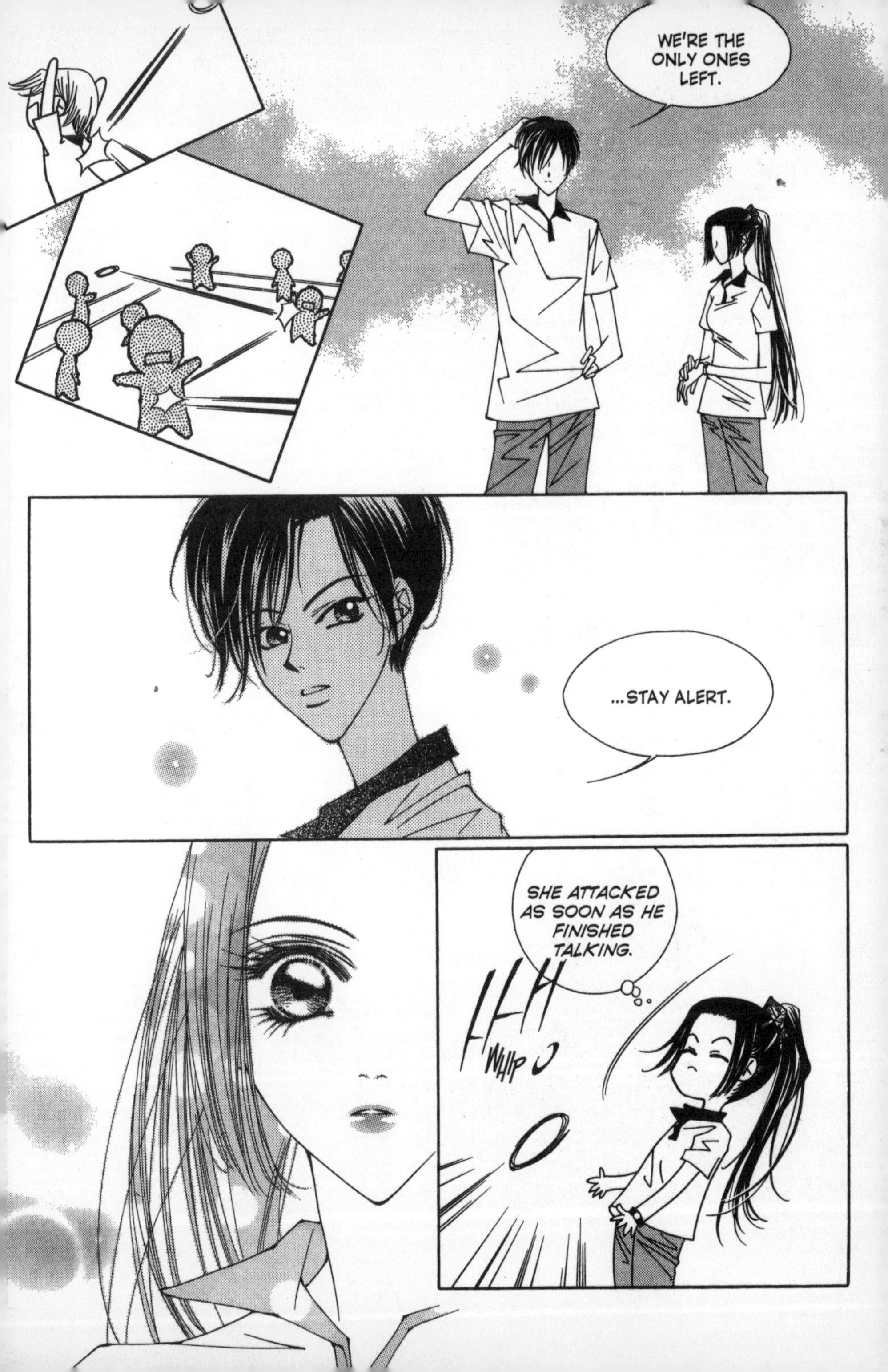
WE'RE THE ONLY ONES LEFT.
...STAY ALERT.
SHE ATTACKED AS SOON AS HE FINISHED TALKING.
WHIP

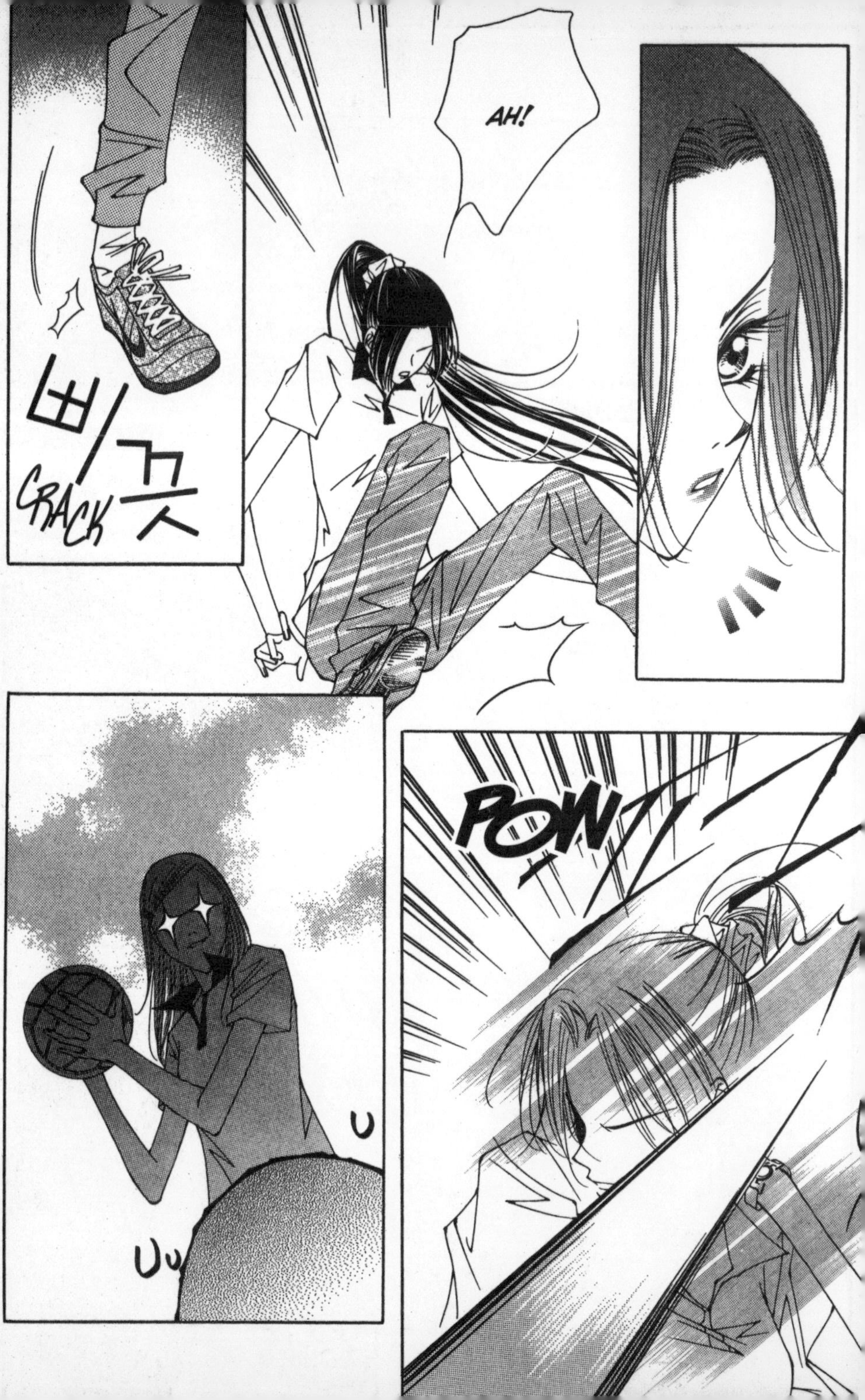
삐끗
CRACK
AH!
U
Uu
POW

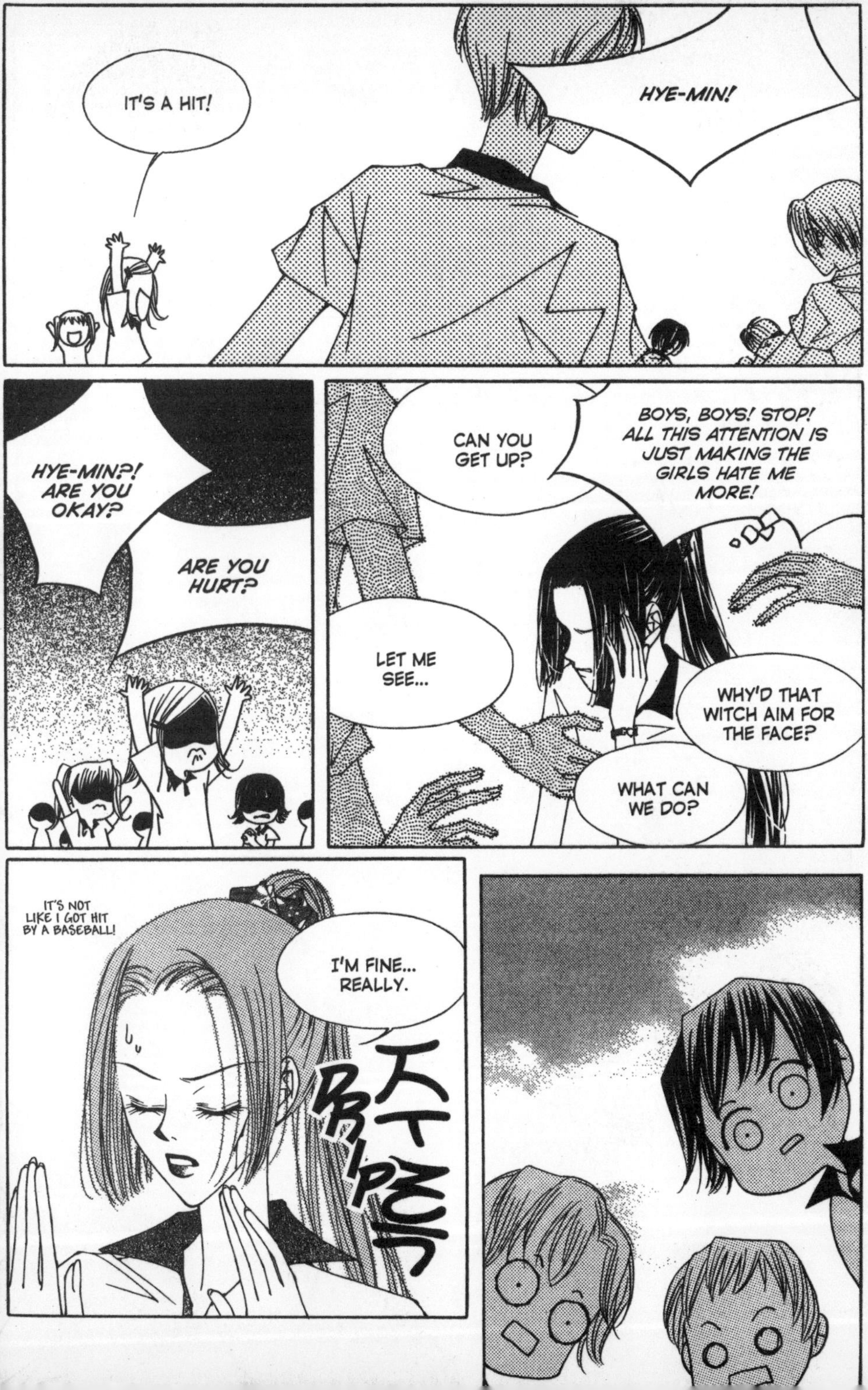
IT'S A HIT!
HYE-MIN!
HYE-MIN?! ARE YOU OKAY?
ARE YOU HURT?
CAN YOU GET UP?
BOYS, BOYS! STOP! ALL THIS ATTENTION IS JUST MAKING THE GIRLS HATE ME MORE!
LET ME SEE...
WHY'D THAT WITCH AIM FOR THE FACE?
WHAT CAN WE DO?
IT'S NOT LIKE I GOT HIT BY A BASEBALL!
I'M FINE... REALLY.
DRIPS

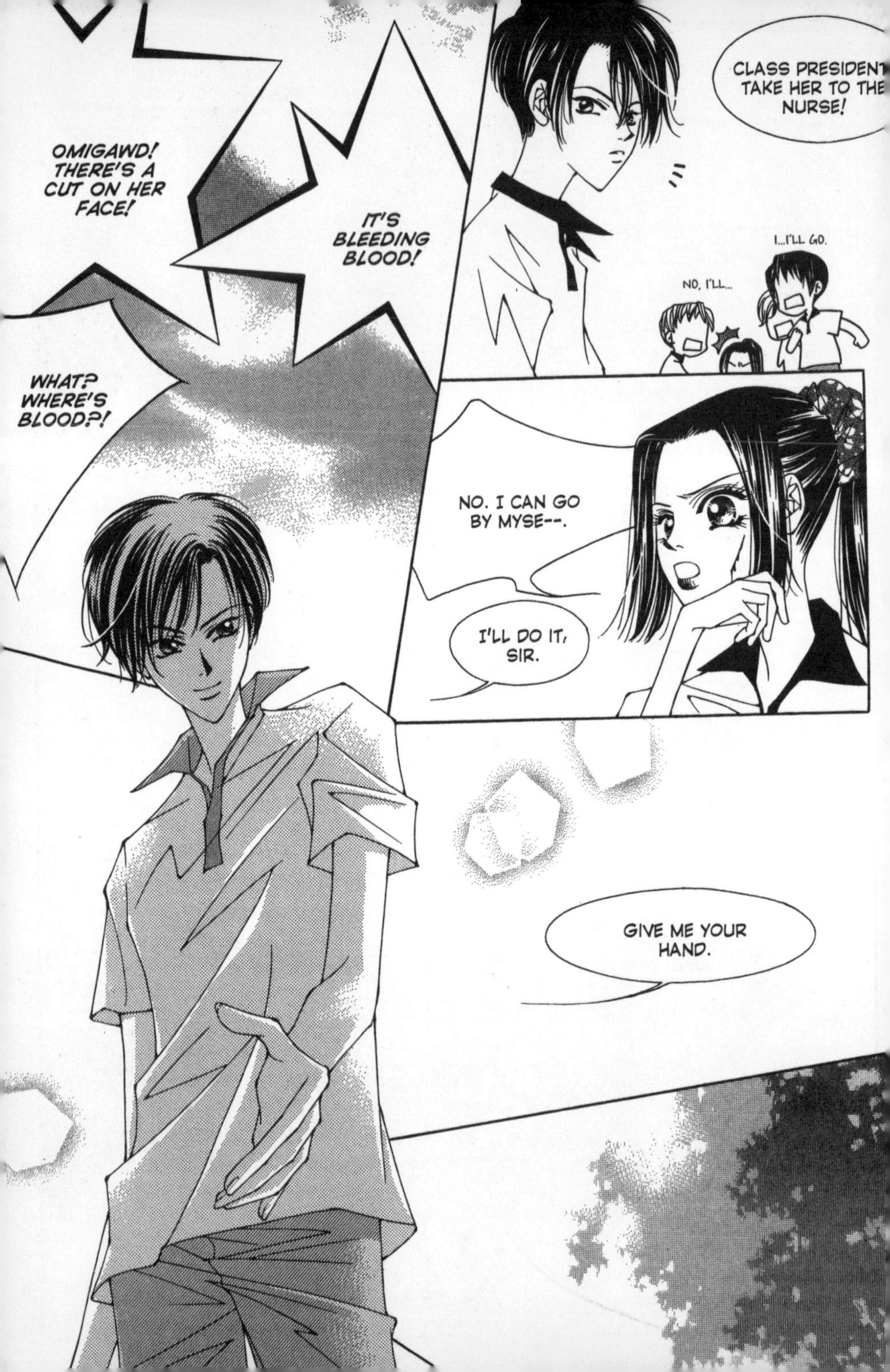
OMIGAWD! THERE'S A CUT ON HER FACE!
IT'S BLEEDING BLOOD!
WHAT? WHERE'S BLOOD?!
CLASS PRESIDENT TAKE HER TO THE NURSE!
NO, I'LL...
I...I'LL GO.
NO. I CAN GO BY MYSE--.
I'LL DO IT, SIR.
GIVE ME YOUR HAND.

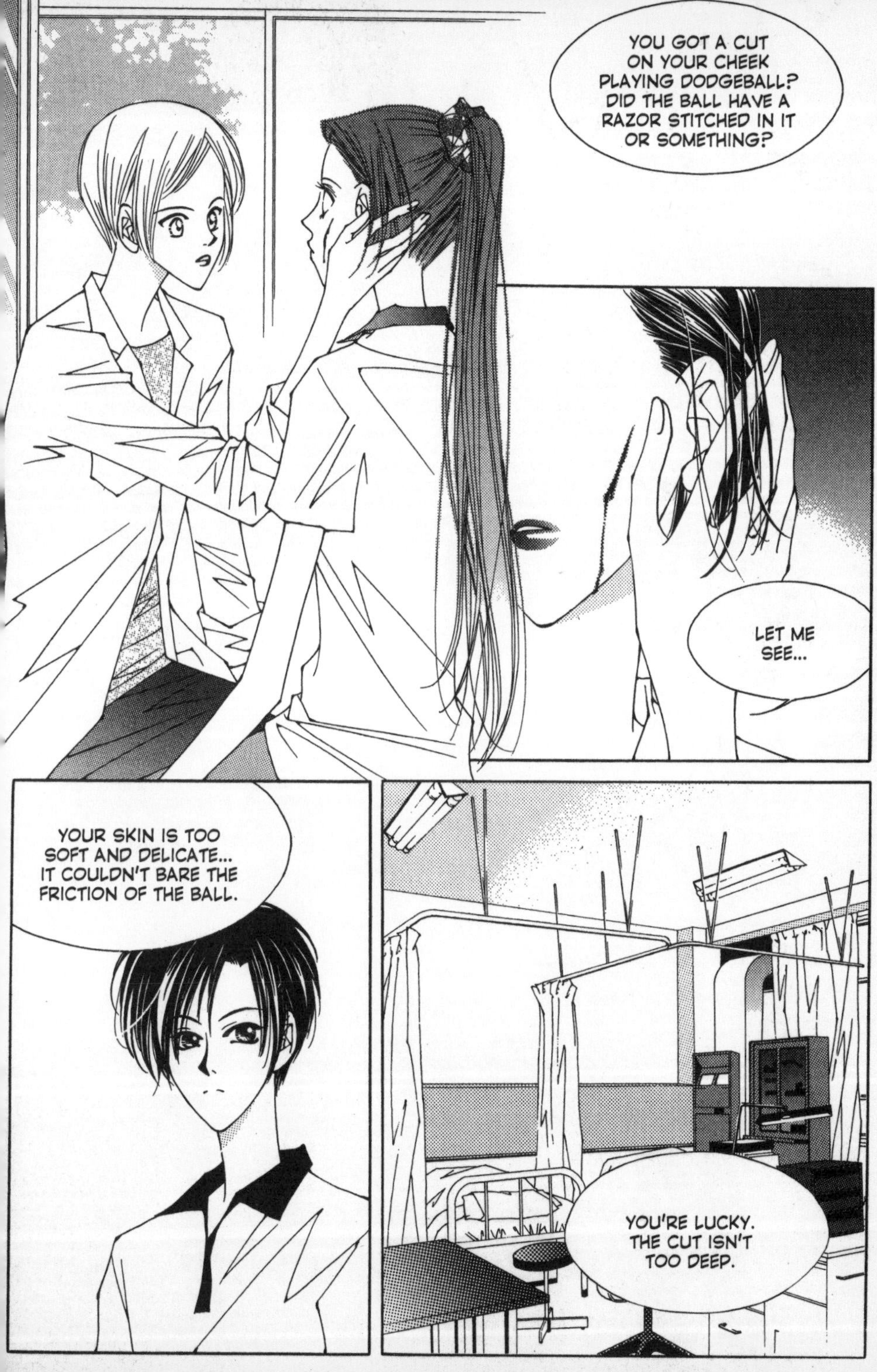
YOU GOT A CUT ON YOUR CHEEK PLAYING DODGEBALL? DID THE BALL HAVE A RAZOR STITCHED IN IT OR SOMETHING?
LET ME SEE...
YOUR SKIN IS TOO SOFT AND DELICATE... IT COULDN'T BARE THE FRICTION OF THE BALL.
YOU'RE LUCKY. THE CUT ISN'T TOO DEEP.

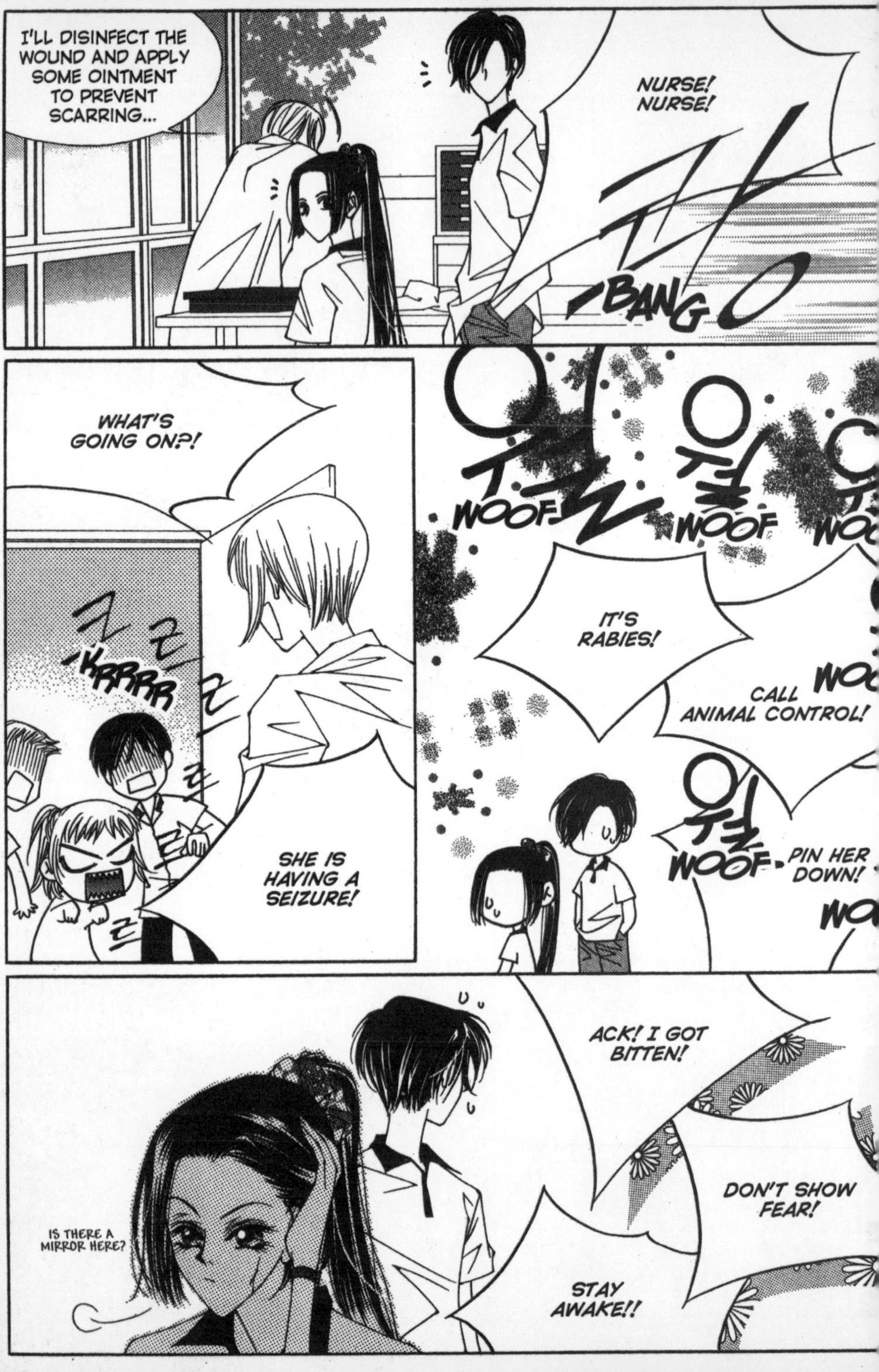
I'LL DISINFECT THE WOUND AND APPLY SOME OINTMENT TO PREVENT SCARRING...
NURSE! NURSE!
BANG
WHAT'S GOING ON?!
KRRRR
SHE IS HAVING A SEIZURE!
WOOF
WOOF
IT'S RABIES!
CALL ANIMAL CONTROL!
WOOF
PIN HER DOWN!
IS THERE A MIRROR HERE?
ACK! I GOT BITTEN!
DON'T SHOW FEAR!
STAY AWAKE!!

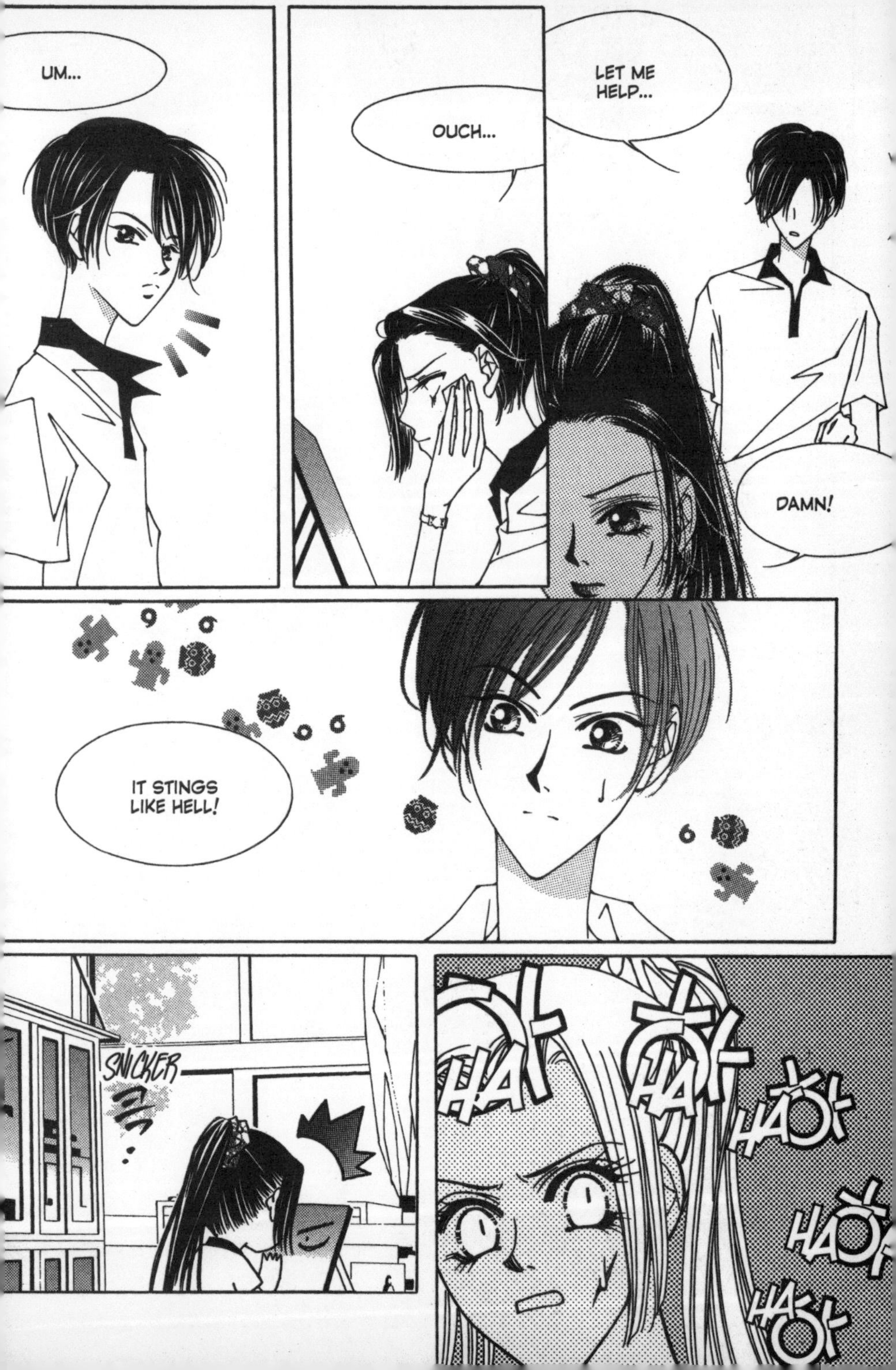
UM...
OUCH...
LET ME HELP...
DAMN!
IT STINGS LIKE HELL!
SNICKER
HA HA HA HA HA

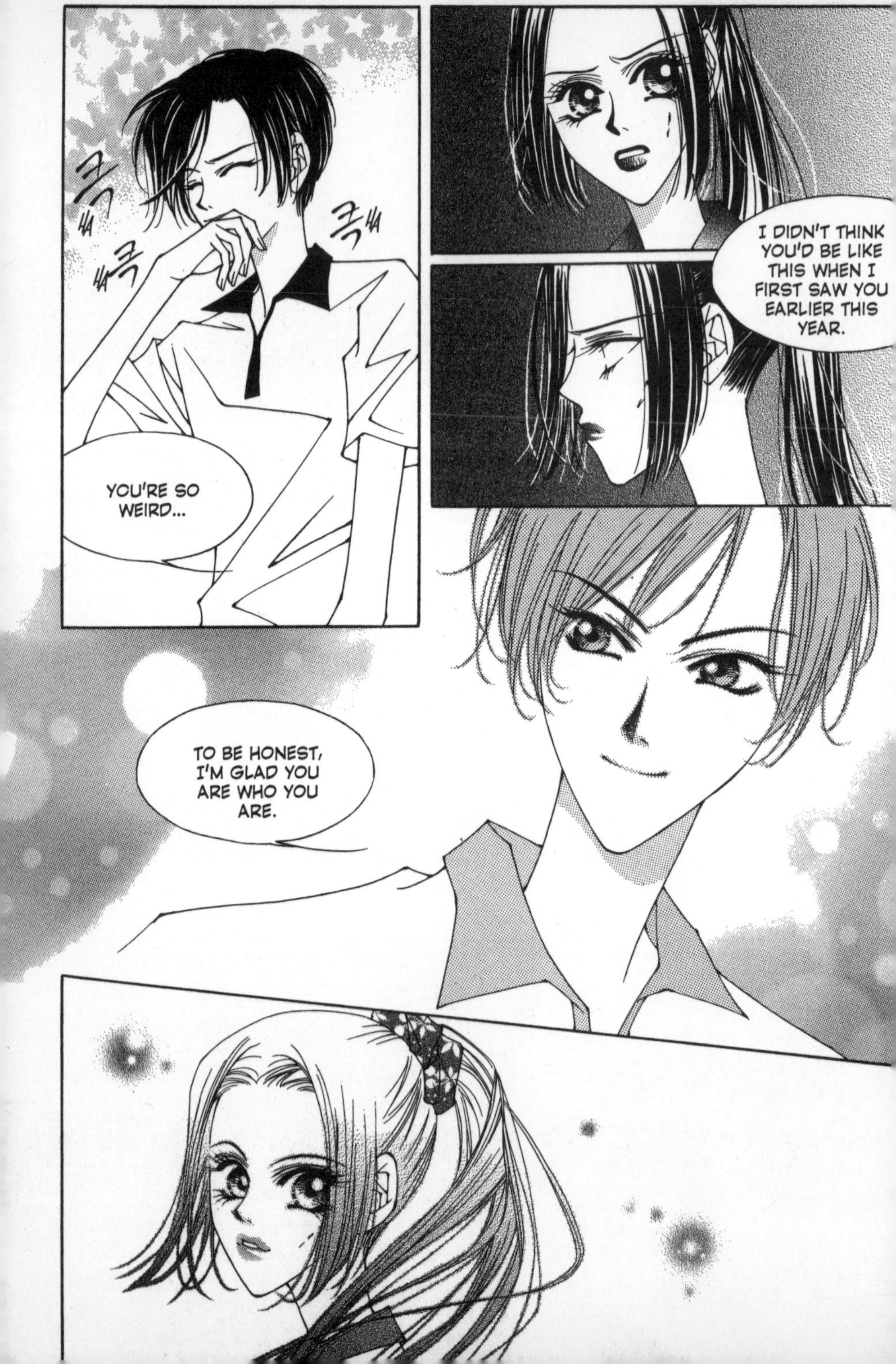
크
크
크
YOU'RE SO WEIRD...
I DIDN'T THINK YOU'D BE LIKE THIS WHEN I FIRST SAW YOU EARLIER THIS YEAR.
TO BE HONEST, I'M GLAD YOU ARE WHO YOU ARE.

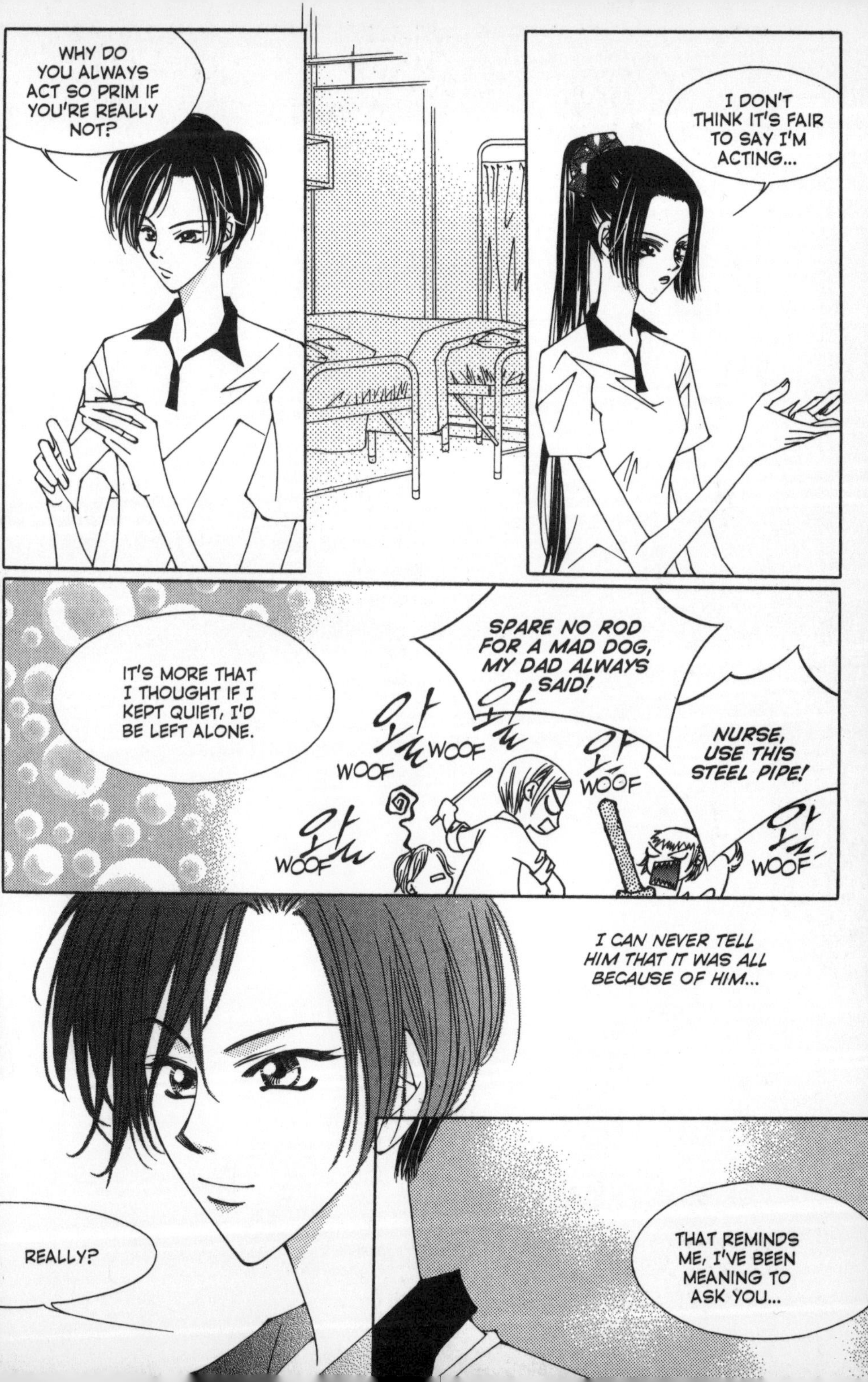
WHY DO YOU ALWAYS ACT SO PRIM IF YOU'RE REALLY NOT?
I DON'T THINK IT'S FAIR TO SAY I'M ACTING...
IT'S MORE THAT I THOUGHT IF I KEPT QUIET, I'D BE LEFT ALONE.
SPARE NO ROD FOR A MAD DOG, MY DAD ALWAYS SAID!
WOOF
WOOF
WOOF
WOOF
NURSE, USE THIS STEEL PIPE!
WOOF
I CAN NEVER TELL HIM THAT IT WAS ALL BECAUSE OF HIM...
REALLY?
THAT REMINDS ME, I'VE BEEN MEANING TO ASK YOU...

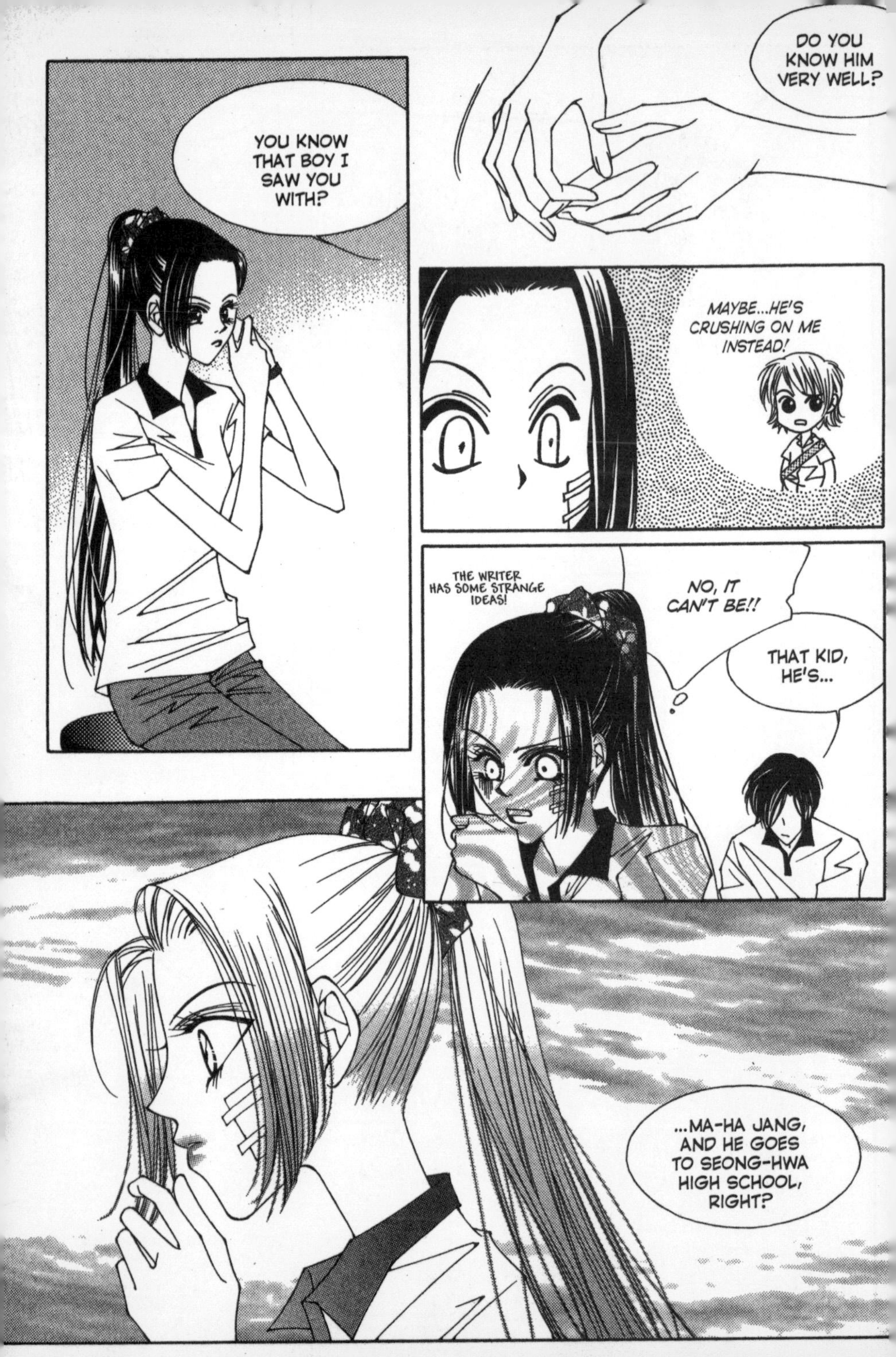
YOU KNOW THAT BOY I SAW YOU WITH?
DO YOU KNOW HIM VERY WELL?
MAYBE...HE'S CRUSHING ON ME INSTEAD!
THE WRITER HAS SOME STRANGE IDEAS!
NO, IT CAN'T BE!!
THAT KID, HE'S...
...MA-HA JANG, AND HE GOES TO SEONG-HWA HIGH SCHOOL, RIGHT?

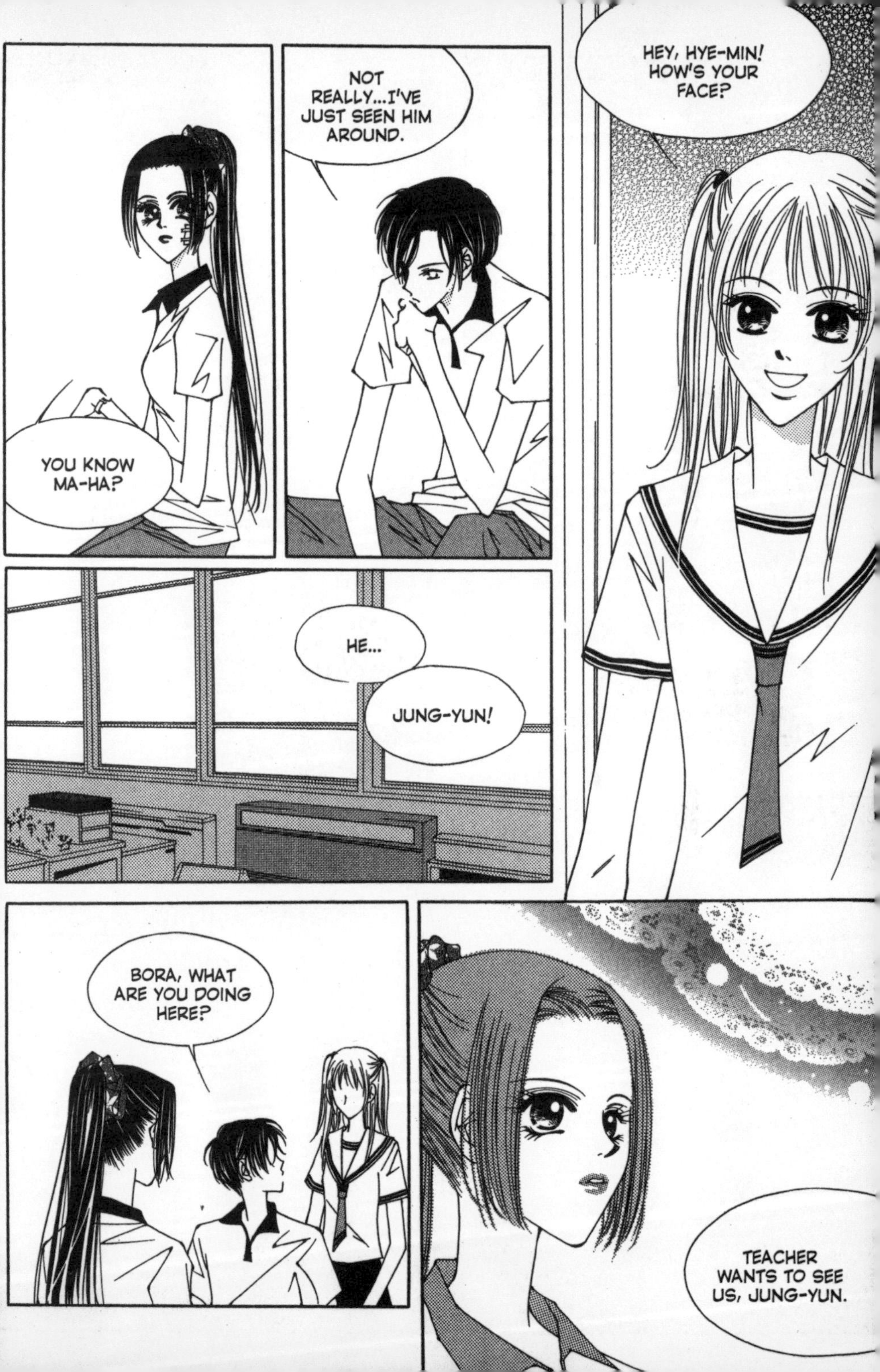
YOU KNOW MA-HA?
NOT REALLY...I'VE JUST SEEN HIM AROUND.
HE...
JUNG-YUN!
HEY, HYE-MIN! HOW'S YOUR FACE?
BORA, WHAT ARE YOU DOING HERE?
TEACHER WANTS TO SEE US, JUNG-YUN.

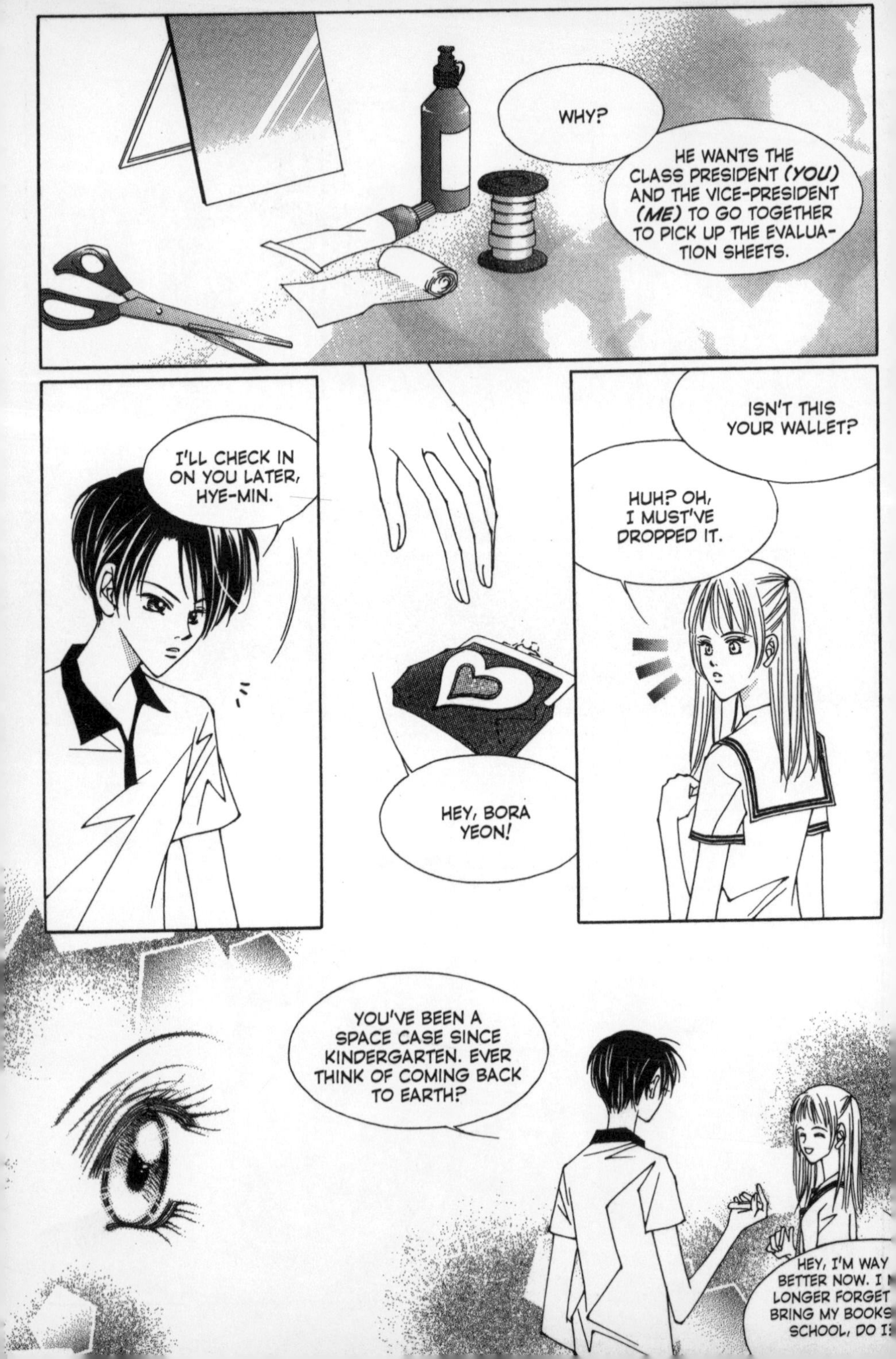
WHY?
HE WANTS THE CLASS PRESIDENT (YOU) AND THE VICE-PRESIDENT (ME) TO GO TOGETHER TO PICK UP THE EVALUATION SHEETS.
I'LL CHECK IN ON YOU LATER, HYE-MIN.
HEY, BORA YEON!
ISN'T THIS YOUR WALLET?
HUH? OH, I MUST'VE DROPPED IT.
YOU'VE BEEN A SPACE CASE SINCE KINDERGARTEN. EVER THINK OF COMING BACK TO EARTH?
HEY, I'M WAY BETTER NOW. I
LONGER FORGET
BRING MY BOOKS
SCHOOL, DO I

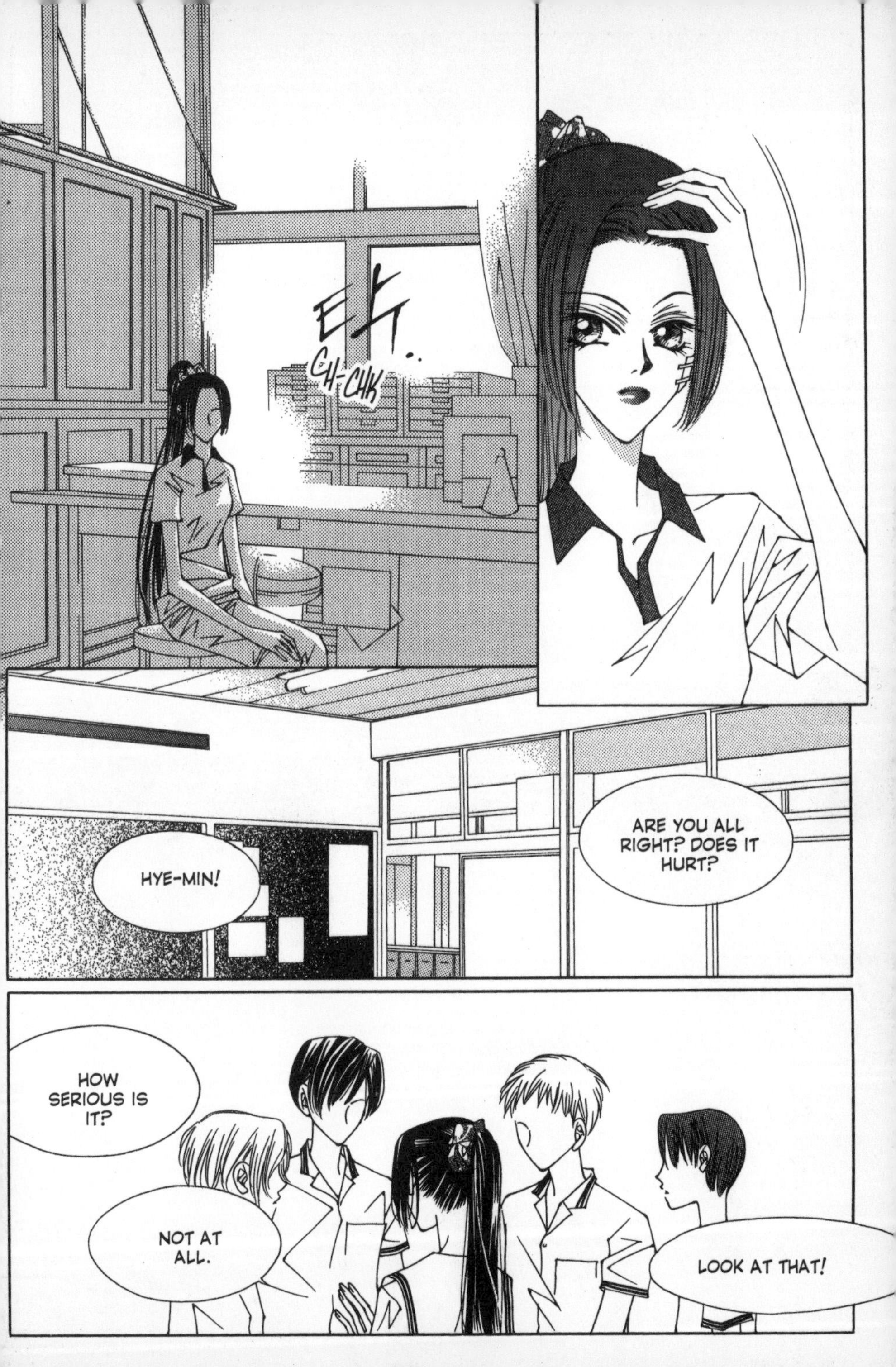
CH-CHK
HYE-MIN!
ARE YOU ALL RIGHT? DOES IT HURT?
HOW SERIOUS IS IT?
NOT AT ALL.
LOOK AT THAT!

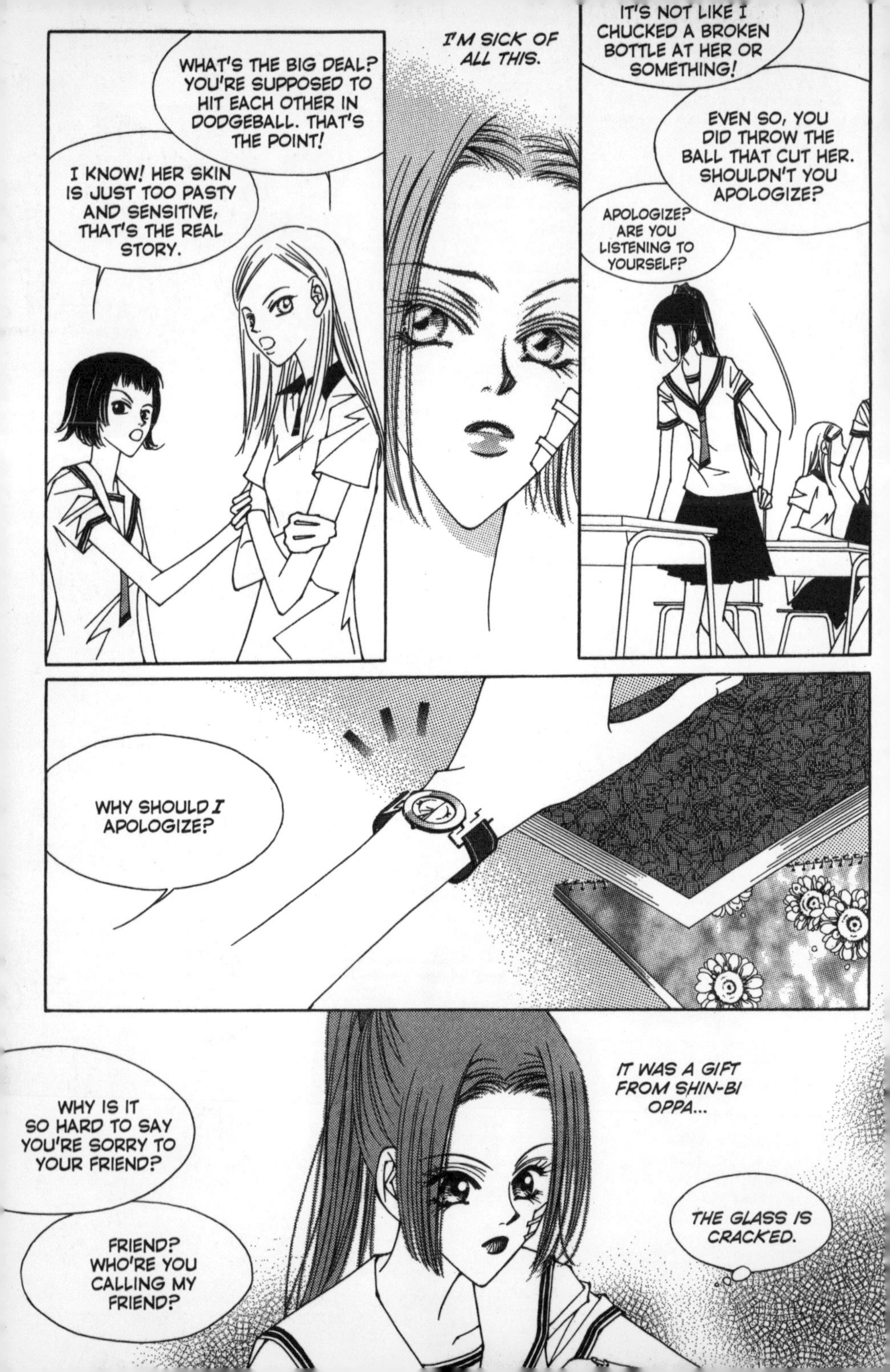
WHAT'S THE BIG DEAL? YOU'RE SUPPOSED TO HIT EACH OTHER IN DODGEBALL. THAT'S THE POINT!
I KNOW! HER SKIN IS JUST TOO PASTY AND SENSITIVE, THAT'S THE REAL STORY.
I'M SICK OF ALL THIS.
IT'S NOT LIKE I CHUCKED A BROKEN BOTTLE AT HER OR SOMETHING!
EVEN SO, YOU DID THROW THE BALL THAT CUT HER. SHOULDN'T YOU APOLOGIZE?
APOLOGIZE? ARE YOU LISTENING TO YOURSELF?
WHY SHOULD I APOLOGIZE?
WHY IS IT SO HARD TO SAY YOU'RE SORRY TO YOUR FRIEND?
FRIEND? WHO'RE YOU CALLING MY FRIEND?
IT WAS A GIFT FROM SHIN-BI OPPA...
THE GLASS IS CRACKED.

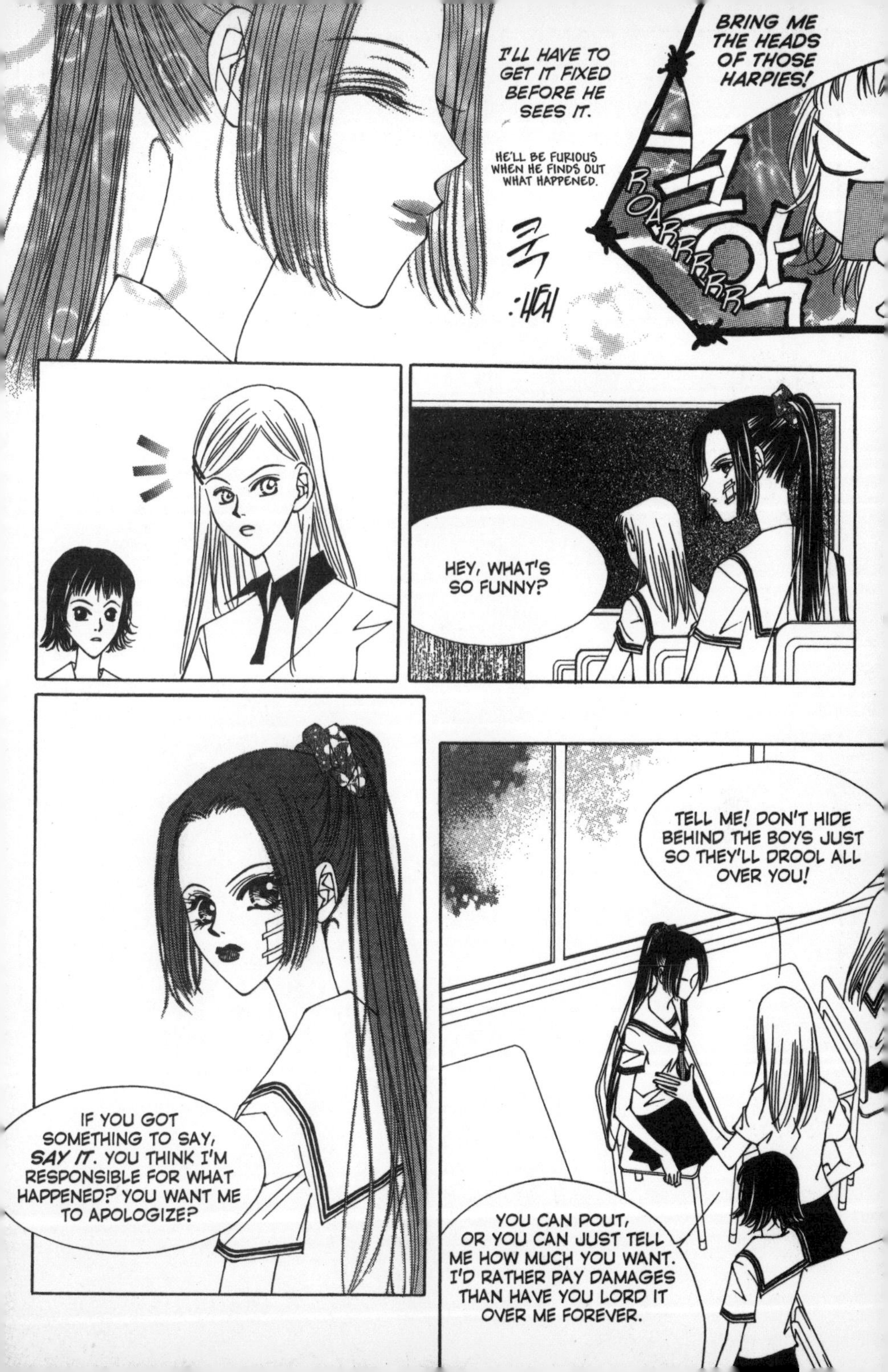
I'LL HAVE TO GET IT FIXED BEFORE HE SEES IT.
HE'LL BE FURIOUS WHEN HE FINDS OUT WHAT HAPPENED.
쿡
:HEH
BRING ME THE HEADS OF THOSE HARPIES!
크아아
ROARRRRRR
HEY, WHAT'S SO FUNNY?
IF YOU GOT SOMETHING TO SAY, SAY IT. YOU THINK I'M RESPONSIBLE FOR WHAT HAPPENED? YOU WANT ME TO APOLOGIZE?
TELL ME! DON'T HIDE BEHIND THE BOYS JUST SO THEY'LL DROOL ALL OVER YOU!
YOU CAN POUT, OR YOU CAN JUST TELL ME HOW MUCH YOU WANT. I'D RATHER PAY DAMAGES THAN HAVE YOU LORD IT OVER ME FOREVER.

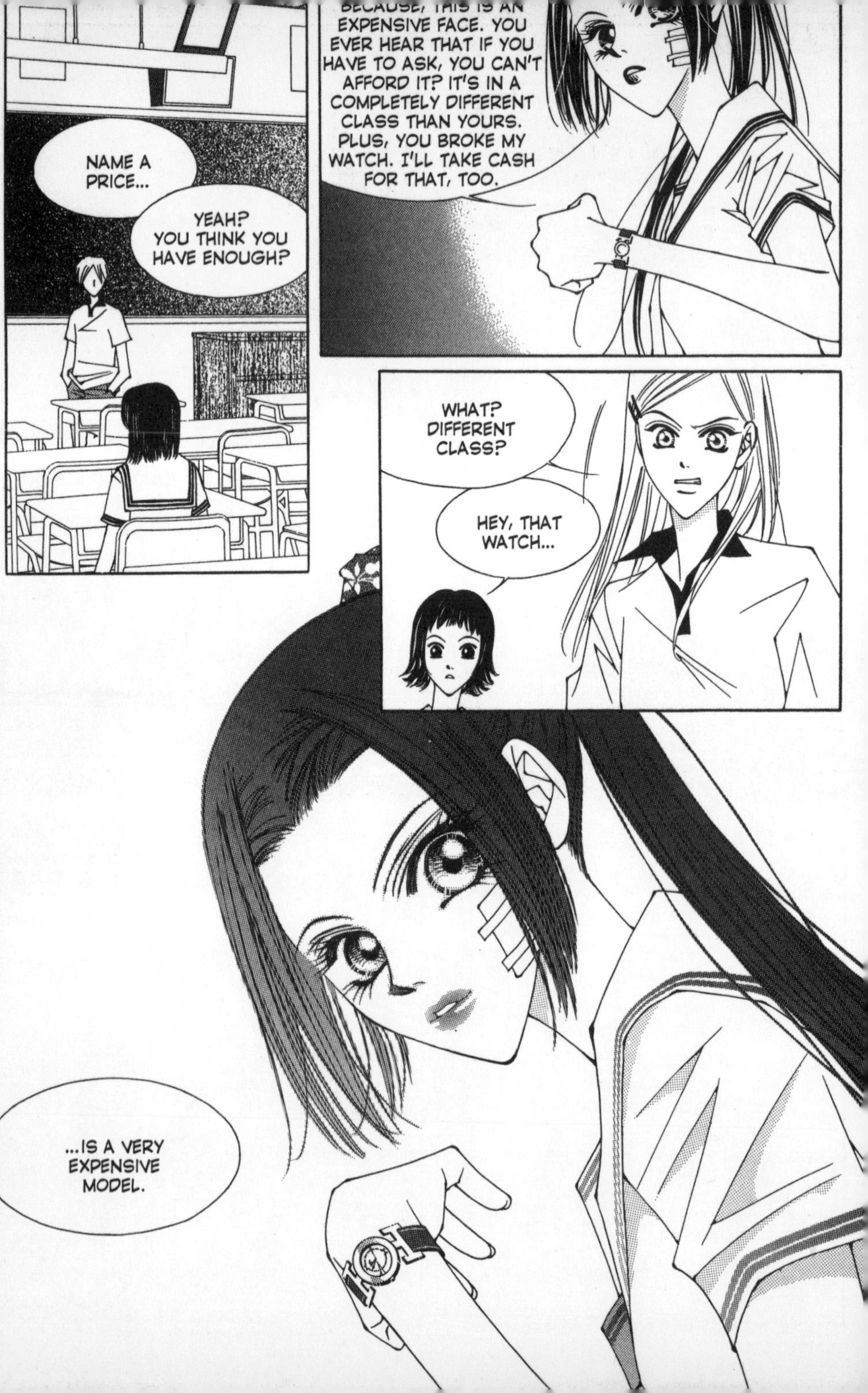
NAME A PRICE...
YEAH? YOU THINK YOU HAVE ENOUGH?
BECAUSE, THIS IS AN EXPENSIVE FACE. YOU EVER HEAR THAT IF YOU HAVE TO ASK, YOU CAN'T AFFORD IT? IT'S IN A COMPLETELY DIFFERENT CLASS THAN YOURS. PLUS, YOU BROKE MY WATCH. I'LL TAKE CASH FOR THAT, TOO.
WHAT? DIFFERENT CLASS?
HEY, THAT WATCH...
...IS A VERY EXPENSIVE MODEL.

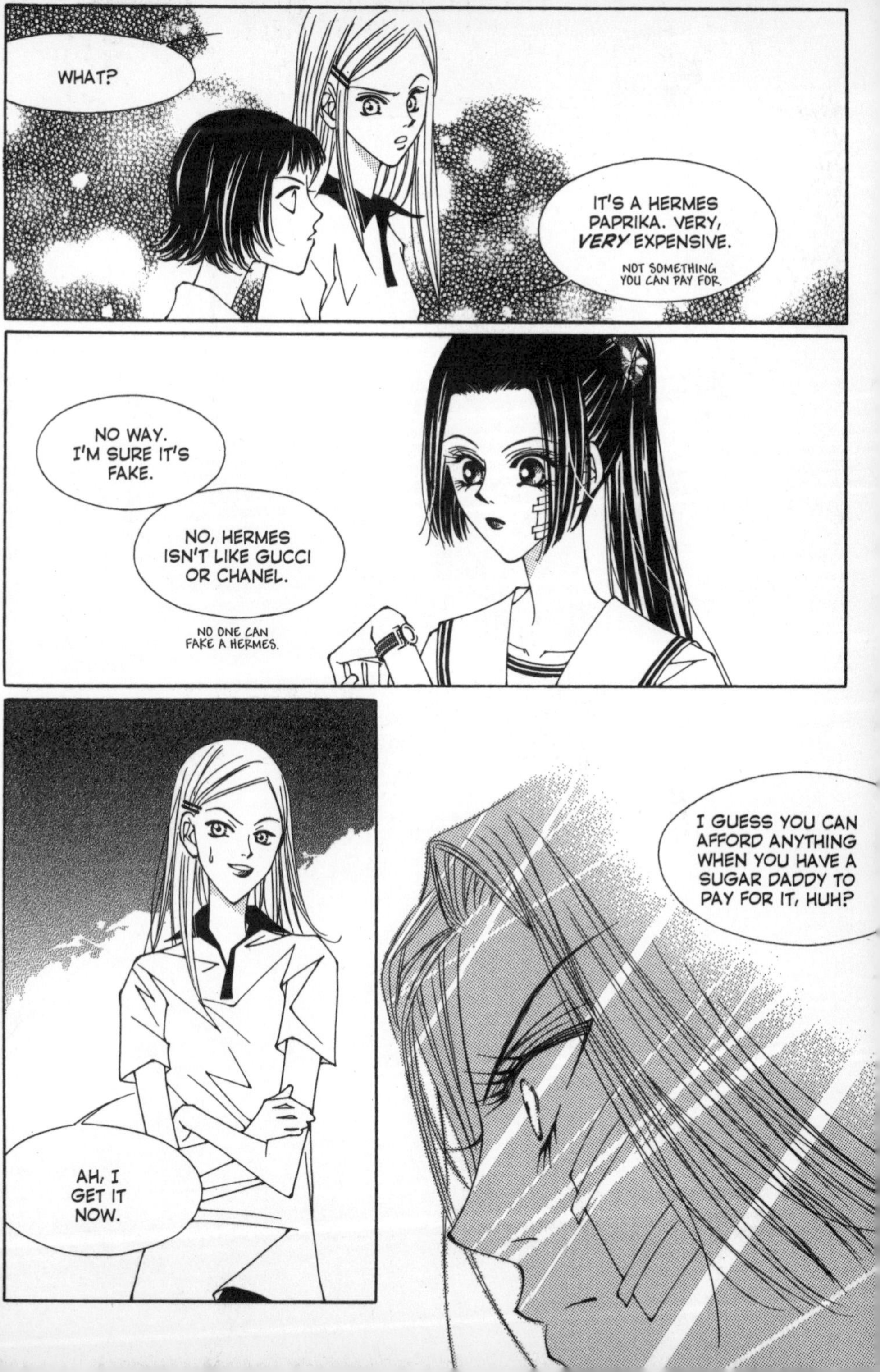
WHAT?
IT'S A HERMES PAPRIKA. VERY, *VERY* EXPENSIVE.
NOT SOMETHING YOU CAN PAY FOR.
NO WAY. I'M SURE IT'S FAKE.
NO, HERMES ISN'T LIKE GUCCI OR CHANEL.
NO ONE CAN FAKE A HERMES.
AH, I GET IT NOW.
I GUESS YOU CAN AFFORD ANYTHING WHEN YOU HAVE A SUGAR DADDY TO PAY FOR IT, HUH?

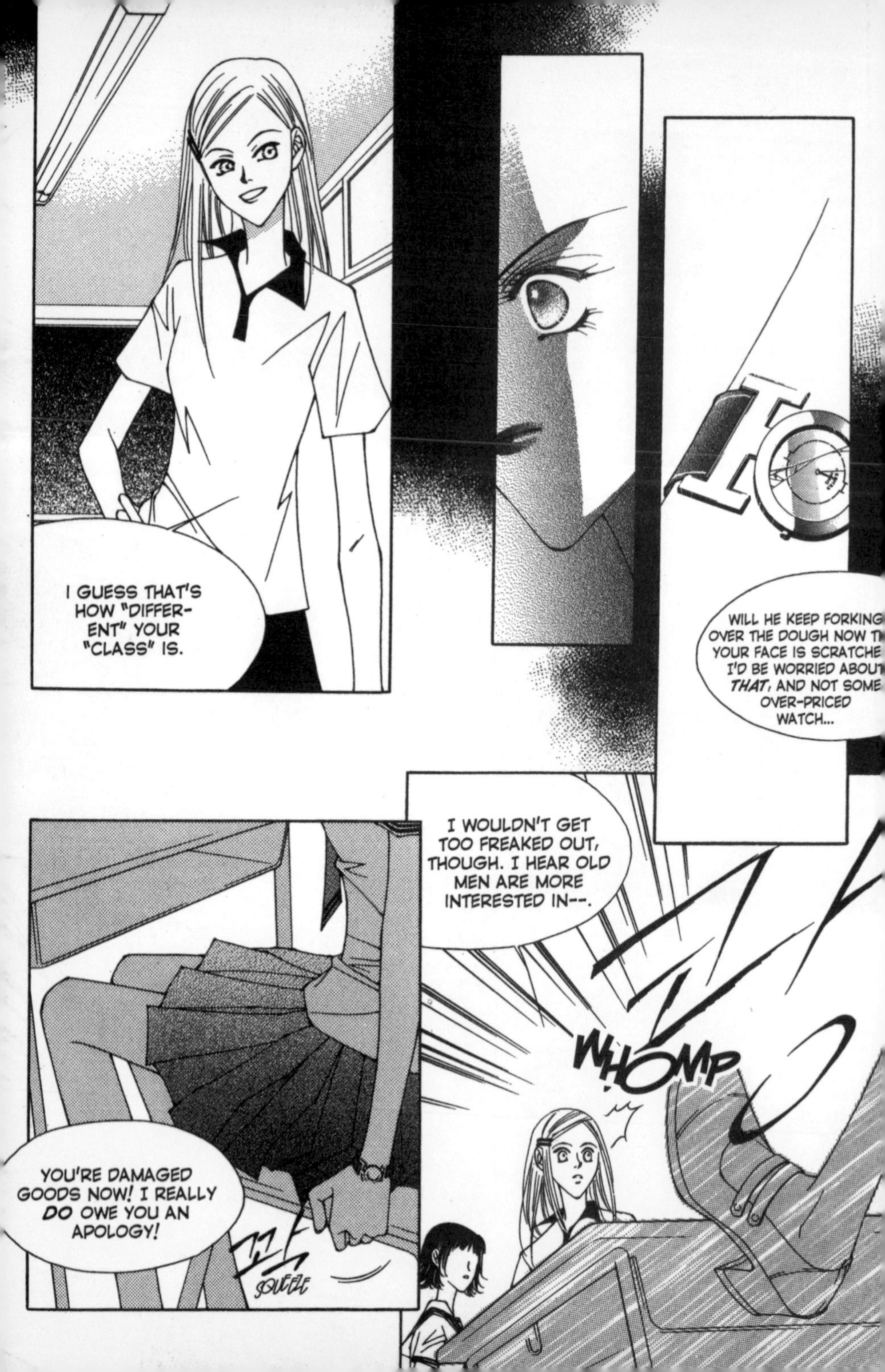
I GUESS THAT'S HOW "DIFFER-ENT" YOUR "CLASS" IS.
WILL HE KEEP FORKING OVER THE DOUGH NOW T YOUR FACE IS SCRATCHE I'D BE WORRIED ABOUT *THAT*, AND NOT SOME OVER-PRICED WATCH...
YOU'RE DAMAGED GOODS NOW! I REALLY *DO* OWE YOU AN APOLOGY!
SQUEEZE
I WOULDN'T GET TOO FREAKED OUT, THOUGH. I HEAR OLD MEN ARE MORE INTERESTED IN--.
WHOMP

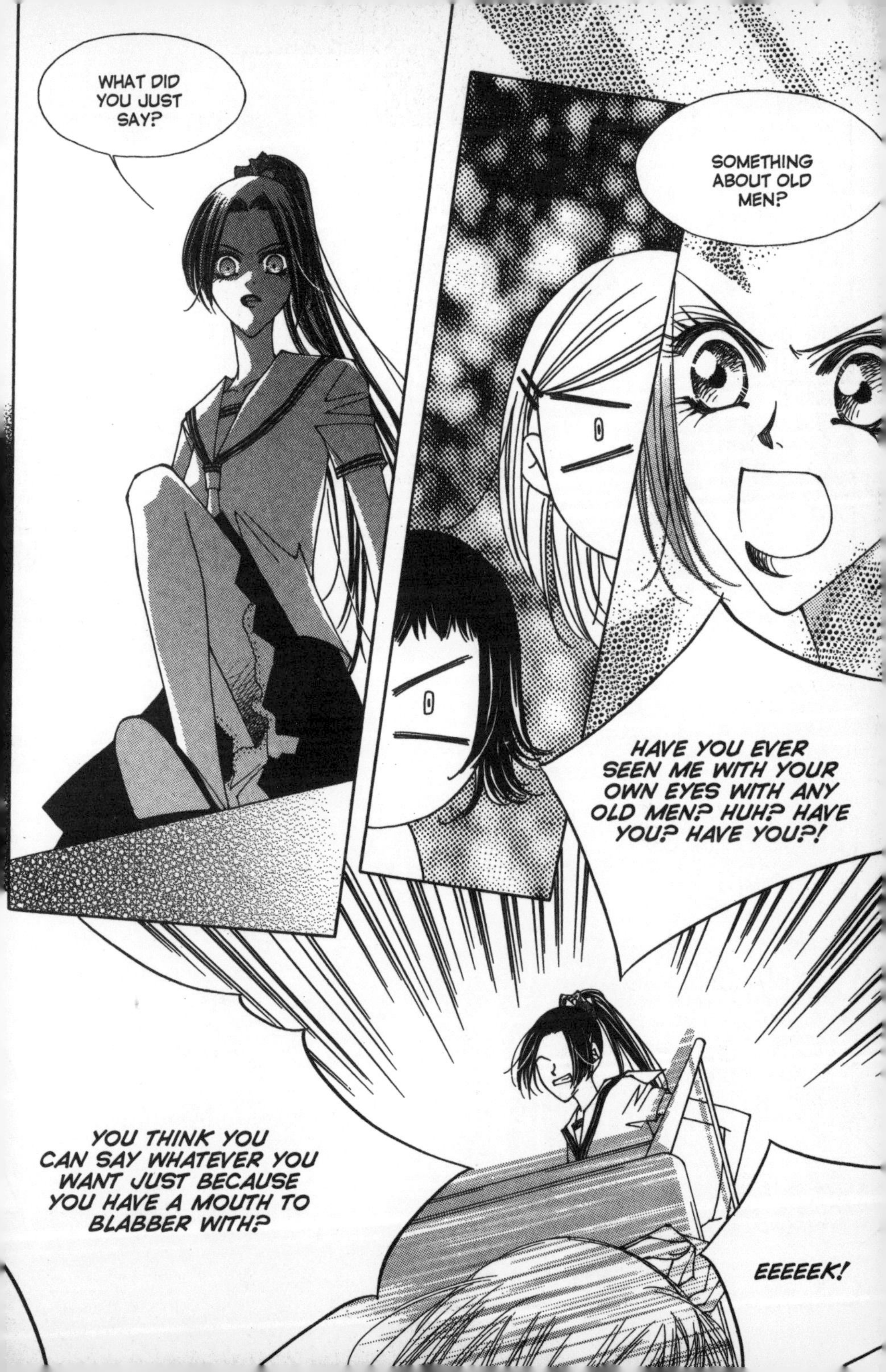
WHAT DID YOU JUST SAY?
SOMETHING ABOUT OLD MEN?
HAVE YOU EVER SEEN ME WITH YOUR OWN EYES WITH ANY OLD MEN? HUH? HAVE YOU? HAVE YOU?!
YOU THINK YOU CAN SAY WHATEVER YOU WANT JUST BECAUSE YOU HAVE A MOUTH TO BLABBER WITH?
EEEEEK!

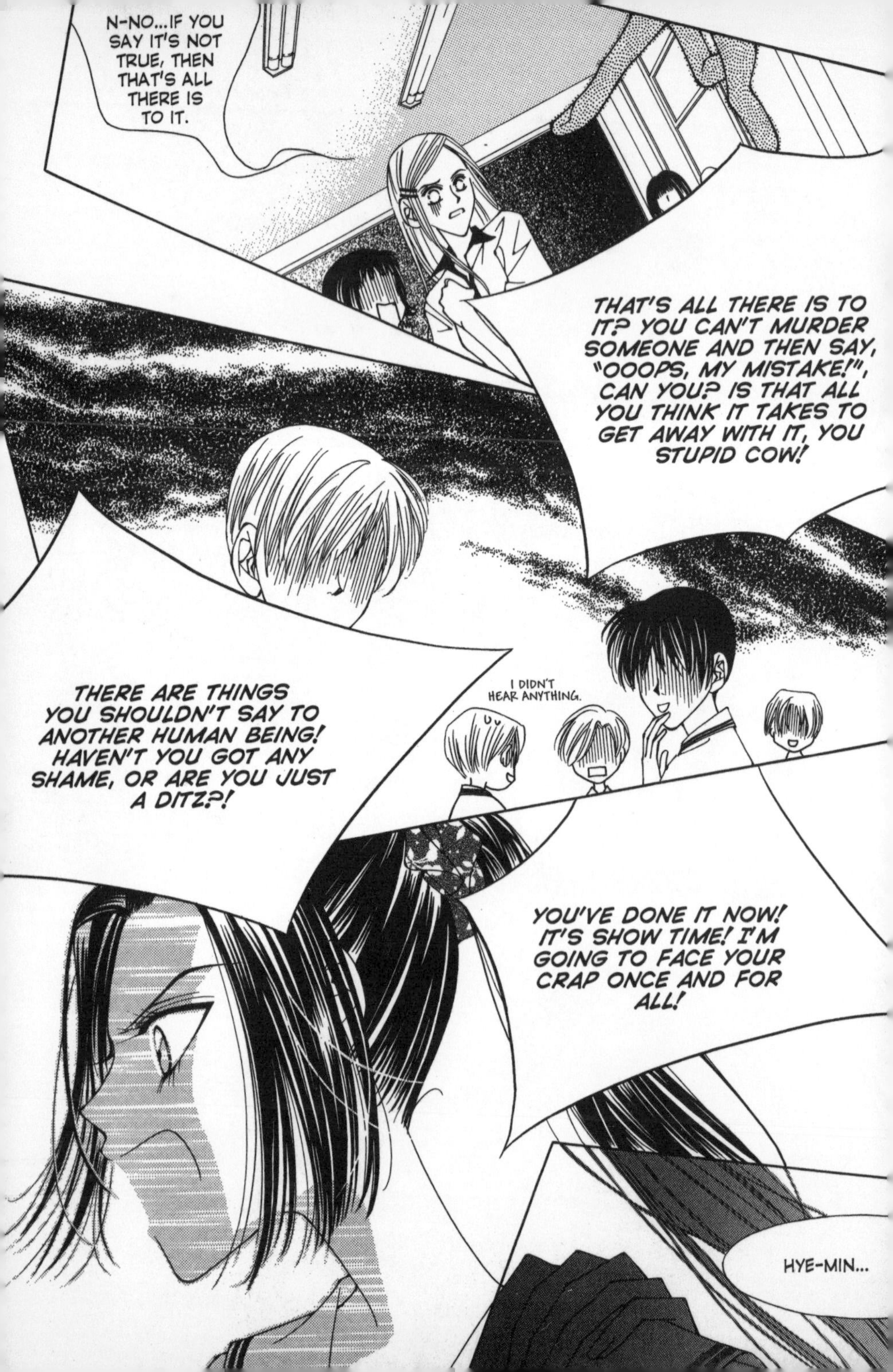
N-NO...IF YOU SAY IT'S NOT TRUE, THEN THAT'S ALL THERE IS TO IT.
THAT'S ALL THERE IS TO IT? YOU CAN'T MURDER SOMEONE AND THEN SAY, "OOOPS, MY MISTAKE!", CAN YOU? IS THAT ALL YOU THINK IT TAKES TO GET AWAY WITH IT, YOU STUPID COW!
THERE ARE THINGS YOU SHOULDN'T SAY TO ANOTHER HUMAN BEING! HAVEN'T YOU GOT ANY SHAME, OR ARE YOU JUST A DITZ?!
I DIDN'T HEAR ANYTHING.
YOU'VE DONE IT NOW! IT'S SHOW TIME! I'M GOING TO FACE YOUR CRAP ONCE AND FOR ALL!
HYE-MIN...

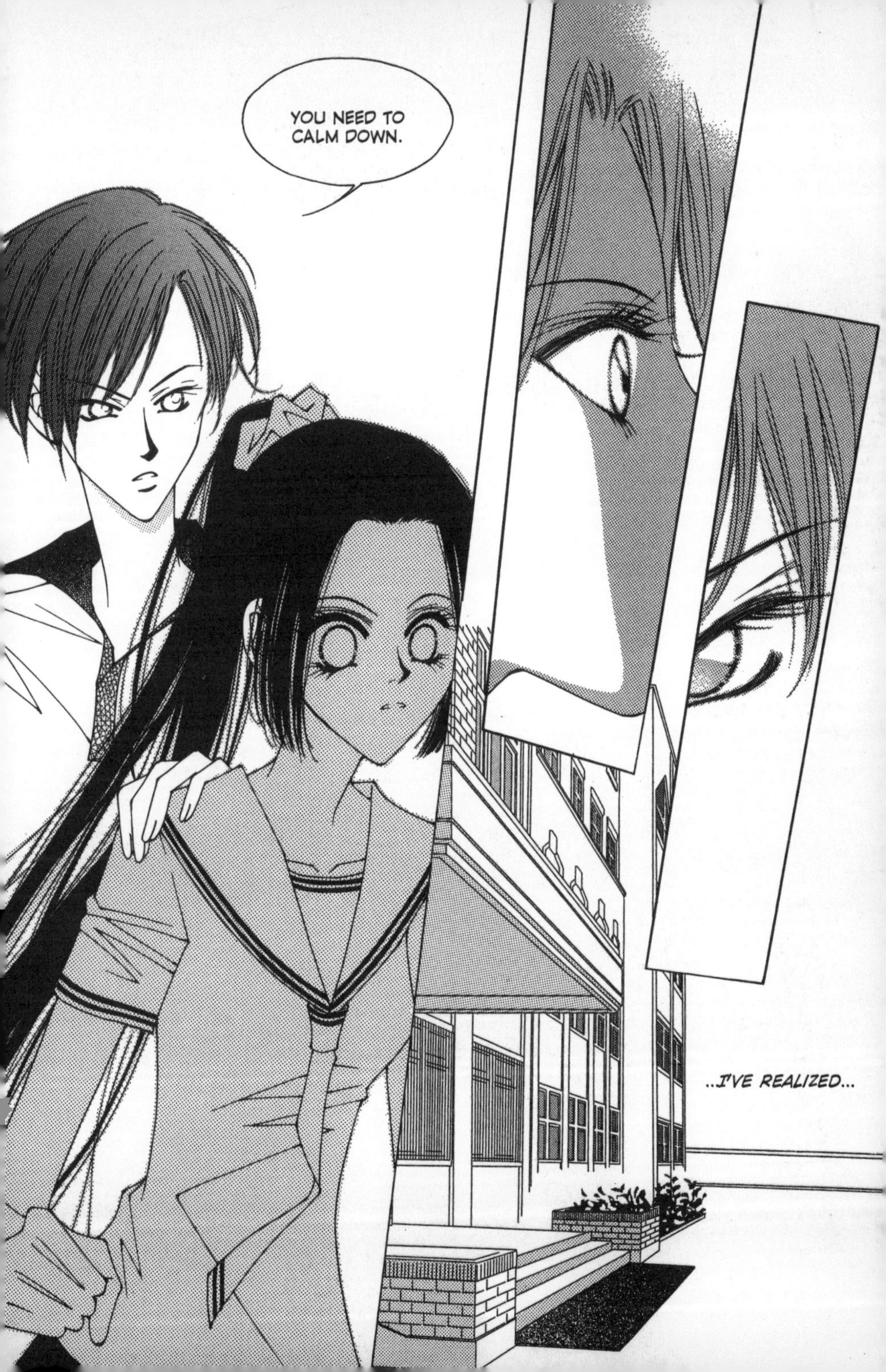
YOU NEED TO CALM DOWN.
...I'VE REALIZED...

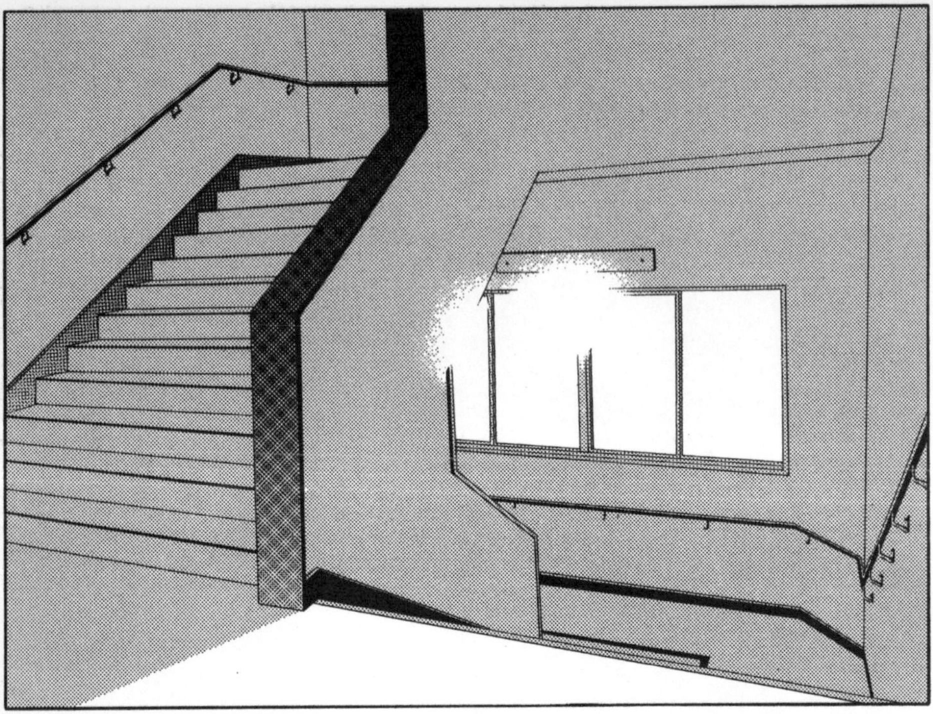

...THAT EVEN THOUGH I TELL MYSELF THAT I HAVE TO BE HONEST WITH MYSELF...

...THAT I DON'T WANT TO HAVE ANY REGRETS...

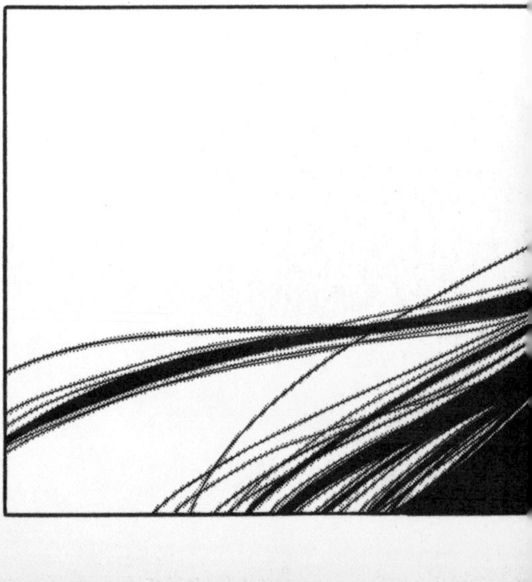

...THE REAL ME...

...IS JUST A BAD-TEMPERED GIRL WITH NOTHING TO OFFER THE WORLD BEYOND A PRETTY FACE.

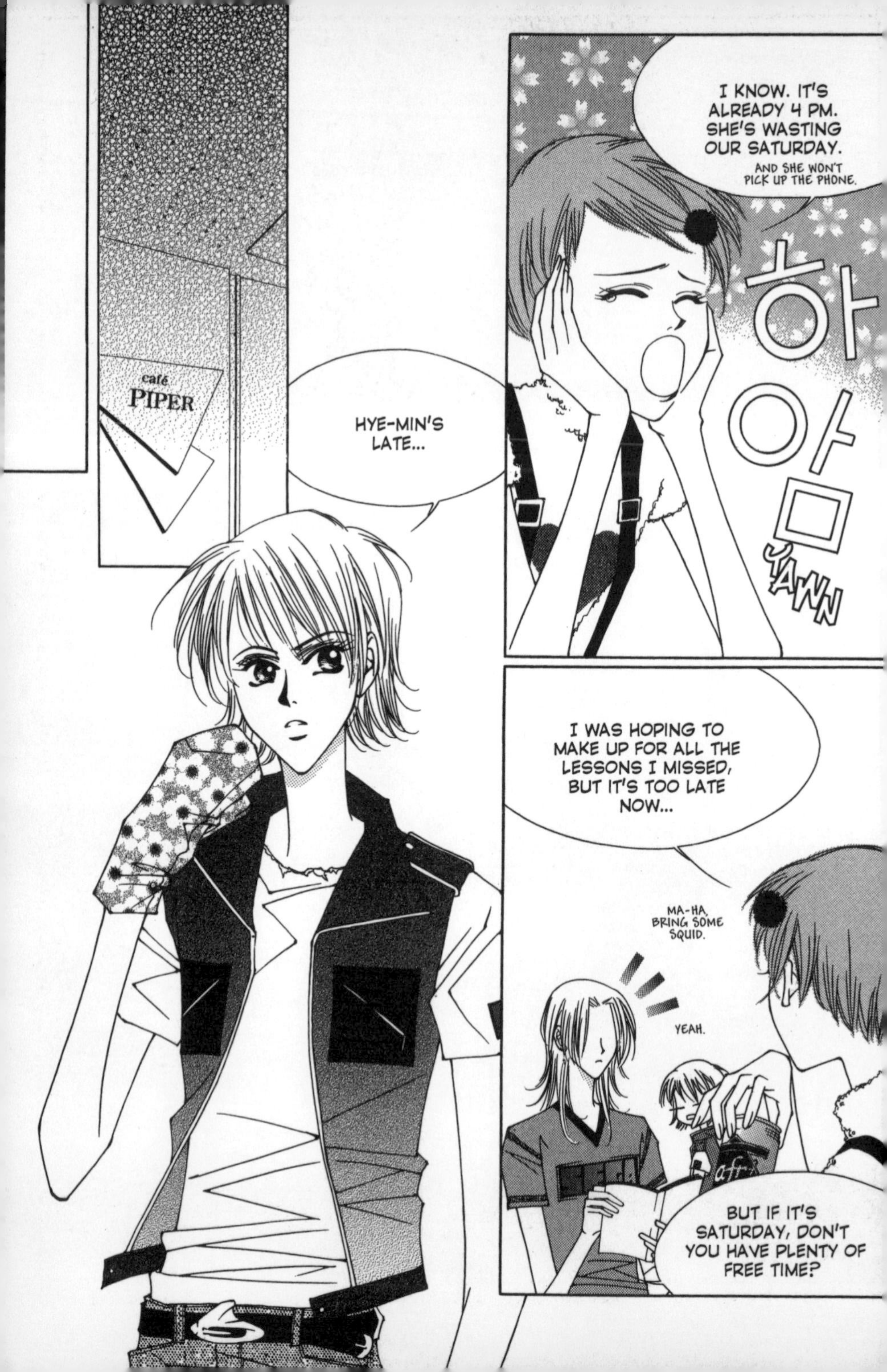
café
PIPER
HYE-MIN'S LATE...
I KNOW. IT'S ALREADY 4 PM. SHE'S WASTING OUR SATURDAY.
AND SHE WON'T PICK UP THE PHONE.
하암
YAWN
I WAS HOPING TO MAKE UP FOR ALL THE LESSONS I MISSED, BUT IT'S TOO LATE NOW...
MA-HA, BRING SOME SQUID.
YEAH.
BUT IF IT'S SATURDAY, DON'T YOU HAVE PLENTY OF FREE TIME?

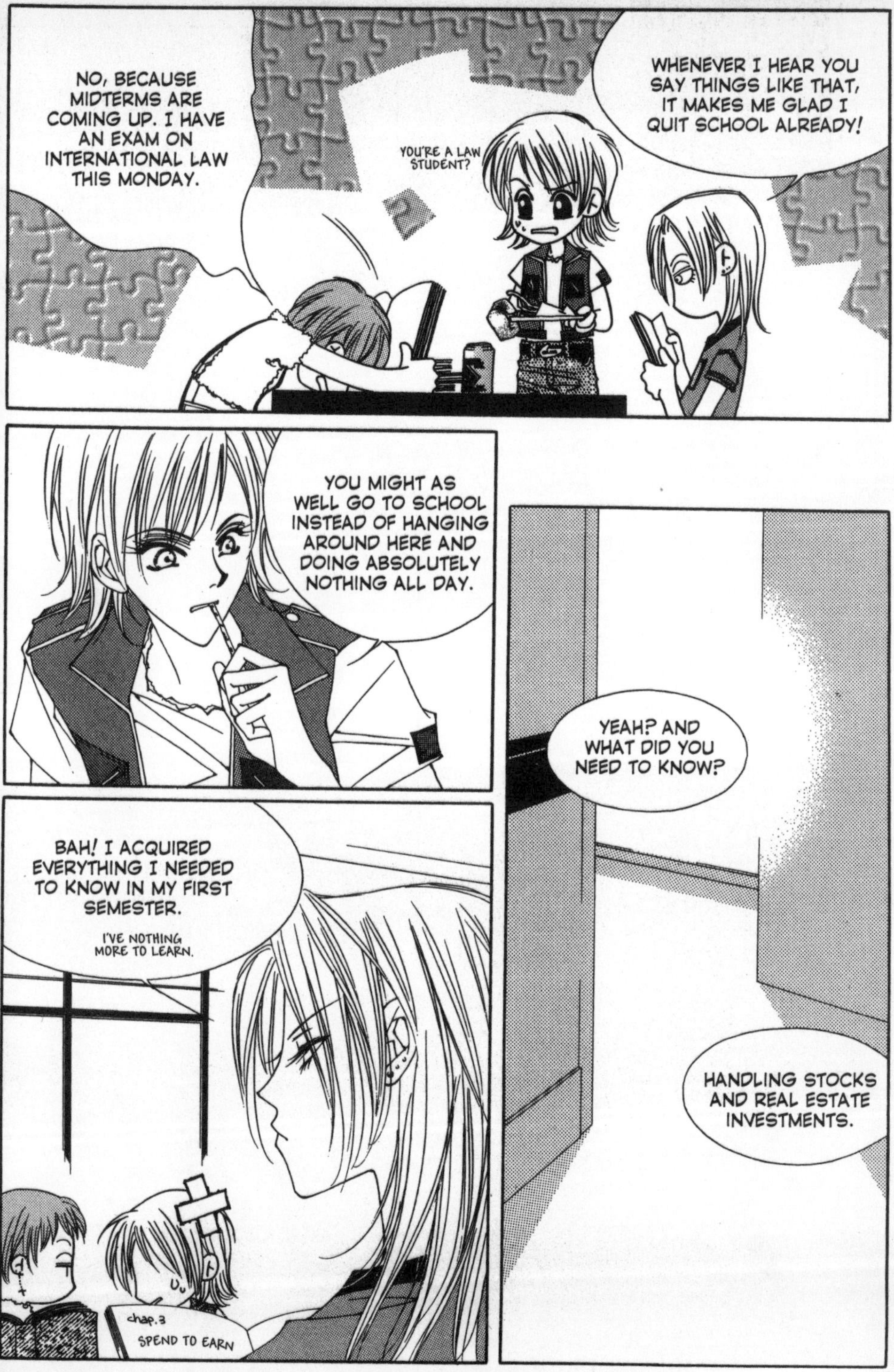
NO, BECAUSE MIDTERMS ARE COMING UP. I HAVE AN EXAM ON INTERNATIONAL LAW THIS MONDAY.
YOU'RE A LAW STUDENT?
WHENEVER I HEAR YOU SAY THINGS LIKE THAT, IT MAKES ME GLAD I QUIT SCHOOL ALREADY!
YOU MIGHT AS WELL GO TO SCHOOL INSTEAD OF HANGING AROUND HERE AND DOING ABSOLUTELY NOTHING ALL DAY.
BAH! I ACQUIRED EVERYTHING I NEEDED TO KNOW IN MY FIRST SEMESTER.
I'VE NOTHING MORE TO LEARN.
chap.3
SPEND TO EARN
YEAH? AND WHAT DID YOU NEED TO KNOW?
HANDLING STOCKS AND REAL ESTATE INVESTMENTS.

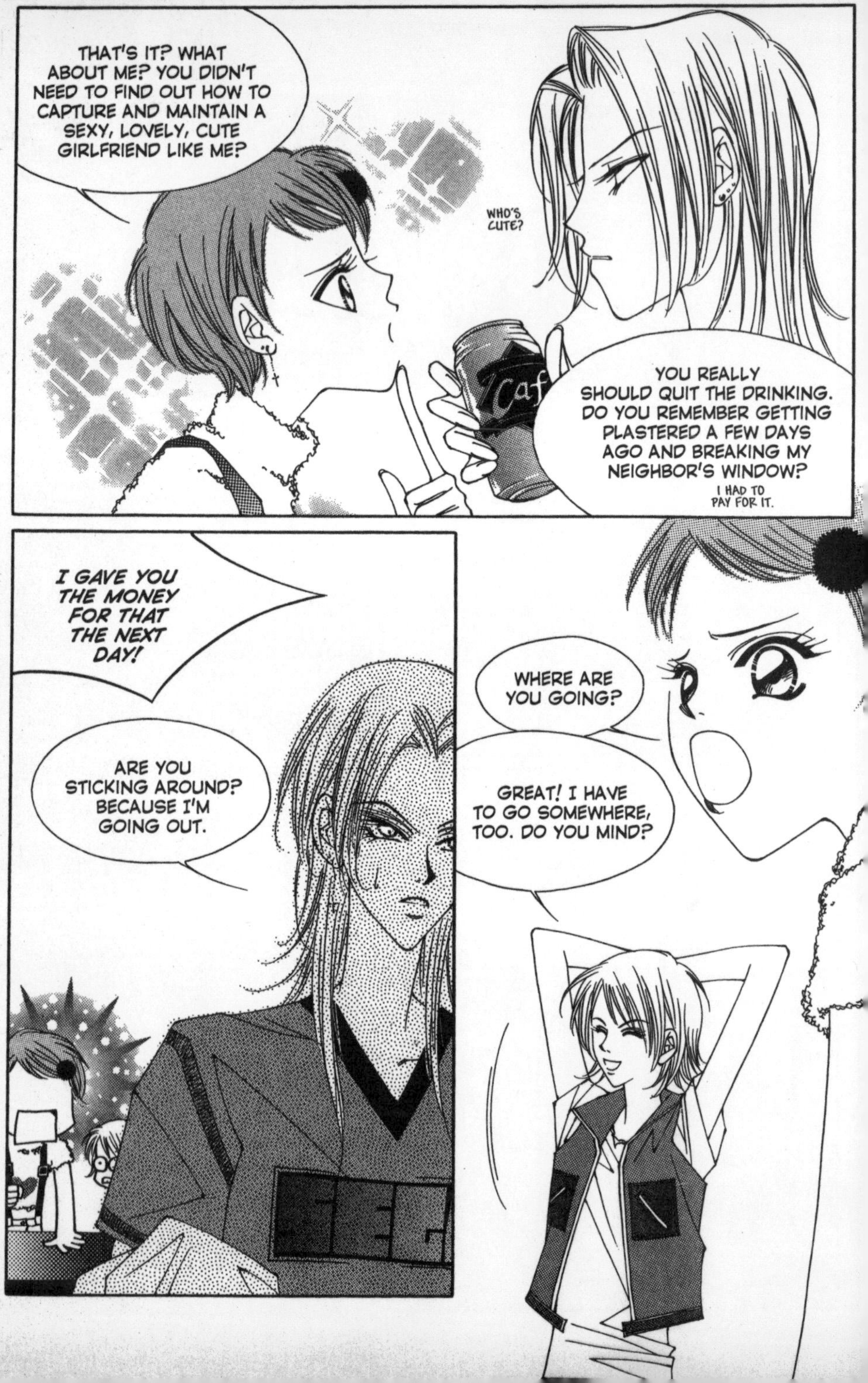
THAT'S IT? WHAT ABOUT ME? YOU DIDN'T NEED TO FIND OUT HOW TO CAPTURE AND MAINTAIN A SEXY, LOVELY, CUTE GIRLFRIEND LIKE ME?
WHO'S CUTE?
Caf
YOU REALLY SHOULD QUIT THE DRINKING. DO YOU REMEMBER GETTING PLASTERED A FEW DAYS AGO AND BREAKING MY NEIGHBOR'S WINDOW?
I HAD TO PAY FOR IT.
I GAVE YOU THE MONEY FOR THAT THE NEXT DAY!
ARE YOU STICKING AROUND? BECAUSE I'M GOING OUT.
WHERE ARE YOU GOING?
GREAT! I HAVE TO GO SOMEWHERE, TOO. DO YOU MIND?

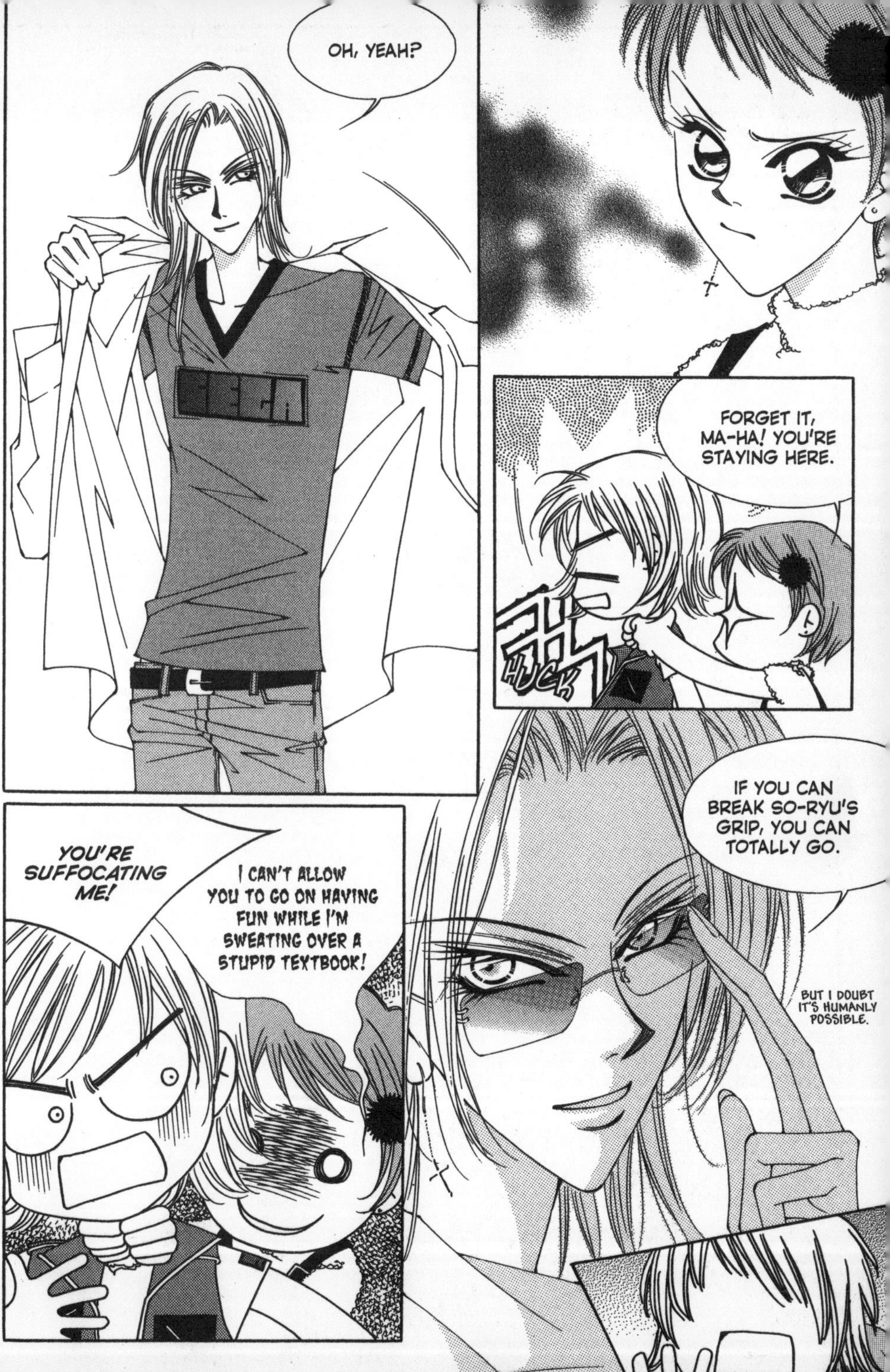
OH, YEAH?
FORGET IT, MA-HA! YOU'RE STAYING HERE.
HUCK
YOU'RE SUFFOCATING ME!
I CAN'T ALLOW YOU TO GO ON HAVING FUN WHILE I'M SWEATING OVER A STUPID TEXTBOOK!
IF YOU CAN BREAK SO-RYU'S GRIP, YOU CAN TOTALLY GO.
BUT I DOUBT IT'S HUMANLY POSSIBLE.

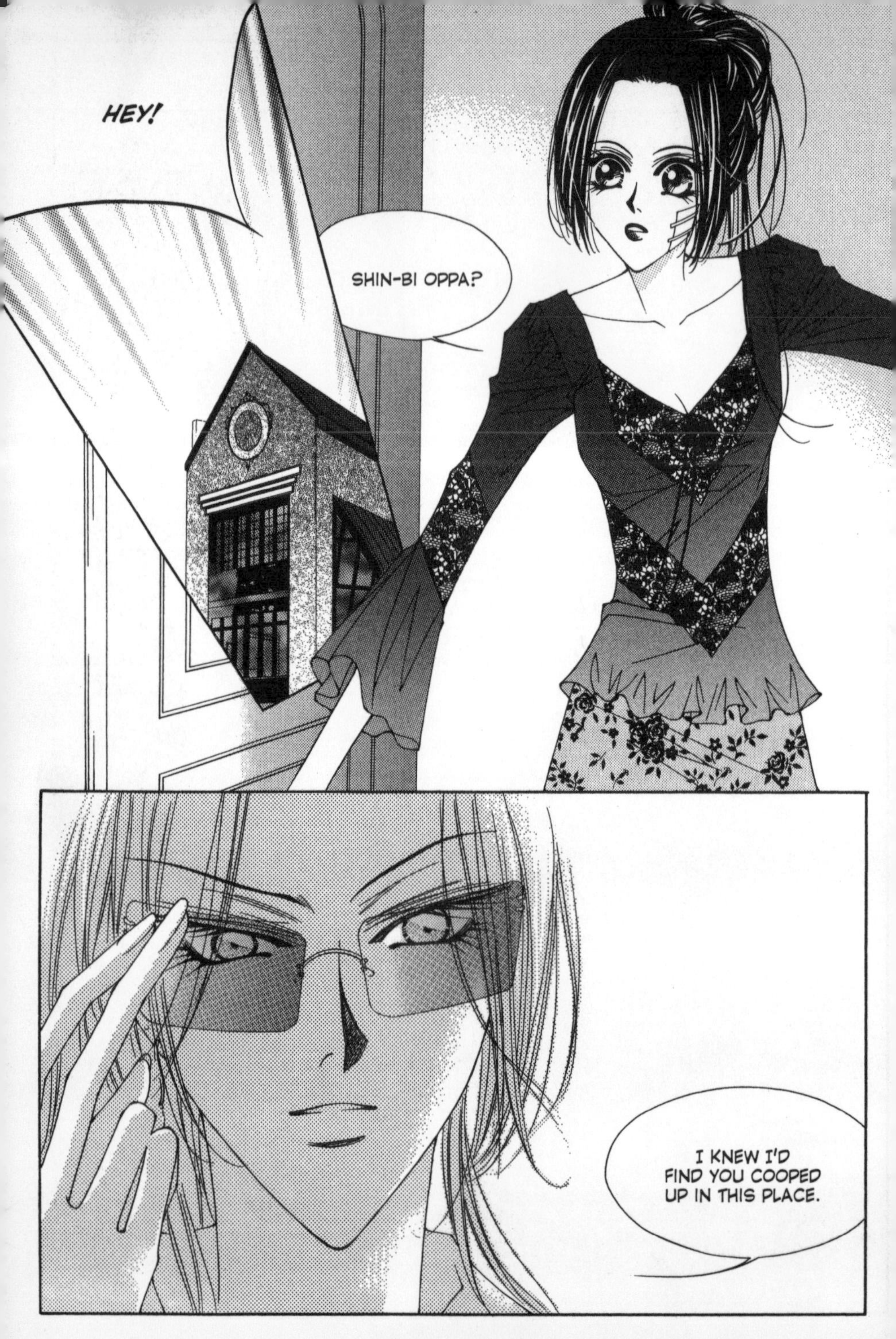
HEY!
SHIN-BI OPPA?
I KNEW I'D FIND YOU COOPED UP IN THIS PLACE.

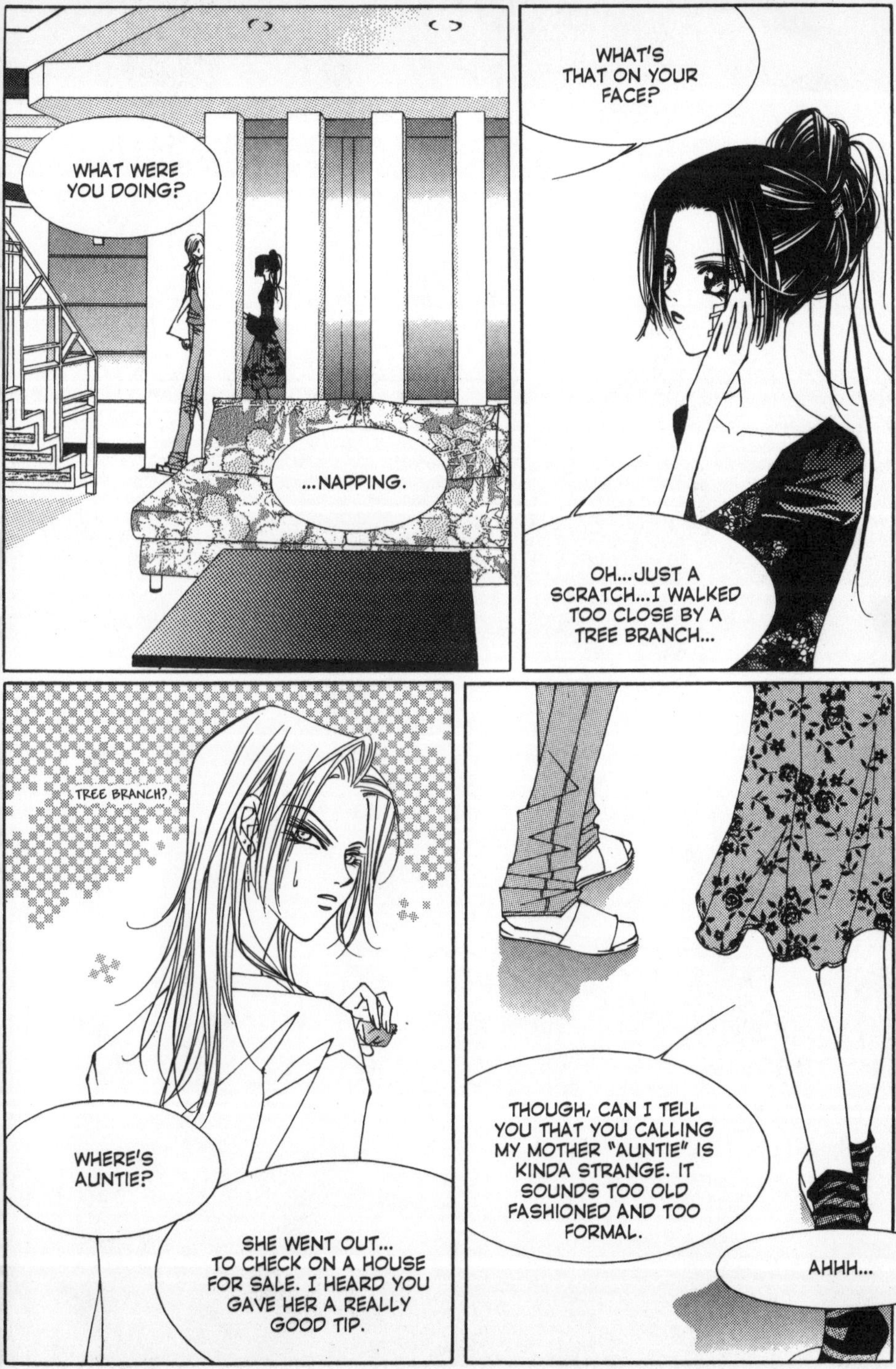
WHAT WERE YOU DOING?
...NAPPING.
WHAT'S THAT ON YOUR FACE?
OH...JUST A SCRATCH...I WALKED TOO CLOSE BY A TREE BRANCH...
TREE BRANCH?
WHERE'S AUNTIE?
SHE WENT OUT... TO CHECK ON A HOUSE FOR SALE. I HEARD YOU GAVE HER A REALLY GOOD TIP.
THOUGH, CAN I TELL YOU THAT YOU CALLING MY MOTHER "AUNTIE" IS KINDA STRANGE. IT SOUNDS TOO OLD FASHIONED AND TOO FORMAL.
AHHH...

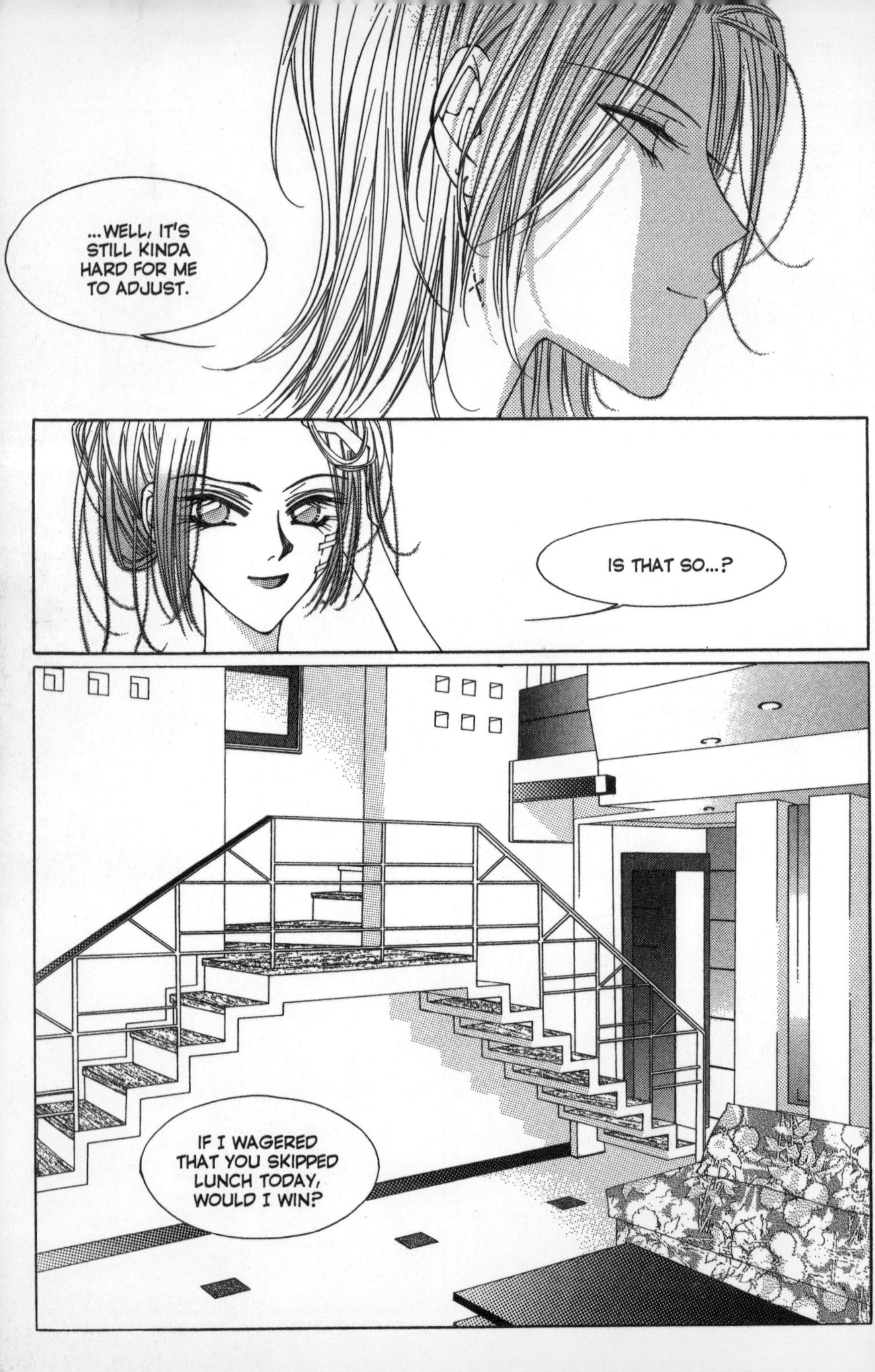
...WELL, IT'S STILL KINDA HARD FOR ME TO ADJUST.
IS THAT SO...?
IF I WAGERED THAT YOU SKIPPED LUNCH TODAY, WOULD I WIN?

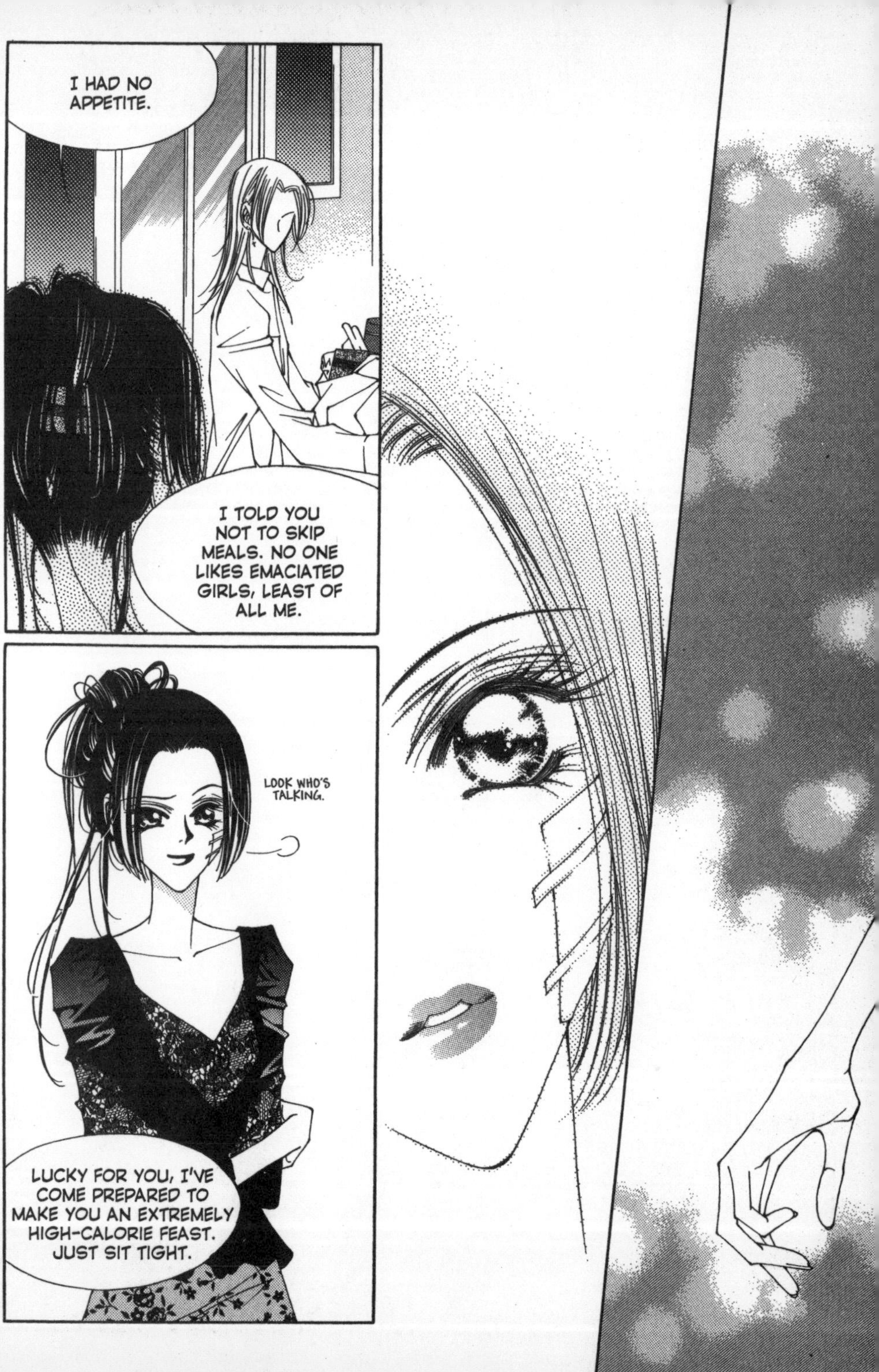
I HAD NO APPETITE.
I TOLD YOU NOT TO SKIP MEALS. NO ONE LIKES EMACIATED GIRLS, LEAST OF ALL ME.
LOOK WHO'S TALKING.
LUCKY FOR YOU, I'VE COME PREPARED TO MAKE YOU AN EXTREMELY HIGH-CALORIE FEAST. JUST SIT TIGHT.

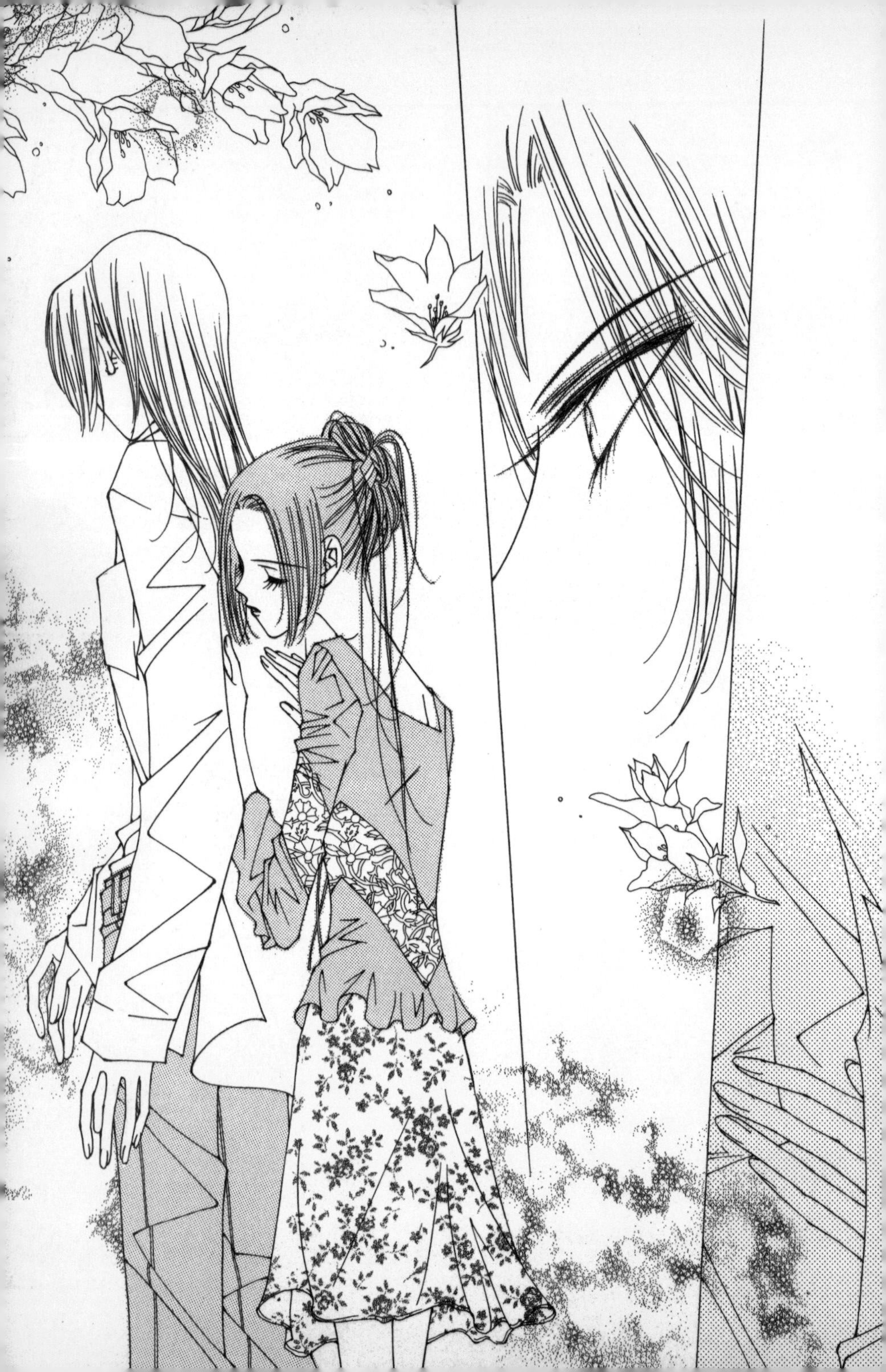

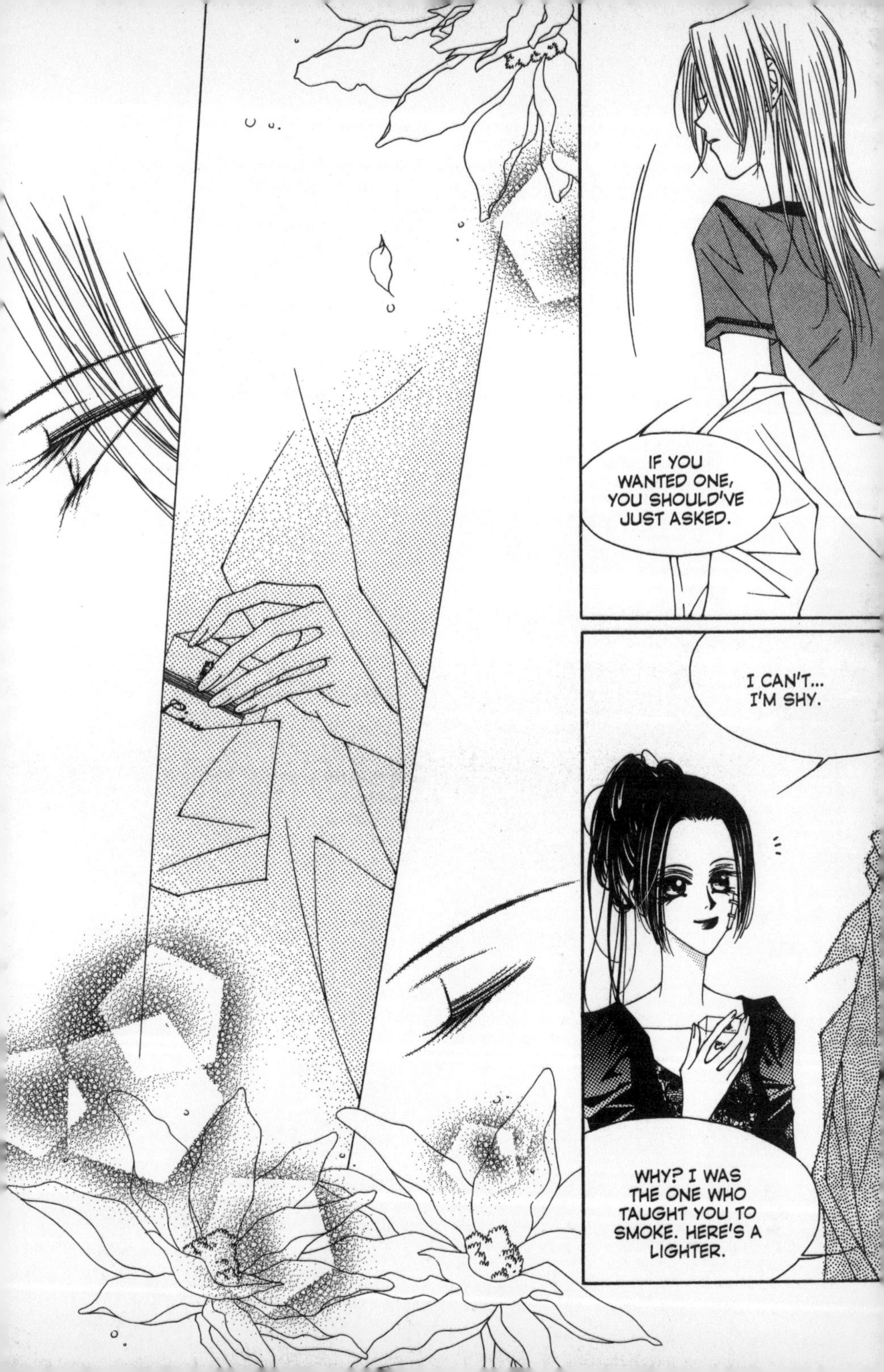
IF YOU WANTED ONE, YOU SHOULD'VE JUST ASKED.
I CAN'T... I'M SHY.
WHY? I WAS THE ONE WHO TAUGHT YOU TO SMOKE. HERE'S A LIGHTER.

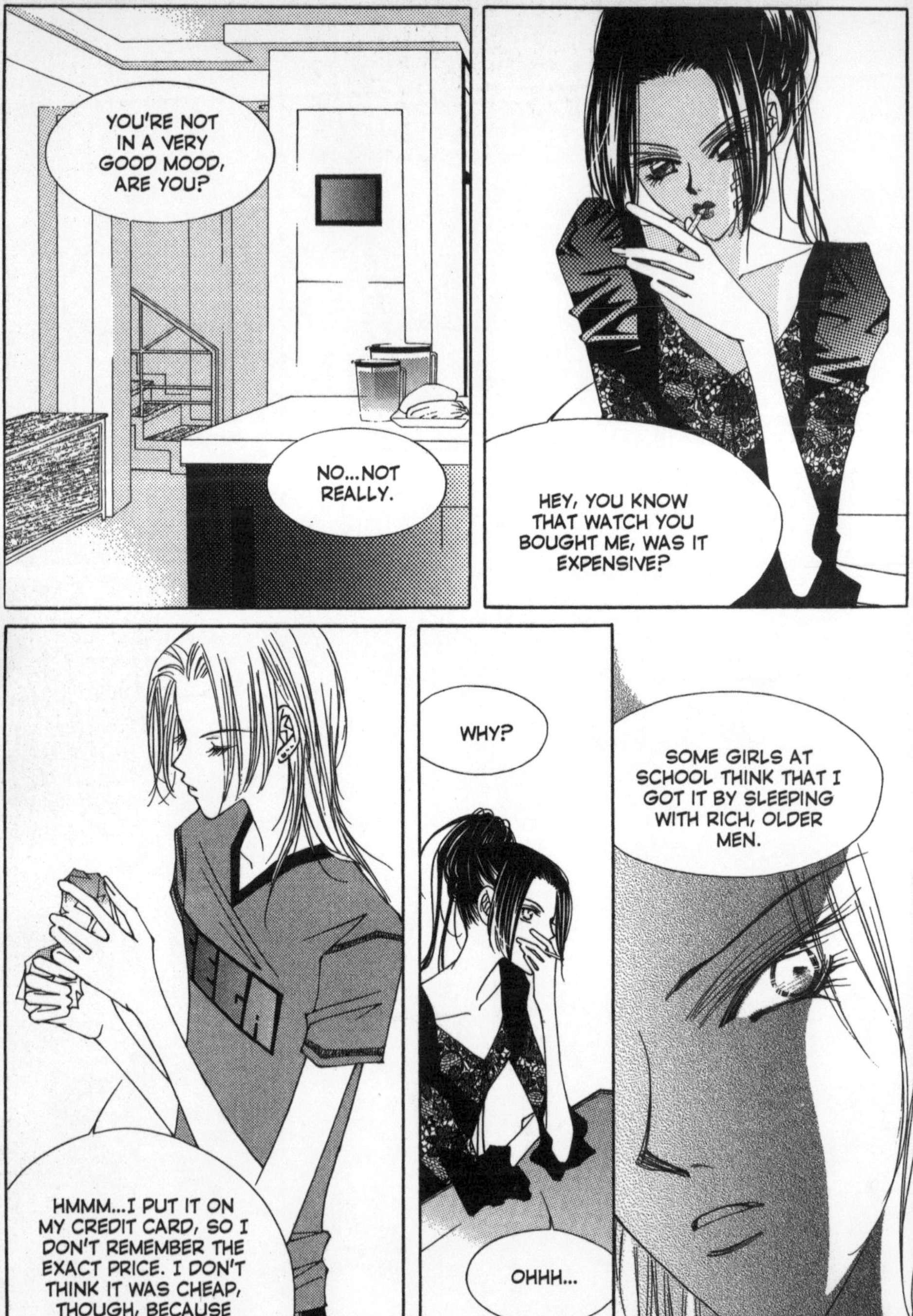
YOU'RE NOT IN A VERY GOOD MOOD, ARE YOU?
NO...NOT REALLY.
HEY, YOU KNOW THAT WATCH YOU BOUGHT ME, WAS IT EXPENSIVE?
HMMM...I PUT IT ON MY CREDIT CARD, SO I DON'T REMEMBER THE EXACT PRICE. I DON'T THINK IT WAS CHEAP, THOUGH, BECAUSE SO-RYU PICKED IT OUT, AND SHE HAS PRETTY EXPENSIVE TASTES.
WHY?
SOME GIRLS AT SCHOOL THINK THAT I GOT IT BY SLEEPING WITH RICH, OLDER MEN.
OHHH...

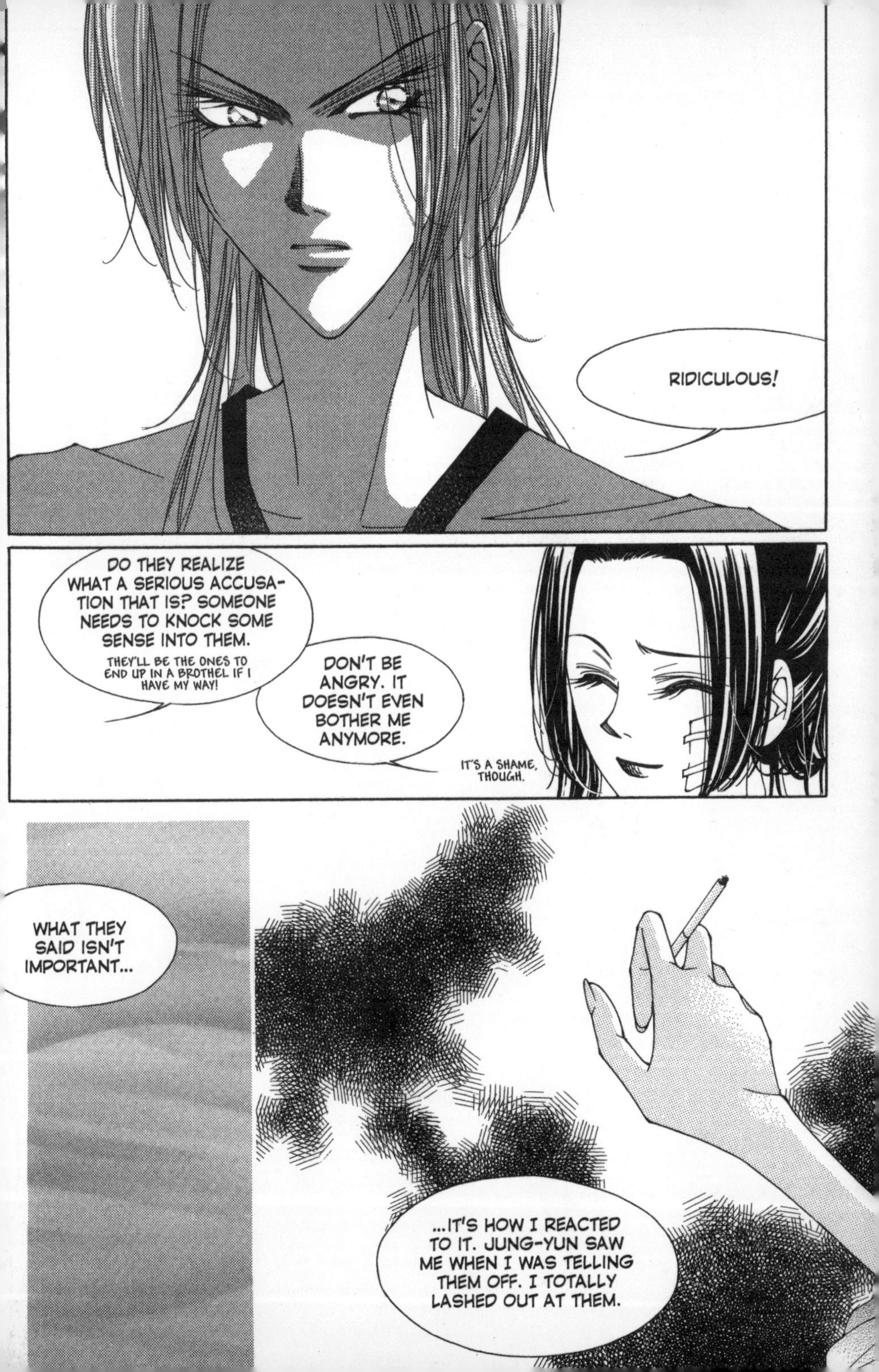
RIDICULOUS!
DO THEY REALIZE WHAT A SERIOUS ACCUSATION THAT IS? SOMEONE NEEDS TO KNOCK SOME SENSE INTO THEM.
THEY'LL BE THE ONES TO END UP IN A BROTHEL IF I HAVE MY WAY!
DON'T BE ANGRY. IT DOESN'T EVEN BOTHER ME ANYMORE.
IT'S A SHAME, THOUGH.
WHAT THEY SAID ISN'T IMPORTANT...
...IT'S HOW I REACTED TO IT. JUNG-YUN SAW ME WHEN I WAS TELLING THEM OFF. I TOTALLY LASHED OUT AT THEM.

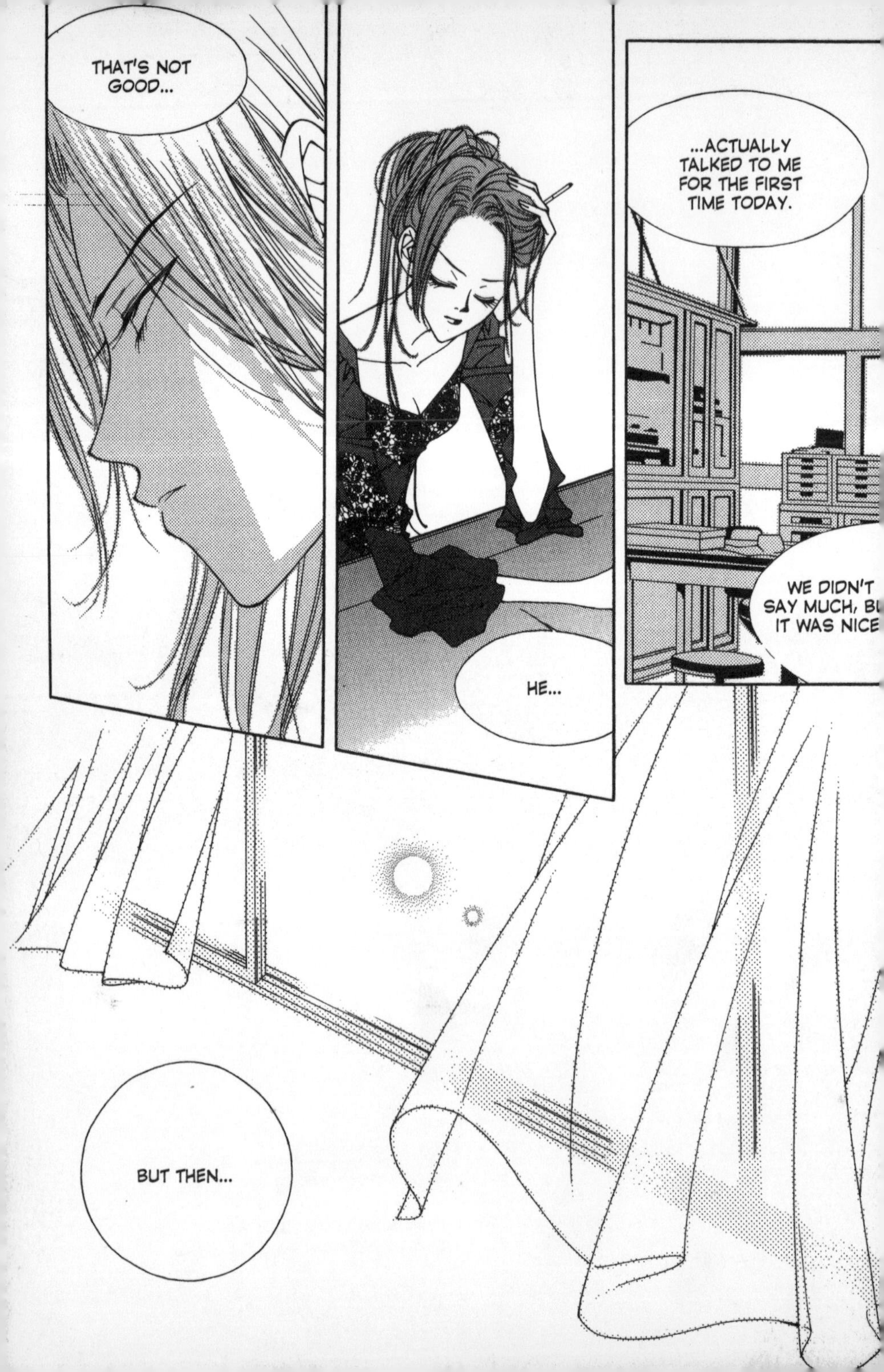
THAT'S NOT GOOD...
HE...
...ACTUALLY TALKED TO ME FOR THE FIRST TIME TODAY.
WE DIDN'T SAY MUCH, B IT WAS NICE
BUT THEN...

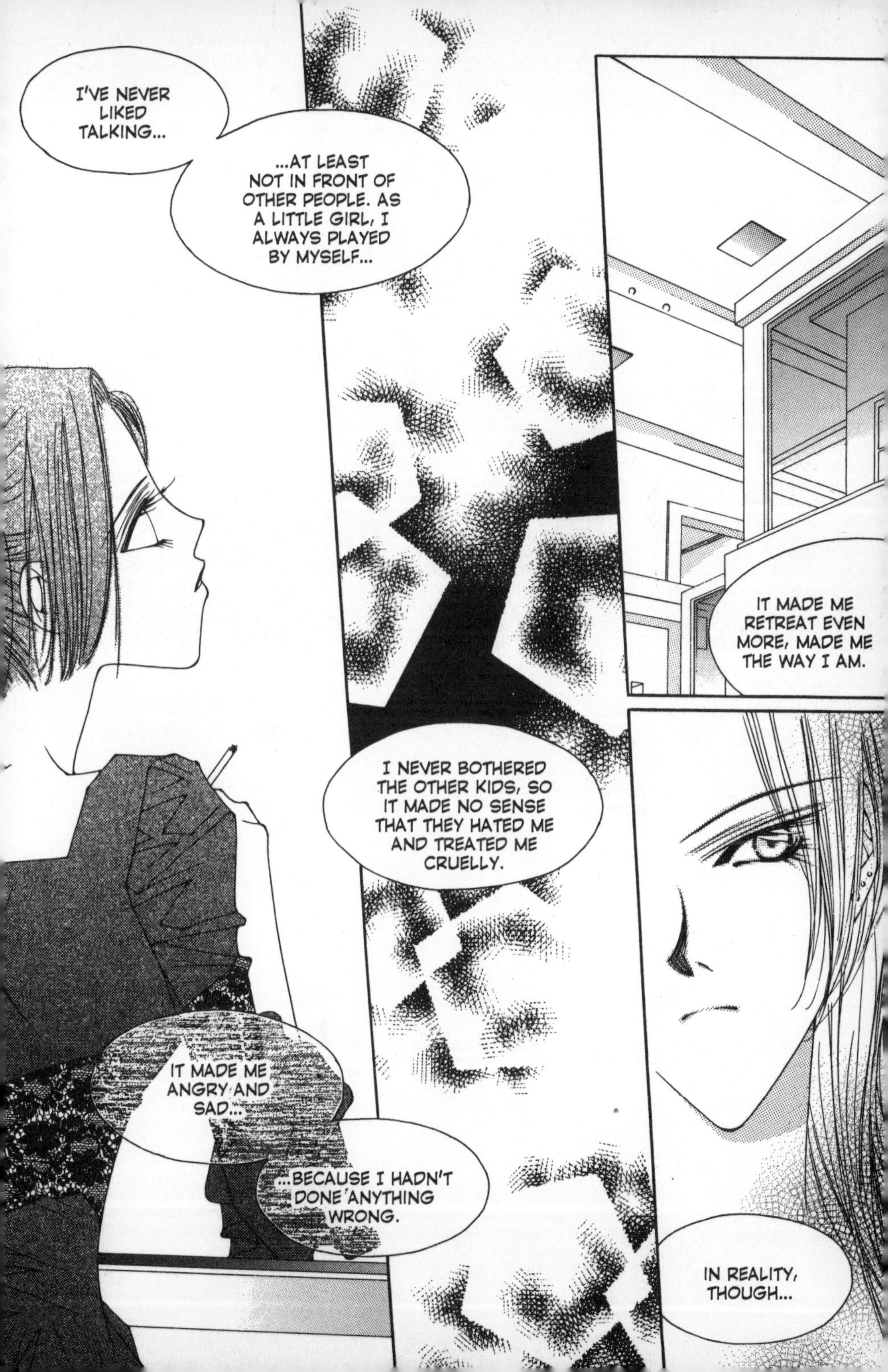
I'VE NEVER LIKED TALKING...
...AT LEAST NOT IN FRONT OF OTHER PEOPLE. AS A LITTLE GIRL, I ALWAYS PLAYED BY MYSELF...
IT MADE ME ANGRY AND SAD...
...BECAUSE I HADN'T DONE ANYTHING WRONG.
I NEVER BOTHERED THE OTHER KIDS, SO IT MADE NO SENSE THAT THEY HATED ME AND TREATED ME CRUELLY.
IT MADE ME RETREAT EVEN MORE, MADE ME THE WAY I AM.
IN REALITY, THOUGH...

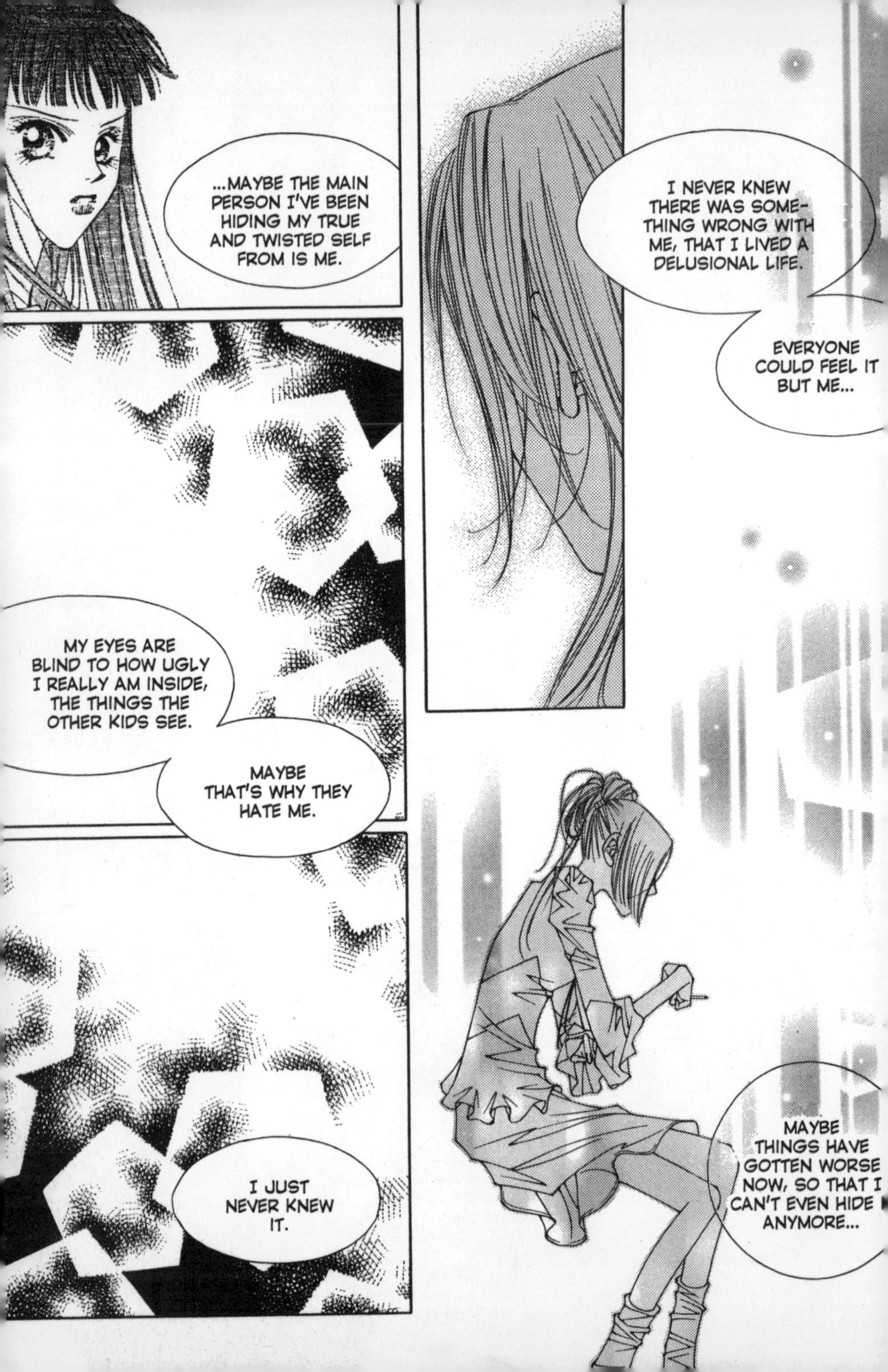
...MAYBE THE MAIN PERSON I'VE BEEN HIDING MY TRUE AND TWISTED SELF FROM IS ME.
MY EYES ARE BLIND TO HOW UGLY I REALLY AM INSIDE, THE THINGS THE OTHER KIDS SEE.
MAYBE THAT'S WHY THEY HATE ME.
I JUST NEVER KNEW IT.
I NEVER KNEW THERE WAS SOME-THING WRONG WITH ME, THAT I LIVED A DELUSIONAL LIFE.
EVERYONE COULD FEEL IT BUT ME...
MAYBE THINGS HAVE GOTTEN WORSE NOW, SO THAT I CAN'T EVEN HIDE ANYMORE...

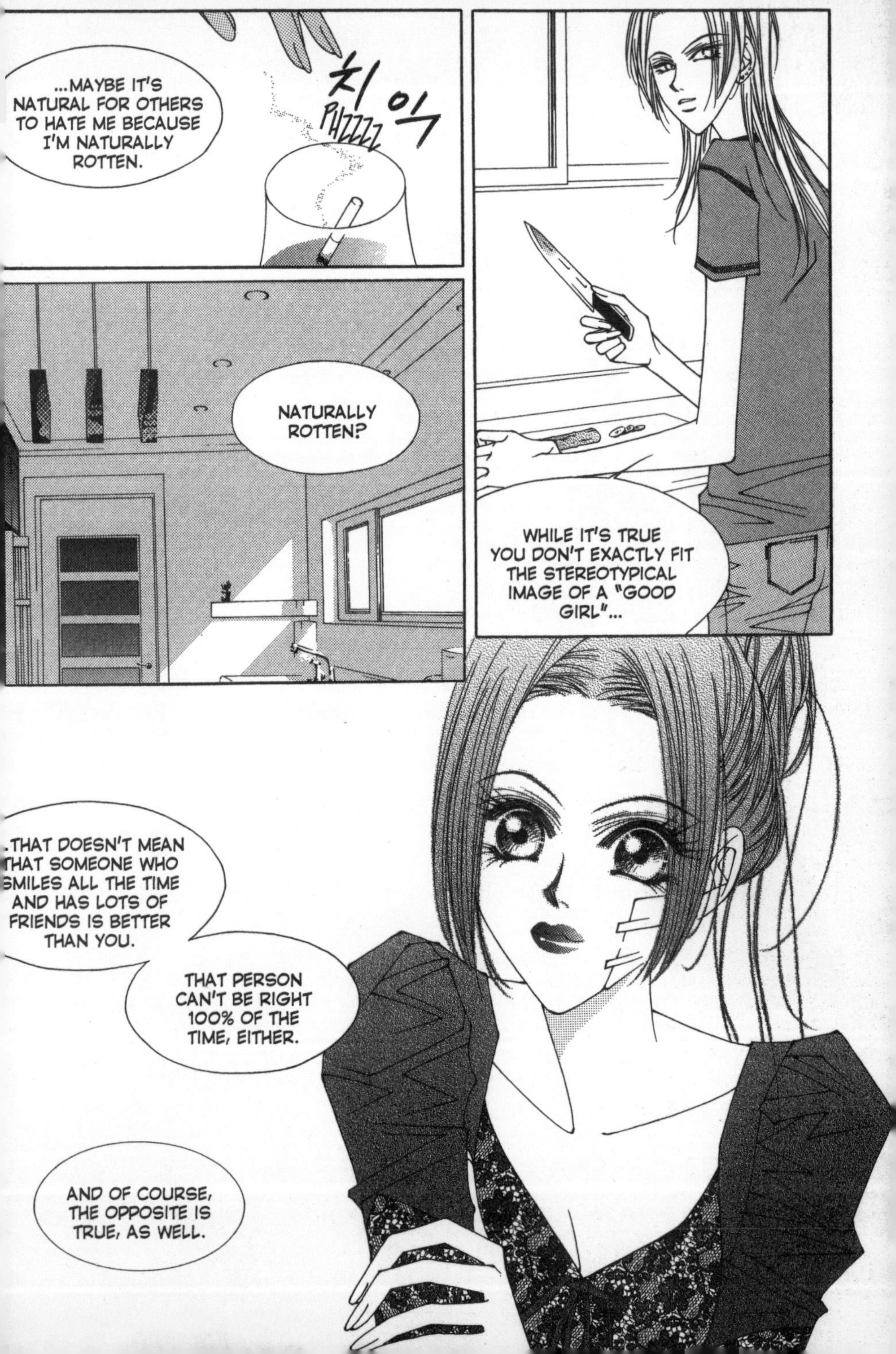
...MAYBE IT'S NATURAL FOR OTHERS TO HATE ME BECAUSE I'M NATURALLY ROTTEN.
치익
PHZZZZ
NATURALLY ROTTEN?
WHILE IT'S TRUE YOU DON'T EXACTLY FIT THE STEREOTYPICAL IMAGE OF A "GOOD GIRL"...
.THAT DOESN'T MEAN THAT SOMEONE WHO SMILES ALL THE TIME AND HAS LOTS OF FRIENDS IS BETTER THAN YOU.
THAT PERSON CAN'T BE RIGHT 100% OF THE TIME, EITHER.
AND OF COURSE, THE OPPOSITE IS TRUE, AS WELL.

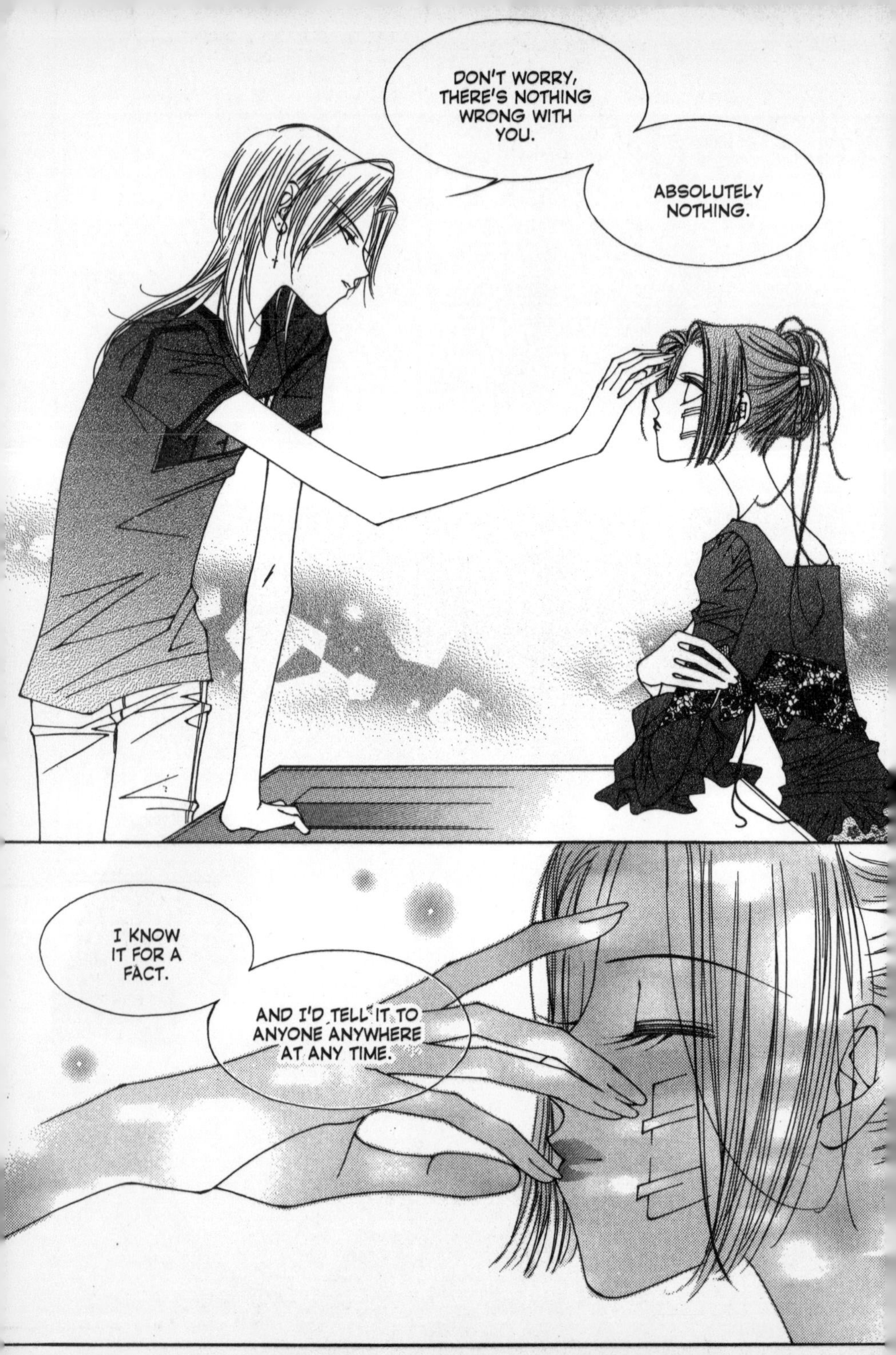
DON'T WORRY, THERE'S NOTHING WRONG WITH YOU.
ABSOLUTELY NOTHING.
I KNOW IT FOR A FACT.
AND I'D TELL IT TO ANYONE ANYWHERE AT ANY TIME.

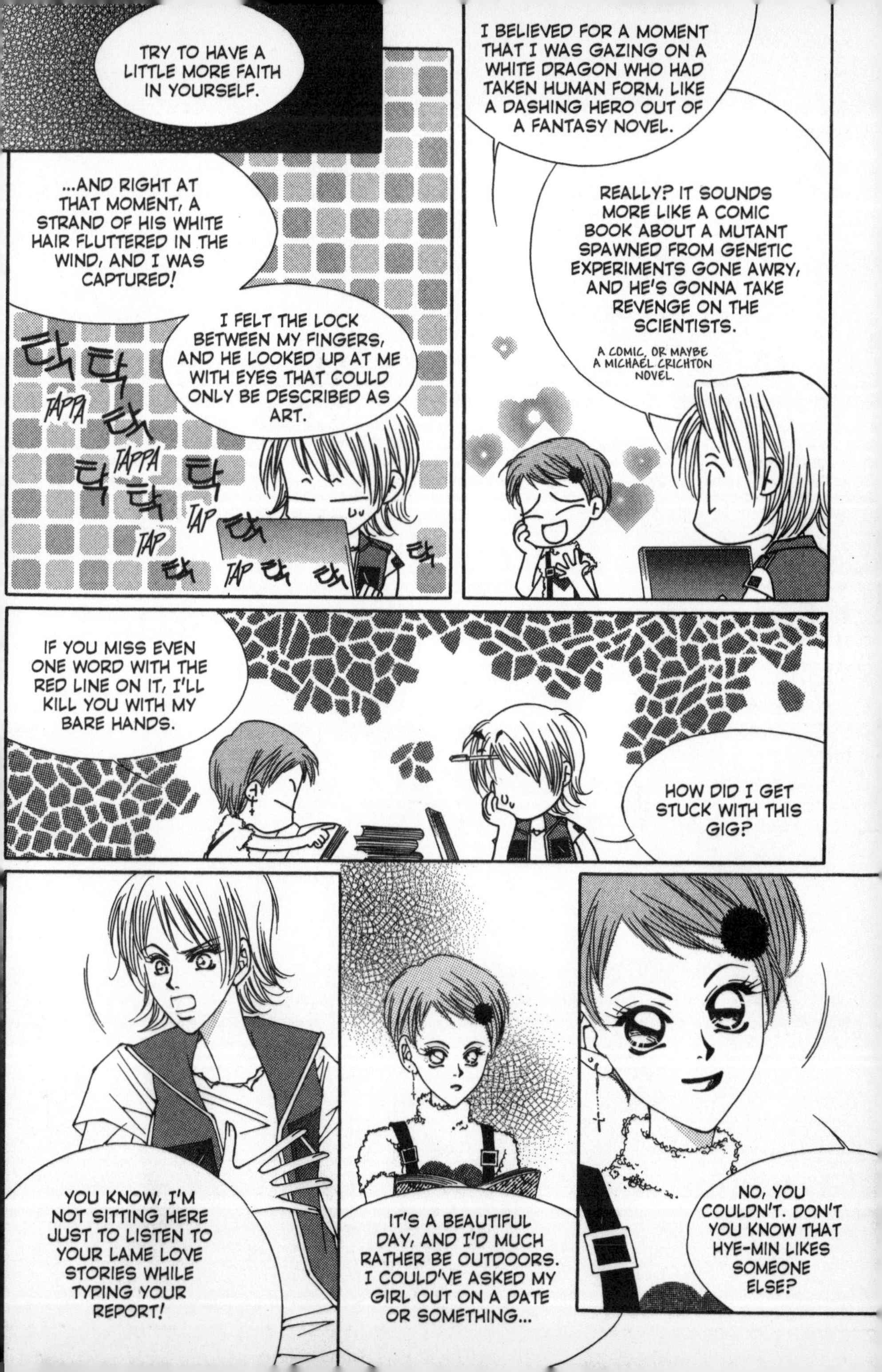
TRY TO HAVE A LITTLE MORE FAITH IN YOURSELF.
...AND RIGHT AT THAT MOMENT, A STRAND OF HIS WHITE HAIR FLUTTERED IN THE WIND, AND I WAS CAPTURED!
I FELT THE LOCK BETWEEN MY FINGERS, AND HE LOOKED UP AT ME WITH EYES THAT COULD ONLY BE DESCRIBED AS ART.
탁 탁 TAPPA 탁 TAPPA 탁 탁 TAP 탁 TAP 탁 TAP 탁 탁 탁
I BELIEVED FOR A MOMENT THAT I WAS GAZING ON A WHITE DRAGON WHO HAD TAKEN HUMAN FORM, LIKE A DASHING HERO OUT OF A FANTASY NOVEL.
REALLY? IT SOUNDS MORE LIKE A COMIC BOOK ABOUT A MUTANT SPAWNED FROM GENETIC EXPERIMENTS GONE AWRY, AND HE'S GONNA TAKE REVENGE ON THE SCIENTISTS.
A COMIC, OR MAYBE A MICHAEL CRICHTON NOVEL.
IF YOU MISS EVEN ONE WORD WITH THE RED LINE ON IT, I'LL KILL YOU WITH MY BARE HANDS.
HOW DID I GET STUCK WITH THIS GIG?
YOU KNOW, I'M NOT SITTING HERE JUST TO LISTEN TO YOUR LAME LOVE STORIES WHILE TYPING YOUR REPORT!
IT'S A BEAUTIFUL DAY, AND I'D MUCH RATHER BE OUTDOORS. I COULD'VE ASKED MY GIRL OUT ON A DATE OR SOMETHING...
NO, YOU COULDN'T. DON'T YOU KNOW THAT HYE-MIN LIKES SOMEONE ELSE?

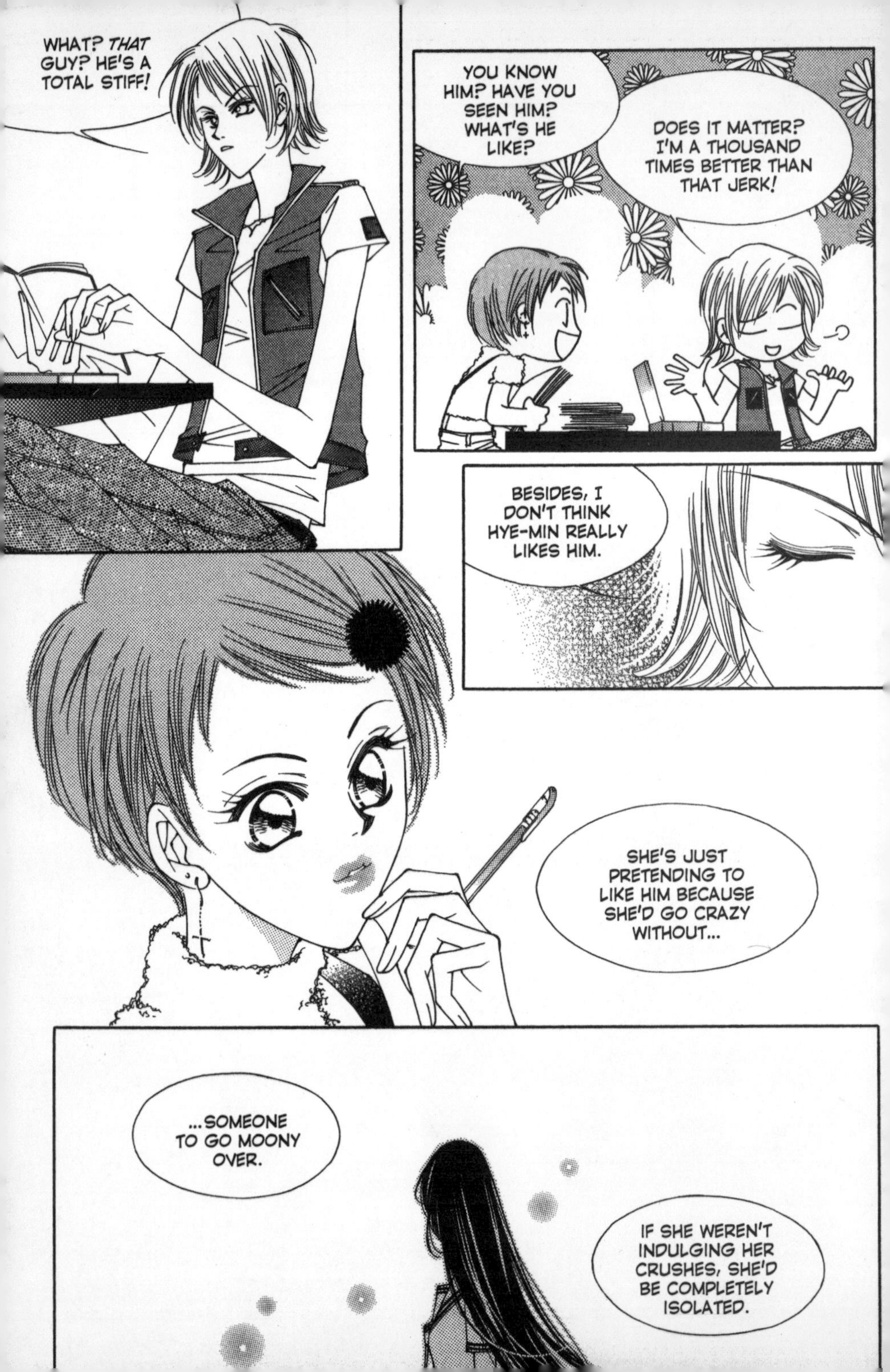
WHAT? THAT GUY? HE'S A TOTAL STIFF!
YOU KNOW HIM? HAVE YOU SEEN HIM? WHAT'S HE LIKE?
DOES IT MATTER? I'M A THOUSAND TIMES BETTER THAN THAT JERK!
BESIDES, I DON'T THINK HYE-MIN REALLY LIKES HIM.
SHE'S JUST PRETENDING TO LIKE HIM BECAUSE SHE'D GO CRAZY WITHOUT...
...SOMEONE TO GO MOONY OVER.
IF SHE WEREN'T INDULGING HER CRUSHES, SHE'D BE COMPLETELY ISOLATED.

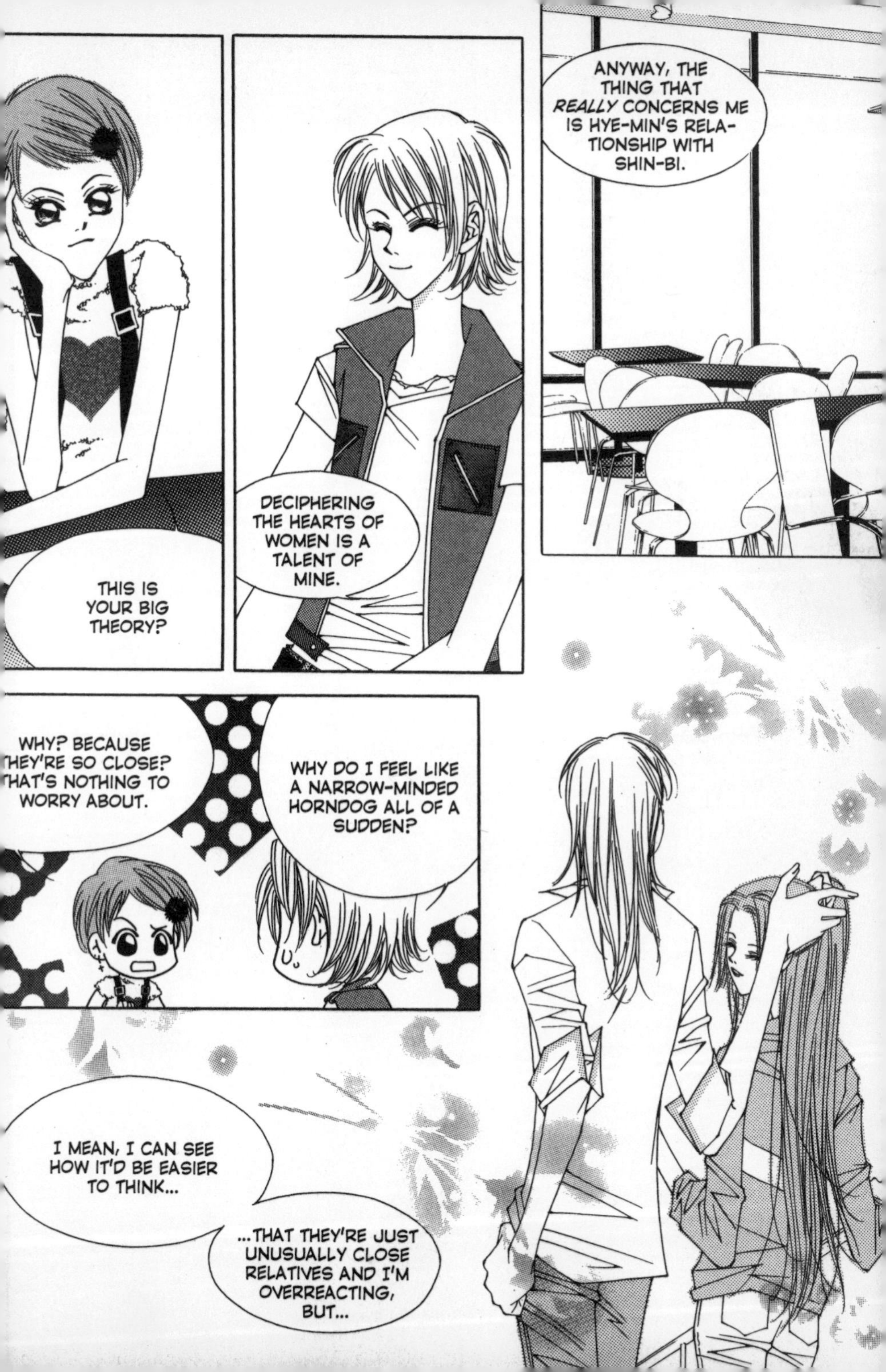
THIS IS YOUR BIG THEORY?
DECIPHERING THE HEARTS OF WOMEN IS A TALENT OF MINE.
ANYWAY, THE THING THAT *REALLY* CONCERNS ME IS HYE-MIN'S RELA-TIONSHIP WITH SHIN-BI.
WHY? BECAUSE THEY'RE SO CLOSE? THAT'S NOTHING TO WORRY ABOUT.
WHY DO I FEEL LIKE A NARROW-MINDED HORNDOG ALL OF A SUDDEN?
I MEAN, I CAN SEE HOW IT'D BE EASIER TO THINK...
...THAT THEY'RE JUST UNUSUALLY CLOSE RELATIVES AND I'M OVERREACTING, BUT...

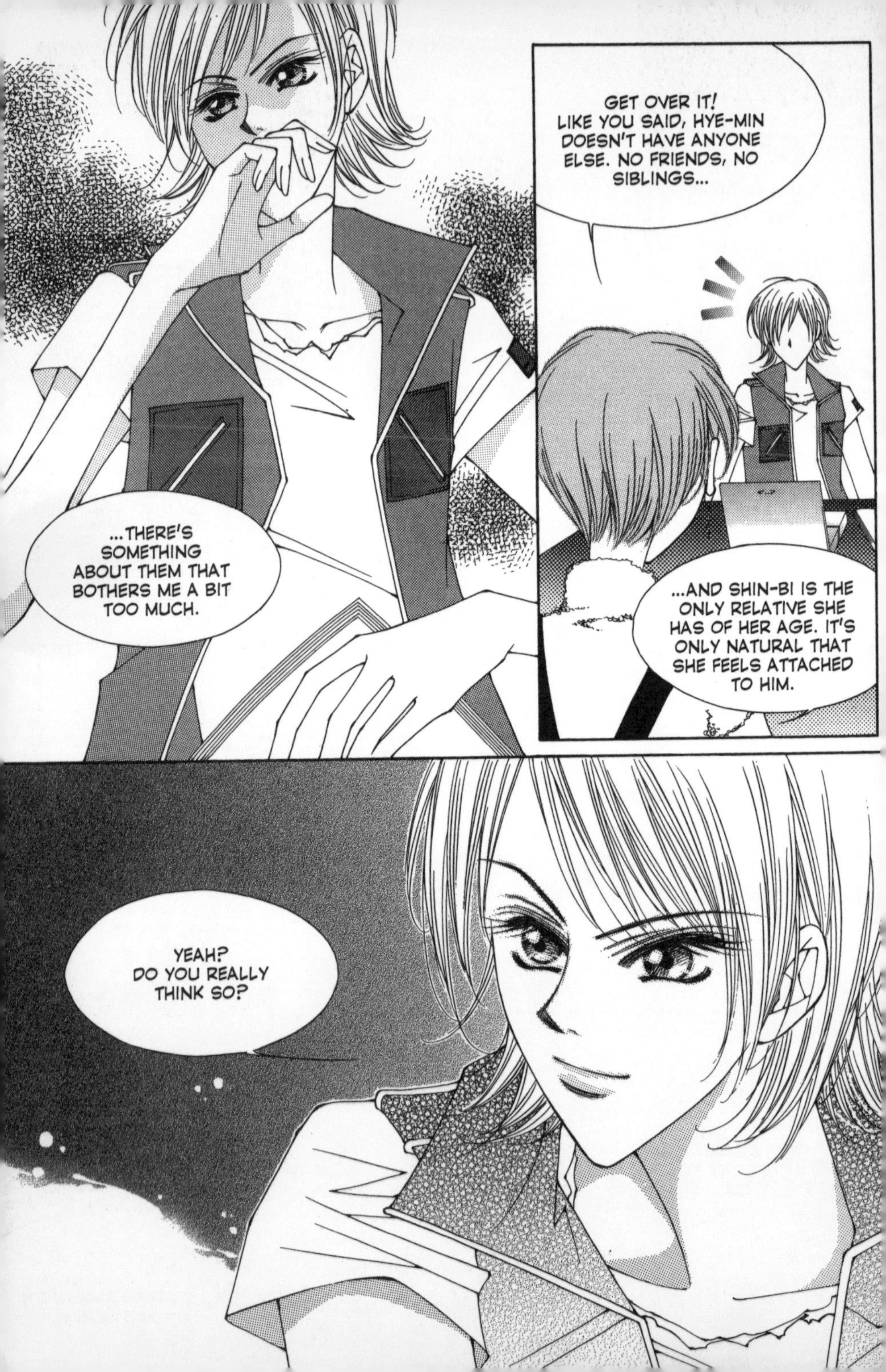
...THERE'S SOMETHING ABOUT THEM THAT BOTHERS ME A BIT TOO MUCH.
GET OVER IT! LIKE YOU SAID, HYE-MIN DOESN'T HAVE ANYONE ELSE. NO FRIENDS, NO SIBLINGS...
...AND SHIN-BI IS THE ONLY RELATIVE SHE HAS OF HER AGE. IT'S ONLY NATURAL THAT SHE FEELS ATTACHED TO HIM.
YEAH? DO YOU REALLY THINK SO?

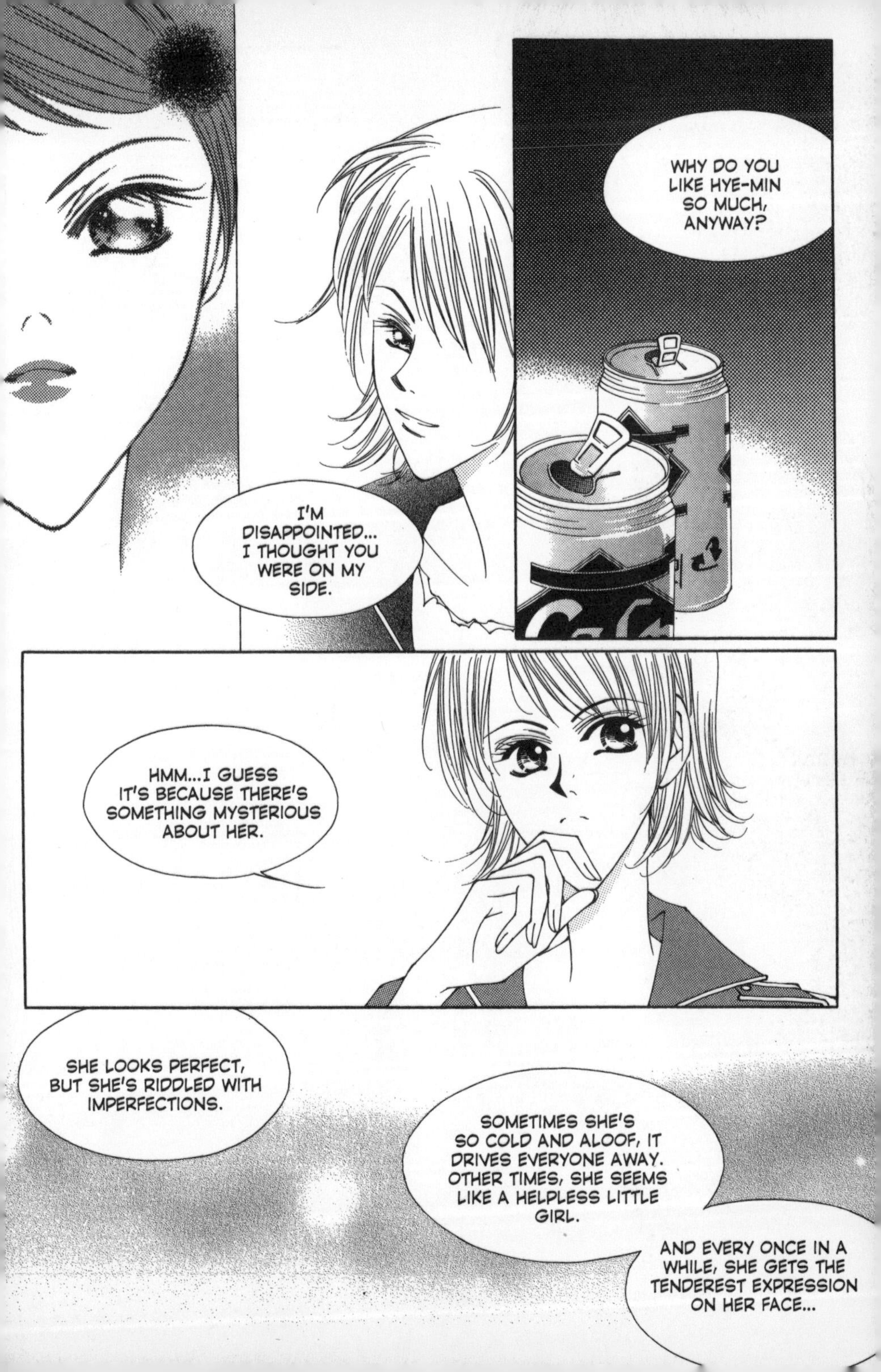
I'M DISAPPOINTED... I THOUGHT YOU WERE ON MY SIDE.
WHY DO YOU LIKE HYE-MIN SO MUCH, ANYWAY?
HMM...I GUESS IT'S BECAUSE THERE'S SOMETHING MYSTERIOUS ABOUT HER.
SHE LOOKS PERFECT, BUT SHE'S RIDDLED WITH IMPERFECTIONS.
SOMETIMES SHE'S SO COLD AND ALOOF, IT DRIVES EVERYONE AWAY. OTHER TIMES, SHE SEEMS LIKE A HELPLESS LITTLE GIRL.
AND EVERY ONCE IN A WHILE, SHE GETS THE TENDEREST EXPRESSION ON HER FACE...

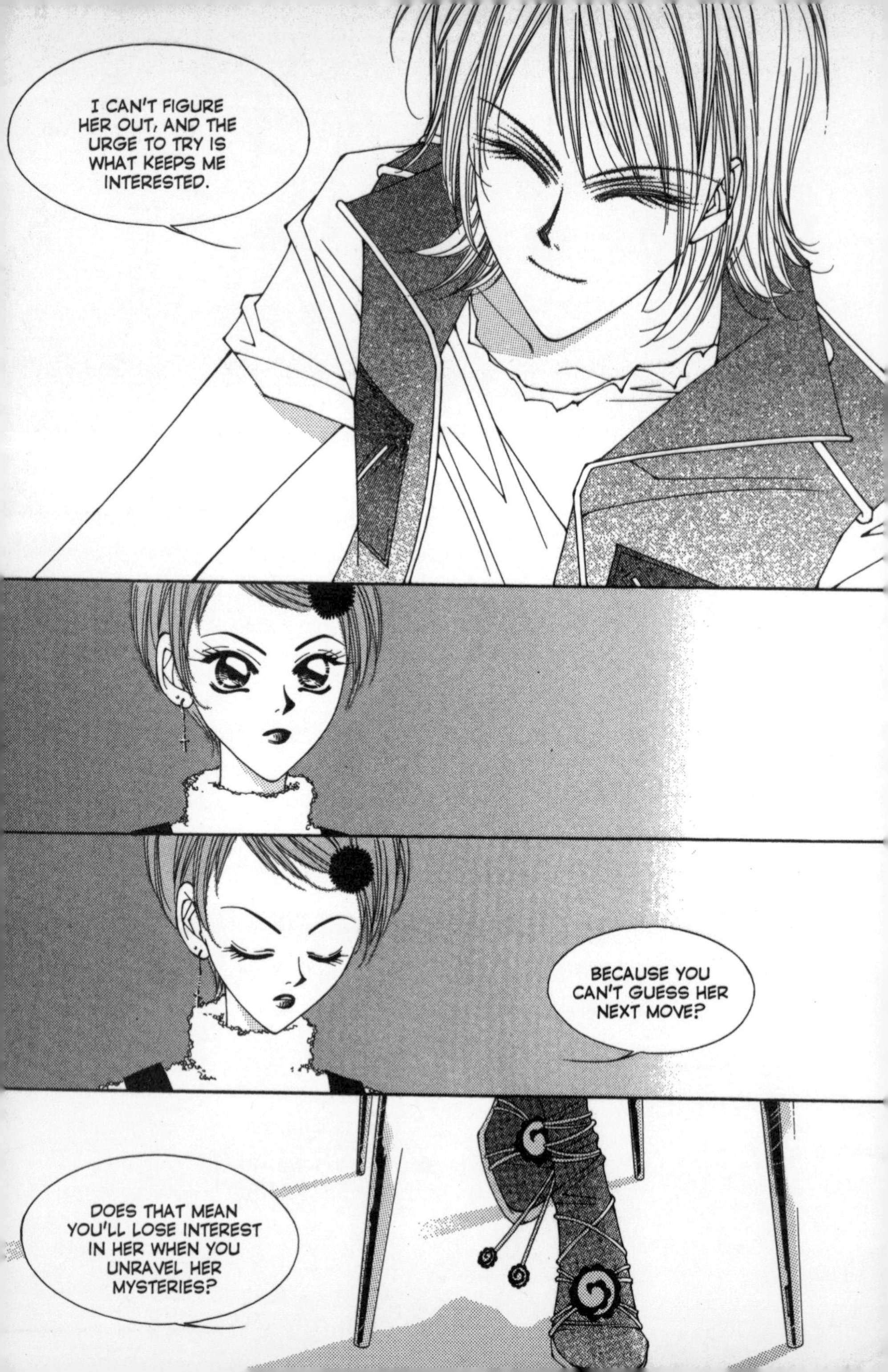
I CAN'T FIGURE HER OUT, AND THE URGE TO TRY IS WHAT KEEPS ME INTERESTED.
BECAUSE YOU CAN'T GUESS HER NEXT MOVE?
DOES THAT MEAN YOU'LL LOSE INTEREST IN HER WHEN YOU UNRAVEL HER MYSTERIES?

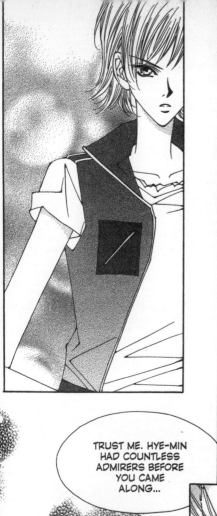

...BUT YOU'RE THE ONLY ONE WHO HAS GOTTEN THIS CLOSE.

MAYBE IT WAS JUST A COINCIDENCE, OR PERHAPS IT WAS FATE...

TRUST ME. HYE-MIN HAD COUNTLESS ADMIRERS BEFORE YOU CAME ALONG...

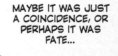

TAB

TAB

...BUT IF YOUR FEELINGS FOR HER ARE REALLY THAT SHALLOW, JUST FORGET ABOUT HER AND LEAVE HERE NOW.

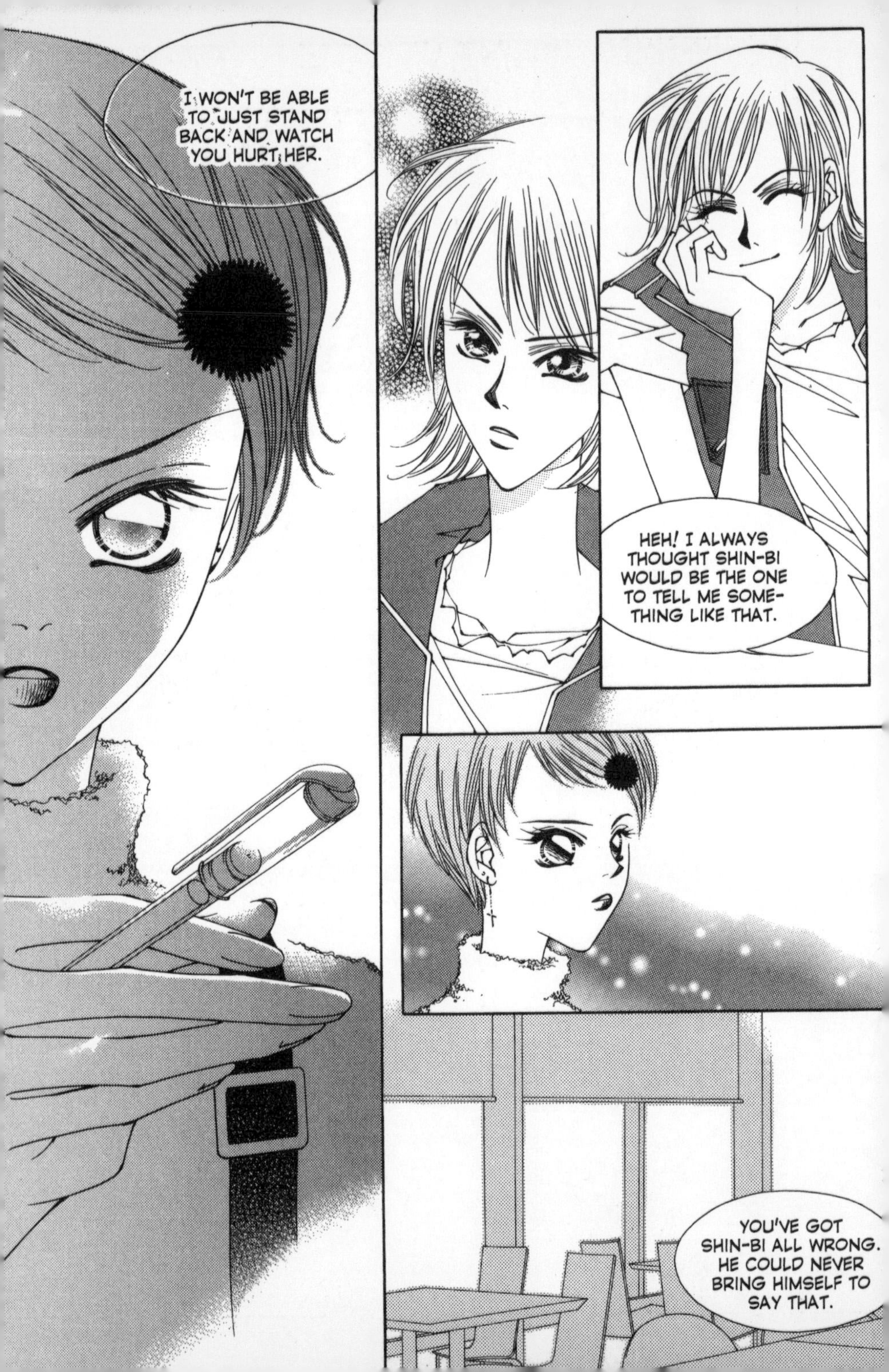
I WON'T BE ABLE TO JUST STAND BACK AND WATCH YOU HURT HER.
HEH! I ALWAYS THOUGHT SHIN-BI WOULD BE THE ONE TO TELL ME SOME-THING LIKE THAT.
YOU'VE GOT SHIN-BI ALL WRONG. HE COULD NEVER BRING HIMSELF TO SAY THAT.

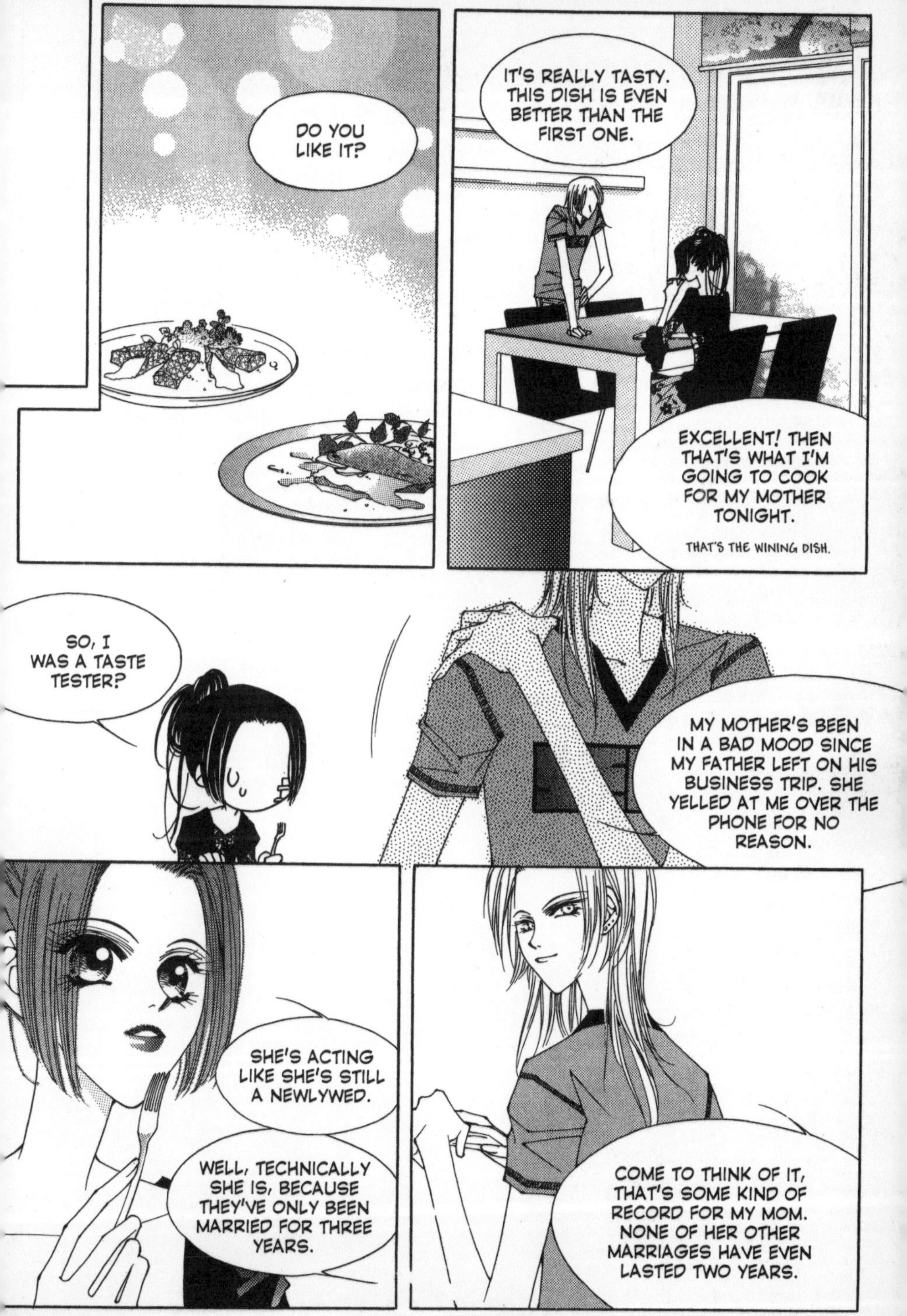
DO YOU LIKE IT?
IT'S REALLY TASTY. THIS DISH IS EVEN BETTER THAN THE FIRST ONE.
EXCELLENT! THEN THAT'S WHAT I'M GOING TO COOK FOR MY MOTHER TONIGHT.
THAT'S THE WINING DISH.
SO, I WAS A TASTE TESTER?
MY MOTHER'S BEEN IN A BAD MOOD SINCE MY FATHER LEFT ON HIS BUSINESS TRIP. SHE YELLED AT ME OVER THE PHONE FOR NO REASON.
SHE'S ACTING LIKE SHE'S STILL A NEWLYWED.
WELL, TECHNICALLY SHE IS, BECAUSE THEY'VE ONLY BEEN MARRIED FOR THREE YEARS.
COME TO THINK OF IT, THAT'S SOME KIND OF RECORD FOR MY MOM. NONE OF HER OTHER MARRIAGES HAVE EVEN LASTED TWO YEARS.

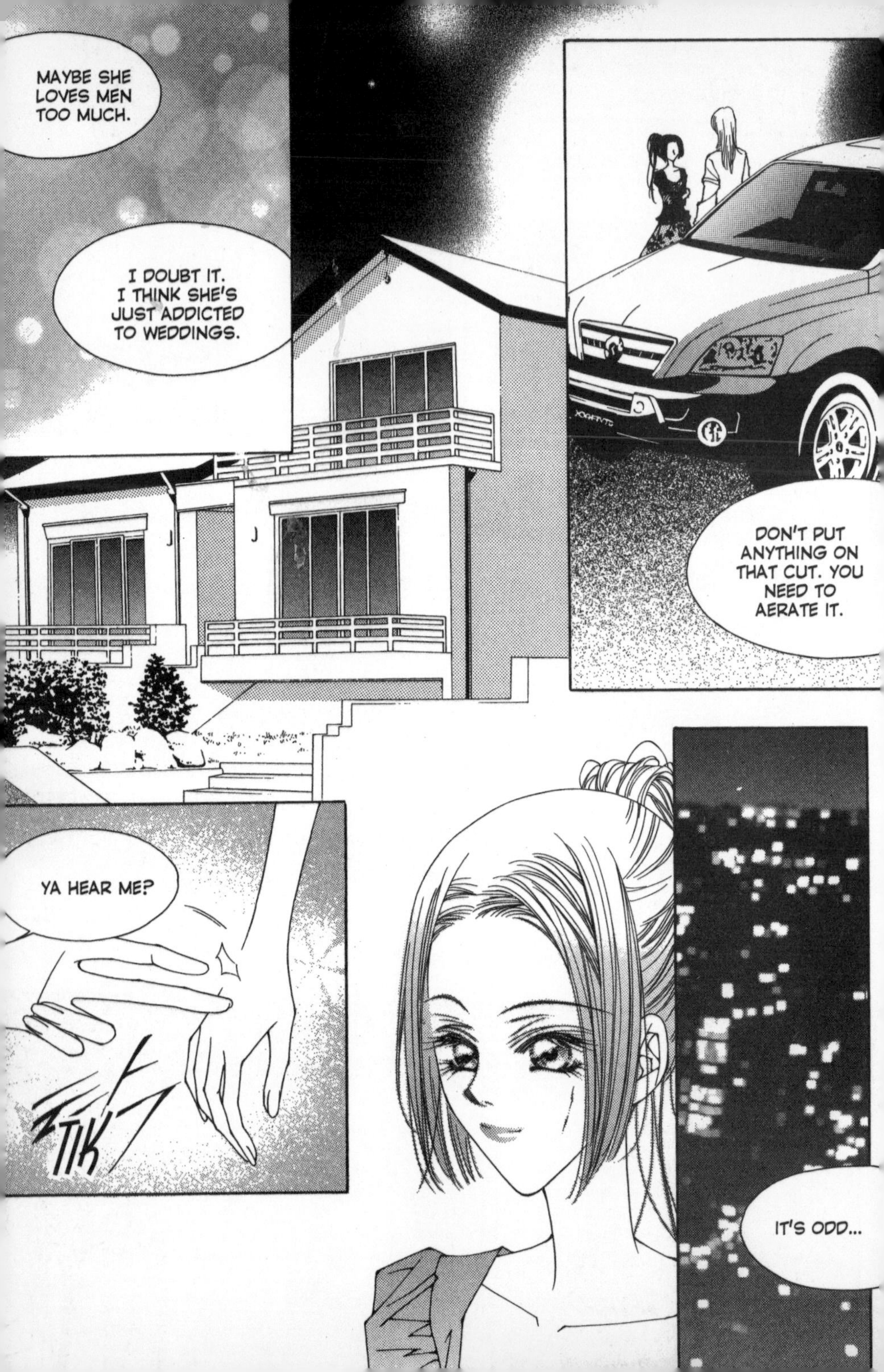
MAYBE SHE LOVES MEN TOO MUCH.
I DOUBT IT. I THINK SHE'S JUST ADDICTED TO WEDDINGS.
DON'T PUT ANYTHING ON THAT CUT. YOU NEED TO AERATE IT.
YA HEAR ME?
TIK
IT'S ODD...

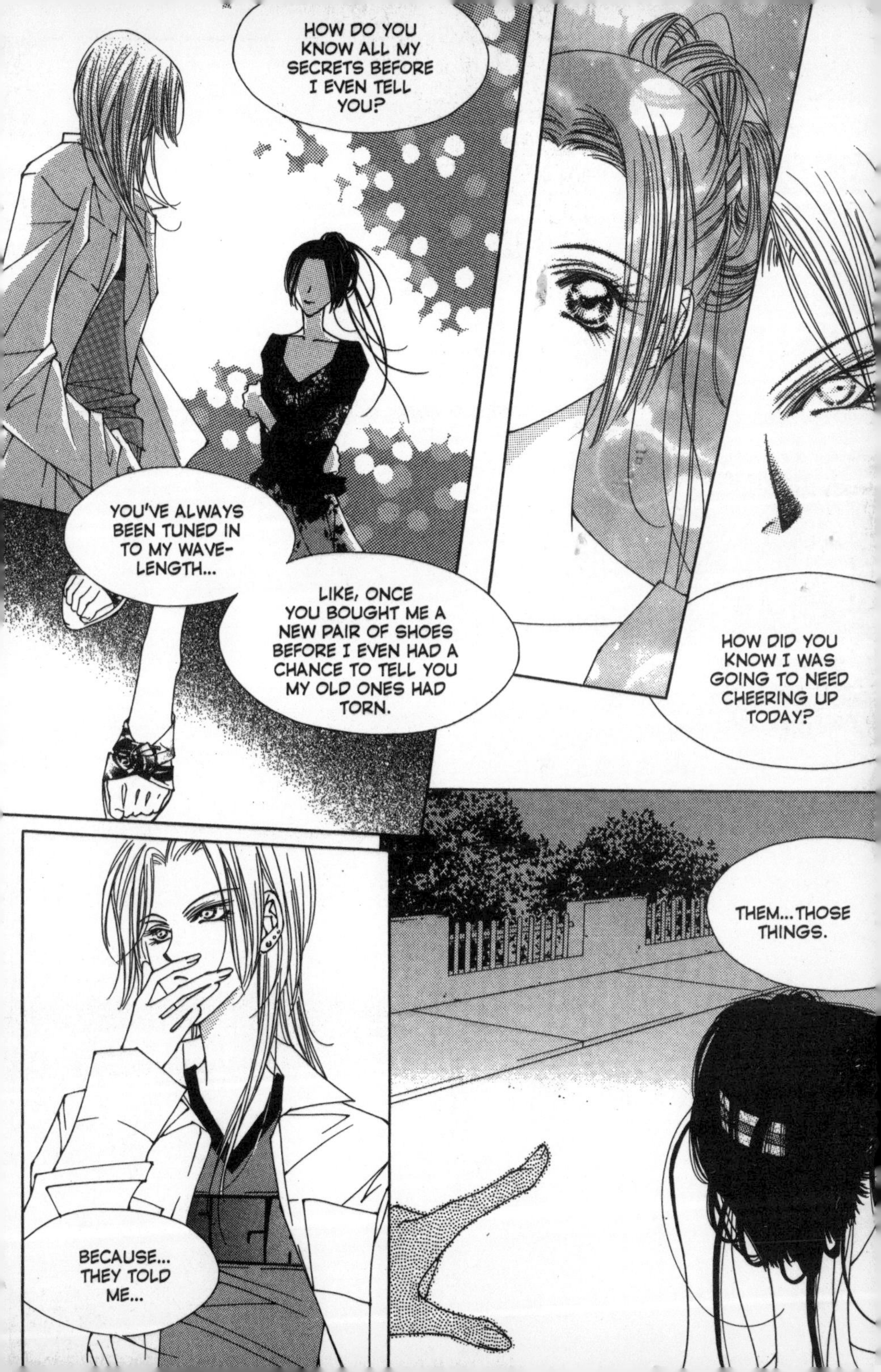
HOW DO YOU KNOW ALL MY SECRETS BEFORE I EVEN TELL YOU?
YOU'VE ALWAYS BEEN TUNED IN TO MY WAVE-LENGTH...
LIKE, ONCE YOU BOUGHT ME A NEW PAIR OF SHOES BEFORE I EVEN HAD A CHANCE TO TELL YOU MY OLD ONES HAD TORN.
HOW DID YOU KNOW I WAS GOING TO NEED CHEERING UP TODAY?
BECAUSE... THEY TOLD ME...
THEM...THOSE THINGS.

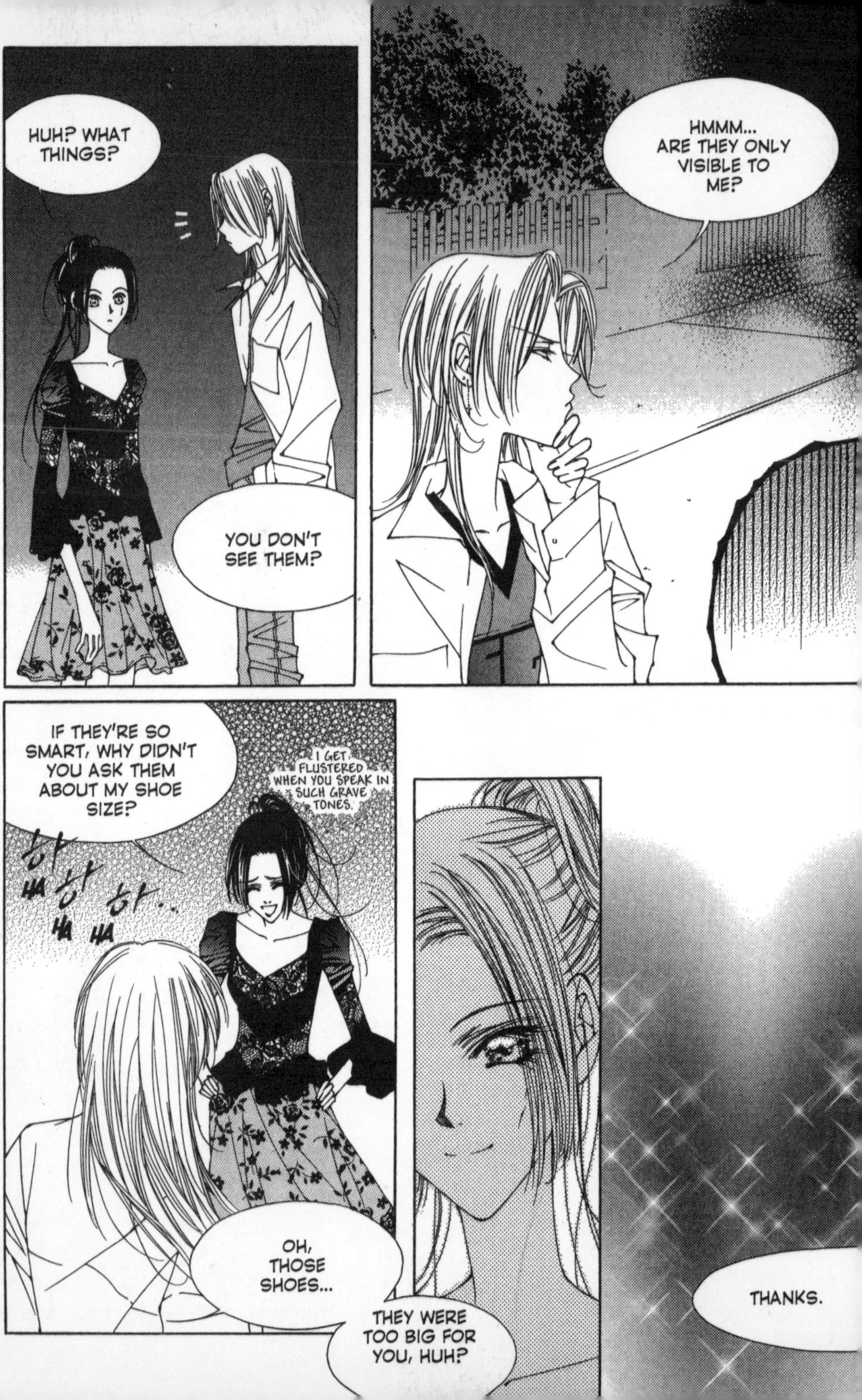
HUH? WHAT THINGS?
YOU DON'T SEE THEM?
HMMM... ARE THEY ONLY VISIBLE TO ME?
IF THEY'RE SO SMART, WHY DIDN'T YOU ASK THEM ABOUT MY SHOE SIZE?
I GET FLUSTERED WHEN YOU SPEAK IN SUCH GRAVE TONES.
하 HA 하 HA 하.. HA
OH, THOSE SHOES...
THEY WERE TOO BIG FOR YOU, HUH?
THANKS.

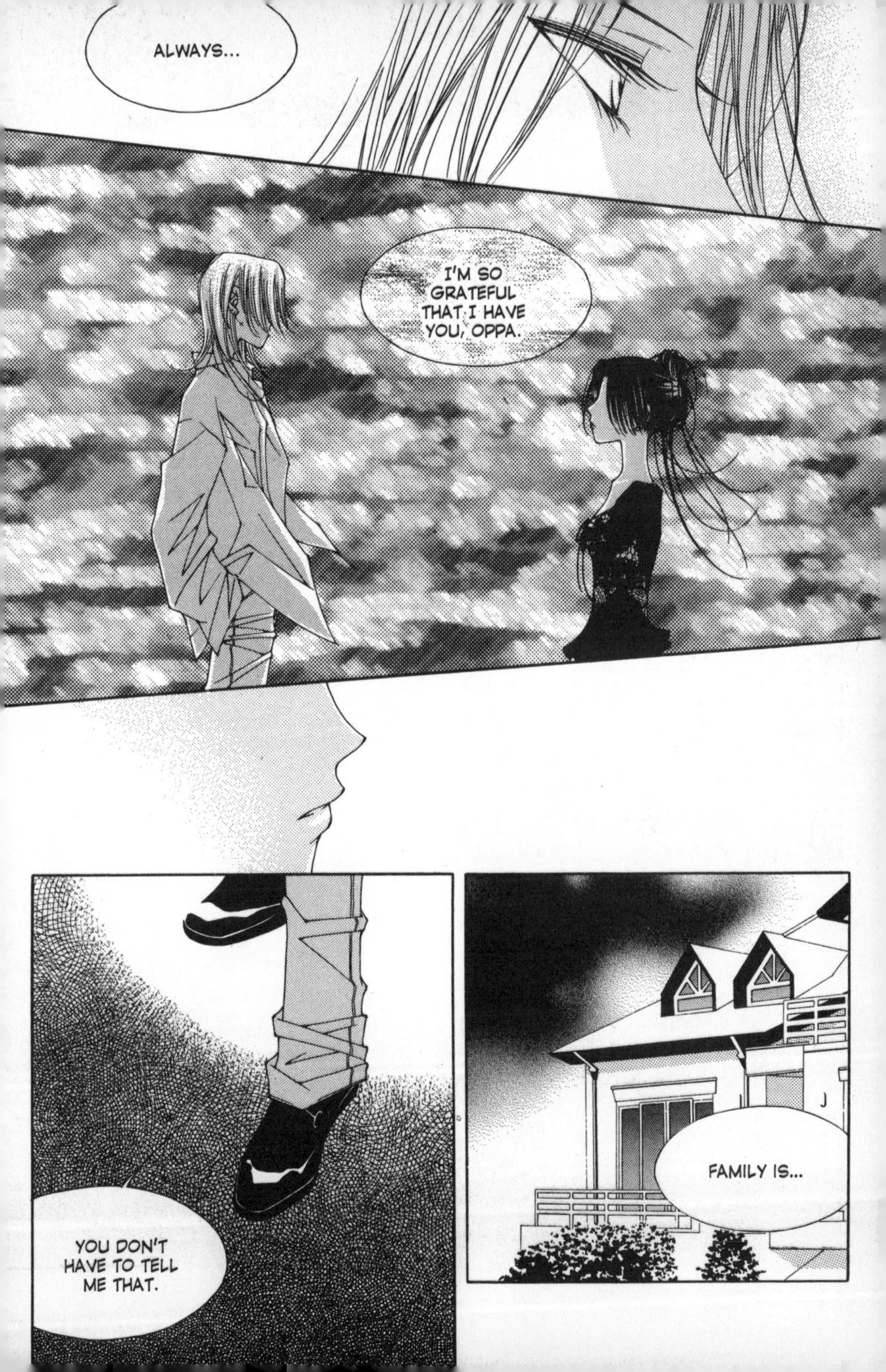
ALWAYS...
I'M SO GRATEFUL THAT I HAVE YOU, OPPA.
YOU DON'T HAVE TO TELL ME THAT.
FAMILY IS...

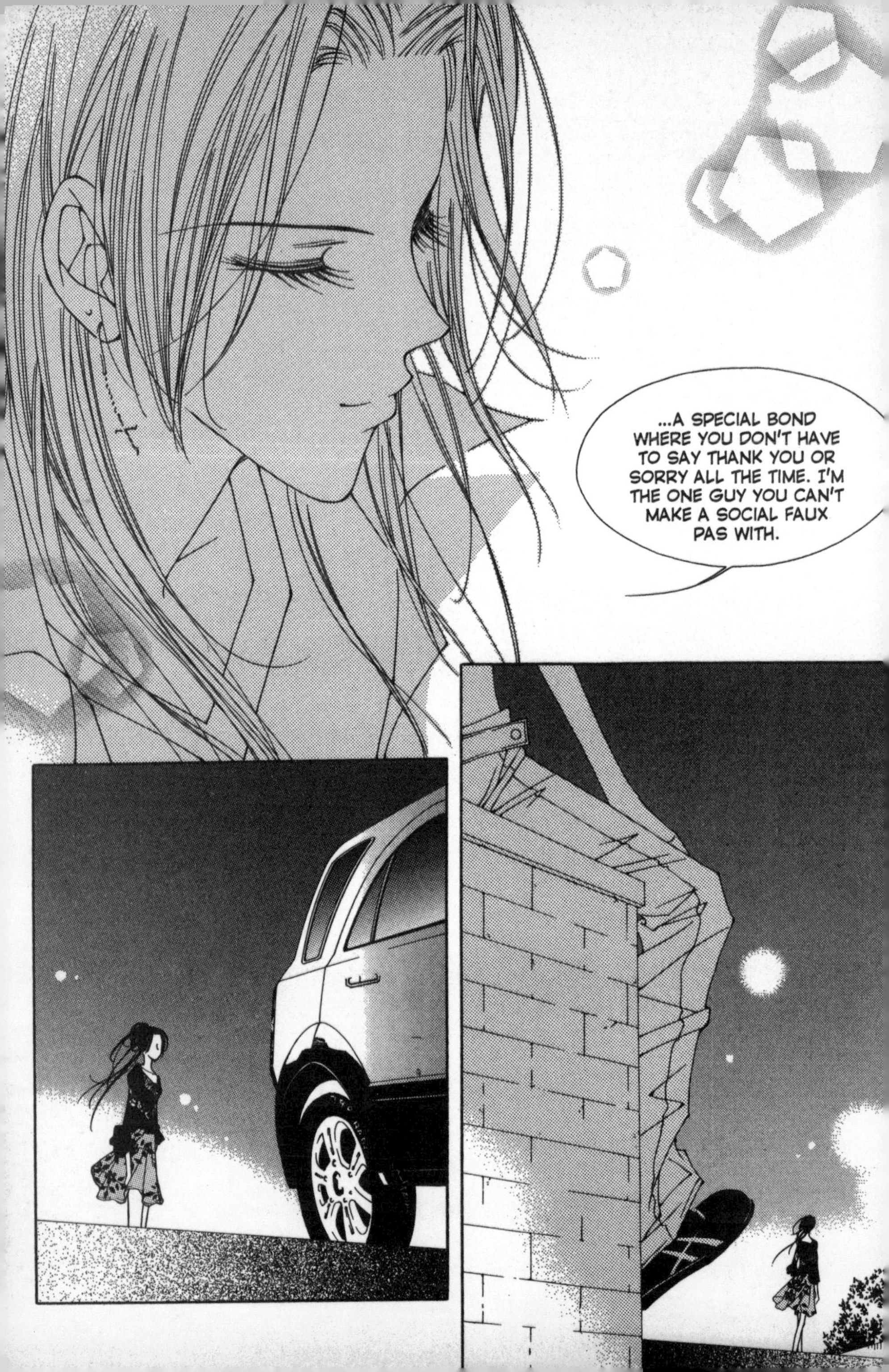
...A SPECIAL BOND WHERE YOU DON'T HAVE TO SAY THANK YOU OR SORRY ALL THE TIME. I'M THE ONE GUY YOU CAN'T MAKE A SOCIAL FAUX PAS WITH.

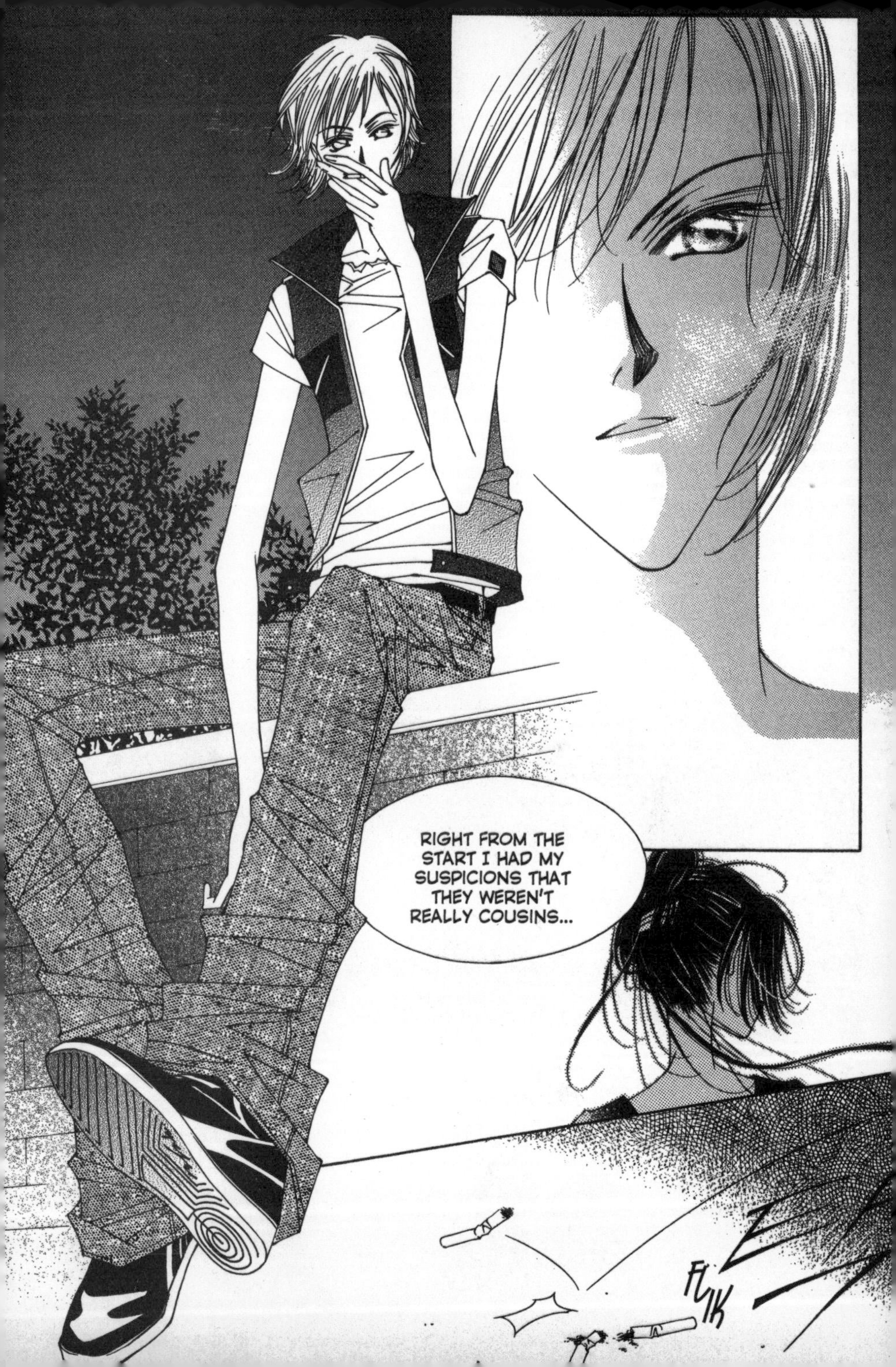
RIGHT FROM THE START I HAD MY SUSPICIONS THAT THEY WEREN'T REALLY COUSINS...
FLIK

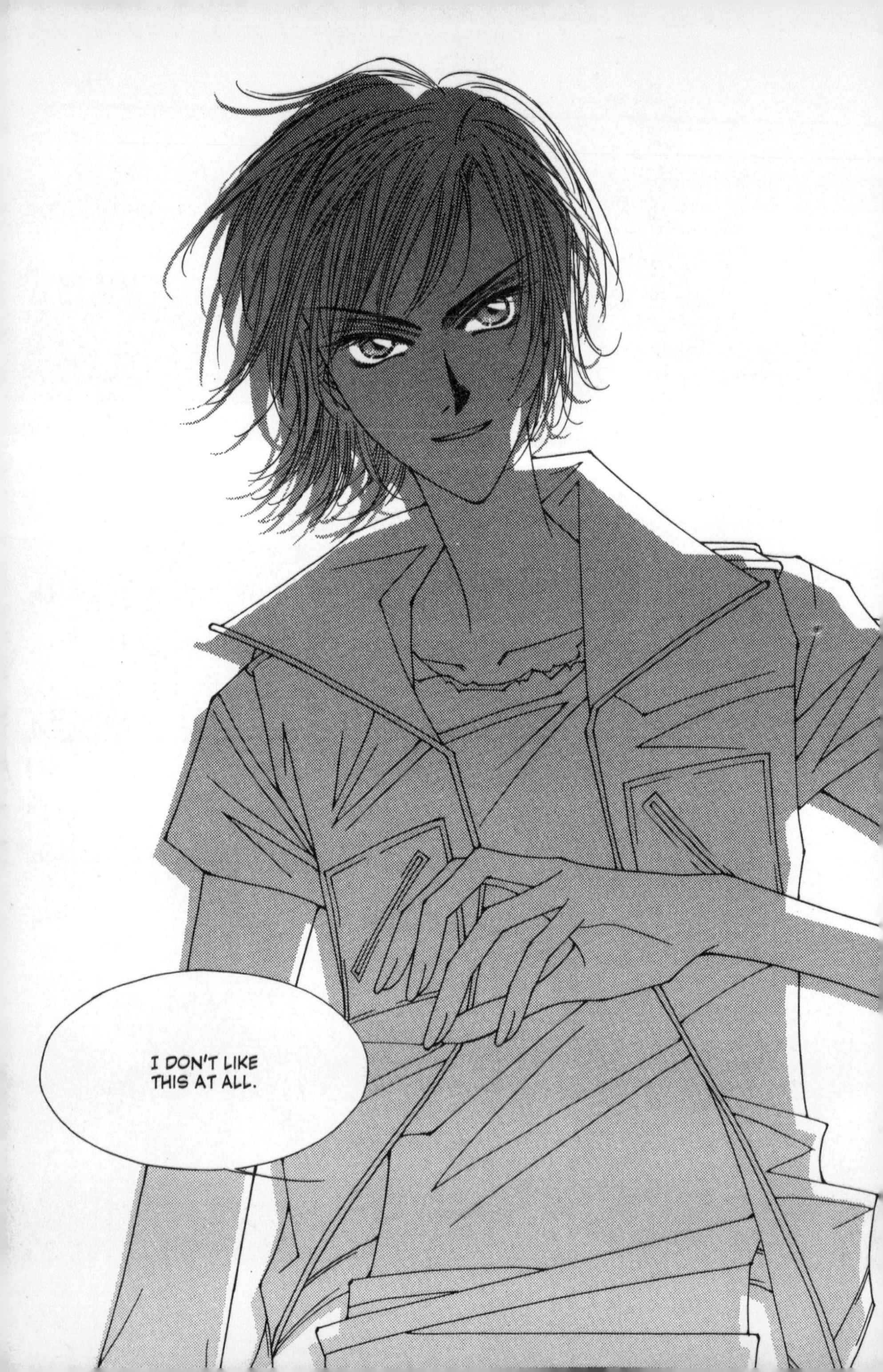
I DON'T LIKE THIS AT ALL.

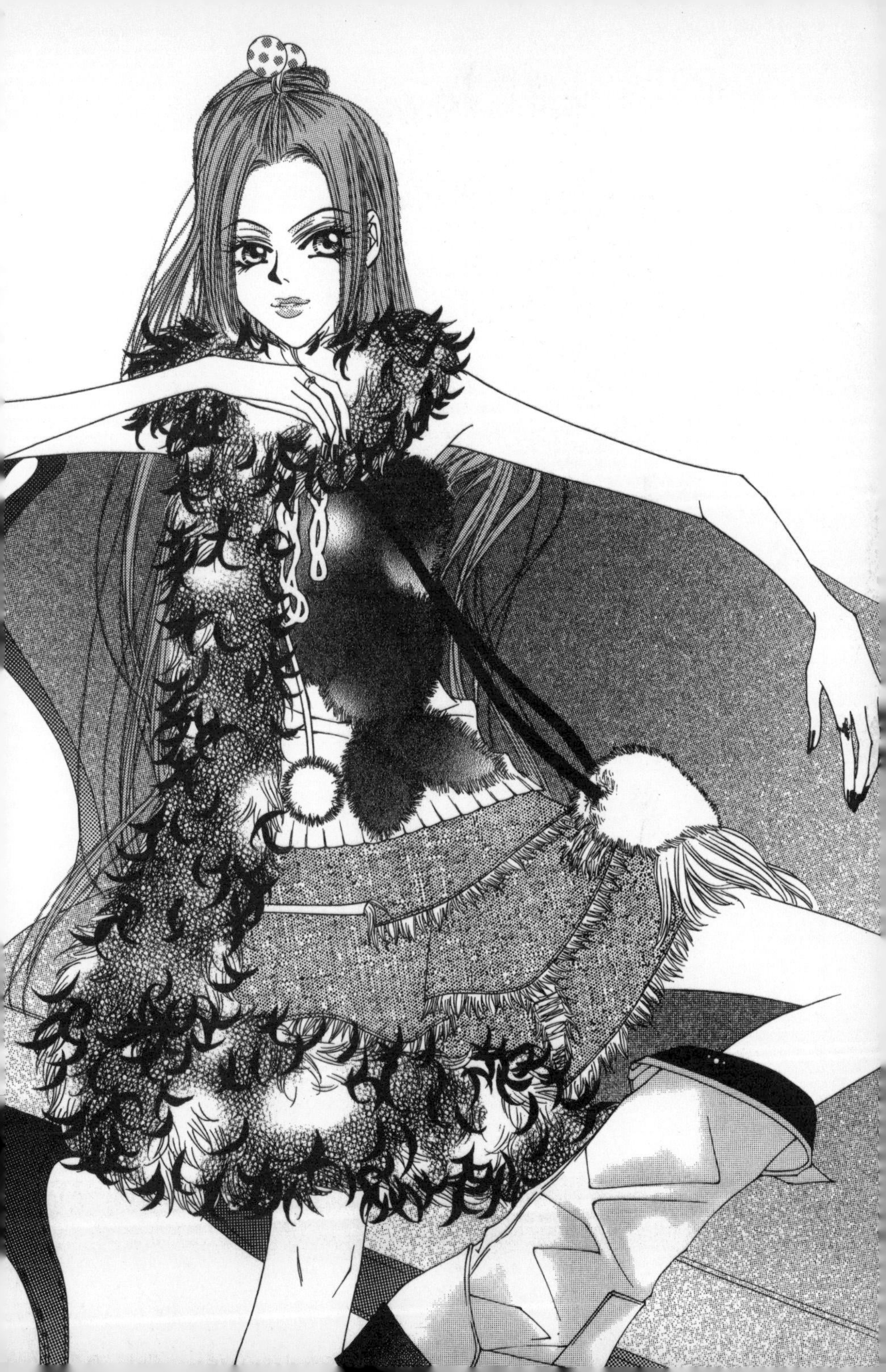

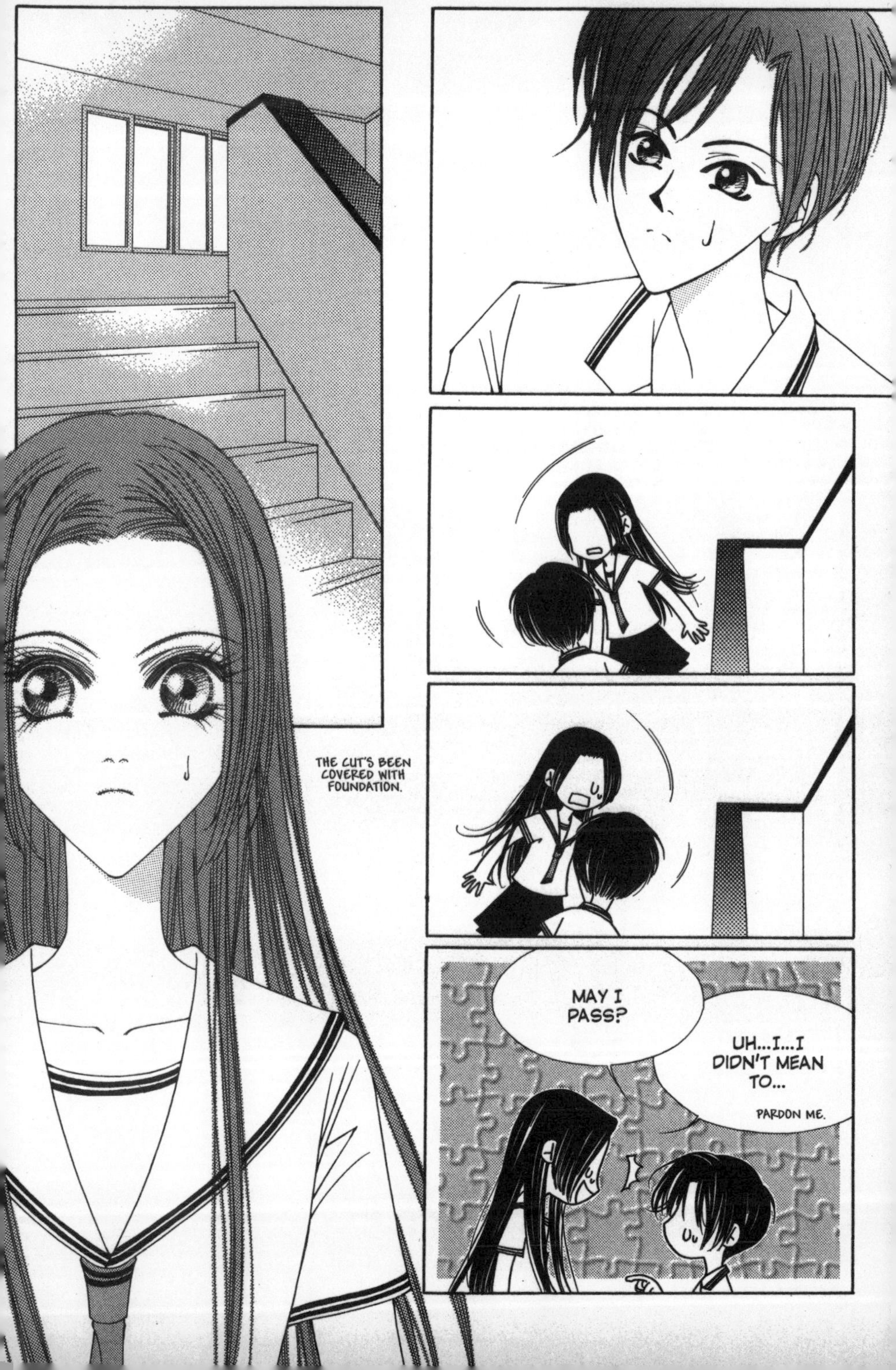
THE CUT'S BEEN COVERED WITH FOUNDATION.
MAY I PASS?
UH...I...I DIDN'T MEAN TO...
PARDON ME.

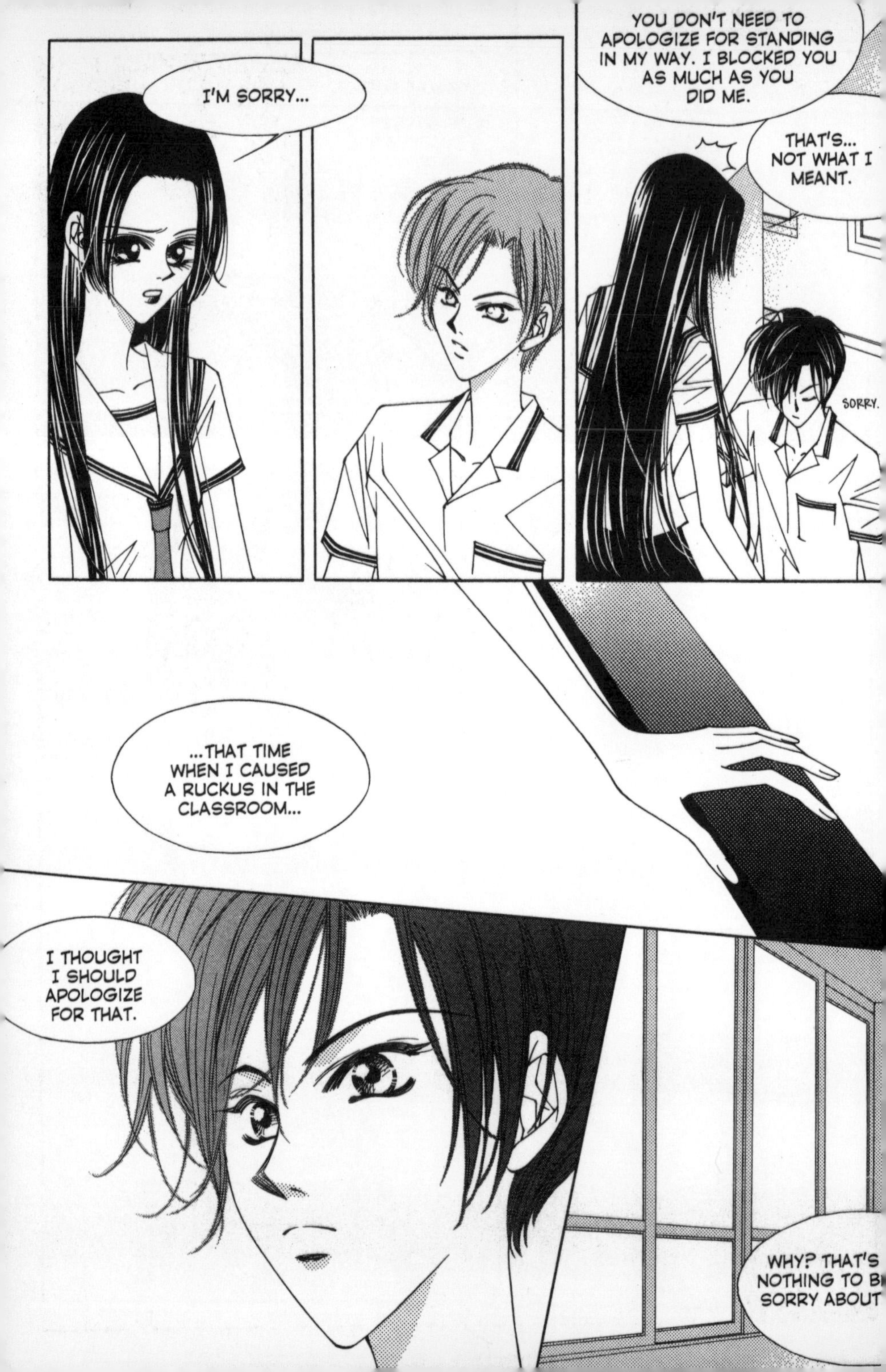
I'M SORRY...
YOU DON'T NEED TO APOLOGIZE FOR STANDING IN MY WAY. I BLOCKED YOU AS MUCH AS YOU DID ME.
THAT'S... NOT WHAT I MEANT.
SORRY.
...THAT TIME WHEN I CAUSED A RUCKUS IN THE CLASSROOM...
I THOUGHT I SHOULD APOLOGIZE FOR THAT.
WHY? THAT'S NOTHING TO B
SORRY ABOUT

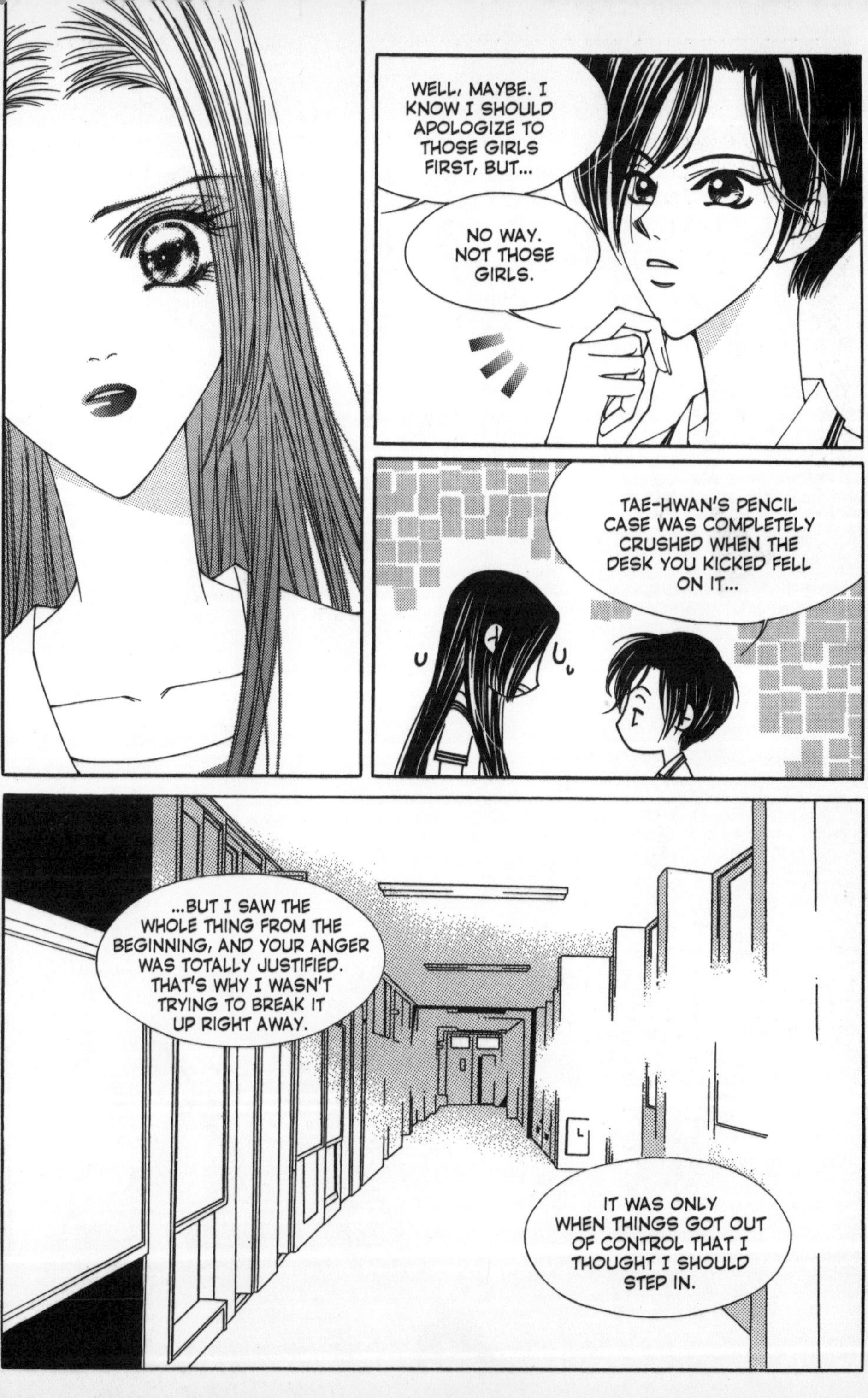
WELL, MAYBE. I KNOW I SHOULD APOLOGIZE TO THOSE GIRLS FIRST, BUT...
NO WAY. NOT THOSE GIRLS.
TAE-HWAN'S PENCIL CASE WAS COMPLETELY CRUSHED WHEN THE DESK YOU KICKED FELL ON IT...
...BUT I SAW THE WHOLE THING FROM THE BEGINNING, AND YOUR ANGER WAS TOTALLY JUSTIFIED. THAT'S WHY I WASN'T TRYING TO BREAK IT UP RIGHT AWAY.
IT WAS ONLY WHEN THINGS GOT OUT OF CONTROL THAT I THOUGHT I SHOULD STEP IN.

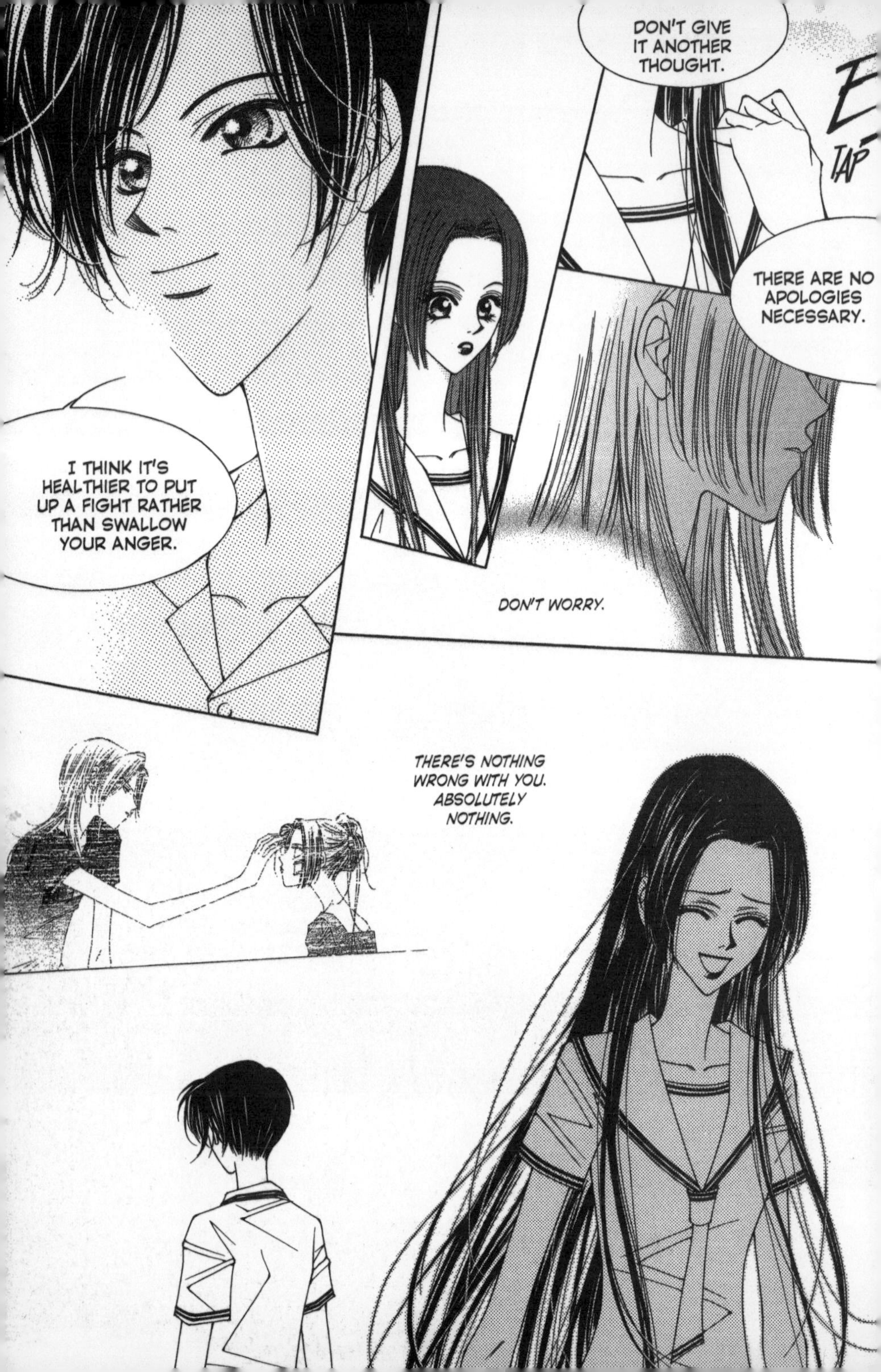
I THINK IT'S HEALTHIER TO PUT UP A FIGHT RATHER THAN SWALLOW YOUR ANGER.
DON'T GIVE IT ANOTHER THOUGHT.
TAP
THERE ARE NO APOLOGIES NECESSARY.
DON'T WORRY.
THERE'S NOTHING WRONG WITH YOU. ABSOLUTELY NOTHING.

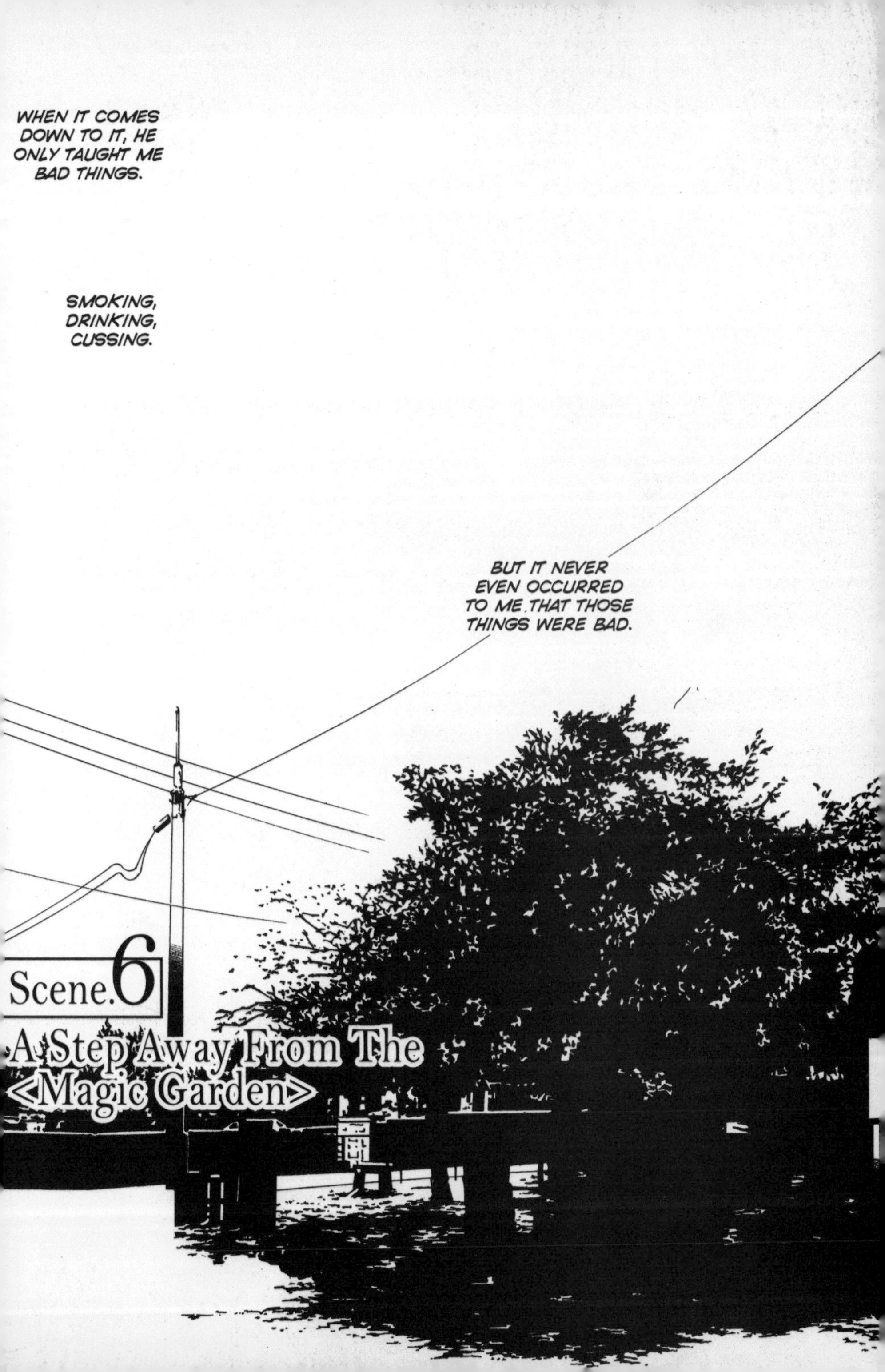
WHEN IT COMES DOWN TO IT, HE ONLY TAUGHT ME BAD THINGS.
SMOKING, DRINKING, CUSSING.
BUT IT NEVER EVEN OCCURRED TO ME THAT THOSE THINGS WERE BAD.

Scene.6 A Step Away From The <Magic Garden>

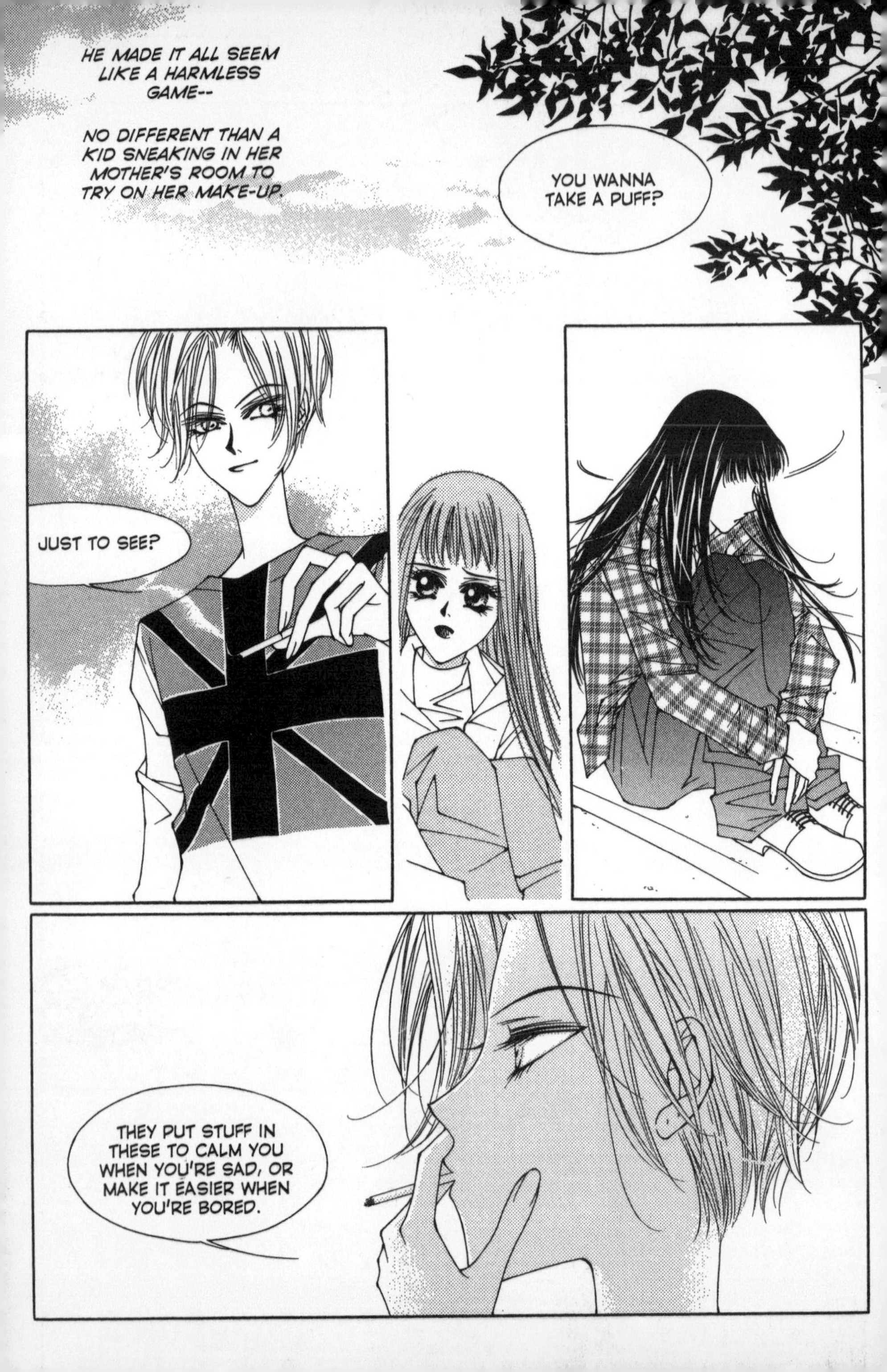
HE MADE IT ALL SEEM LIKE A HARMLESS GAME--
NO DIFFERENT THAN A KID SNEAKING IN HER MOTHER'S ROOM TO TRY ON HER MAKE-UP.
YOU WANNA TAKE A PUFF?
JUST TO SEE?
THEY PUT STUFF IN THESE TO CALM YOU WHEN YOU'RE SAD, OR MAKE IT EASIER WHEN YOU'RE BORED.

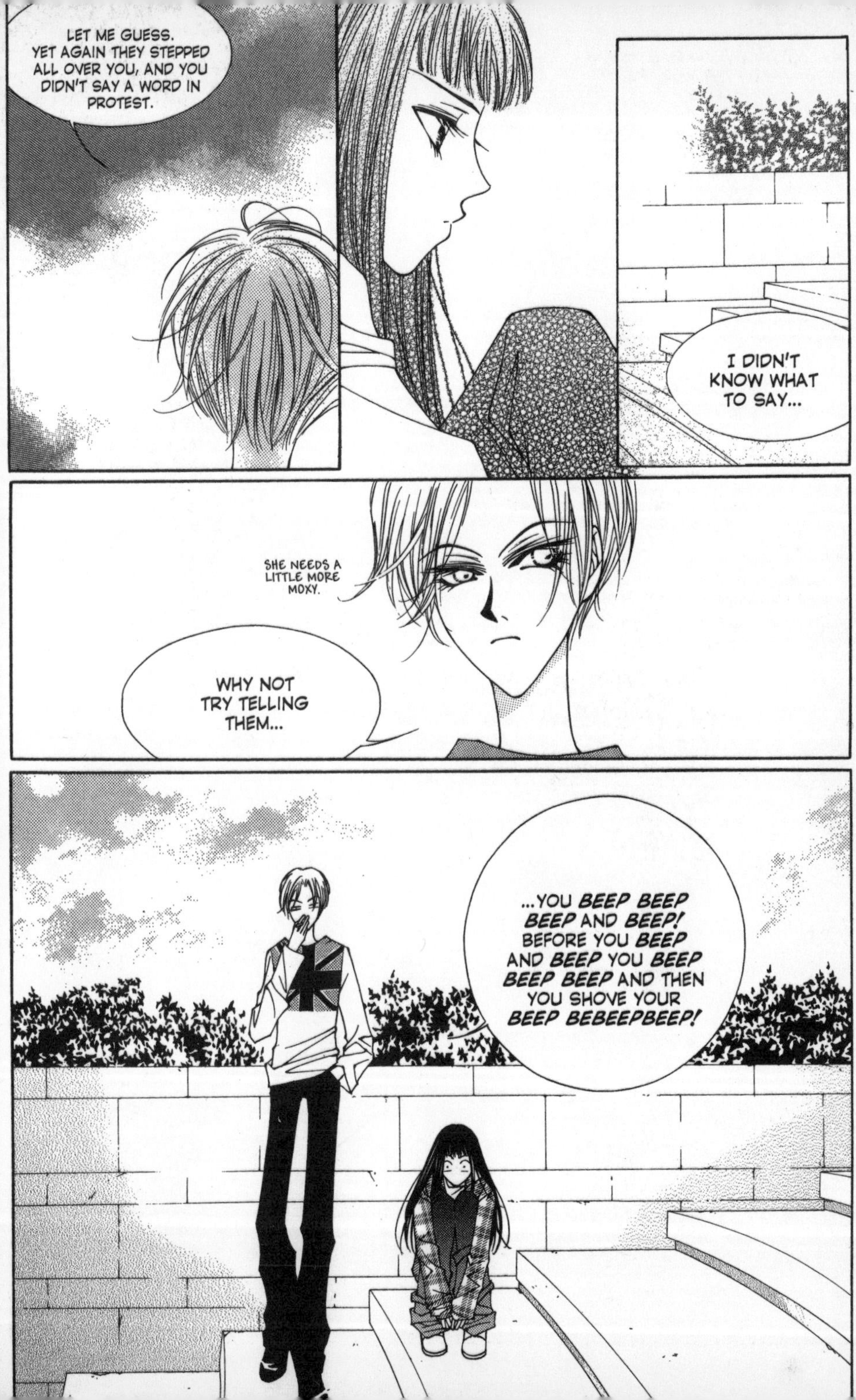
LET ME GUESS. YET AGAIN THEY STEPPED ALL OVER YOU, AND YOU DIDN'T SAY A WORD IN PROTEST.
I DIDN'T KNOW WHAT TO SAY...
SHE NEEDS A LITTLE MORE MOXY.
WHY NOT TRY TELLING THEM...
...YOU BEEP BEEP BEEP AND BEEP! BEFORE YOU BEEP AND BEEP YOU BEEP BEEP BEEP AND THEN YOU SHOVE YOUR BEEP BEBEEPBEEP!

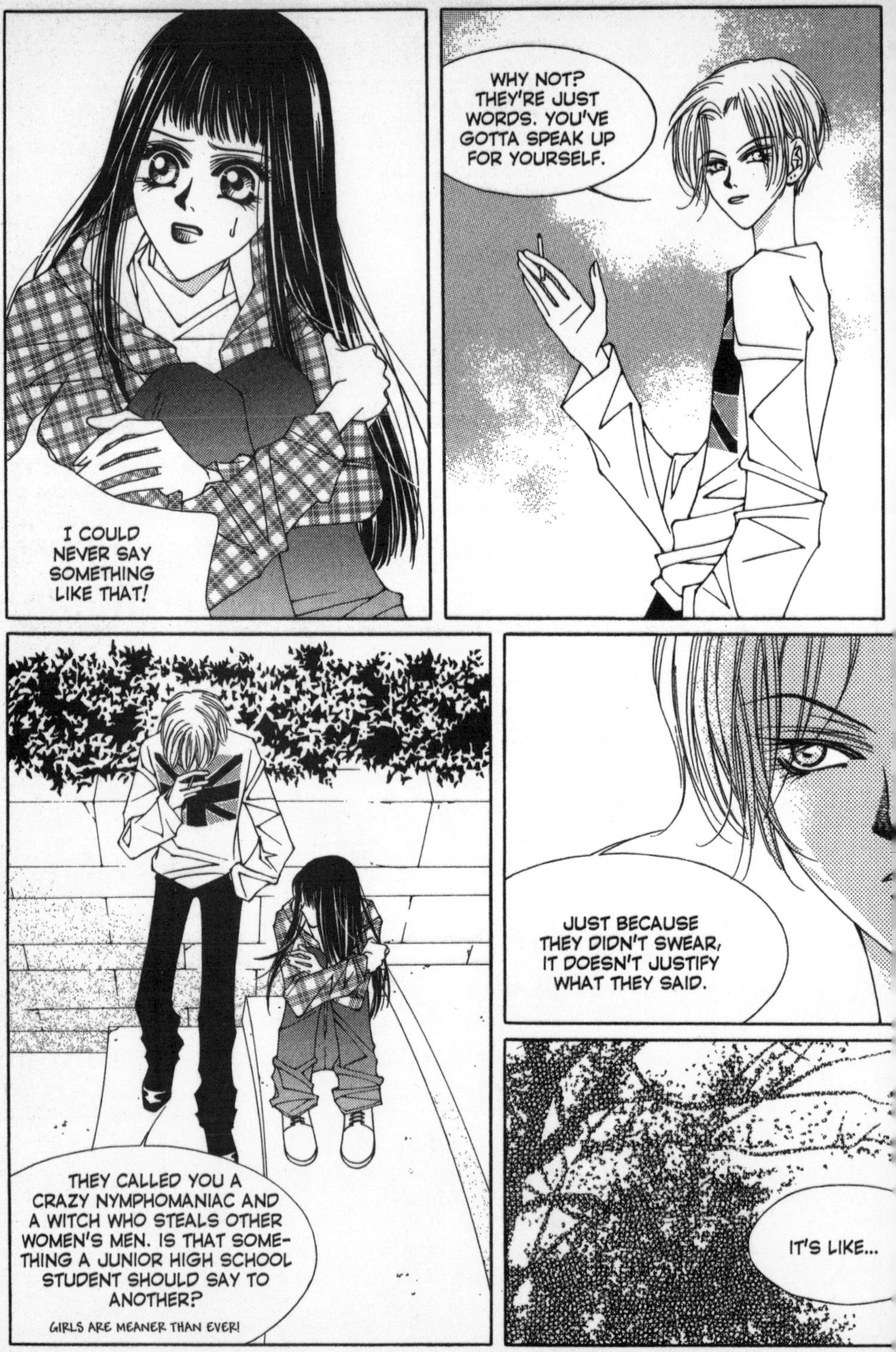
I COULD NEVER SAY SOMETHING LIKE THAT!
WHY NOT? THEY'RE JUST WORDS. YOU'VE GOTTA SPEAK UP FOR YOURSELF.
THEY CALLED YOU A CRAZY NYMPHOMANIAC AND A WITCH WHO STEALS OTHER WOMEN'S MEN. IS THAT SOMETHING A JUNIOR HIGH SCHOOL STUDENT SHOULD SAY TO ANOTHER?
GIRLS ARE MEANER THAN EVER!
JUST BECAUSE THEY DIDN'T SWEAR, IT DOESN'T JUSTIFY WHAT THEY SAID.
IT'S LIKE...

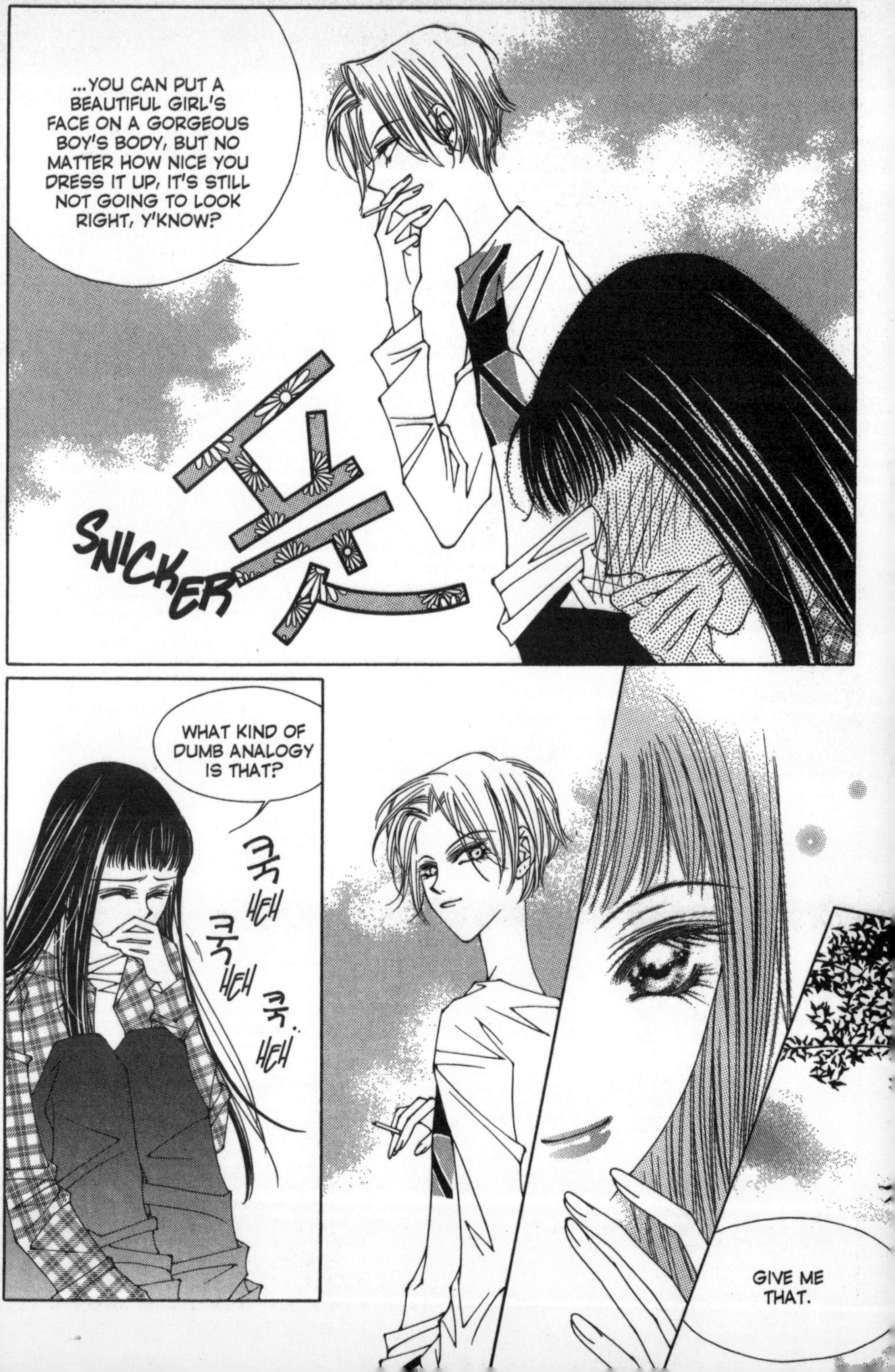
...YOU CAN PUT A BEAUTIFUL GIRL'S FACE ON A GORGEOUS BOY'S BODY, BUT NO MATTER HOW NICE YOU DRESS IT UP, IT'S STILL NOT GOING TO LOOK RIGHT, Y'KNOW?
풋
SNICKER
WHAT KIND OF DUMB ANALOGY IS THAT?
쿡 HEH
쿡 HEH
쿡.. HEH
GIVE ME THAT.

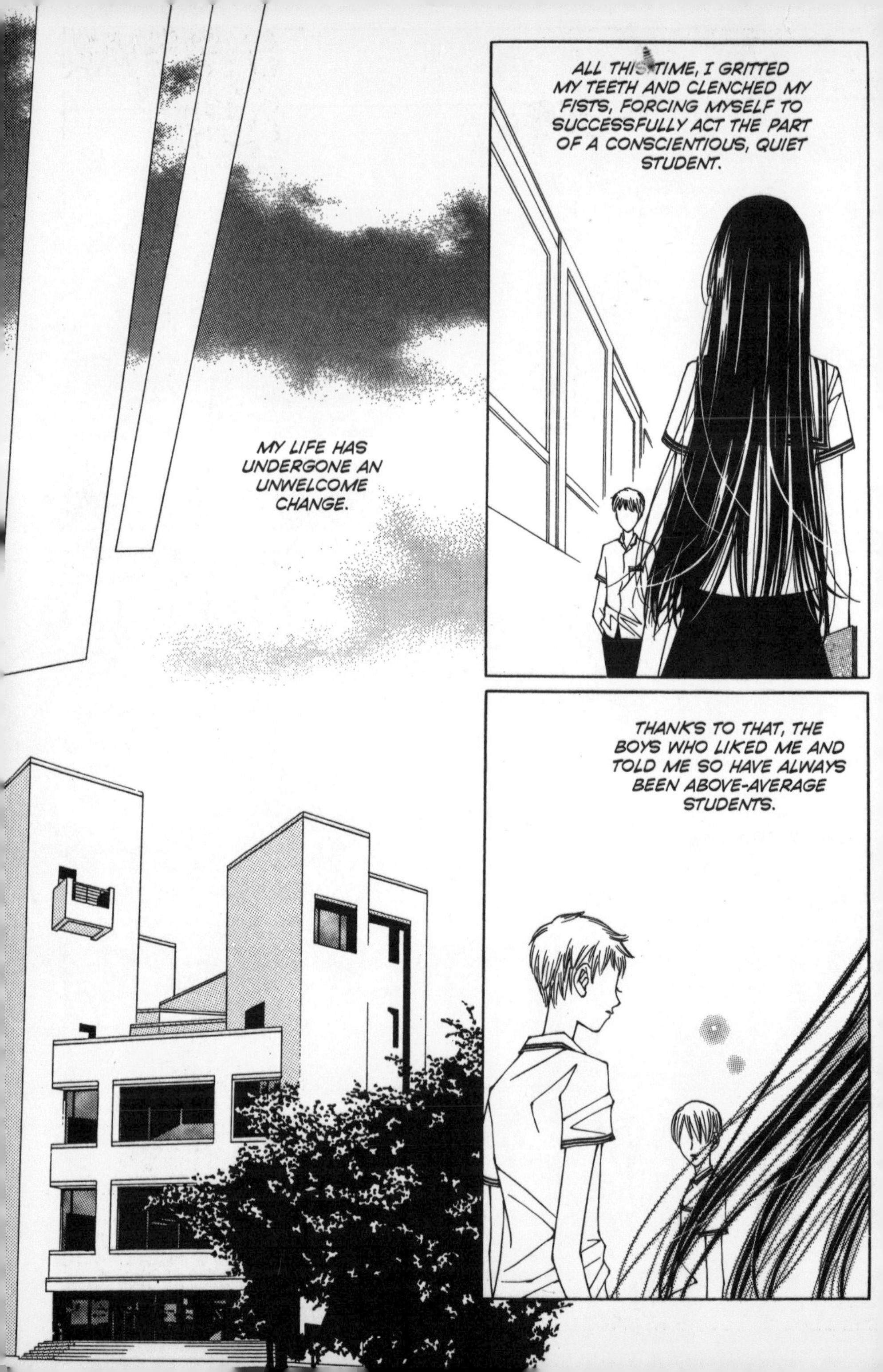
MY LIFE HAS UNDERGONE AN UNWELCOME CHANGE.
ALL THIS TIME, I GRITTED MY TEETH AND CLENCHED MY FISTS, FORCING MYSELF TO SUCCESSFULLY ACT THE PART OF A CONSCIENTIOUS, QUIET STUDENT.
THANKS TO THAT, THE BOYS WHO LIKED ME AND TOLD ME SO HAVE ALWAYS BEEN ABOVE-AVERAGE STUDENTS.

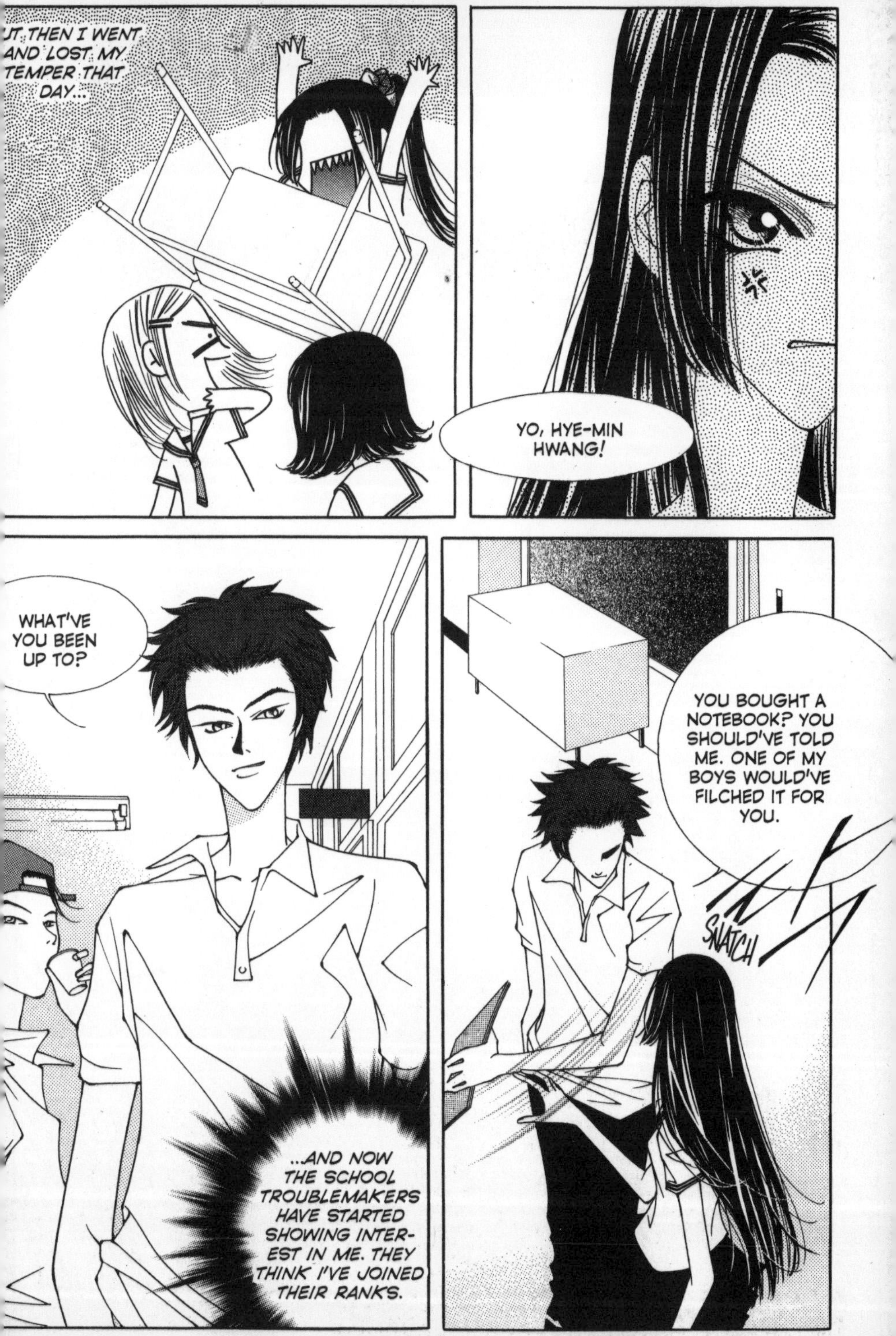
UT THEN I WENT AND LOST MY TEMPER THAT DAY...
YO, HYE-MIN HWANG!
WHAT'VE YOU BEEN UP TO?
...AND NOW THE SCHOOL TROUBLEMAKERS HAVE STARTED SHOWING INTER-EST IN ME. THEY THINK I'VE JOINED THEIR RANKS.
YOU BOUGHT A NOTEBOOK? YOU SHOULD'VE TOLD ME. ONE OF MY BOYS WOULD'VE FILCHED IT FOR YOU.
SNATCH

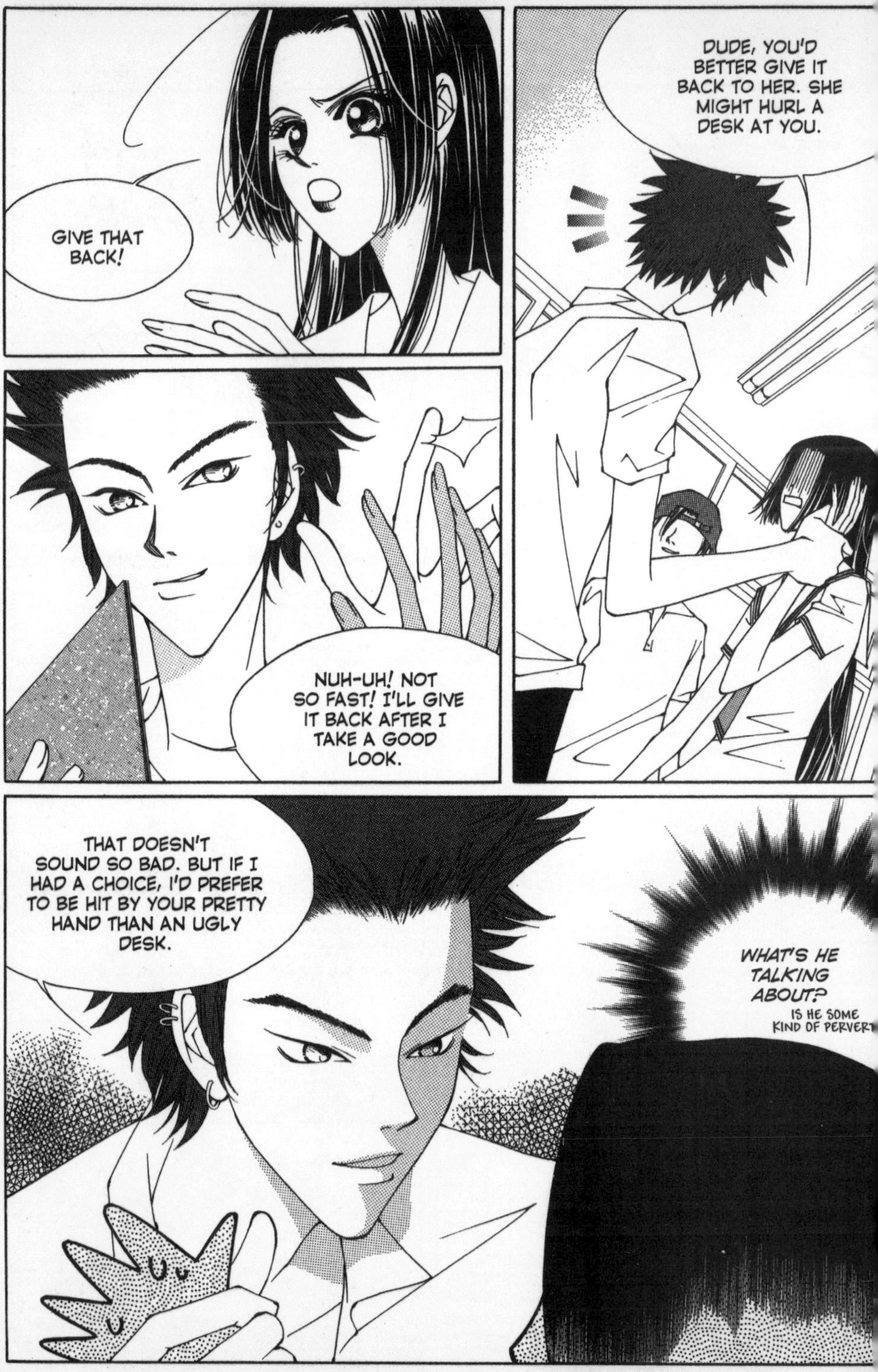
GIVE THAT BACK!
NUH-UH! NOT SO FAST! I'LL GIVE IT BACK AFTER I TAKE A GOOD LOOK.
DUDE, YOU'D BETTER GIVE IT BACK TO HER. SHE MIGHT HURL A DESK AT YOU.
THAT DOESN'T SOUND SO BAD. BUT IF I HAD A CHOICE, I'D PREFER TO BE HIT BY YOUR PRETTY HAND THAN AN UGLY DESK.
WHAT'S HE TALKING ABOUT?
IS HE SOME KIND OF PERVERT

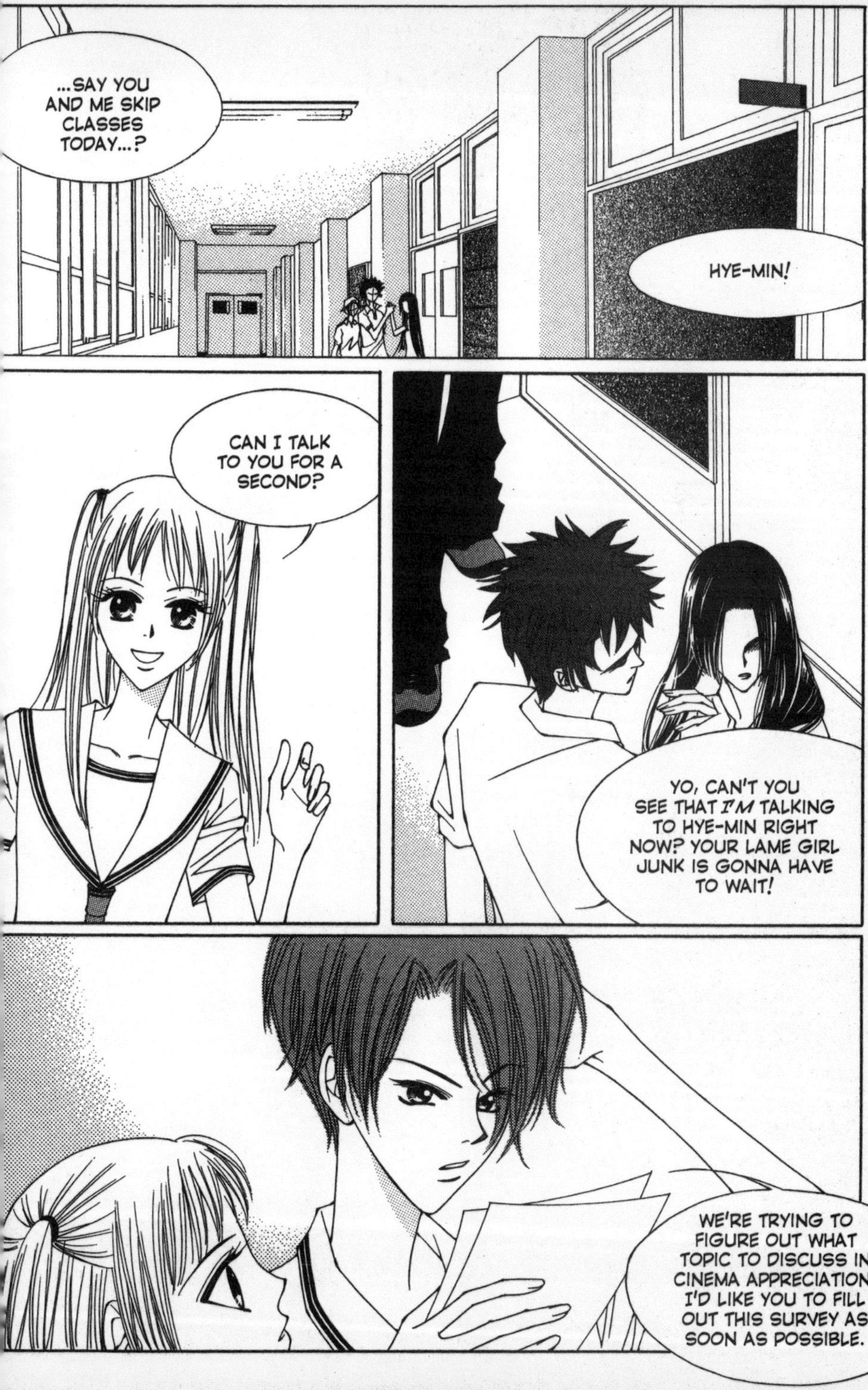
...SAY YOU AND ME SKIP CLASSES TODAY...?
HYE-MIN!
CAN I TALK TO YOU FOR A SECOND?
YO, CAN'T YOU SEE THAT *I'M* TALKING TO HYE-MIN RIGHT NOW? YOUR LAME GIRL JUNK IS GONNA HAVE TO WAIT!
WE'RE TRYING TO FIGURE OUT WHAT TOPIC TO DISCUSS IN CINEMA APPRECIATION. I'D LIKE YOU TO FILL OUT THIS SURVEY AS SOON AS POSSIBLE.

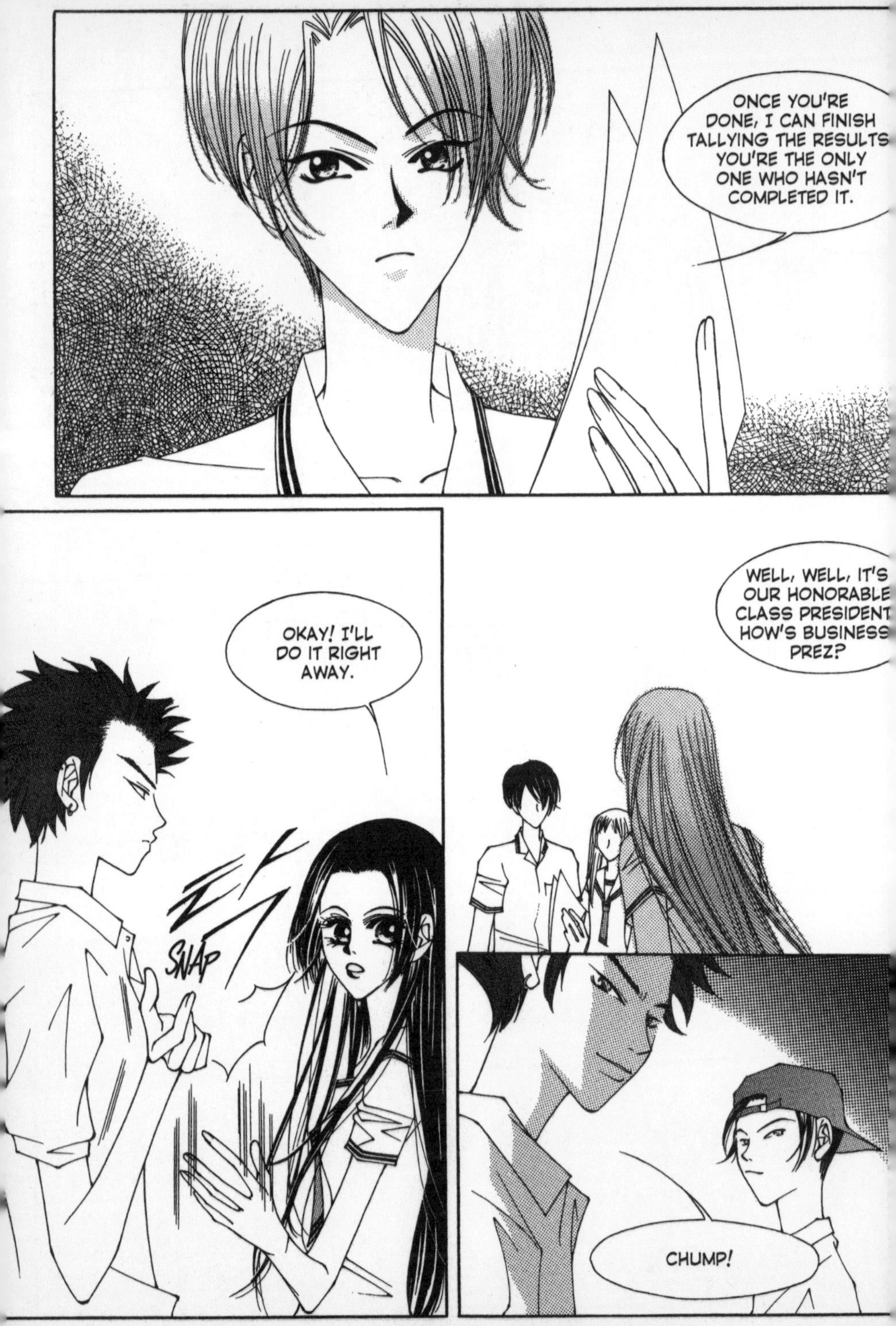
ONCE YOU'RE DONE, I CAN FINISH TALLYING THE RESULTS YOU'RE THE ONLY ONE WHO HASN'T COMPLETED IT.
OKAY! I'LL DO IT RIGHT AWAY.
SNAP
WELL, WELL, IT'S OUR HONORABLE CLASS PRESIDENT HOW'S BUSINESS PREZ?
CHUMP!

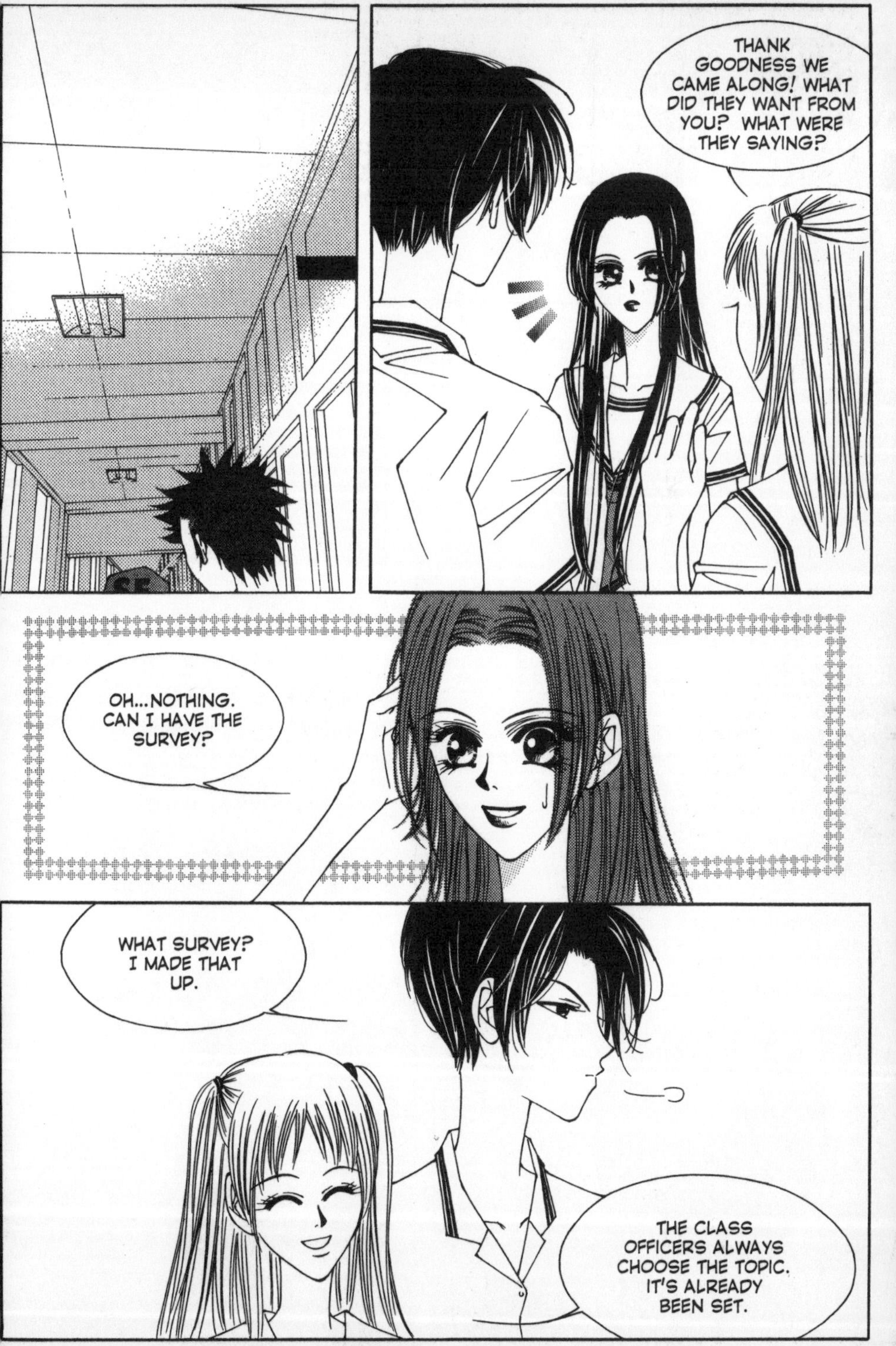
THANK GOODNESS WE CAME ALONG! WHAT DID THEY WANT FROM YOU? WHAT WERE THEY SAYING?
OH...NOTHING. CAN I HAVE THE SURVEY?
WHAT SURVEY? I MADE THAT UP.
THE CLASS OFFICERS ALWAYS CHOOSE THE TOPIC. IT'S ALREADY BEEN SET.

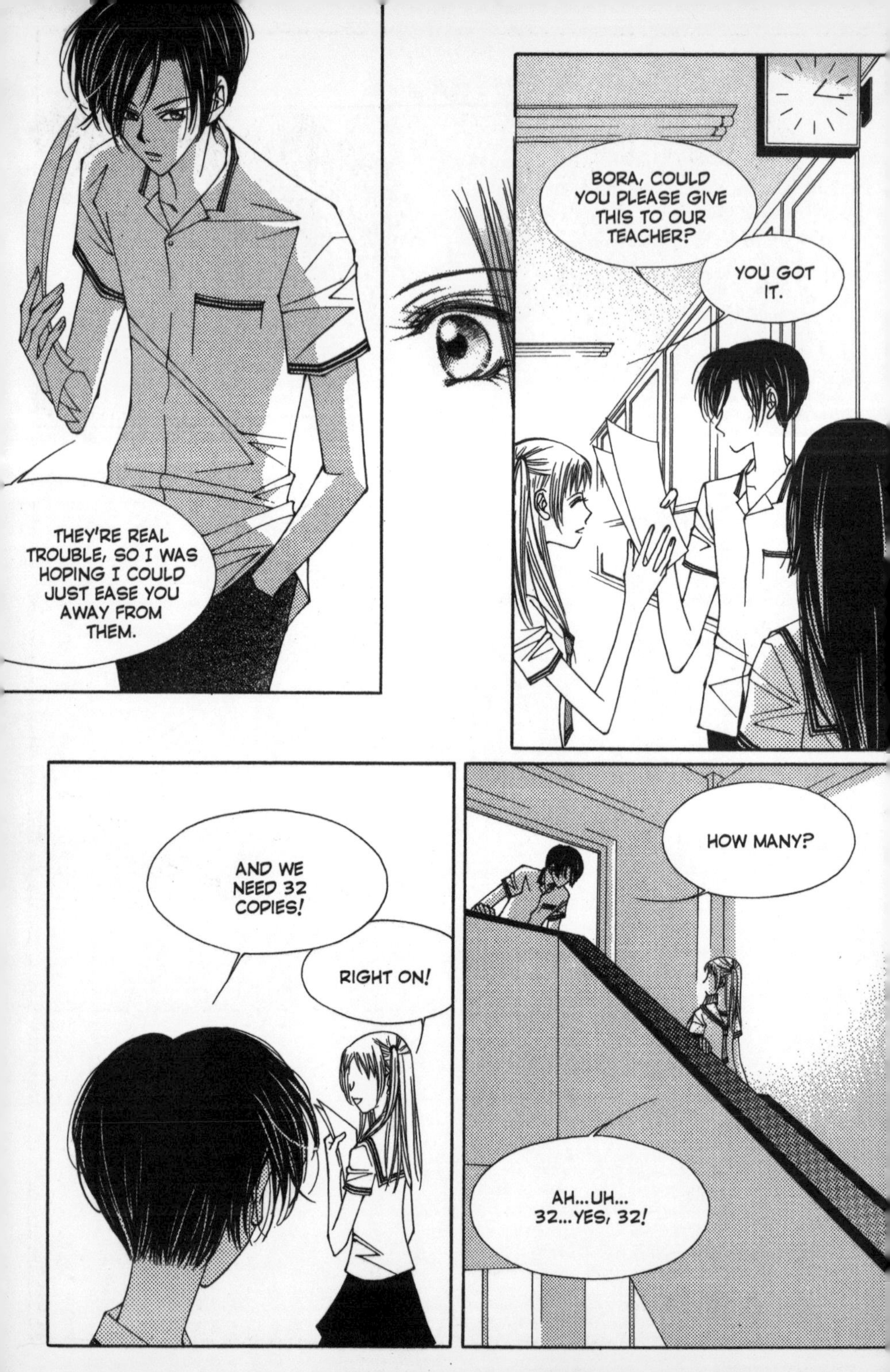
THEY'RE REAL TROUBLE, SO I WAS HOPING I COULD JUST EASE YOU AWAY FROM THEM.
BORA, COULD YOU PLEASE GIVE THIS TO OUR TEACHER?
YOU GOT IT.
AND WE NEED 32 COPIES!
RIGHT ON!
HOW MANY?
AH...UH... 32...YES, 32!

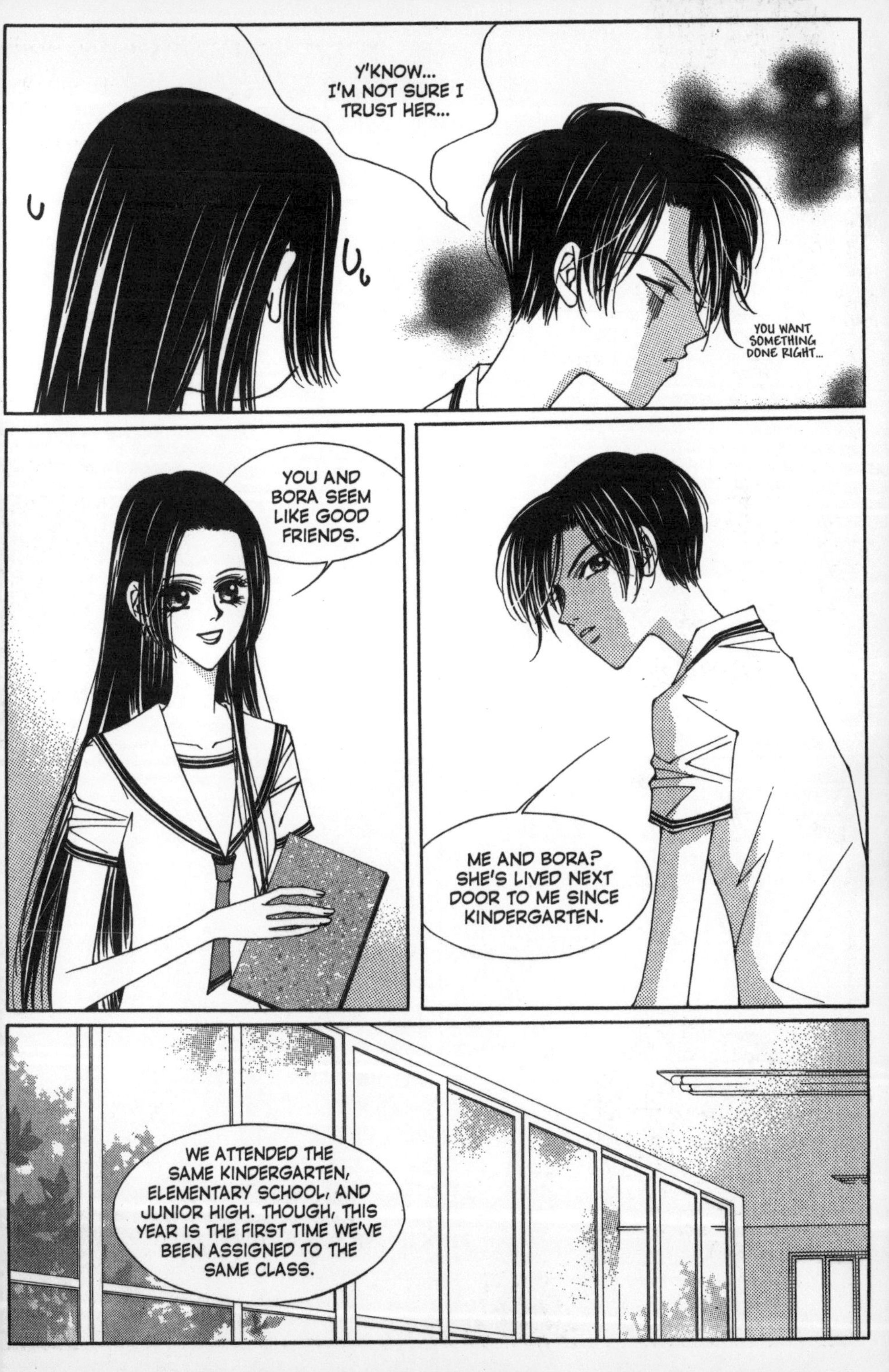

Y'KNOW... I'M NOT SURE I TRUST HER...
U
U
YOU WANT SOMETHING DONE RIGHT...
YOU AND BORA SEEM LIKE GOOD FRIENDS.
ME AND BORA? SHE'S LIVED NEXT DOOR TO ME SINCE KINDERGARTEN.
WE ATTENDED THE SAME KINDERGARTEN, ELEMENTARY SCHOOL, AND JUNIOR HIGH. THOUGH, THIS YEAR IS THE FIRST TIME WE'VE BEEN ASSIGNED TO THE SAME CLASS.

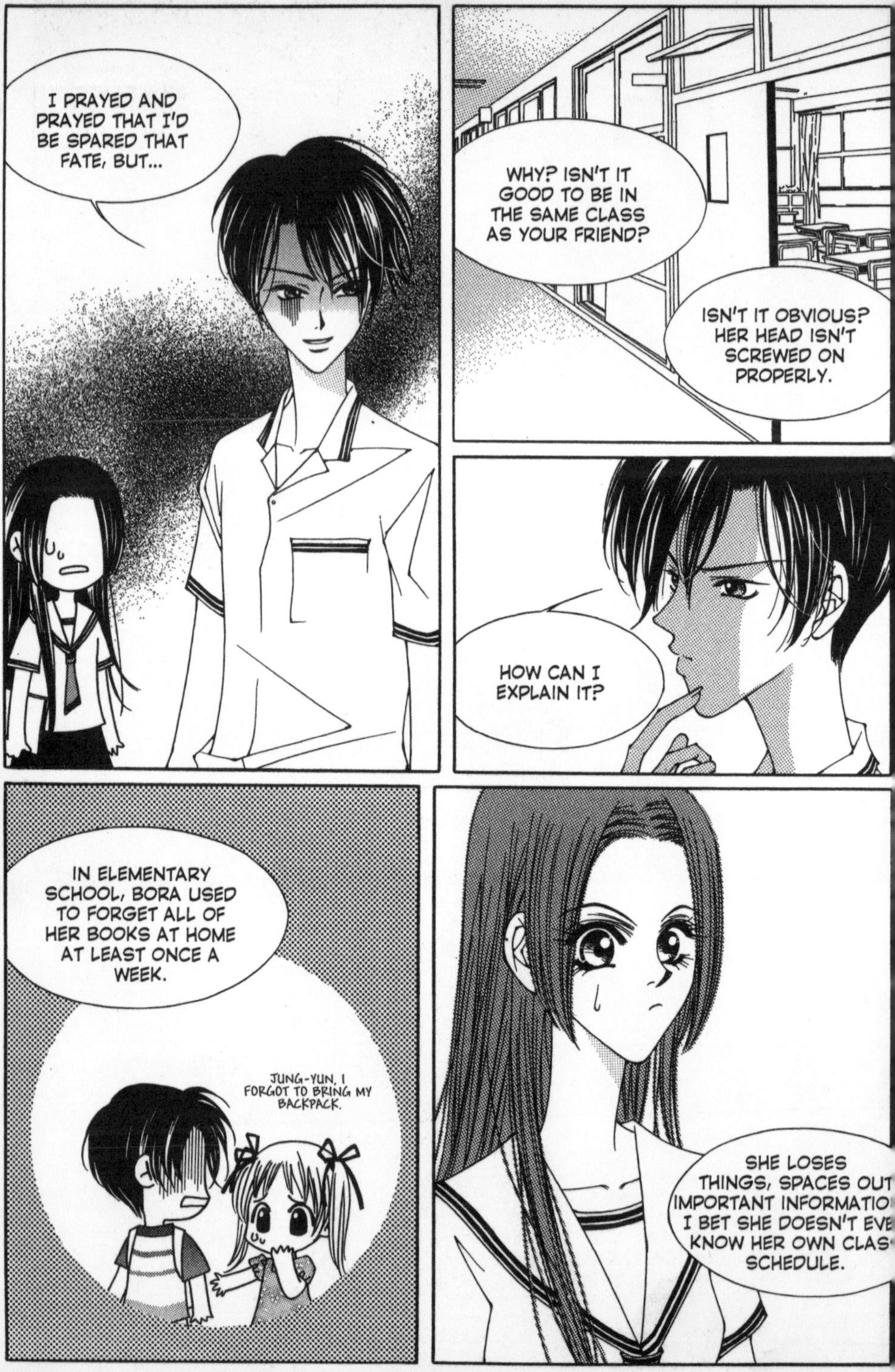
I PRAYED AND PRAYED THAT I'D BE SPARED THAT FATE, BUT...
WHY? ISN'T IT GOOD TO BE IN THE SAME CLASS AS YOUR FRIEND?
ISN'T IT OBVIOUS? HER HEAD ISN'T SCREWED ON PROPERLY.
HOW CAN I EXPLAIN IT?
IN ELEMENTARY SCHOOL, BORA USED TO FORGET ALL OF HER BOOKS AT HOME AT LEAST ONCE A WEEK.
JUNG-YUN, I FORGOT TO BRING MY BACKPACK.
SHE LOSES THINGS, SPACES OUT IMPORTANT INFORMATIO I BET SHE DOESN'T EVE KNOW HER OWN CLAS SCHEDULE.

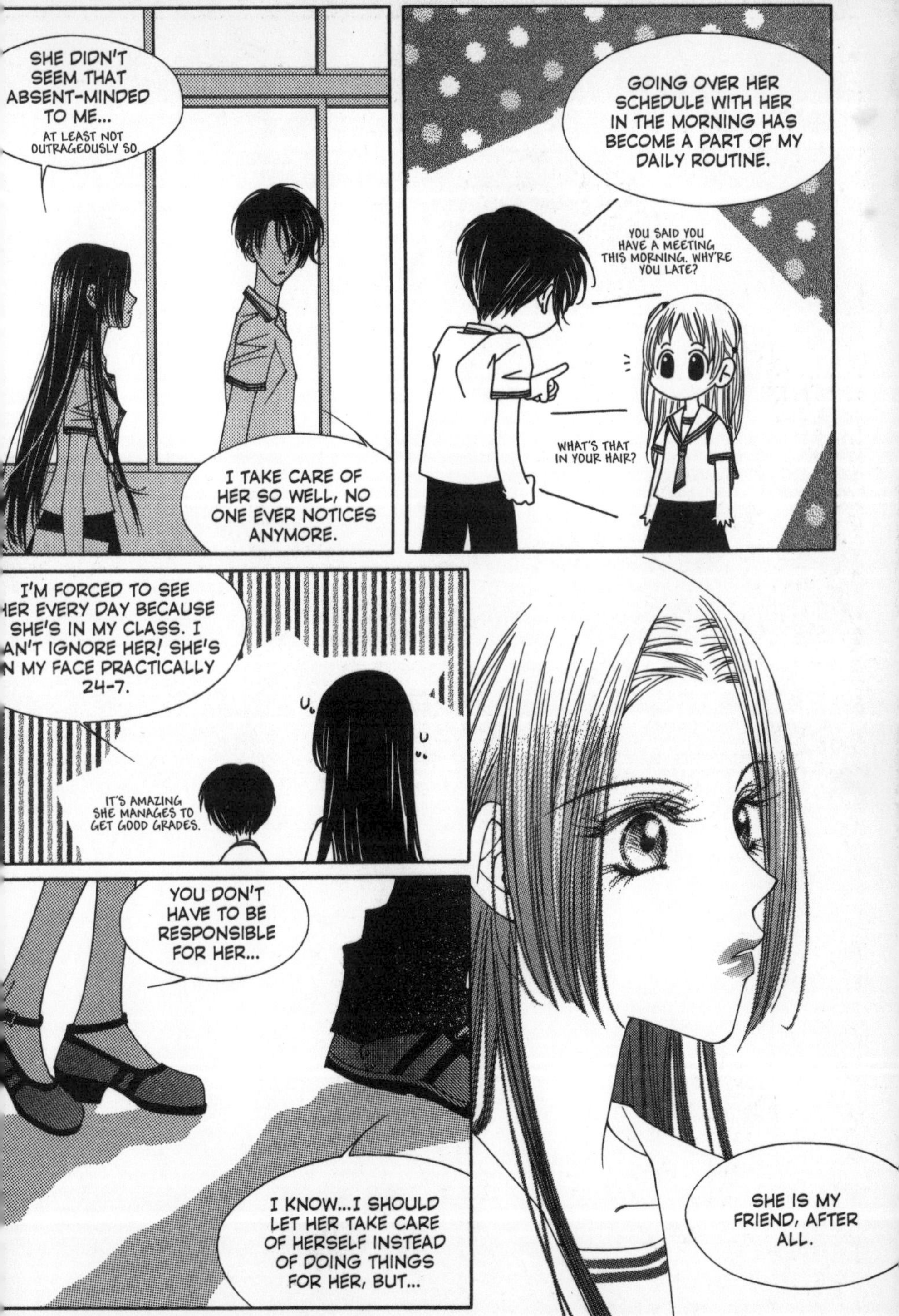
SHE DIDN'T SEEM THAT ABSENT-MINDED TO ME...
AT LEAST NOT OUTRAGEOUSLY SO.
I TAKE CARE OF HER SO WELL, NO ONE EVER NOTICES ANYMORE.
GOING OVER HER SCHEDULE WITH HER IN THE MORNING HAS BECOME A PART OF MY DAILY ROUTINE.
YOU SAID YOU HAVE A MEETING THIS MORNING. WHY'RE YOU LATE?
WHAT'S THAT IN YOUR HAIR?
I'M FORCED TO SEE HER EVERY DAY BECAUSE SHE'S IN MY CLASS. I AN'T IGNORE HER! SHE'S N MY FACE PRACTICALLY 24-7.
IT'S AMAZING SHE MANAGES TO GET GOOD GRADES.
YOU DON'T HAVE TO BE RESPONSIBLE FOR HER...
I KNOW...I SHOULD LET HER TAKE CARE OF HERSELF INSTEAD OF DOING THINGS FOR HER, BUT...
SHE IS MY FRIEND, AFTER ALL.

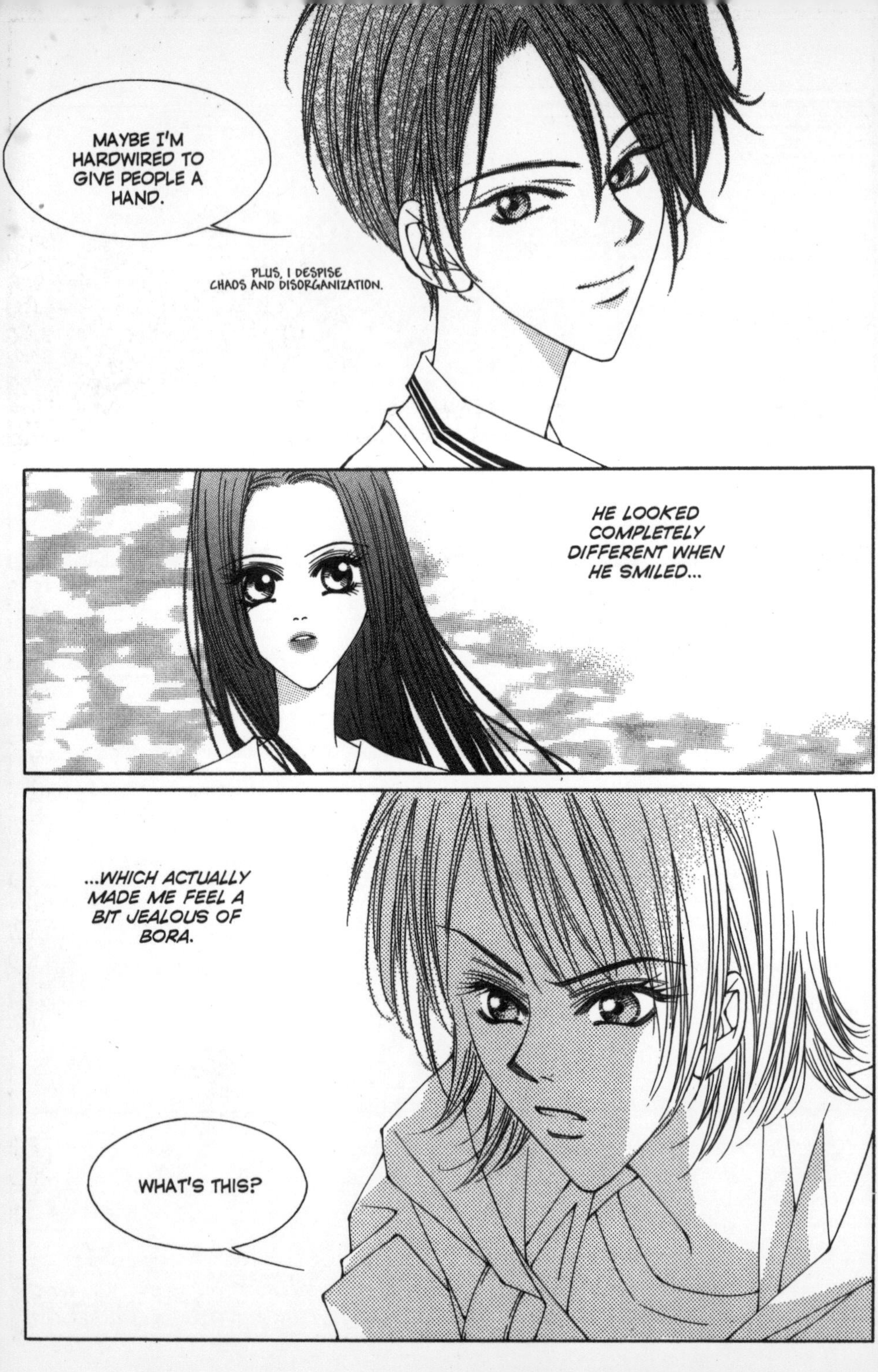
MAYBE I'M HARDWIRED TO GIVE PEOPLE A HAND.
PLUS, I DESPISE CHAOS AND DISORGANIZATION.
HE LOOKED COMPLETELY DIFFERENT WHEN HE SMILED...
...WHICH ACTUALLY MADE ME FEEL A BIT JEALOUS OF BORA.
WHAT'S THIS?

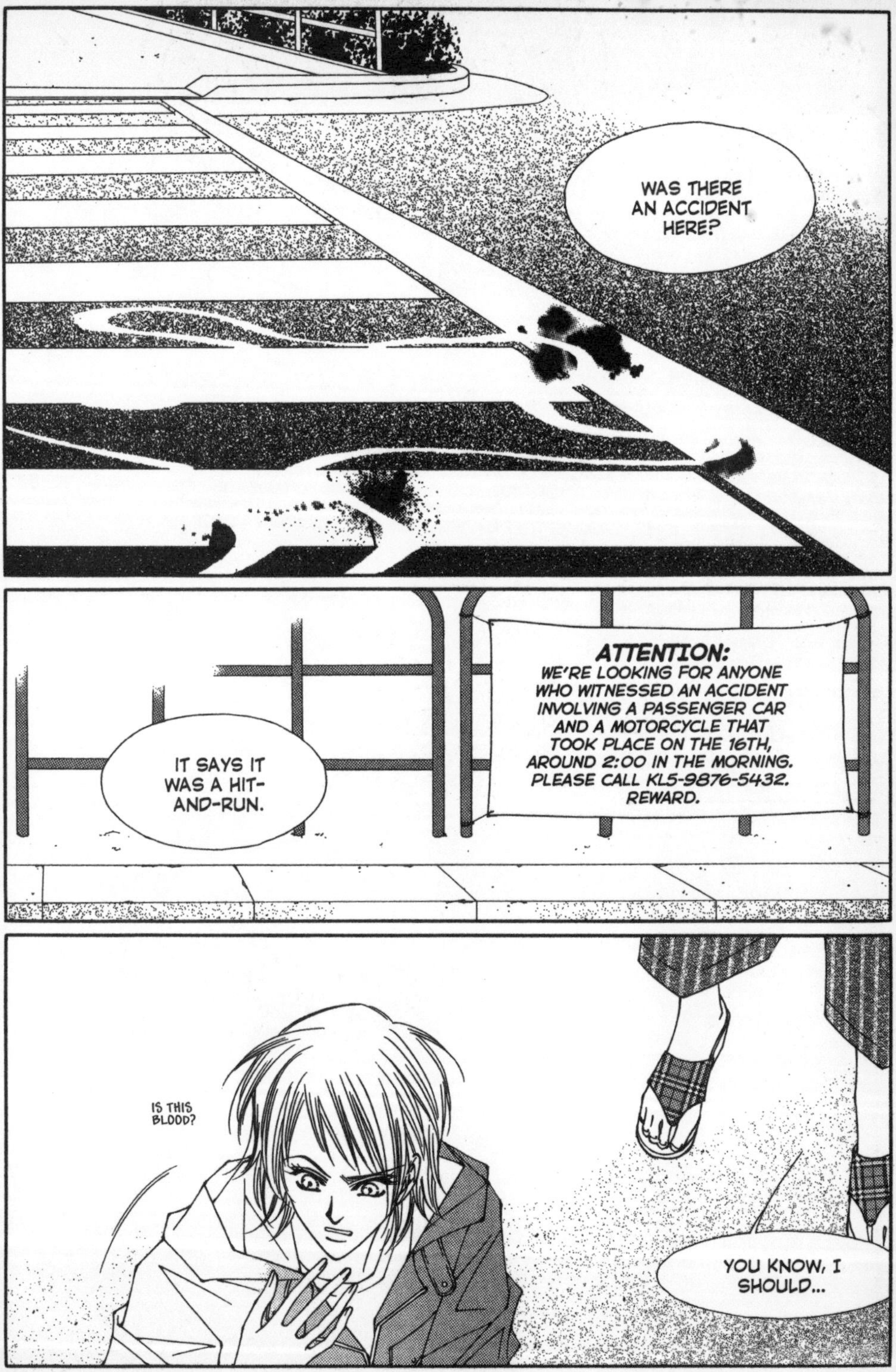
WAS THERE AN ACCIDENT HERE?
IT SAYS IT WAS A HIT-AND-RUN.
ATTENTION:
WE'RE LOOKING FOR ANYONE WHO WITNESSED AN ACCIDENT INVOLVING A PASSENGER CAR AND A MOTORCYCLE THAT TOOK PLACE ON THE 16TH, AROUND 2:00 IN THE MORNING. PLEASE CALL KL5-9876-5432. REWARD.
IS THIS BLOOD?
YOU KNOW, I SHOULD...

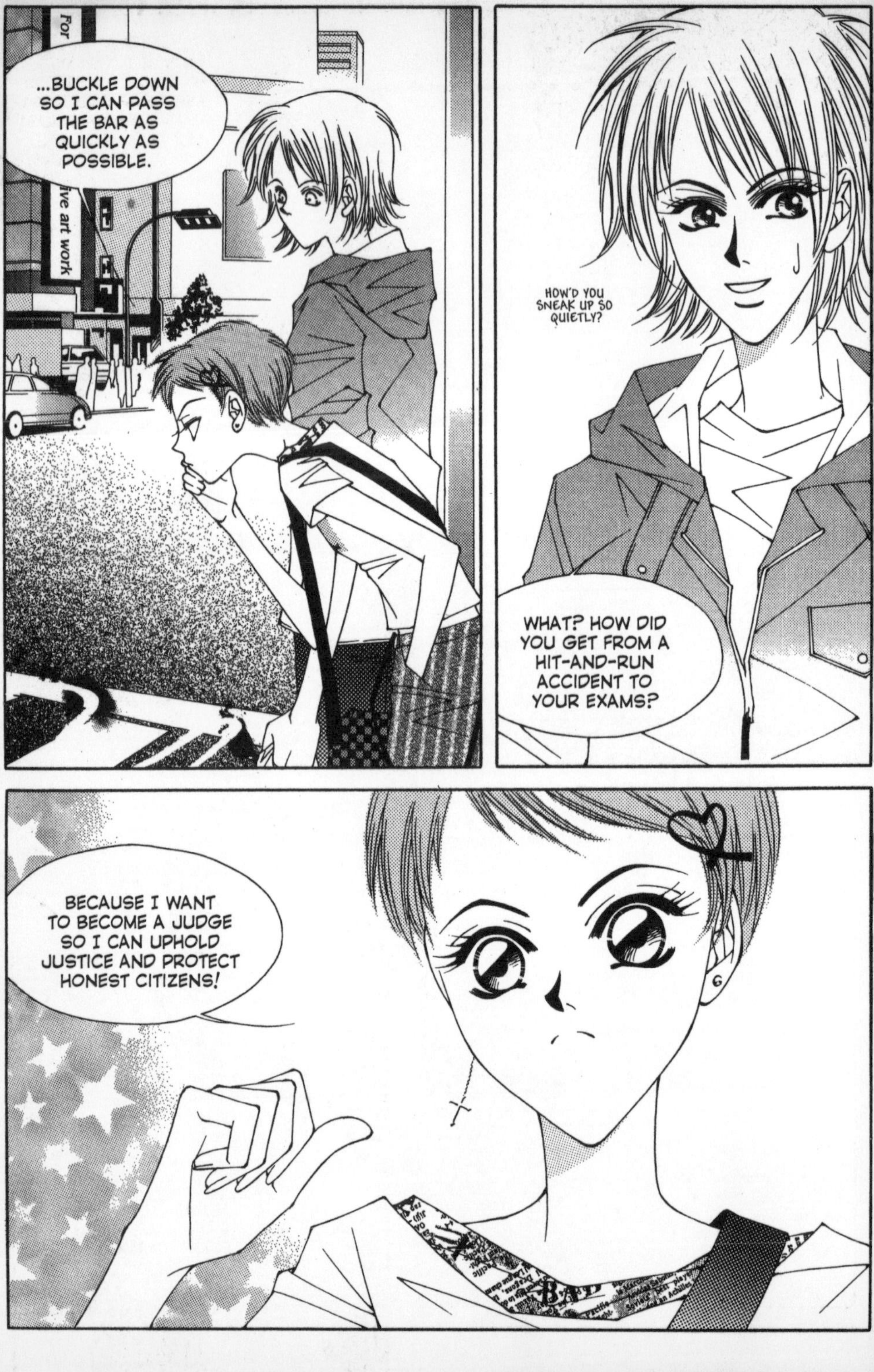
...BUCKLE DOWN SO I CAN PASS THE BAR AS QUICKLY AS POSSIBLE.
For
ive art work
HOW'D YOU SNEAK UP SO QUIETLY?
WHAT? HOW DID YOU GET FROM A HIT-AND-RUN ACCIDENT TO YOUR EXAMS?
BECAUSE I WANT TO BECOME A JUDGE SO I CAN UPHOLD JUSTICE AND PROTECT HONEST CITIZENS!

STOP STARING AT THAT.

LOOK AT ALL THE BLOODSTAINS. WHOEVER'S RESPONSIBLE FOR THIS MUST BE CAUGHT! WE MUST BE VIGILANT. WE'LL CHASE HIM TO THE ENDS OF THE EARTH IF NECESSARY!

IF THAT'S WHAT YOU WANT TO DO, WHY NOT BECOME A POLICEWOMAN AND PATROL THE STREETS?

AN EYE FOR AN EYE, A TOOTH FOR A TOOTH! A HIT-AND-RUN FOR A HIT-AND-RUN!

IF I WERE THE JUDGE IN THIS CASE, I WOULD RULE THAT THE OFFENDER MUST EXPERIENCE THE SAME PAIN HE CAUSED HIS VICTIM!

NOW I UNDERSTAND WHY YOU AND SHIN-BI ARE TOGETHER.

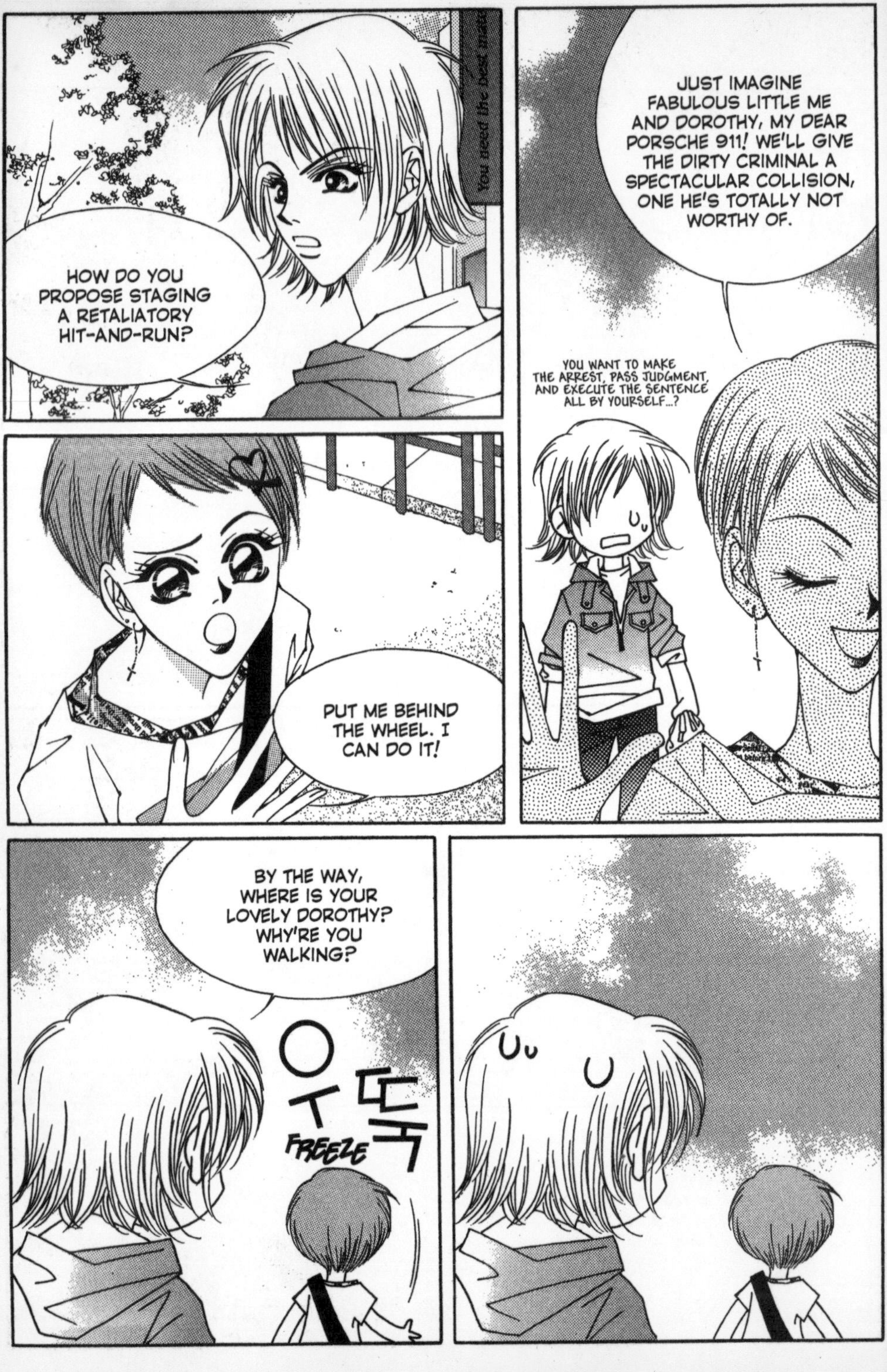
HOW DO YOU PROPOSE STAGING A RETALIATORY HIT-AND-RUN?
PUT ME BEHIND THE WHEEL. I CAN DO IT!
JUST IMAGINE FABULOUS LITTLE ME AND DOROTHY, MY DEAR PORSCHE 911! WE'LL GIVE THE DIRTY CRIMINAL A SPECTACULAR COLLISION, ONE HE'S TOTALLY NOT WORTHY OF.
YOU WANT TO MAKE THE ARREST, PASS JUDGMENT, AND EXECUTE THE SENTENCE ALL BY YOURSELF...?
BY THE WAY, WHERE IS YOUR LOVELY DOROTHY? WHY'RE YOU WALKING?
FREEZE

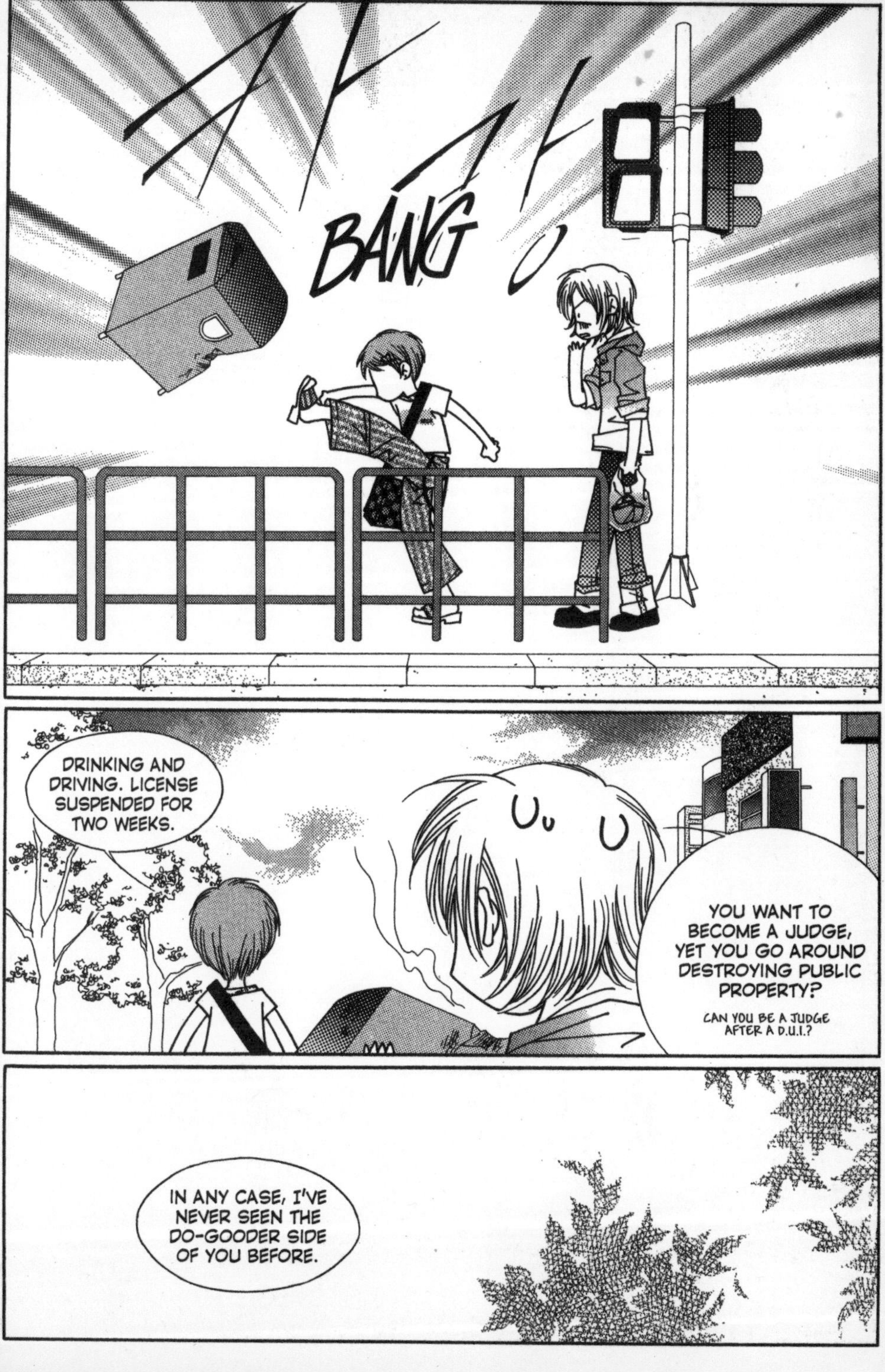
BANG
DRINKING AND DRIVING. LICENSE SUSPENDED FOR TWO WEEKS.
YOU WANT TO BECOME A JUDGE, YET YOU GO AROUND DESTROYING PUBLIC PROPERTY?
CAN YOU BE A JUDGE AFTER A D.U.I.?
IN ANY CASE, I'VE NEVER SEEN THE DO-GOODER SIDE OF YOU BEFORE.

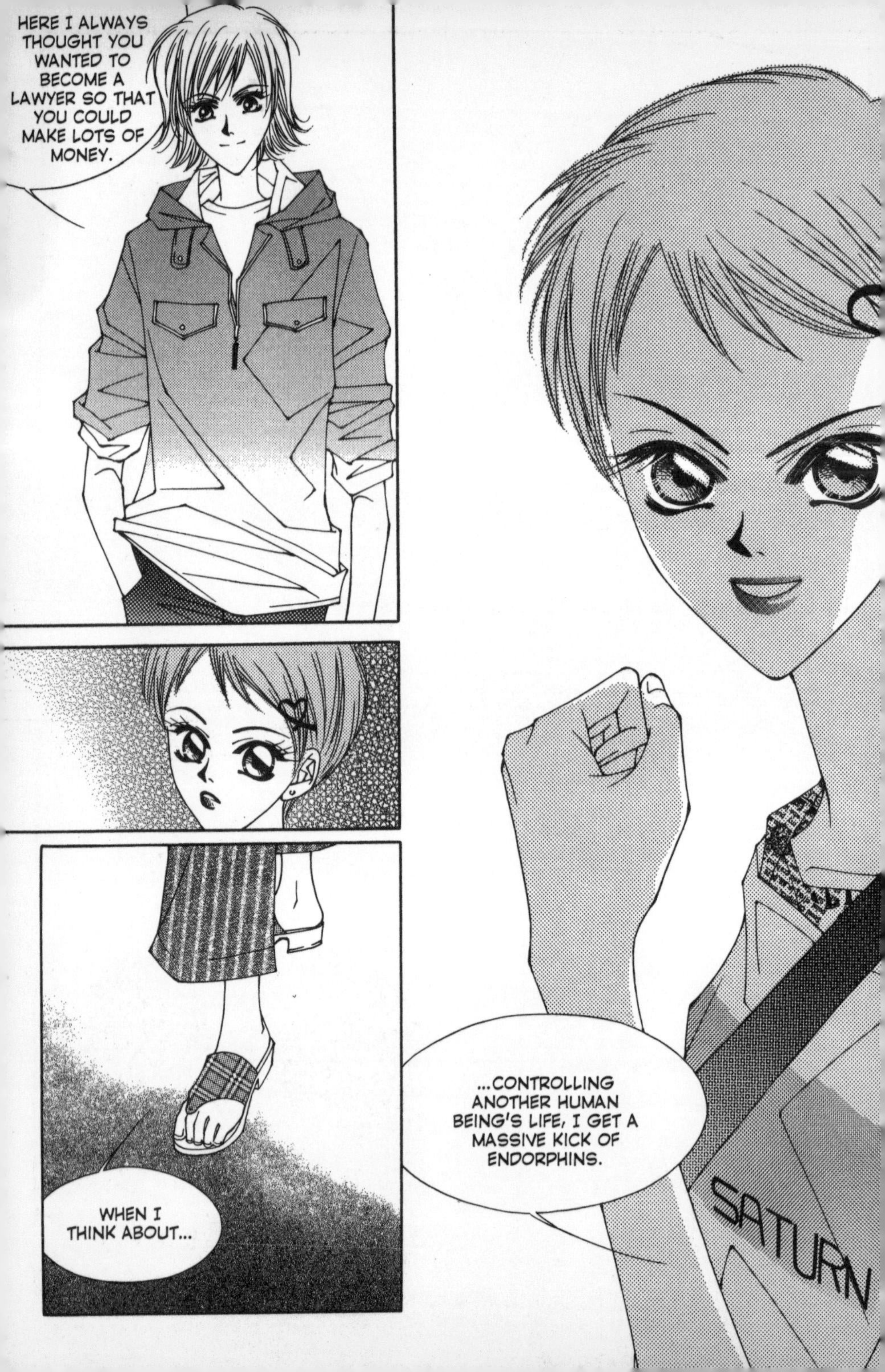
HERE I ALWAYS THOUGHT YOU WANTED TO BECOME A LAWYER SO THAT YOU COULD MAKE LOTS OF MONEY.
WHEN I THINK ABOUT...
...CONTROLLING ANOTHER HUMAN BEING'S LIFE, I GET A MASSIVE KICK OF ENDORPHINS.
SATURN

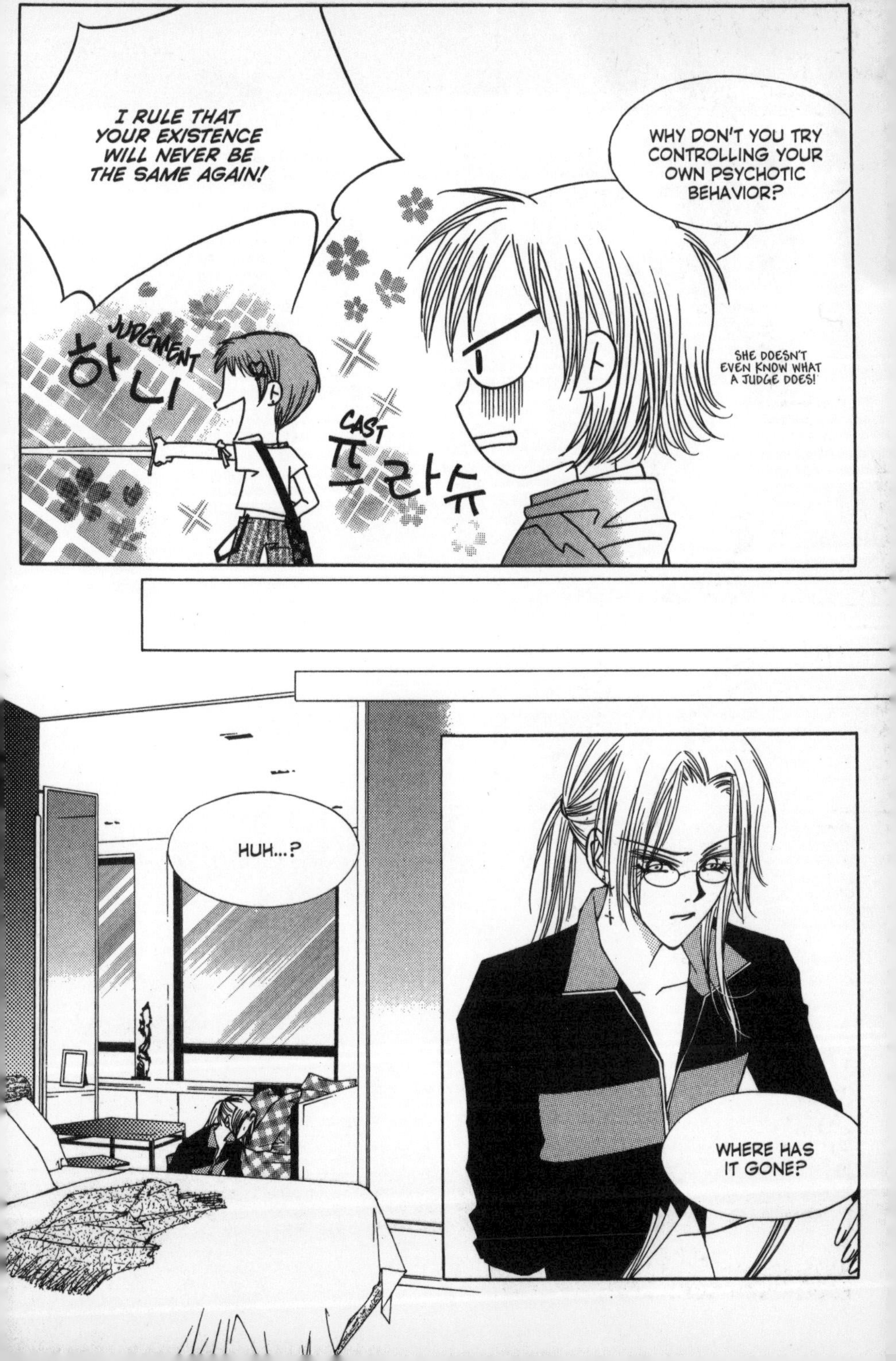
I RULE THAT YOUR EXISTENCE WILL NEVER BE THE SAME AGAIN!
JUDGMENT
하니
CAST
뜨라슈
WHY DON'T YOU TRY CONTROLLING YOUR OWN PSYCHOTIC BEHAVIOR?
SHE DOESN'T EVEN KNOW WHAT A JUDGE DOES!
HUH...?
WHERE HAS IT GONE?

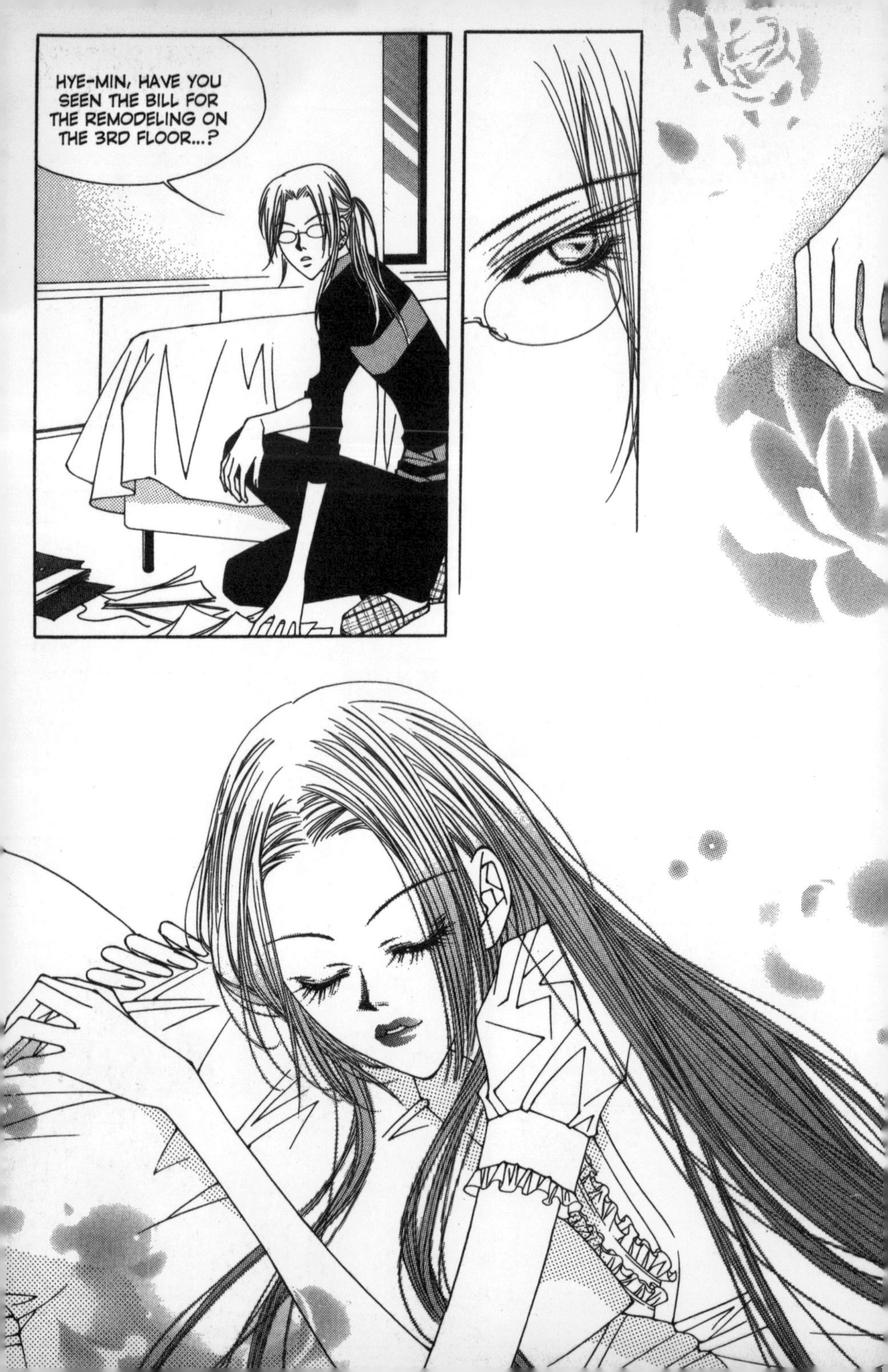
HYE-MIN, HAVE YOU SEEN THE BILL FOR THE REMODELING ON THE 3RD FLOOR...?

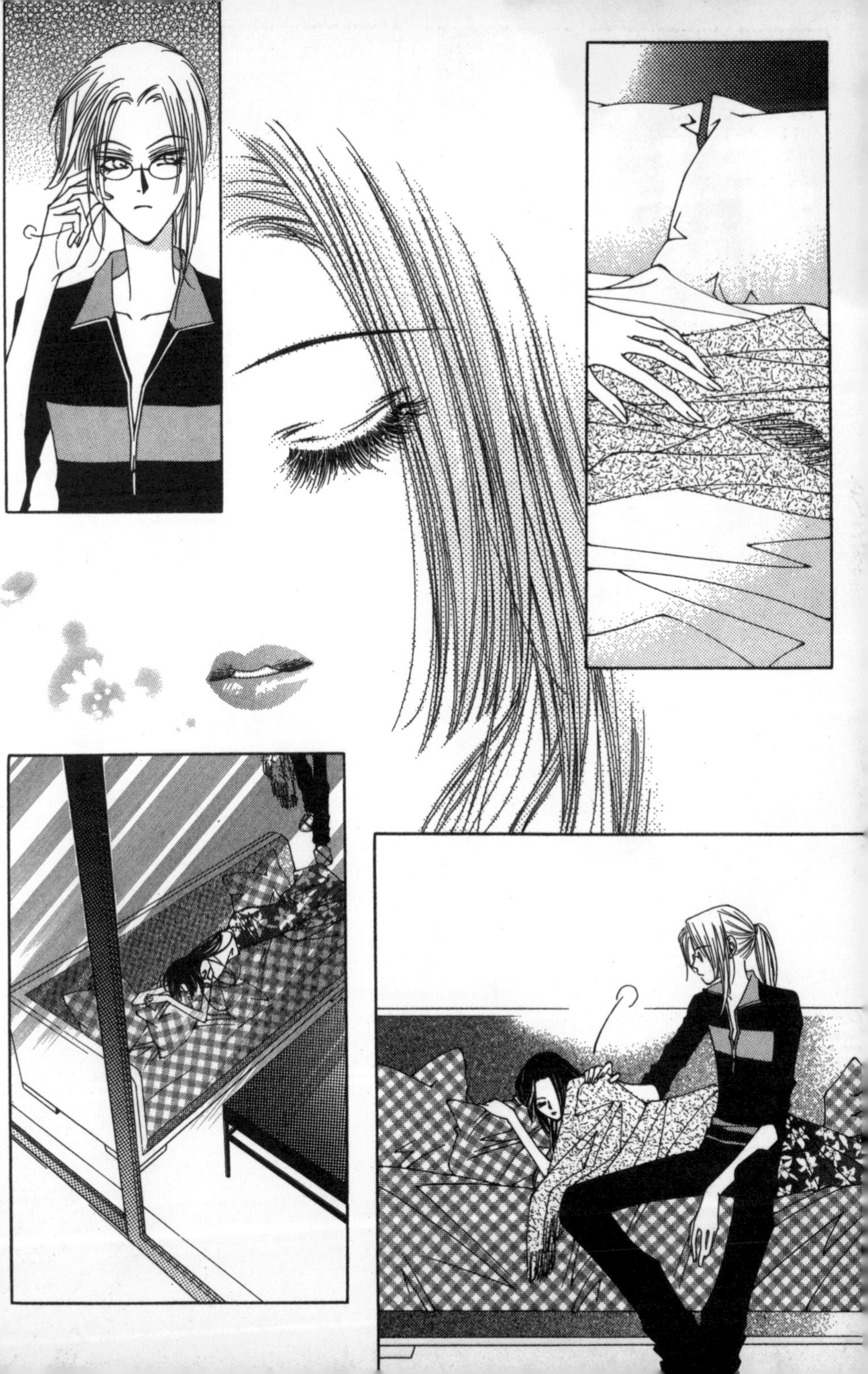

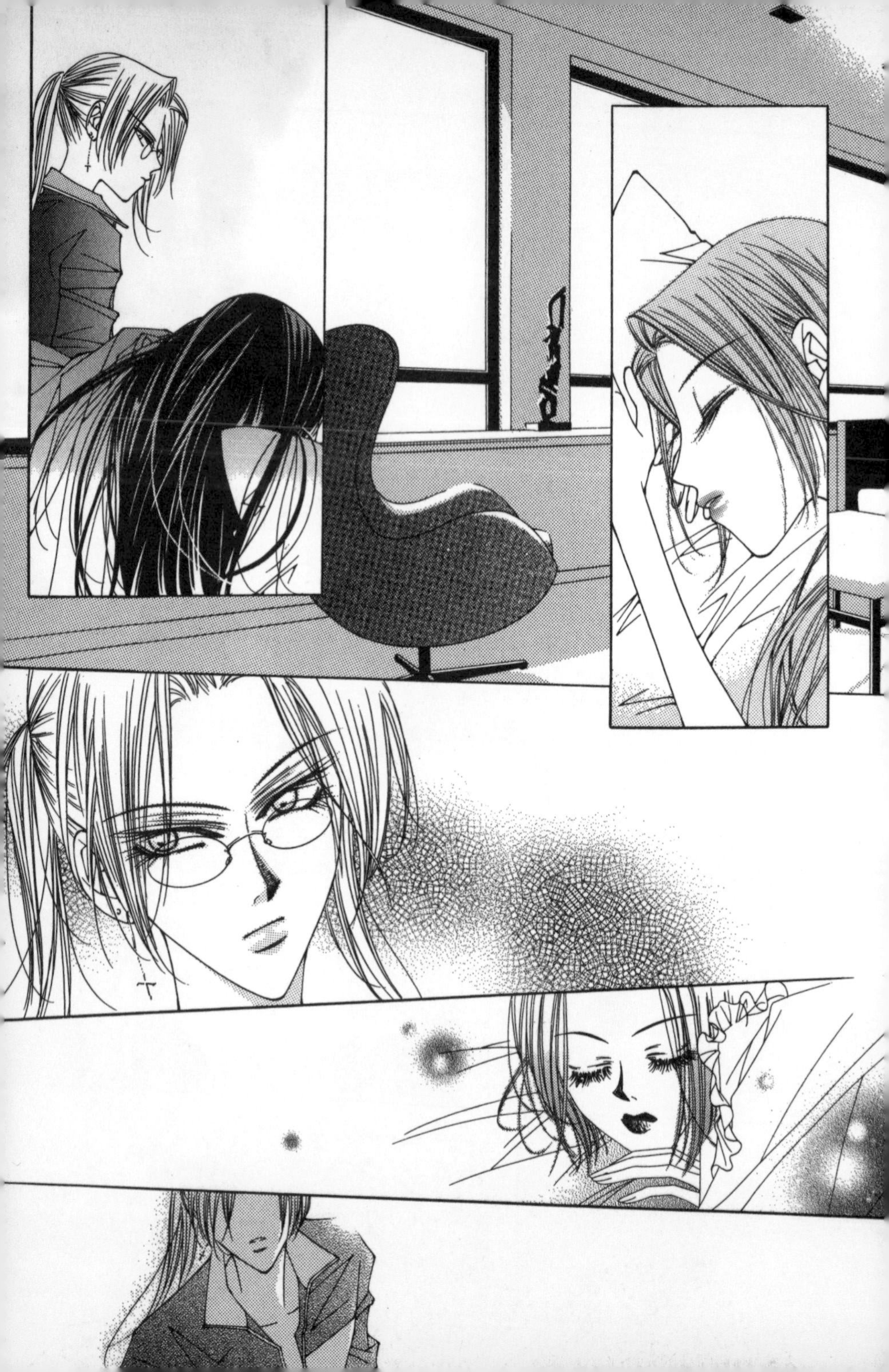

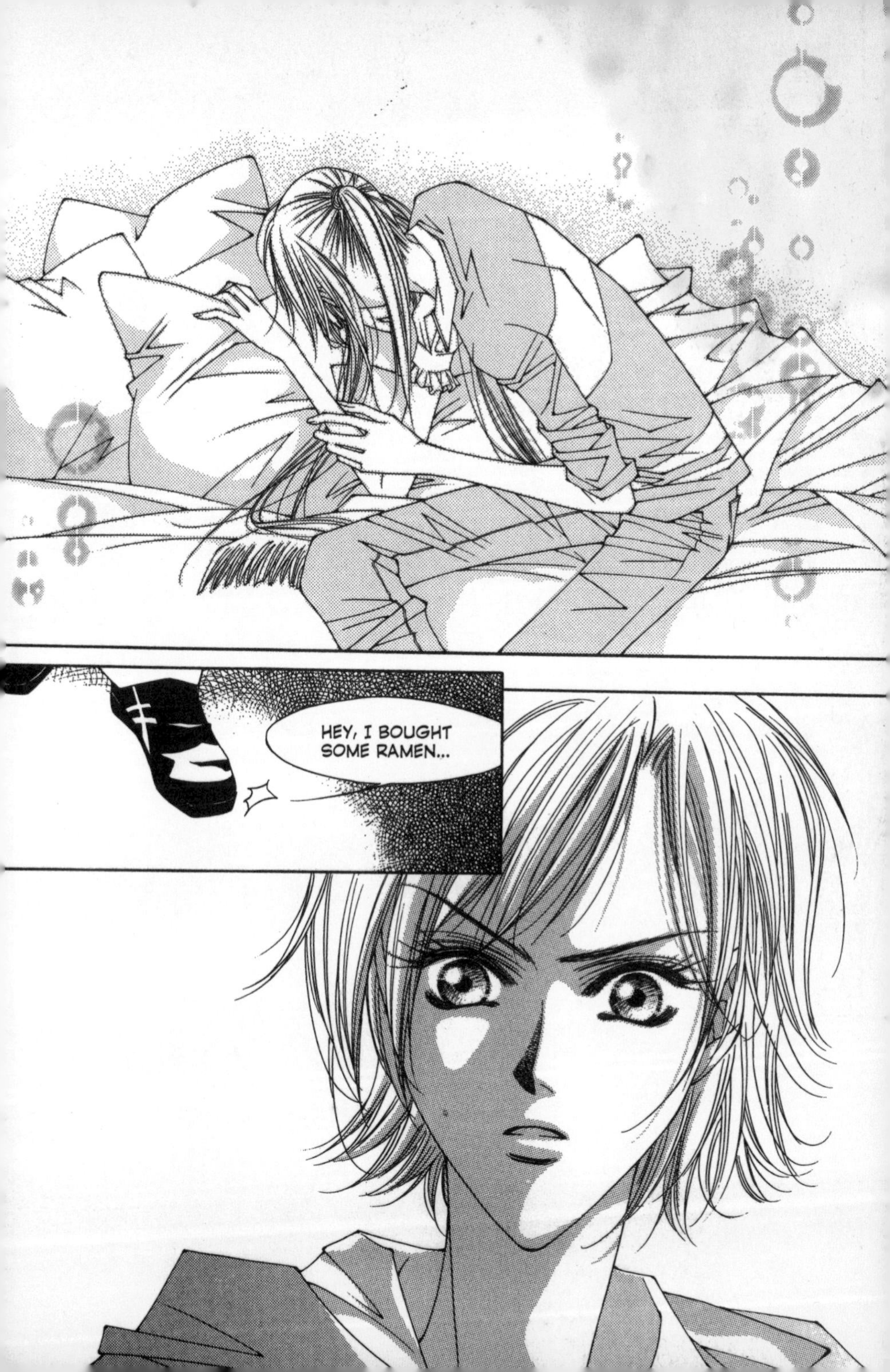
HEY, I BOUGHT SOME RAMEN...

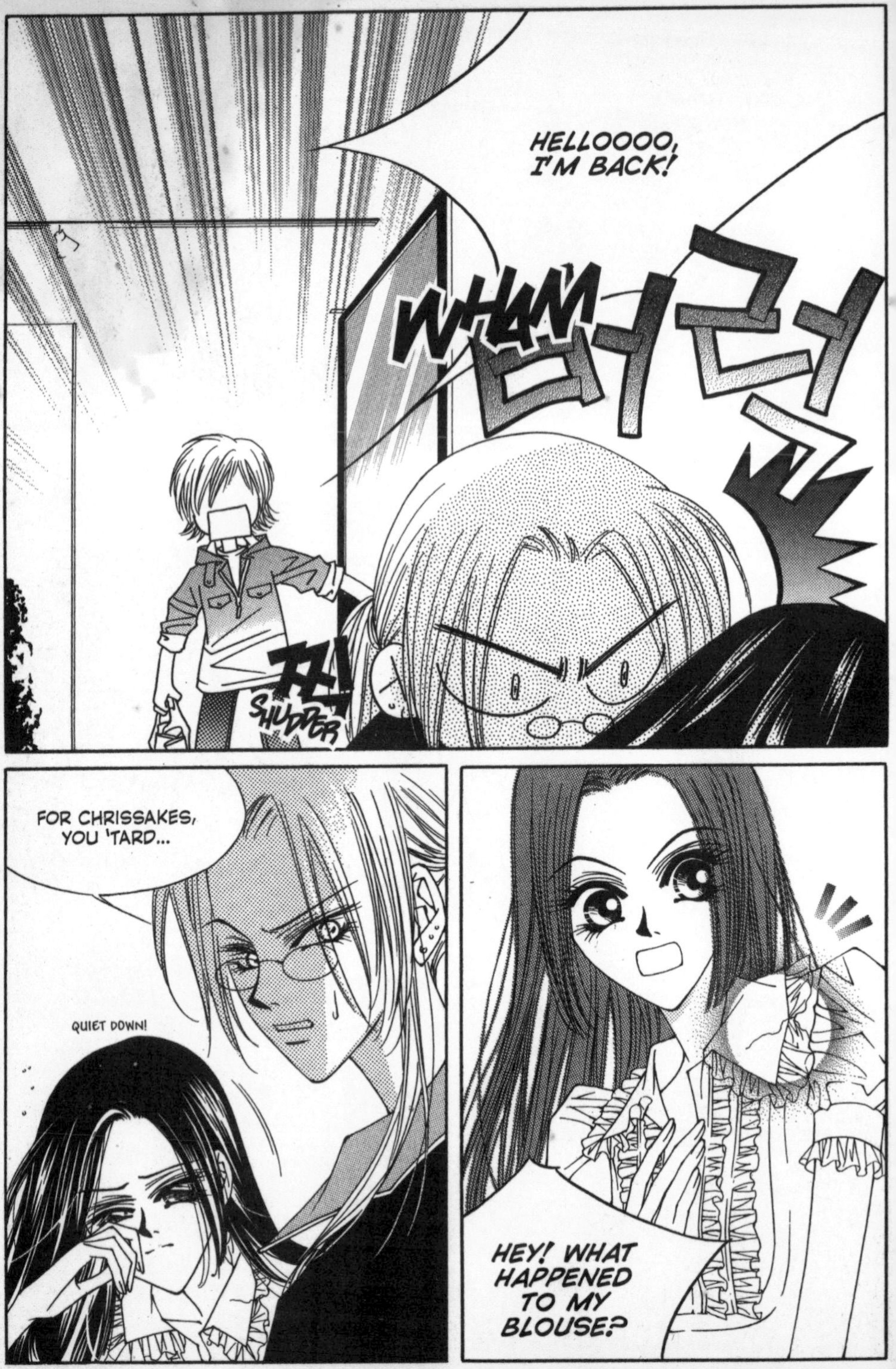
HELLOOOO, I'M BACK!
WHAM
SHUDDER
FOR CHRISSAKES, YOU 'TARD...
QUIET DOWN!
HEY! WHAT HAPPENED TO MY BLOUSE?

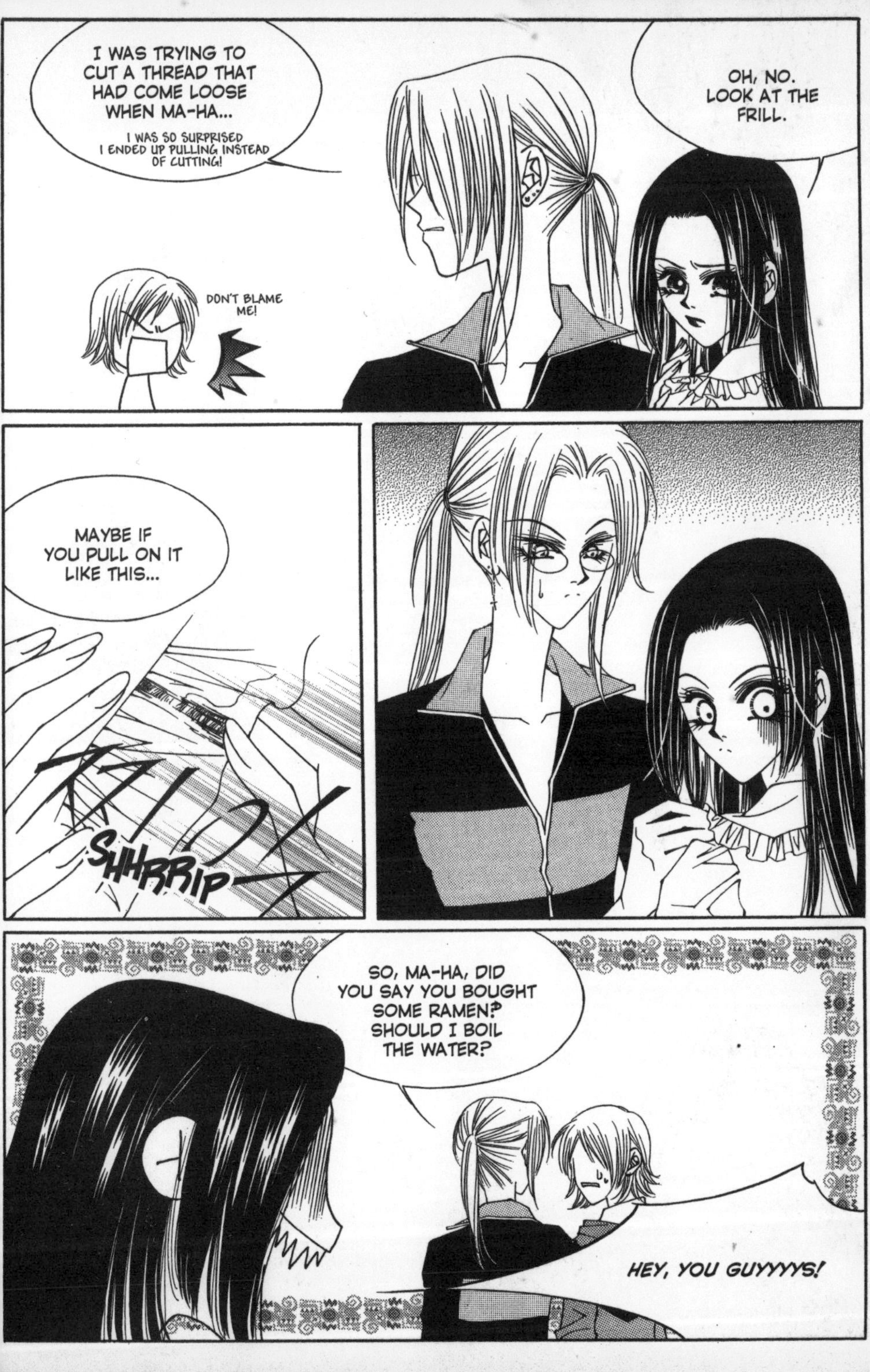
I WAS TRYING TO CUT A THREAD THAT HAD COME LOOSE WHEN MA-HA...
I WAS SO SURPRISED I ENDED UP PULLING INSTEAD OF CUTTING!
OH, NO. LOOK AT THE FRILL.
DON'T BLAME ME!
MAYBE IF YOU PULL ON IT LIKE THIS...
SHHRRIP
SO, MA-HA, DID YOU SAY YOU BOUGHT SOME RAMEN? SHOULD I BOIL THE WATER?
HEY, YOU GUYYYYS!

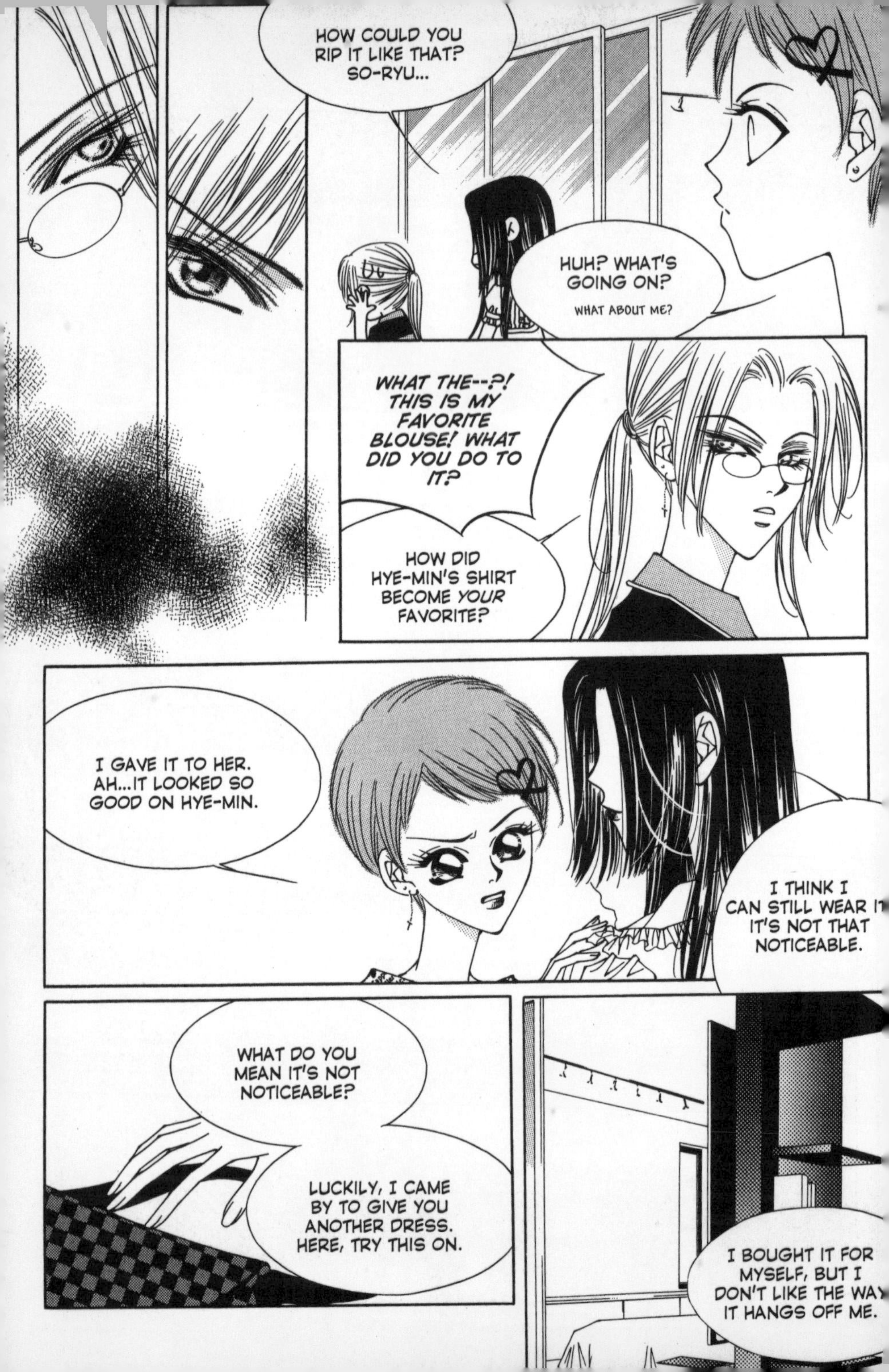
HOW COULD YOU RIP IT LIKE THAT? SO-RYU...
HUH? WHAT'S GOING ON?
WHAT ABOUT ME?
WHAT THE--?! THIS IS MY FAVORITE BLOUSE! WHAT DID YOU DO TO IT?
HOW DID HYE-MIN'S SHIRT BECOME YOUR FAVORITE?
I GAVE IT TO HER. AH...IT LOOKED SO GOOD ON HYE-MIN.
I THINK I CAN STILL WEAR IT. IT'S NOT THAT NOTICEABLE.
WHAT DO YOU MEAN IT'S NOT NOTICEABLE?
LUCKILY, I CAME BY TO GIVE YOU ANOTHER DRESS. HERE, TRY THIS ON.
I BOUGHT IT FOR MYSELF, BUT I DON'T LIKE THE WAY IT HANGS OFF ME.

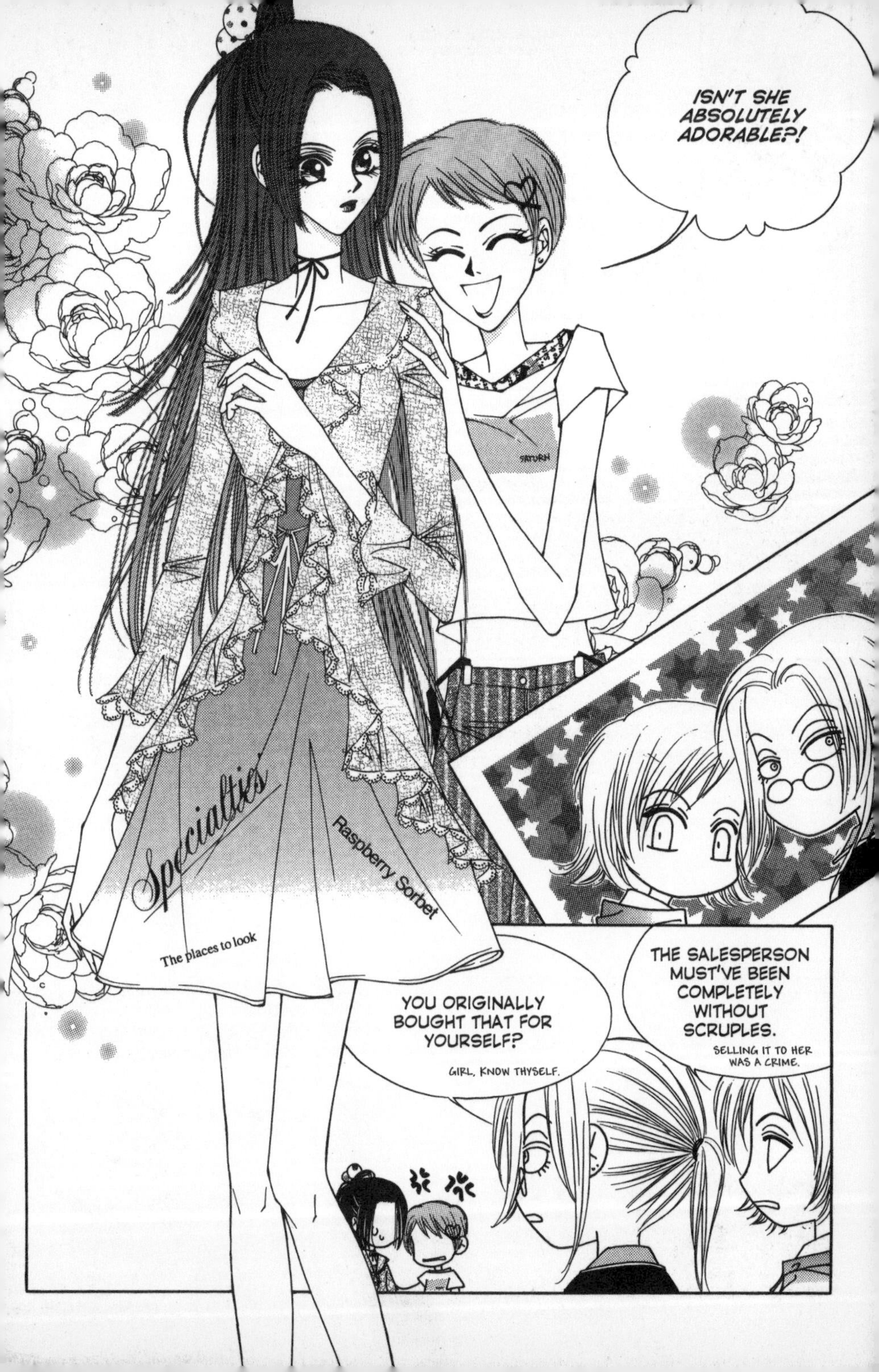
ISN'T SHE ABSOLUTELY ADORABLE?!
SATURN
Specialties
Raspberry Sorbet
The places to look
YOU ORIGINALLY BOUGHT THAT FOR YOURSELF?
GIRL, KNOW THYSELF.
THE SALESPERSON MUST'VE BEEN COMPLETELY WITHOUT SCRUPLES.
SELLING IT TO HER WAS A CRIME.

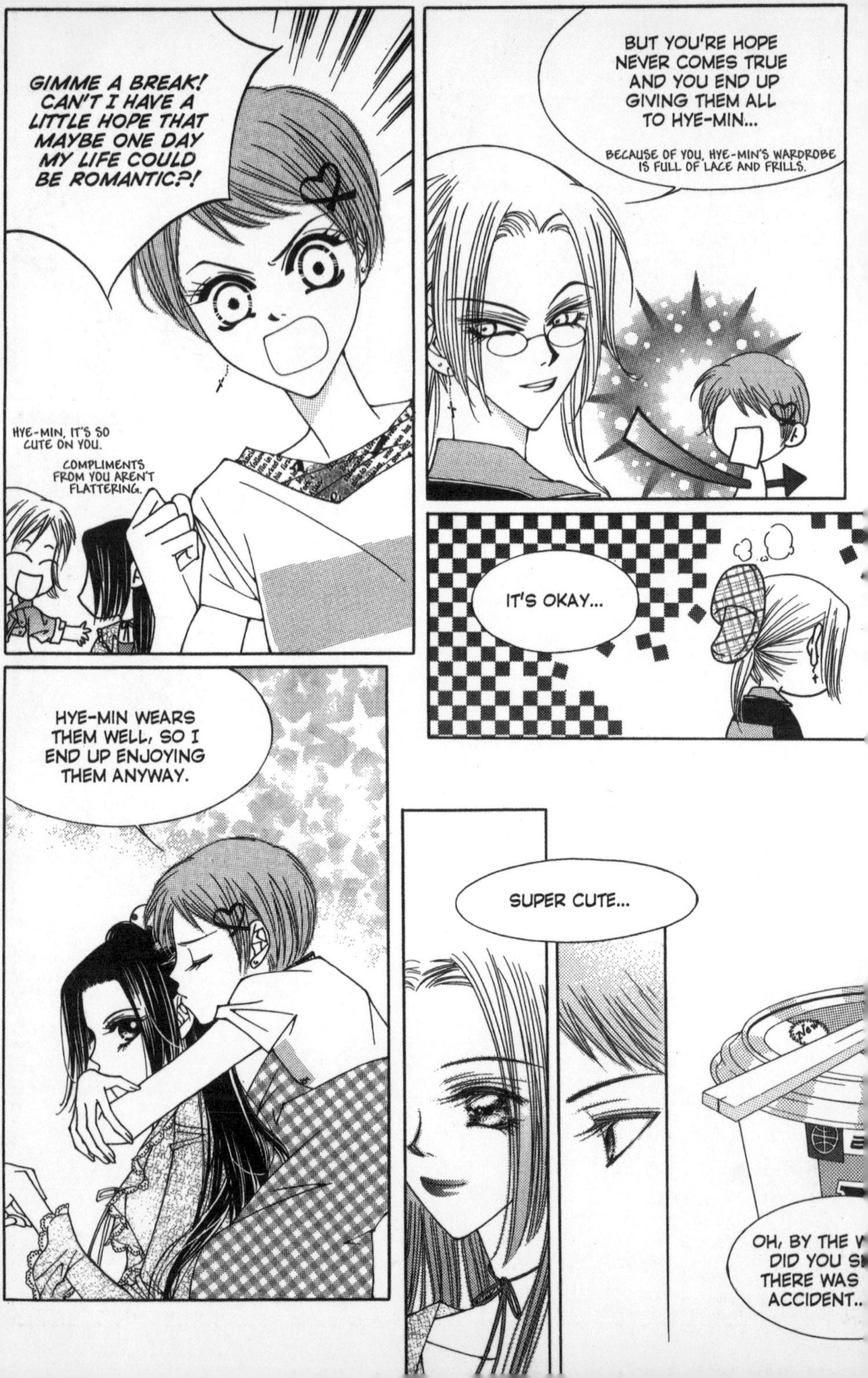
GIMME A BREAK! CAN'T I HAVE A LITTLE HOPE THAT MAYBE ONE DAY MY LIFE COULD BE ROMANTIC?!
HYE-MIN, IT'S SO CUTE ON YOU.
COMPLIMENTS FROM YOU AREN'T FLATTERING.
BUT YOU'RE HOPE NEVER COMES TRUE AND YOU END UP GIVING THEM ALL TO HYE-MIN...
BECAUSE OF YOU, HYE-MIN'S WARDROBE IS FULL OF LACE AND FRILLS.
IT'S OKAY...
HYE-MIN WEARS THEM WELL, SO I END UP ENJOYING THEM ANYWAY.
SUPER CUTE...
OH, BY THE W
DID YOU S
THERE WAS
ACCIDENT..

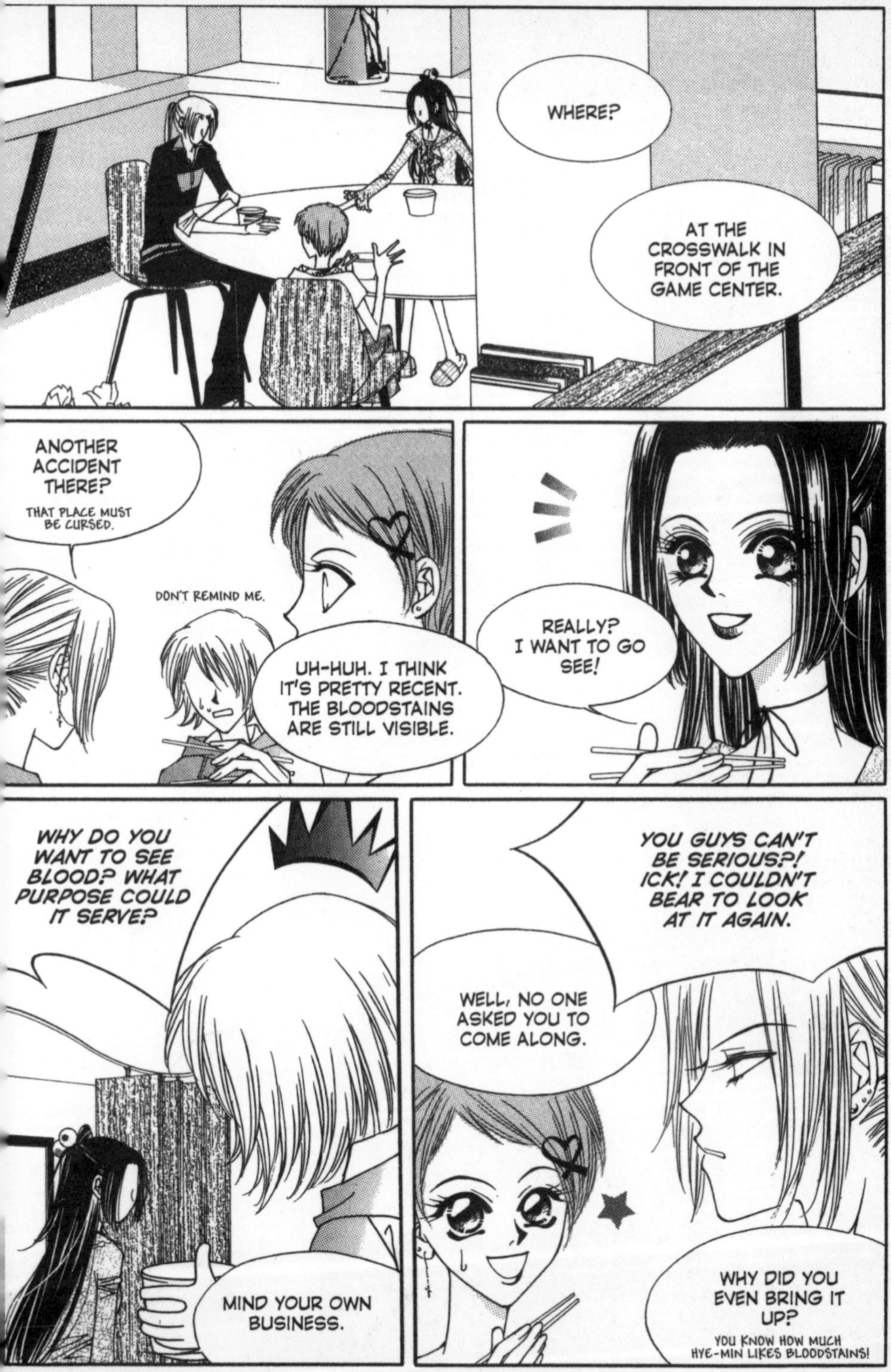
WHERE?
AT THE CROSSWALK IN FRONT OF THE GAME CENTER.
ANOTHER ACCIDENT THERE?
THAT PLACE MUST BE CURSED.
DON'T REMIND ME.
UH-HUH. I THINK IT'S PRETTY RECENT. THE BLOODSTAINS ARE STILL VISIBLE.
REALLY? I WANT TO GO SEE!
WHY DO YOU WANT TO SEE BLOOD? WHAT PURPOSE COULD IT SERVE?
MIND YOUR OWN BUSINESS.
YOU GUYS CAN'T BE SERIOUS?! ICK! I COULDN'T BEAR TO LOOK AT IT AGAIN.
WELL, NO ONE ASKED YOU TO COME ALONG.
WHY DID YOU EVEN BRING IT UP?
YOU KNOW HOW MUCH HYE-MIN LIKES BLOODSTAINS!

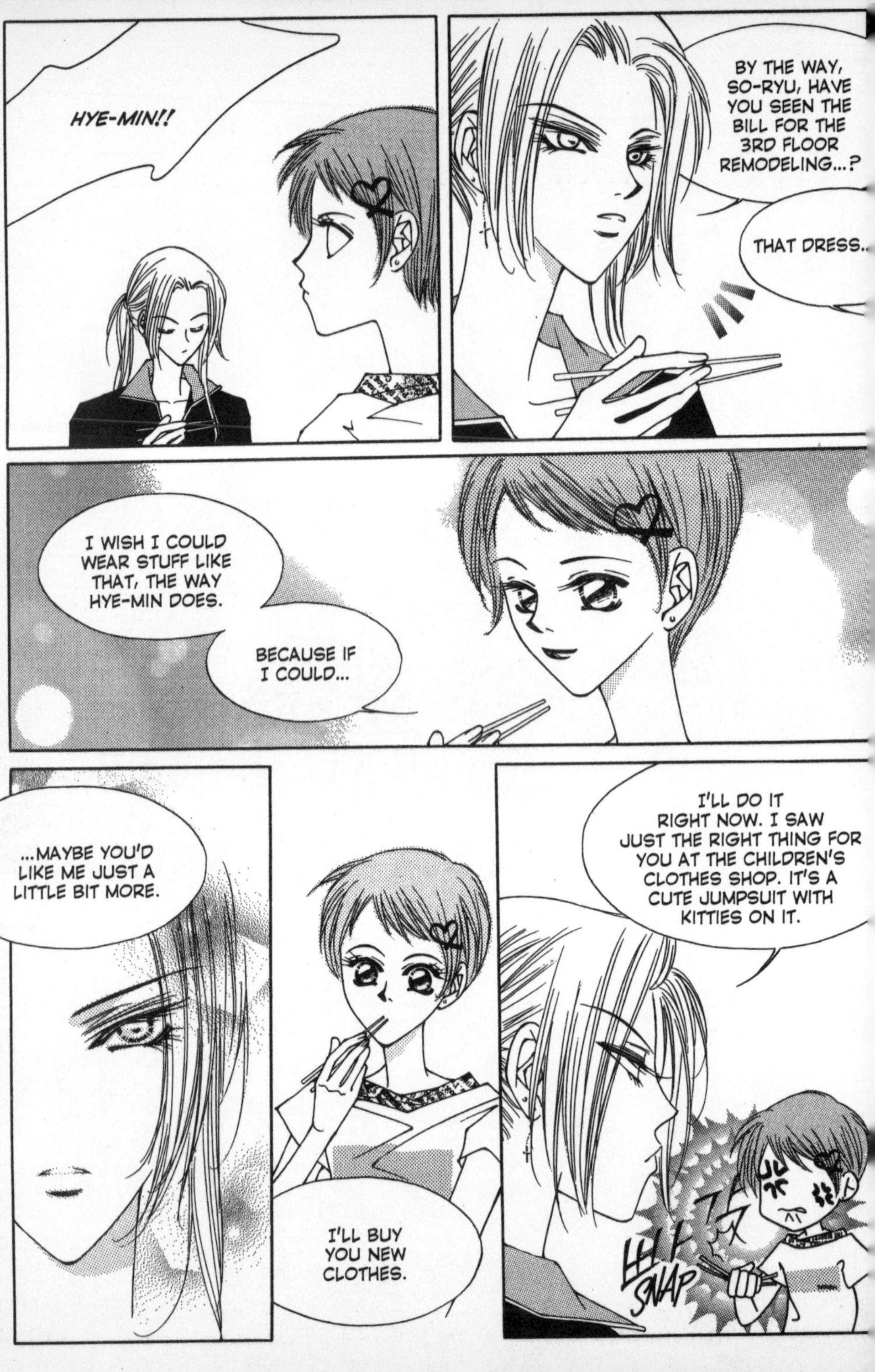
HYE-MIN!!
BY THE WAY, SO-RYU, HAVE YOU SEEN THE BILL FOR THE 3RD FLOOR REMODELING...?
THAT DRESS...
I WISH I COULD WEAR STUFF LIKE THAT, THE WAY HYE-MIN DOES.
BECAUSE IF I COULD...
...MAYBE YOU'D LIKE ME JUST A LITTLE BIT MORE.
I'LL BUY YOU NEW CLOTHES.
I'LL DO IT RIGHT NOW. I SAW JUST THE RIGHT THING FOR YOU AT THE CHILDREN'S CLOTHES SHOP. IT'S A CUTE JUMPSUIT WITH KITTIES ON IT.
SNAP

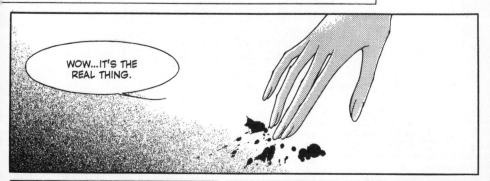

WOW...IT'S THE REAL THING.

I WISH I COULD'VE SEEN IT WHILE THE RED WAS STILL BRIGHT.

I BET YOU SOMEBODY DIED IN THIS...

I SAW AN ACCIDENT ONCE. A MAN WAS THROWN WAY UP INTO THE AIR...

ULP...

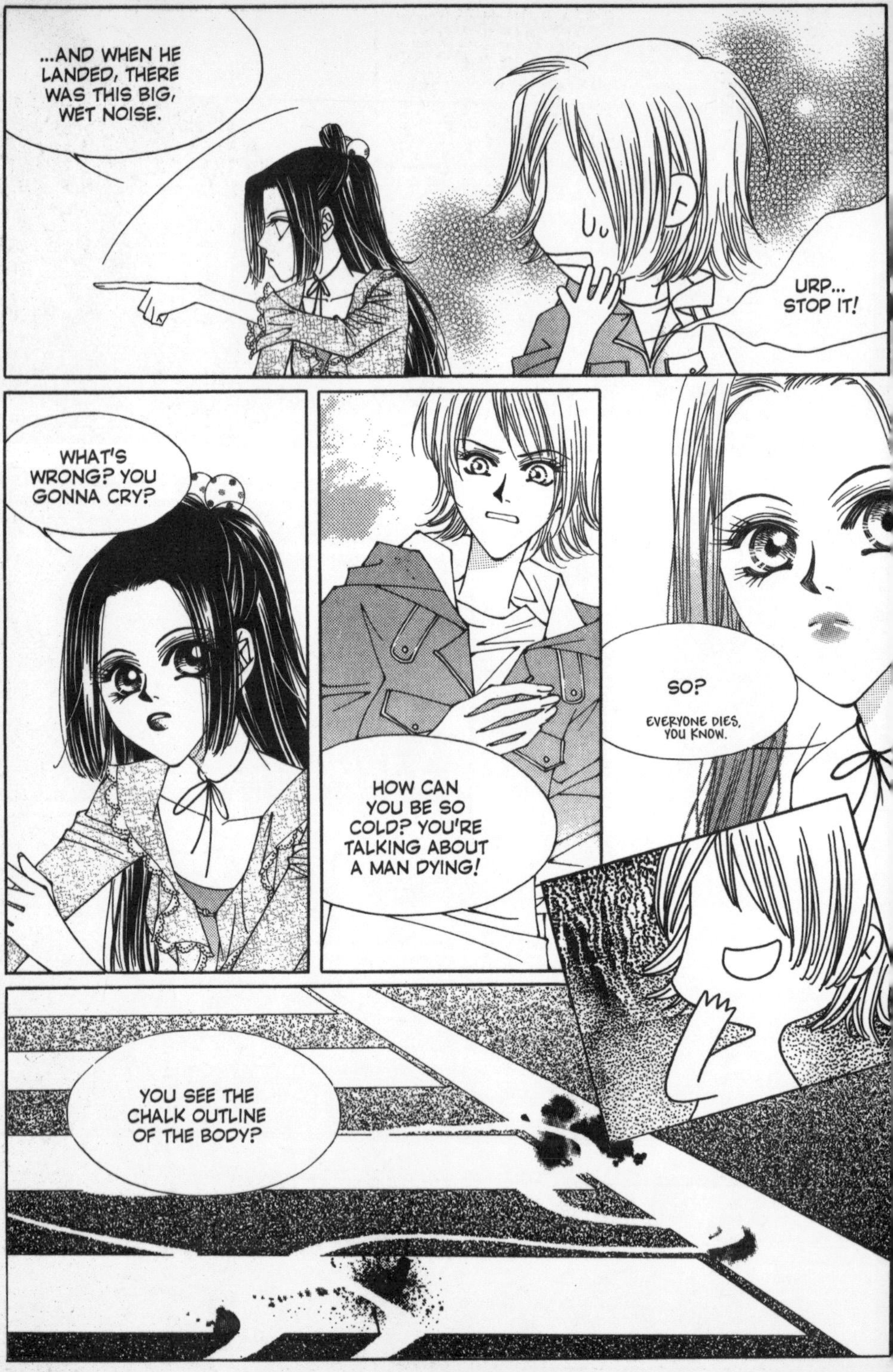
...AND WHEN HE LANDED, THERE WAS THIS BIG, WET NOISE.
URP... STOP IT!
WHAT'S WRONG? YOU GONNA CRY?
HOW CAN YOU BE SO COLD? YOU'RE TALKING ABOUT A MAN DYING!
SO?
EVERYONE DIES, YOU KNOW.
YOU SEE THE CHALK OUTLINE OF THE BODY?

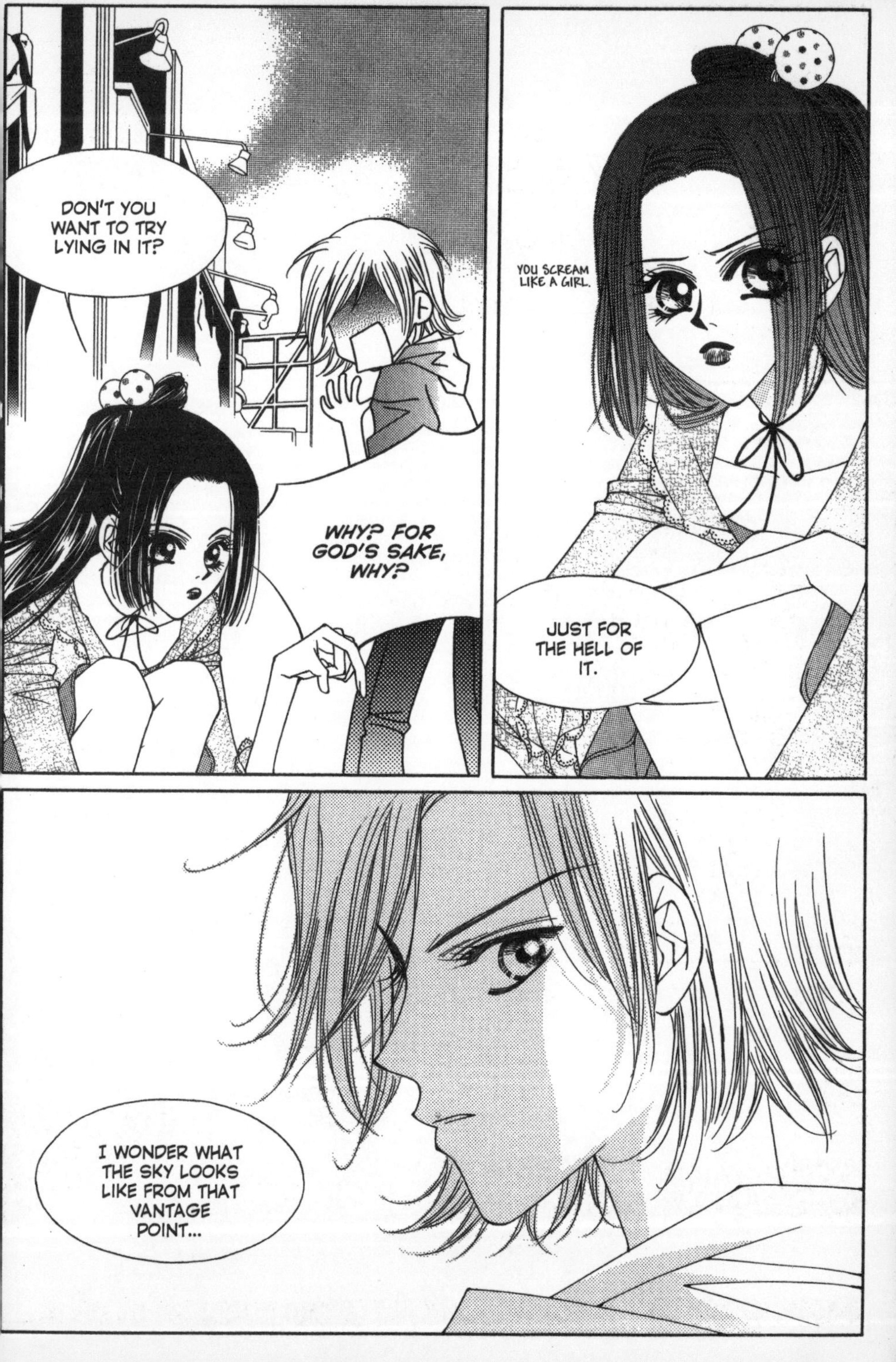
DON'T YOU WANT TO TRY LYING IN IT?
WHY? FOR GOD'S SAKE, WHY?
YOU SCREAM LIKE A GIRL.
JUST FOR THE HELL OF IT.
I WONDER WHAT THE SKY LOOKS LIKE FROM THAT VANTAGE POINT...

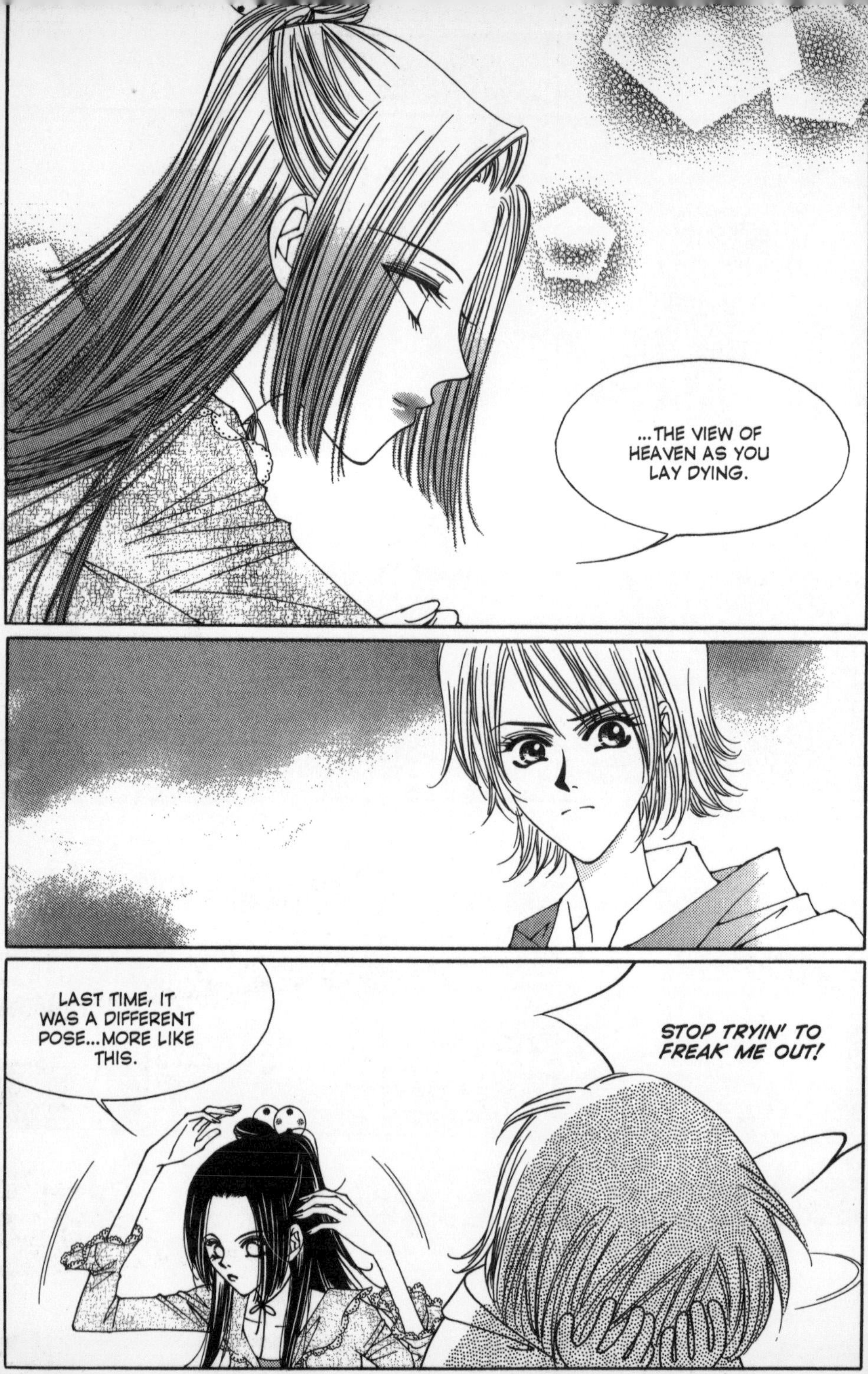
...THE VIEW OF HEAVEN AS YOU LAY DYING.
LAST TIME, IT WAS A DIFFERENT POSE...MORE LIKE THIS.
STOP TRYIN' TO FREAK ME OUT!

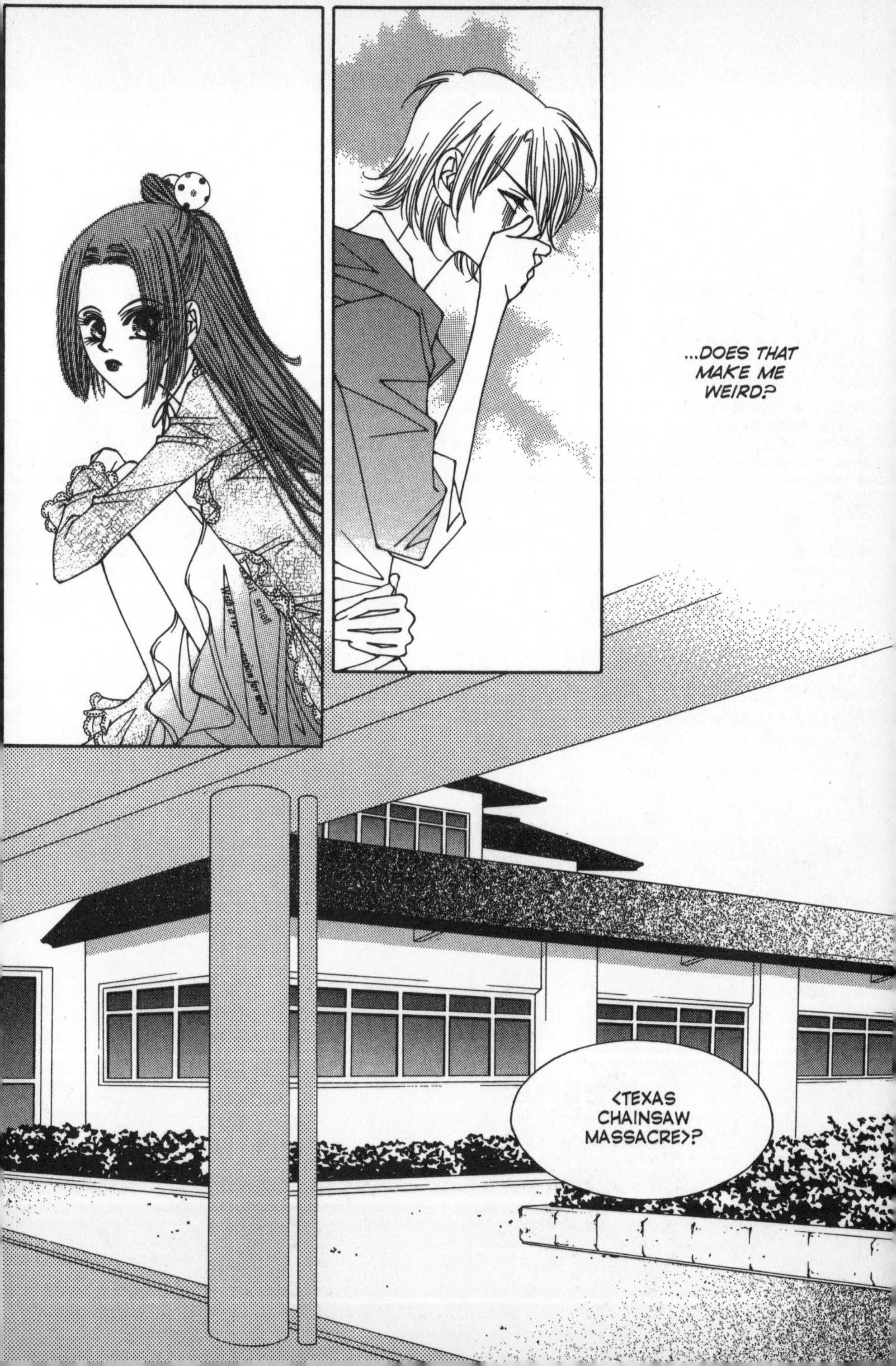
...DOES THAT MAKE ME WEIRD?
<TEXAS CHAINSAW MASSACRE>?

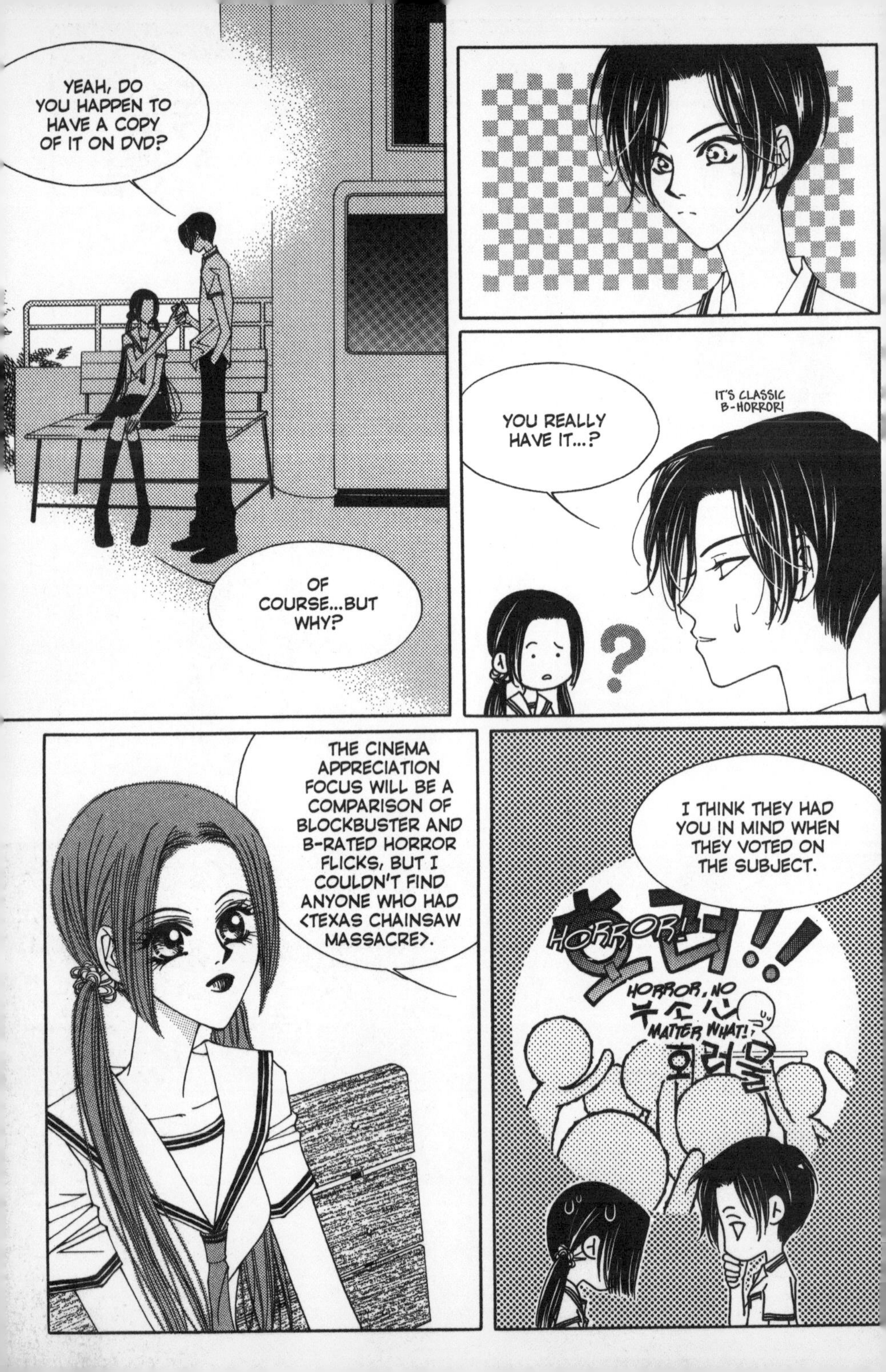
YEAH, DO YOU HAPPEN TO HAVE A COPY OF IT ON DVD?
OF COURSE...BUT WHY?
YOU REALLY HAVE IT...?
IT'S CLASSIC B-HORROR!
?
THE CINEMA APPRECIATION FOCUS WILL BE A COMPARISON OF BLOCKBUSTER AND B-RATED HORROR FLICKS, BUT I COULDN'T FIND ANYONE WHO HAD <TEXAS CHAINSAW MASSACRE>.
I THINK THEY HAD YOU IN MIND WHEN THEY VOTED ON THE SUBJECT.
HORROR!
HORROR, NO MATTER WHAT!

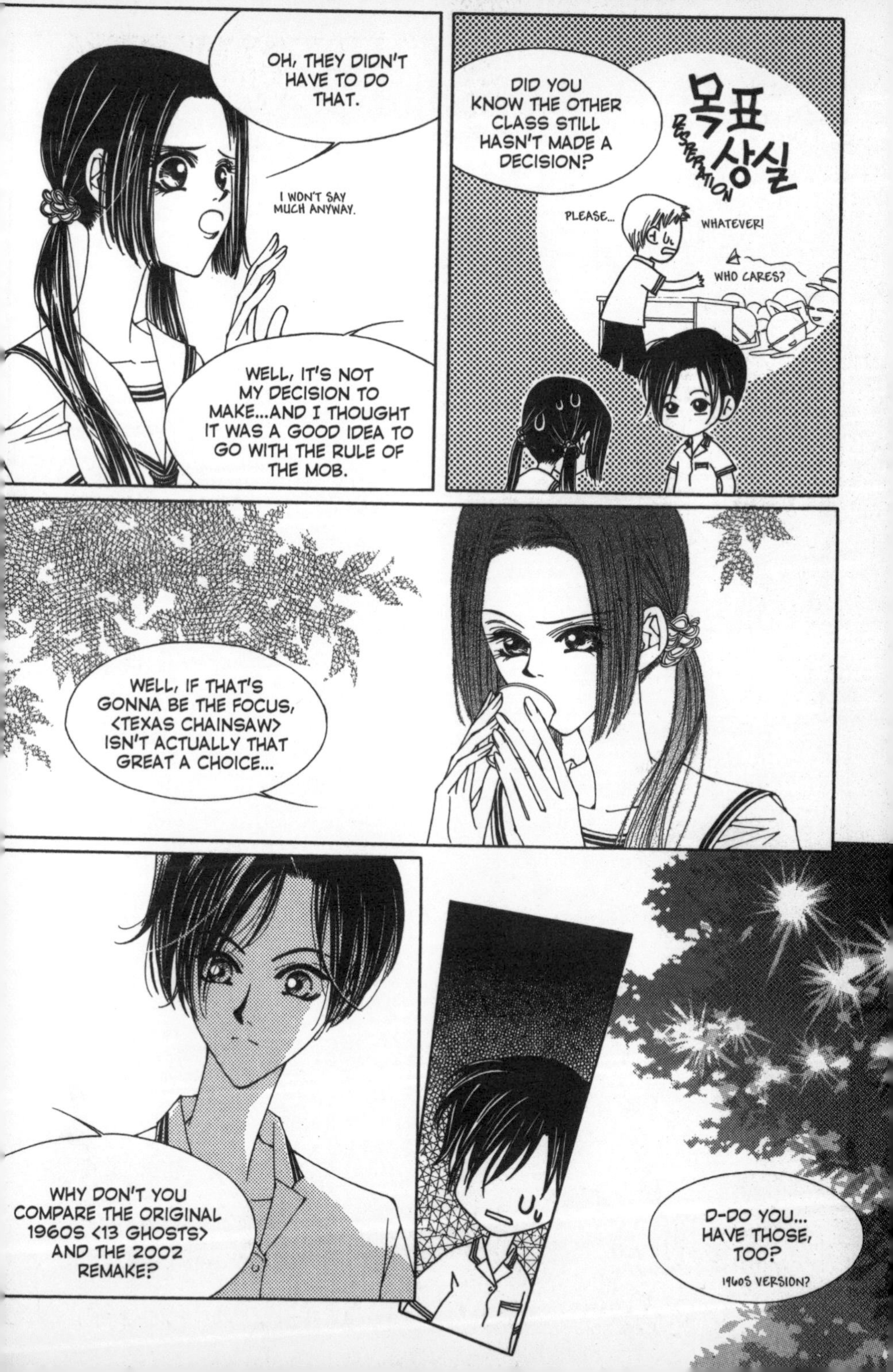
OH, THEY DIDN'T HAVE TO DO THAT.
I WON'T SAY MUCH ANYWAY.
WELL, IT'S NOT MY DECISION TO MAKE...AND I THOUGHT IT WAS A GOOD IDEA TO GO WITH THE RULE OF THE MOB.
DID YOU KNOW THE OTHER CLASS STILL HASN'T MADE A DECISION?
목표 상실
DESPERATION
PLEASE...
WHATEVER!
WHO CARES?
WELL, IF THAT'S GONNA BE THE FOCUS, <TEXAS CHAINSAW> ISN'T ACTUALLY THAT GREAT A CHOICE...
WHY DON'T YOU COMPARE THE ORIGINAL 1960S <13 GHOSTS> AND THE 2002 REMAKE?
D-DO YOU... HAVE THOSE, TOO?
1960S VERSION?

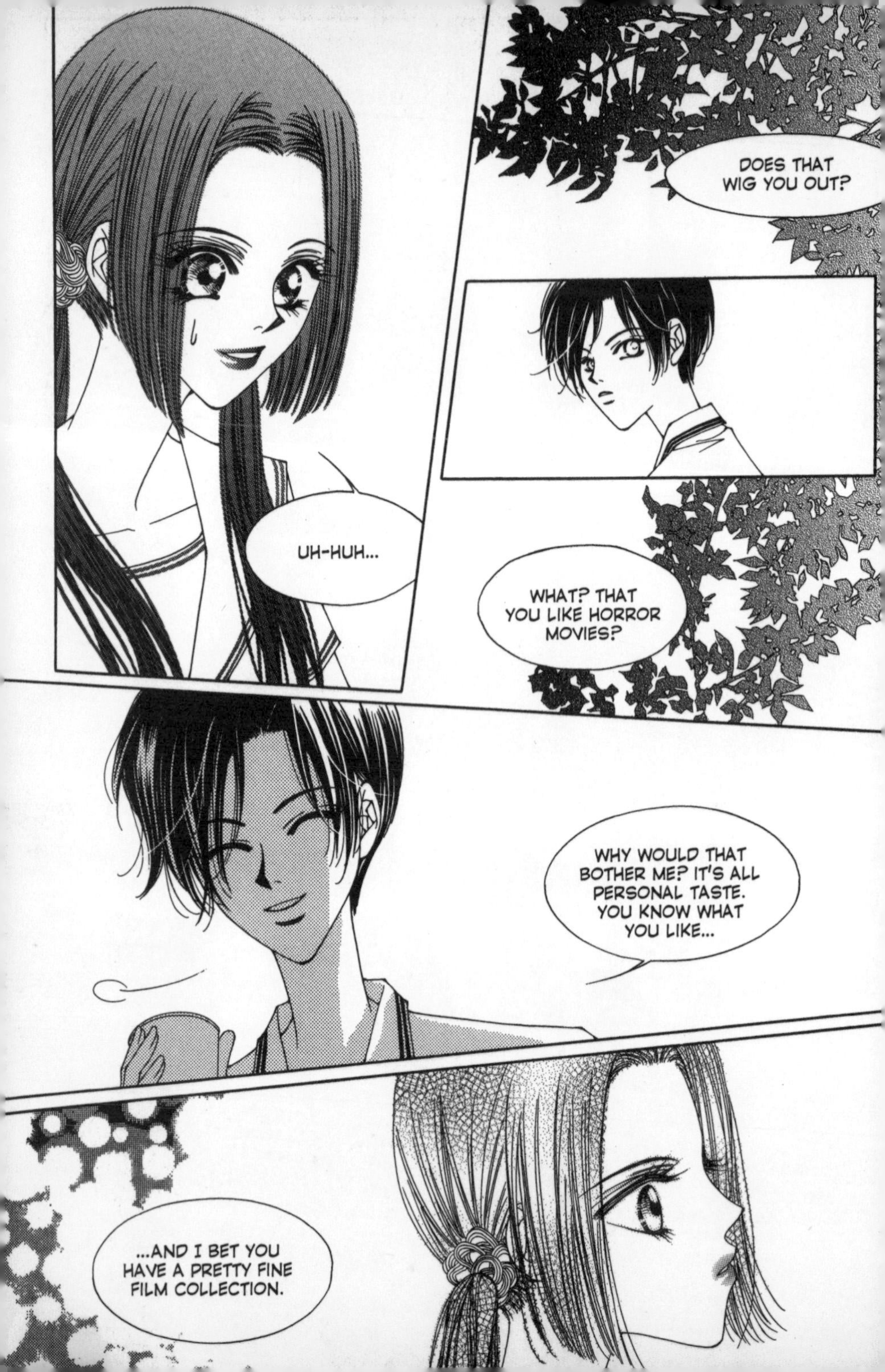
UH-HUH...
DOES THAT WIG YOU OUT?
WHAT? THAT YOU LIKE HORROR MOVIES?
WHY WOULD THAT BOTHER ME? IT'S ALL PERSONAL TASTE. YOU KNOW WHAT YOU LIKE...
...AND I BET YOU HAVE A PRETTY FINE FILM COLLECTION.

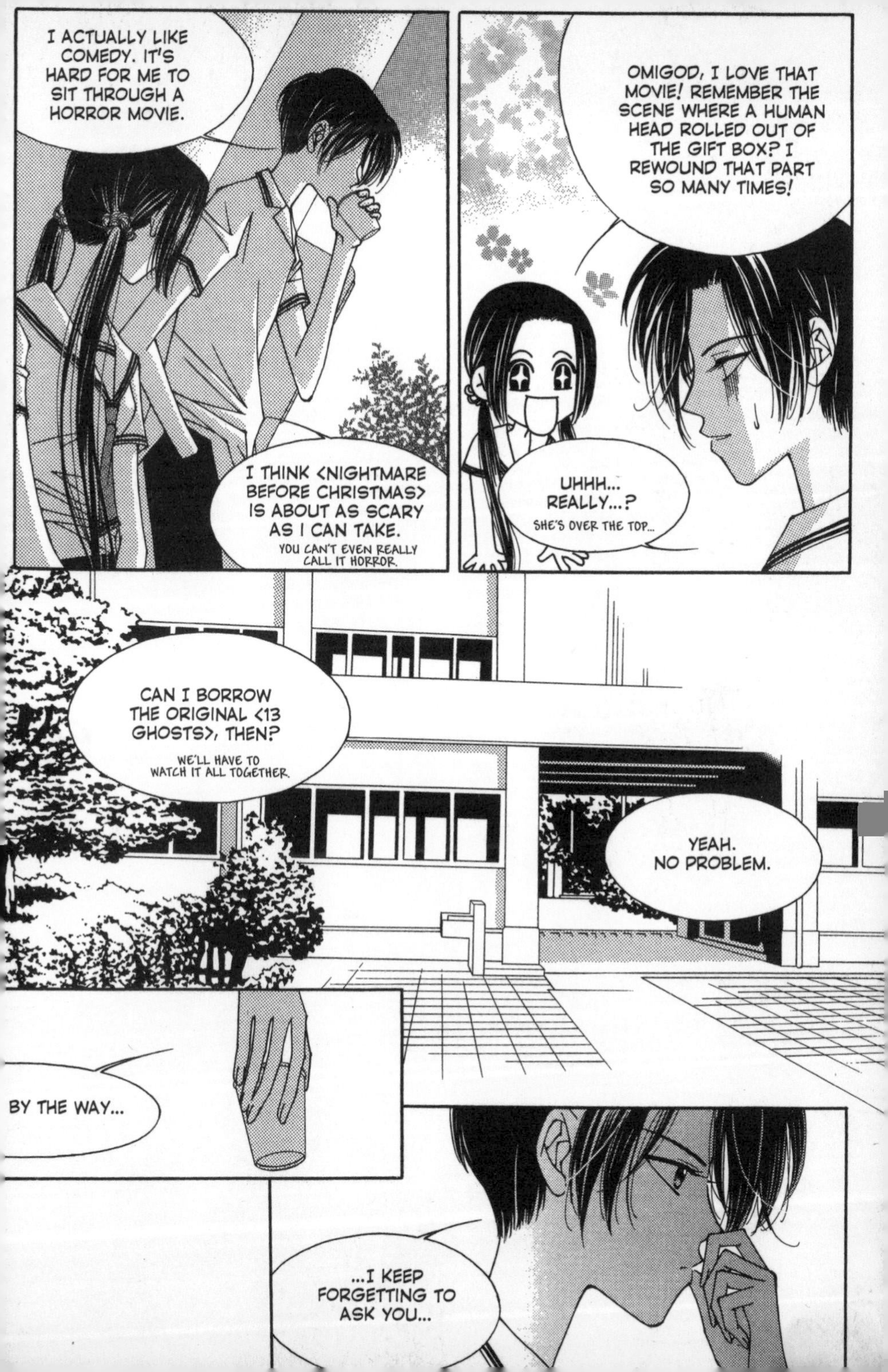
I ACTUALLY LIKE COMEDY. IT'S HARD FOR ME TO SIT THROUGH A HORROR MOVIE.
I THINK <NIGHTMARE BEFORE CHRISTMAS> IS ABOUT AS SCARY AS I CAN TAKE.
YOU CAN'T EVEN REALLY CALL IT HORROR.
OMIGOD, I LOVE THAT MOVIE! REMEMBER THE SCENE WHERE A HUMAN HEAD ROLLED OUT OF THE GIFT BOX? I REWOUND THAT PART SO MANY TIMES!
UHHH... REALLY...?
SHE'S OVER THE TOP...
CAN I BORROW THE ORIGINAL <13 GHOSTS>, THEN?
WE'LL HAVE TO WATCH IT ALL TOGETHER.
YEAH. NO PROBLEM.
BY THE WAY...
...I KEEP FORGETTING TO ASK YOU...

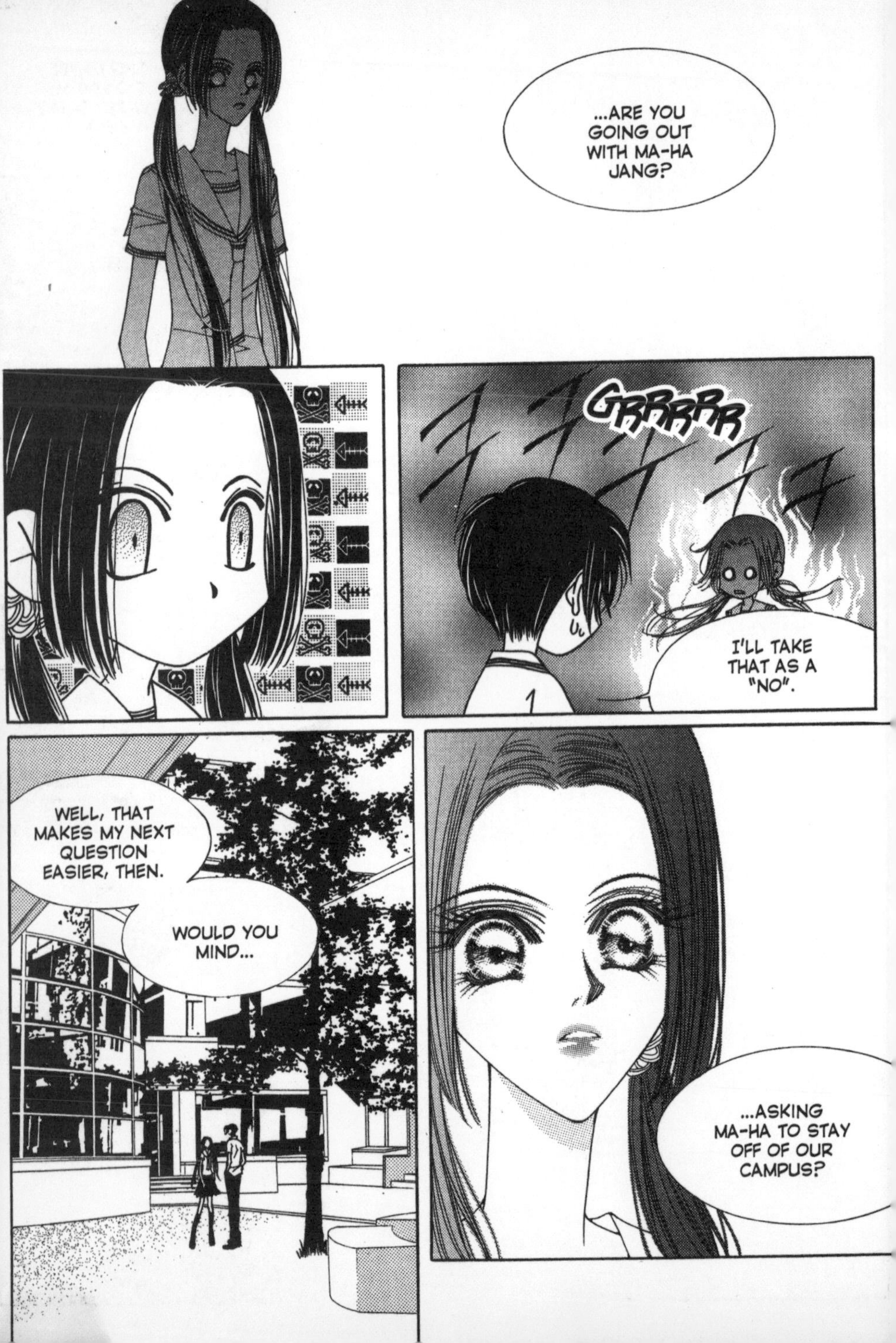
...ARE YOU GOING OUT WITH MA-HA JANG?
GRRRRR
I'LL TAKE THAT AS A "NO".
WELL, THAT MAKES MY NEXT QUESTION EASIER, THEN.
WOULD YOU MIND...
...ASKING MA-HA TO STAY OFF OF OUR CAMPUS?

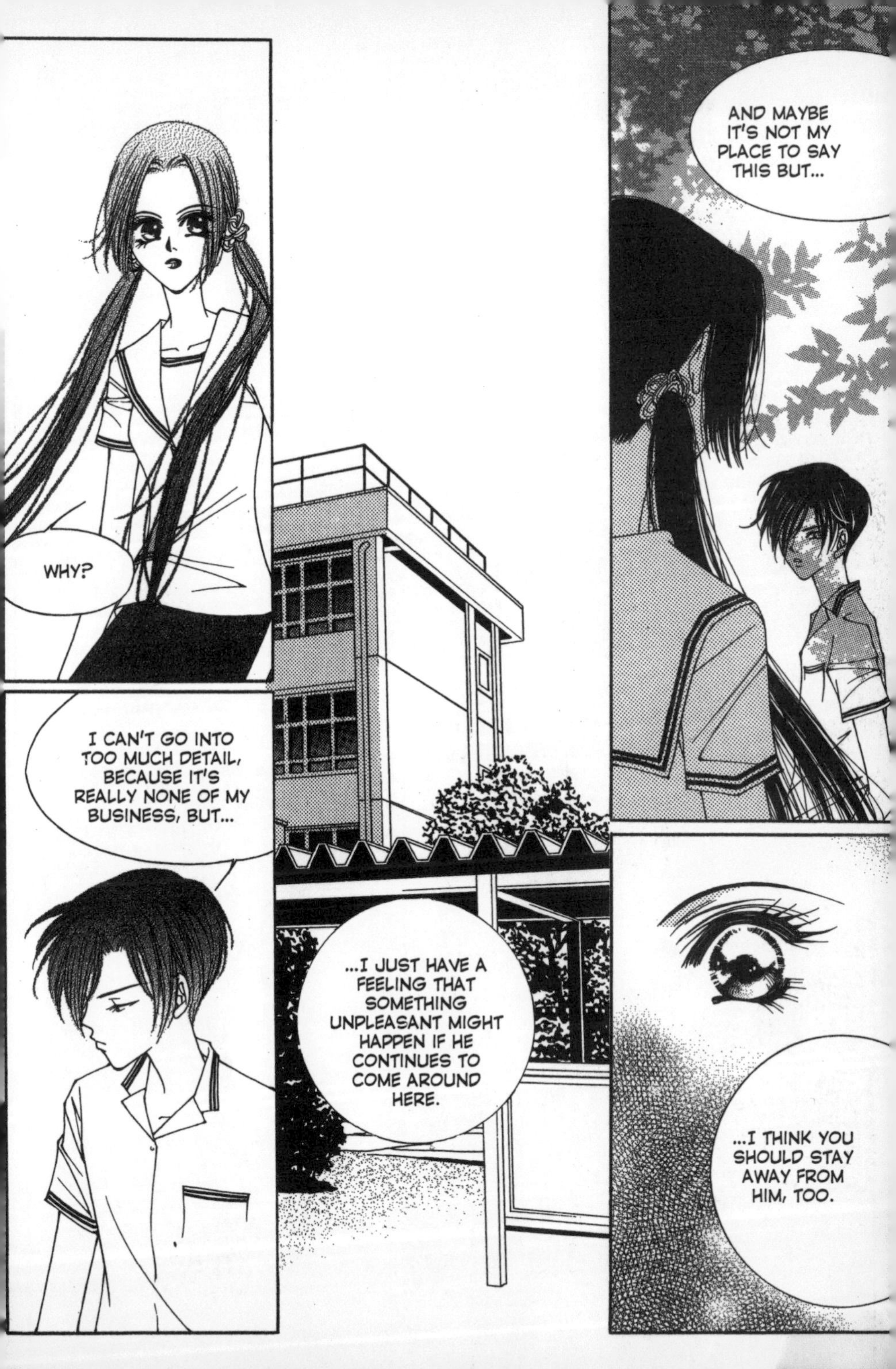
WHY?
AND MAYBE IT'S NOT MY PLACE TO SAY THIS BUT...
I CAN'T GO INTO TOO MUCH DETAIL, BECAUSE IT'S REALLY NONE OF MY BUSINESS, BUT...
...I JUST HAVE A FEELING THAT SOMETHING UNPLEASANT MIGHT HAPPEN IF HE CONTINUES TO COME AROUND HERE.
...I THINK YOU SHOULD STAY AWAY FROM HIM, TOO.

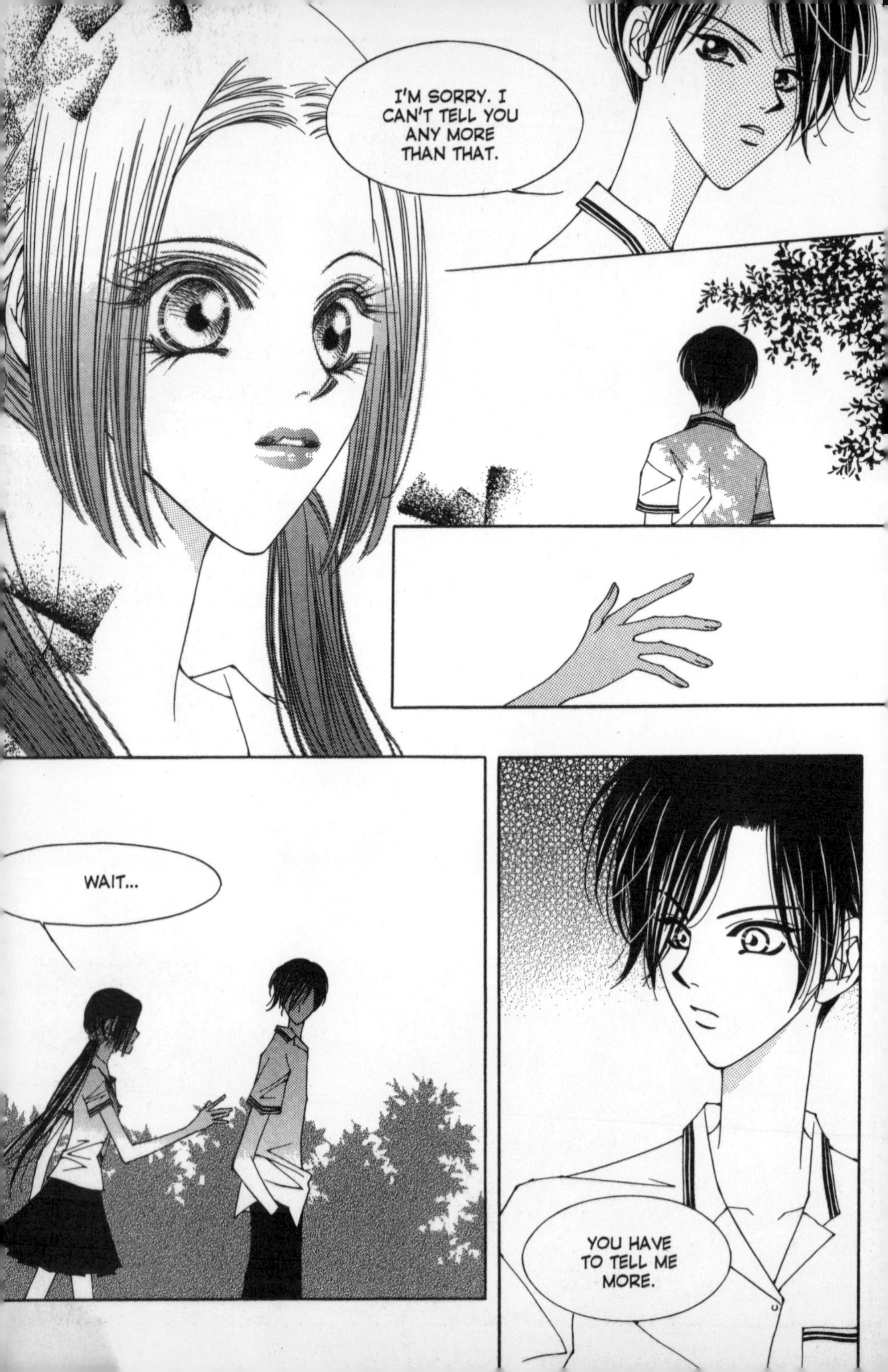
I'M SORRY. I CAN'T TELL YOU ANY MORE THAN THAT.
WAIT...
YOU HAVE TO TELL ME MORE.

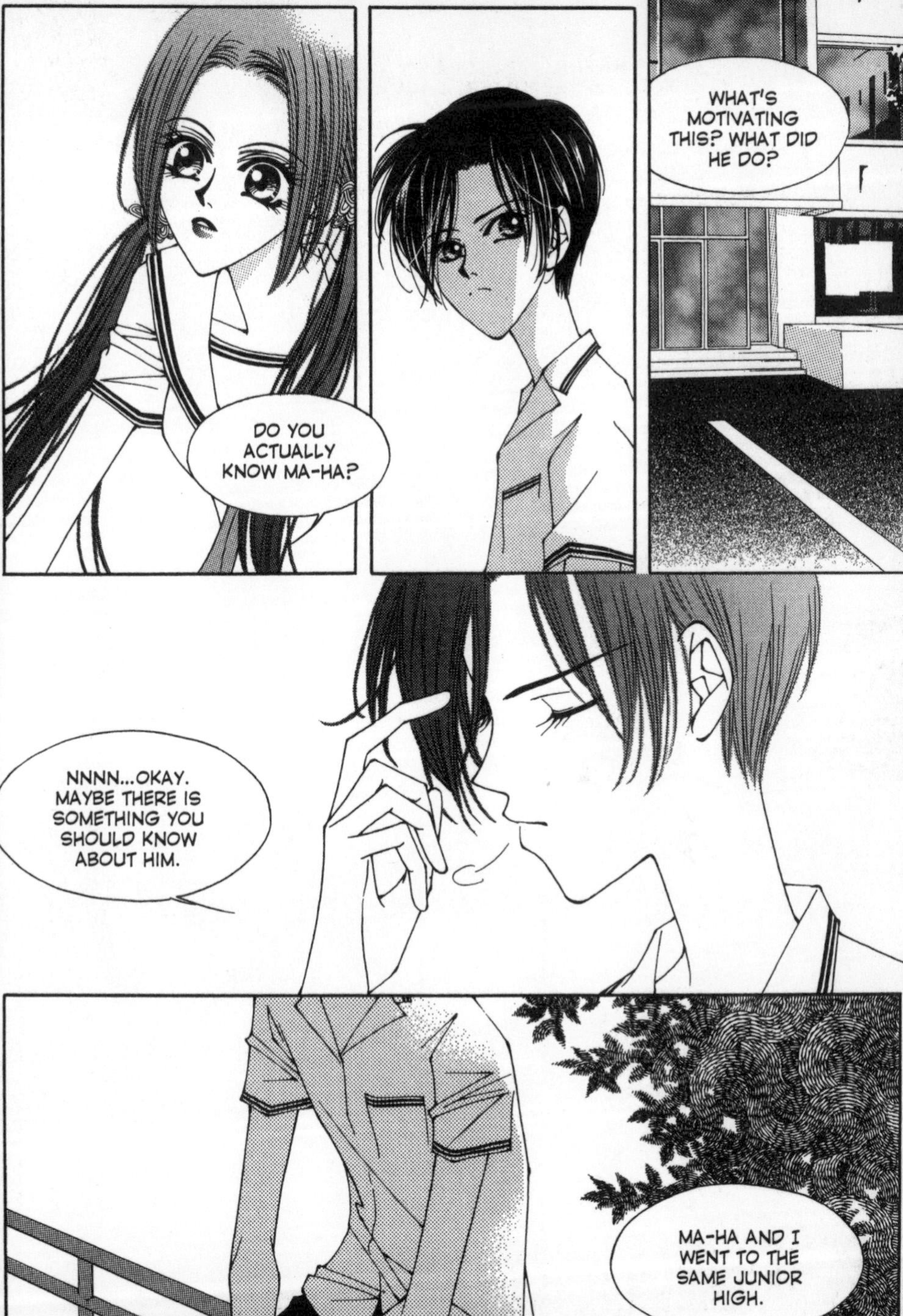
DO YOU ACTUALLY KNOW MA-HA?
WHAT'S MOTIVATING THIS? WHAT DID HE DO?
NNNN...OKAY. MAYBE THERE IS SOMETHING YOU SHOULD KNOW ABOUT HIM.
MA-HA AND I WENT TO THE SAME JUNIOR HIGH.

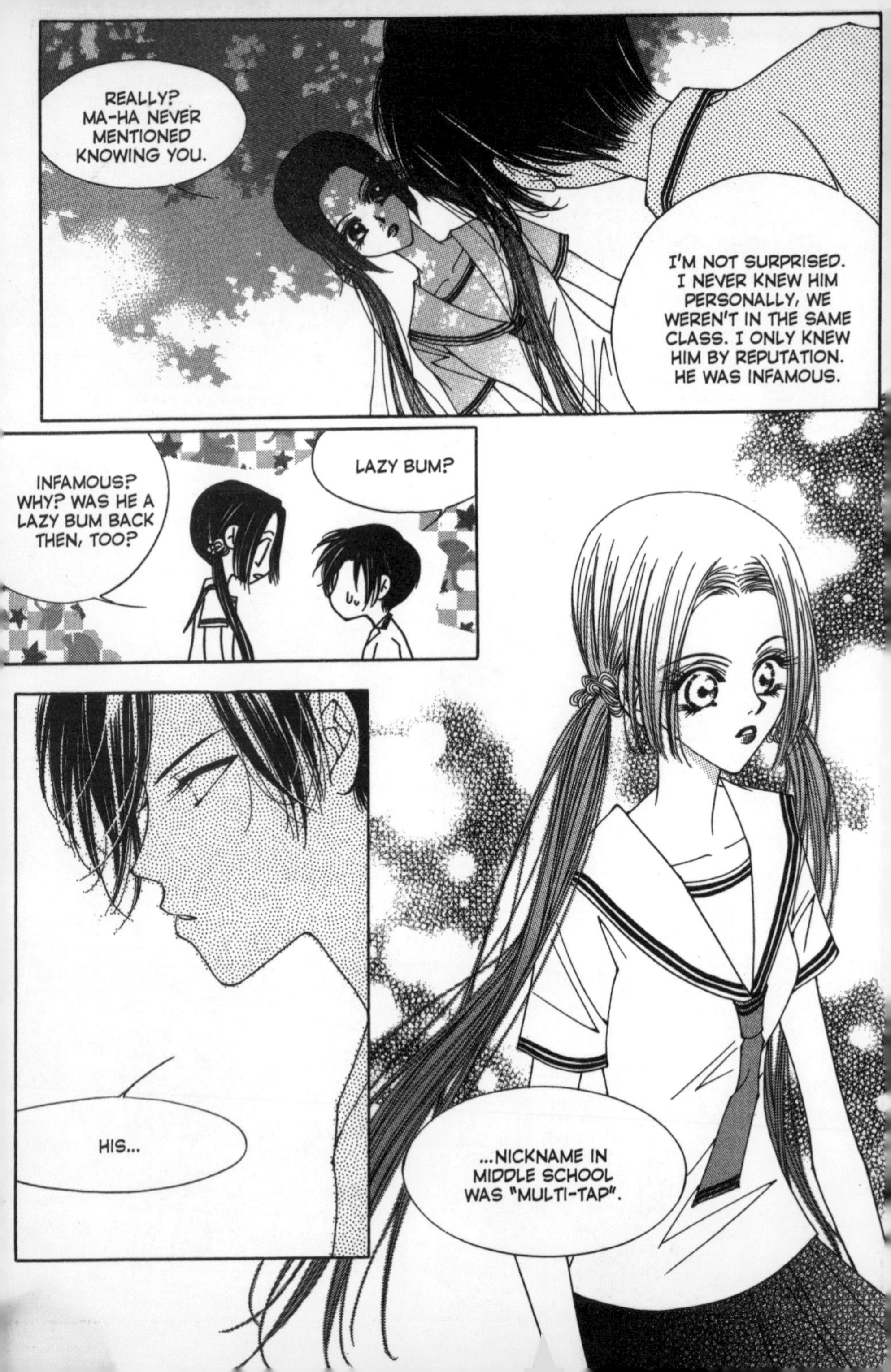
REALLY? MA-HA NEVER MENTIONED KNOWING YOU.
I'M NOT SURPRISED. I NEVER KNEW HIM PERSONALLY, WE WEREN'T IN THE SAME CLASS. I ONLY KNEW HIM BY REPUTATION. HE WAS INFAMOUS.
INFAMOUS? WHY? WAS HE A LAZY BUM BACK THEN, TOO?
LAZY BUM?
HIS...
...NICKNAME IN MIDDLE SCHOOL WAS "MULTI-TAP".

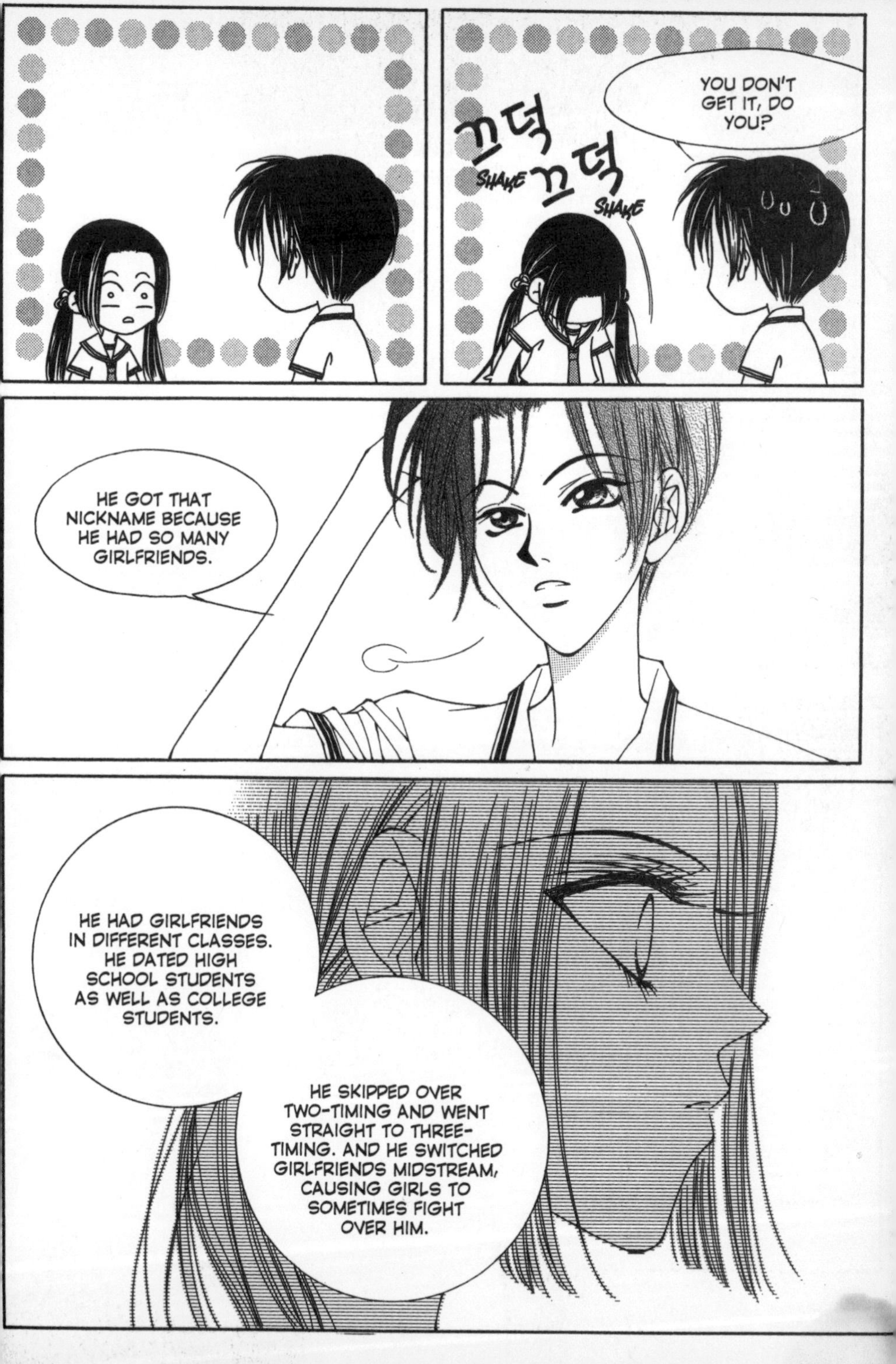
끄덕
SHAKE
끄덕
SHAKE
YOU DON'T GET IT, DO YOU?
HE GOT THAT NICKNAME BECAUSE HE HAD SO MANY GIRLFRIENDS.
HE HAD GIRLFRIENDS IN DIFFERENT CLASSES. HE DATED HIGH SCHOOL STUDENTS AS WELL AS COLLEGE STUDENTS.
HE SKIPPED OVER TWO-TIMING AND WENT STRAIGHT TO THREE-TIMING. AND HE SWITCHED GIRLFRIENDS MIDSTREAM, CAUSING GIRLS TO SOMETIMES FIGHT OVER HIM.

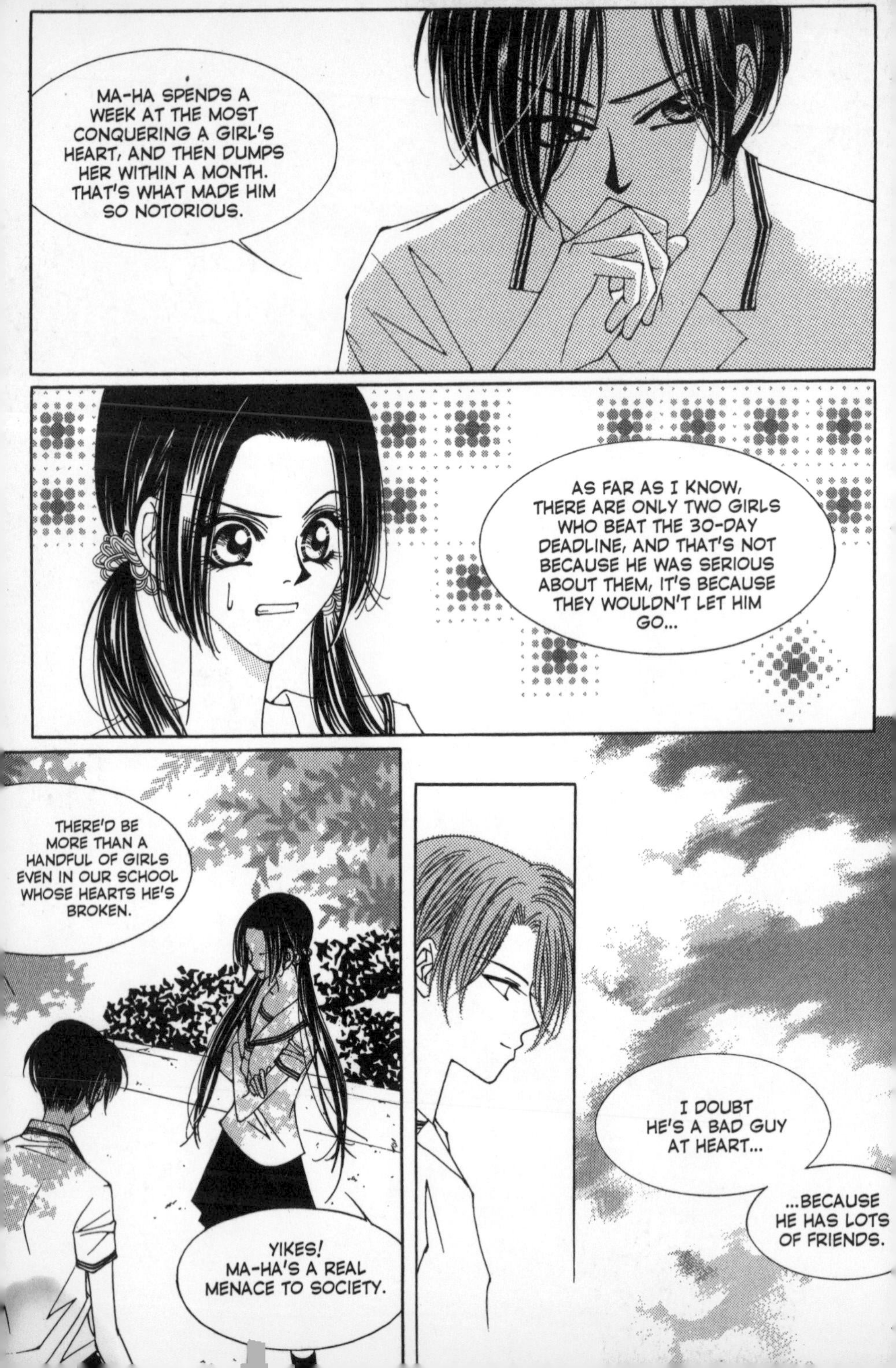
MA-HA SPENDS A WEEK AT THE MOST CONQUERING A GIRL'S HEART, AND THEN DUMPS HER WITHIN A MONTH. THAT'S WHAT MADE HIM SO NOTORIOUS.
AS FAR AS I KNOW, THERE ARE ONLY TWO GIRLS WHO BEAT THE 30-DAY DEADLINE, AND THAT'S NOT BECAUSE HE WAS SERIOUS ABOUT THEM, IT'S BECAUSE THEY WOULDN'T LET HIM GO...
THERE'D BE MORE THAN A HANDFUL OF GIRLS EVEN IN OUR SCHOOL WHOSE HEARTS HE'S BROKEN.
YIKES! MA-HA'S A REAL MENACE TO SOCIETY.
I DOUBT HE'S A BAD GUY AT HEART...
...BECAUSE HE HAS LOTS OF FRIENDS.

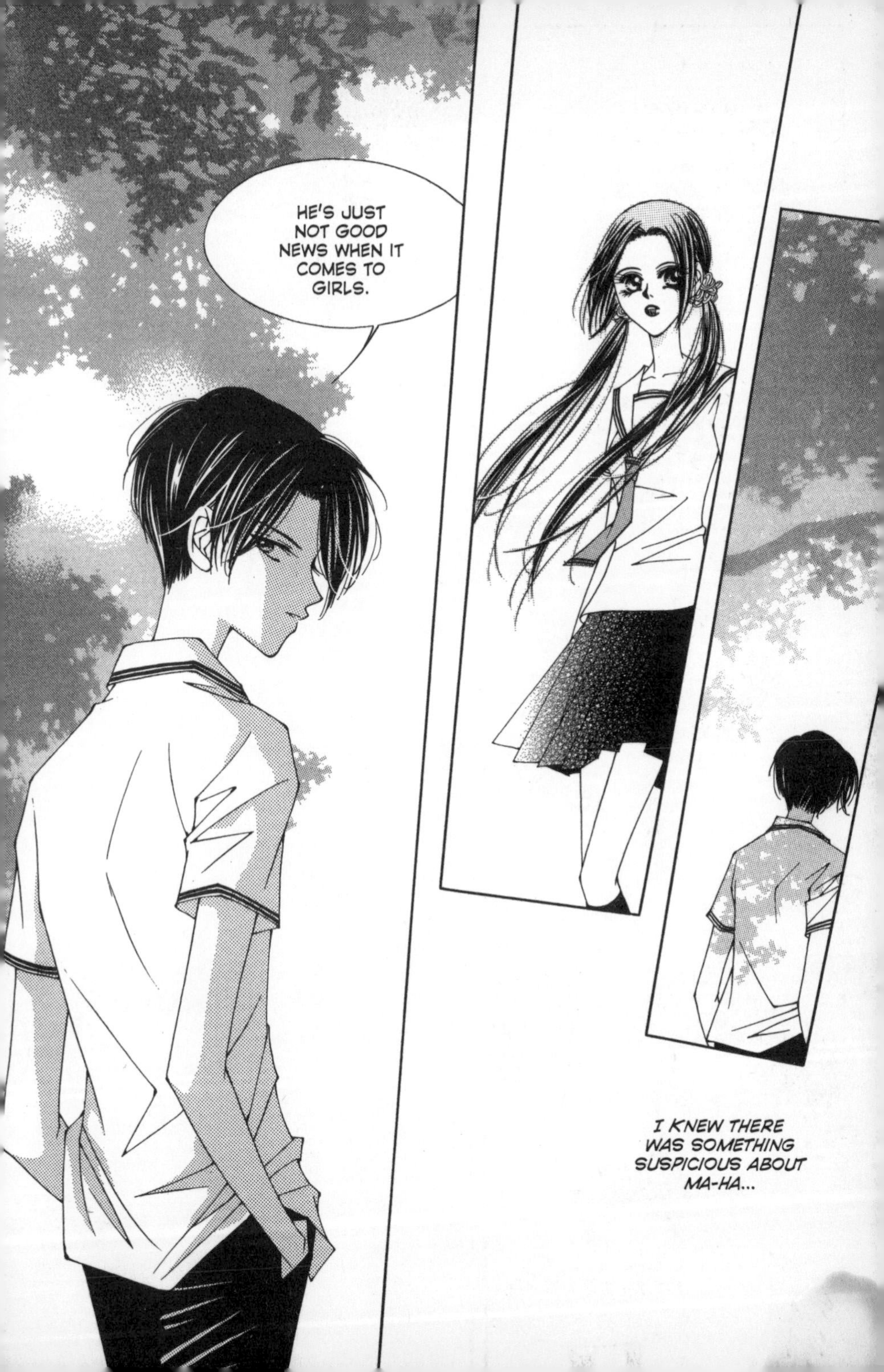
HE'S JUST NOT GOOD NEWS WHEN IT COMES TO GIRLS.
I KNEW THERE WAS SOMETHING SUSPICIOUS ABOUT MA-HA...

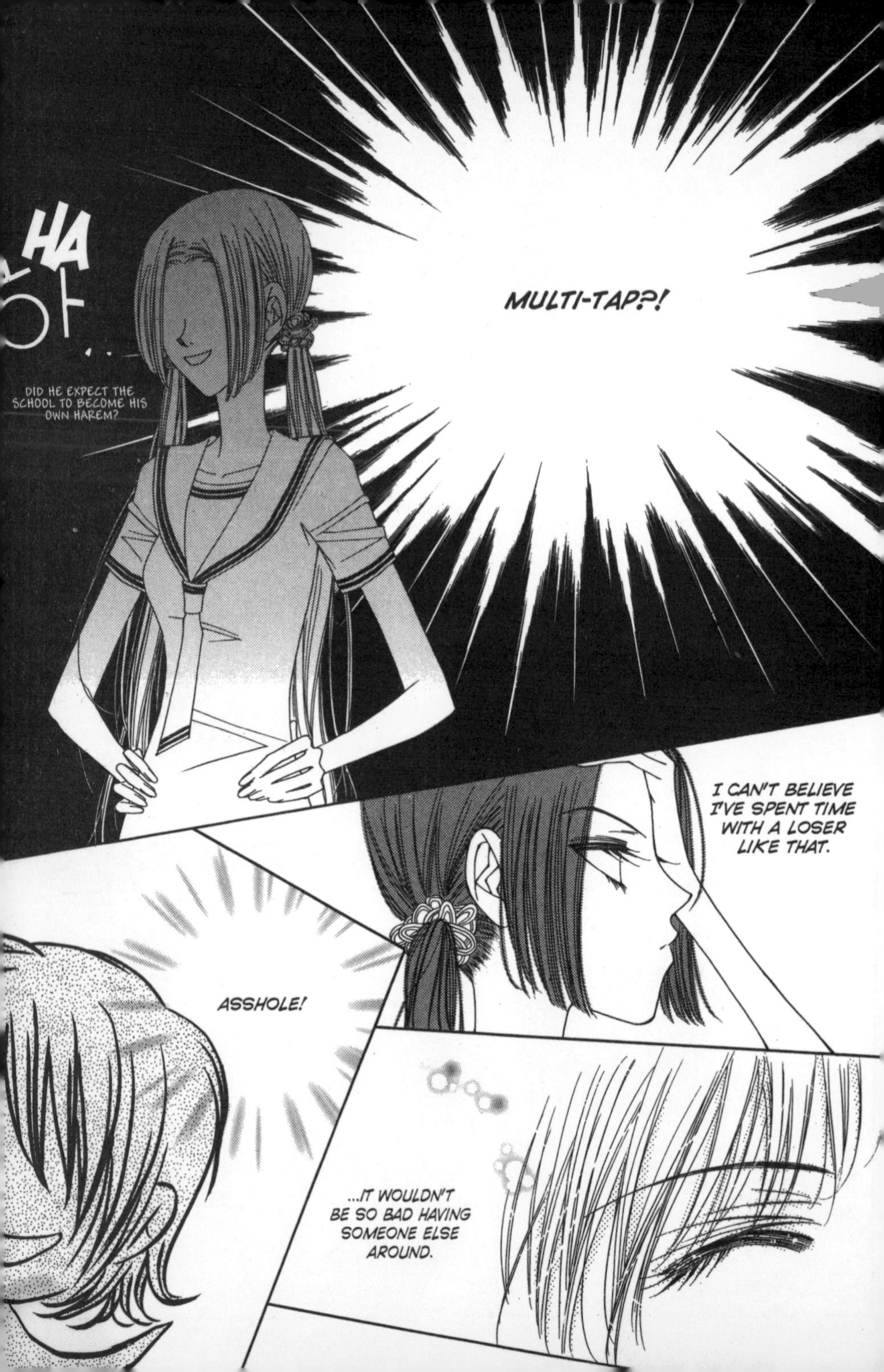
HA
DID HE EXPECT THE SCHOOL TO BECOME HIS OWN HAREM?
MULTI-TAP?!
ASSHOLE!
I CAN'T BELIEVE I'VE SPENT TIME WITH A LOSER LIKE THAT.
...IT WOULDN'T BE SO BAD HAVING SOMEONE ELSE AROUND.

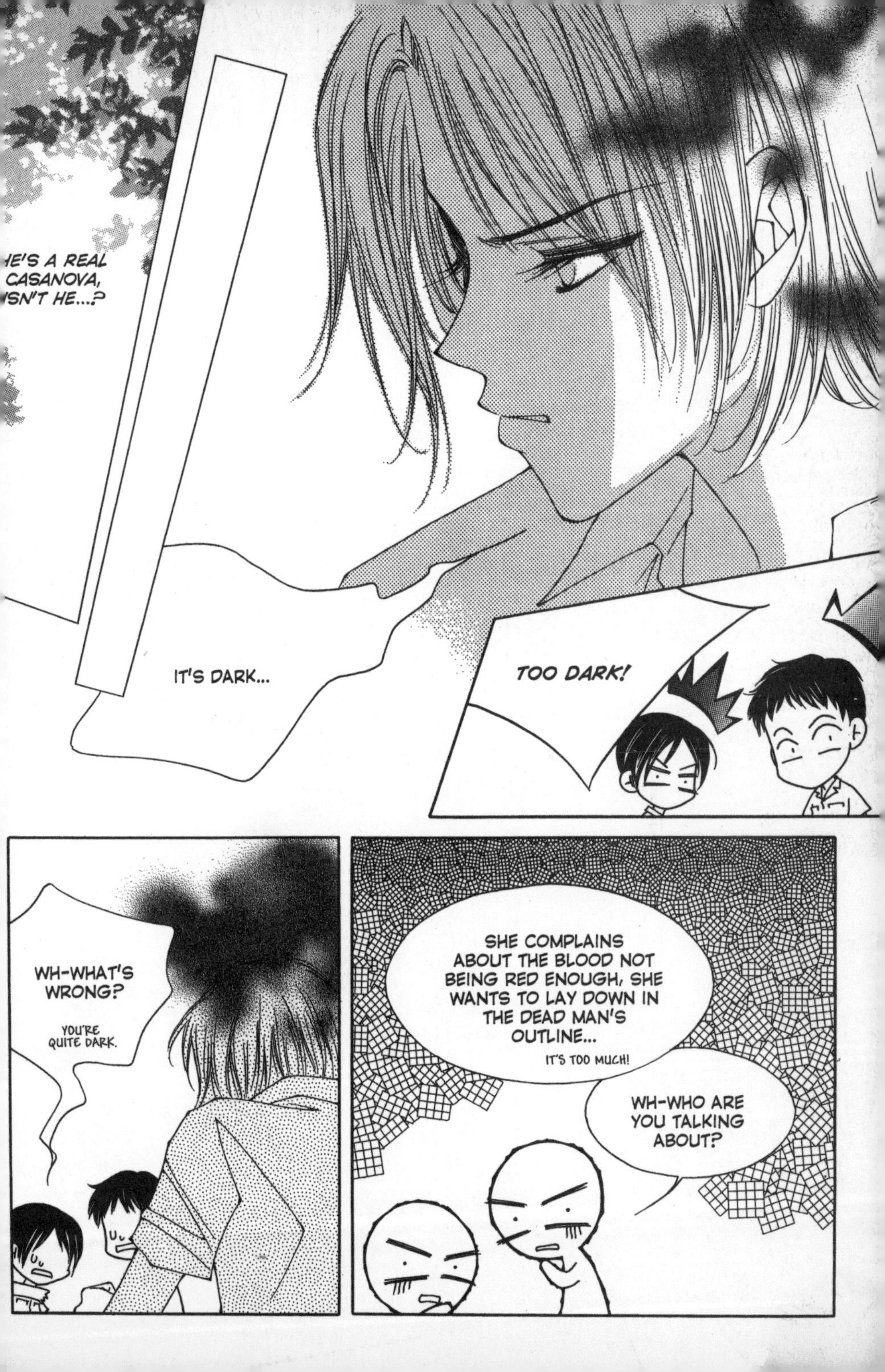
E'S A REAL CASANOVA, SN'T HE...?
IT'S DARK...
TOO DARK!
WH-WHAT'S WRONG?
YOU'RE QUITE DARK.
SHE COMPLAINS ABOUT THE BLOOD NOT BEING RED ENOUGH, SHE WANTS TO LAY DOWN IN THE DEAD MAN'S OUTLINE...
IT'S TOO MUCH!
WH-WHO ARE YOU TALKING ABOUT?

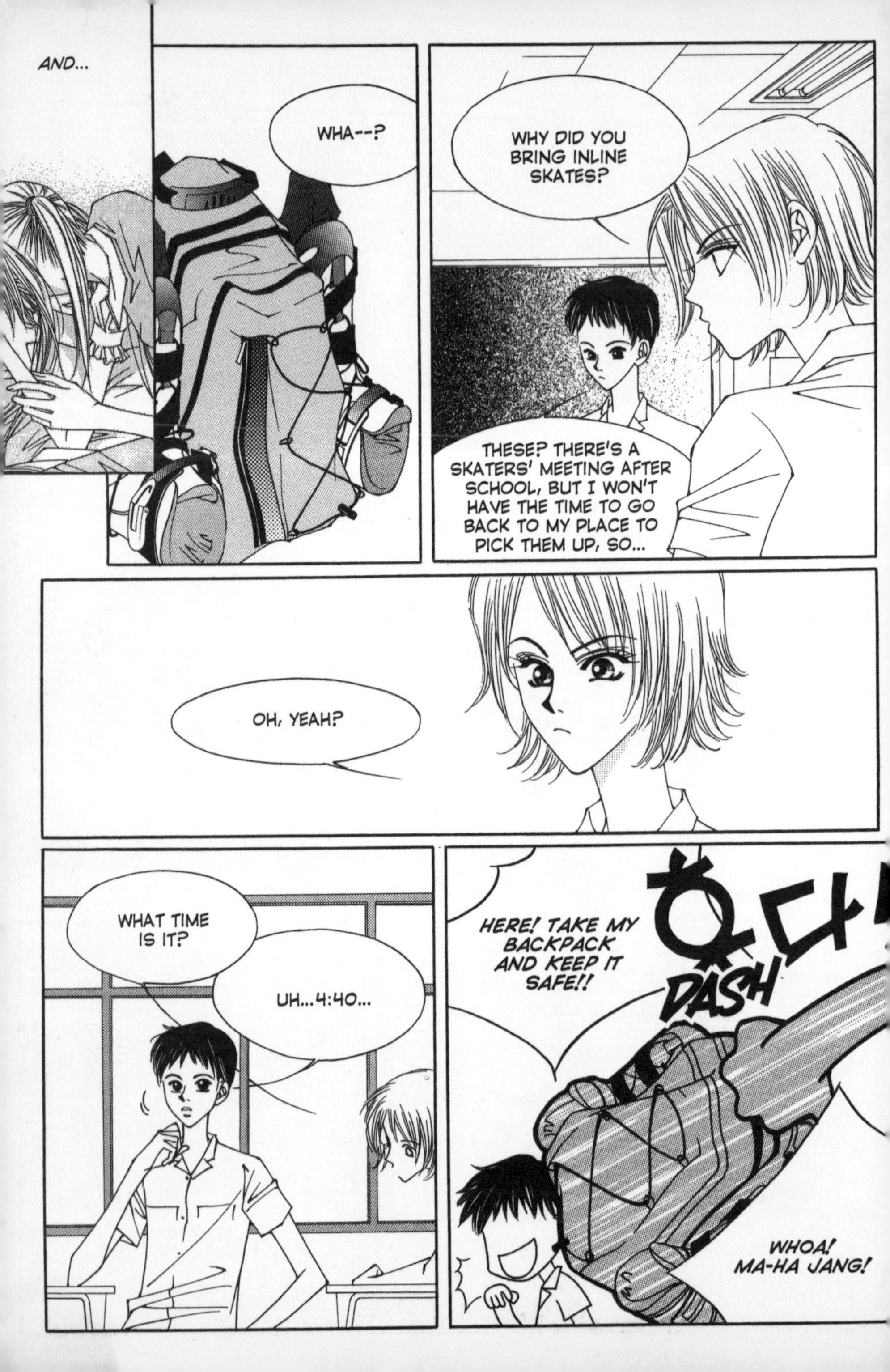
AND...
WHA--?
WHY DID YOU BRING INLINE SKATES?
THESE? THERE'S A SKATERS' MEETING AFTER SCHOOL, BUT I WON'T HAVE THE TIME TO GO BACK TO MY PLACE TO PICK THEM UP, SO...
OH, YEAH?
WHAT TIME IS IT?
UH...4:40...
HERE! TAKE MY BACKPACK AND KEEP IT SAFE!!
후다
DASH
WHOA! MA-HA JANG!

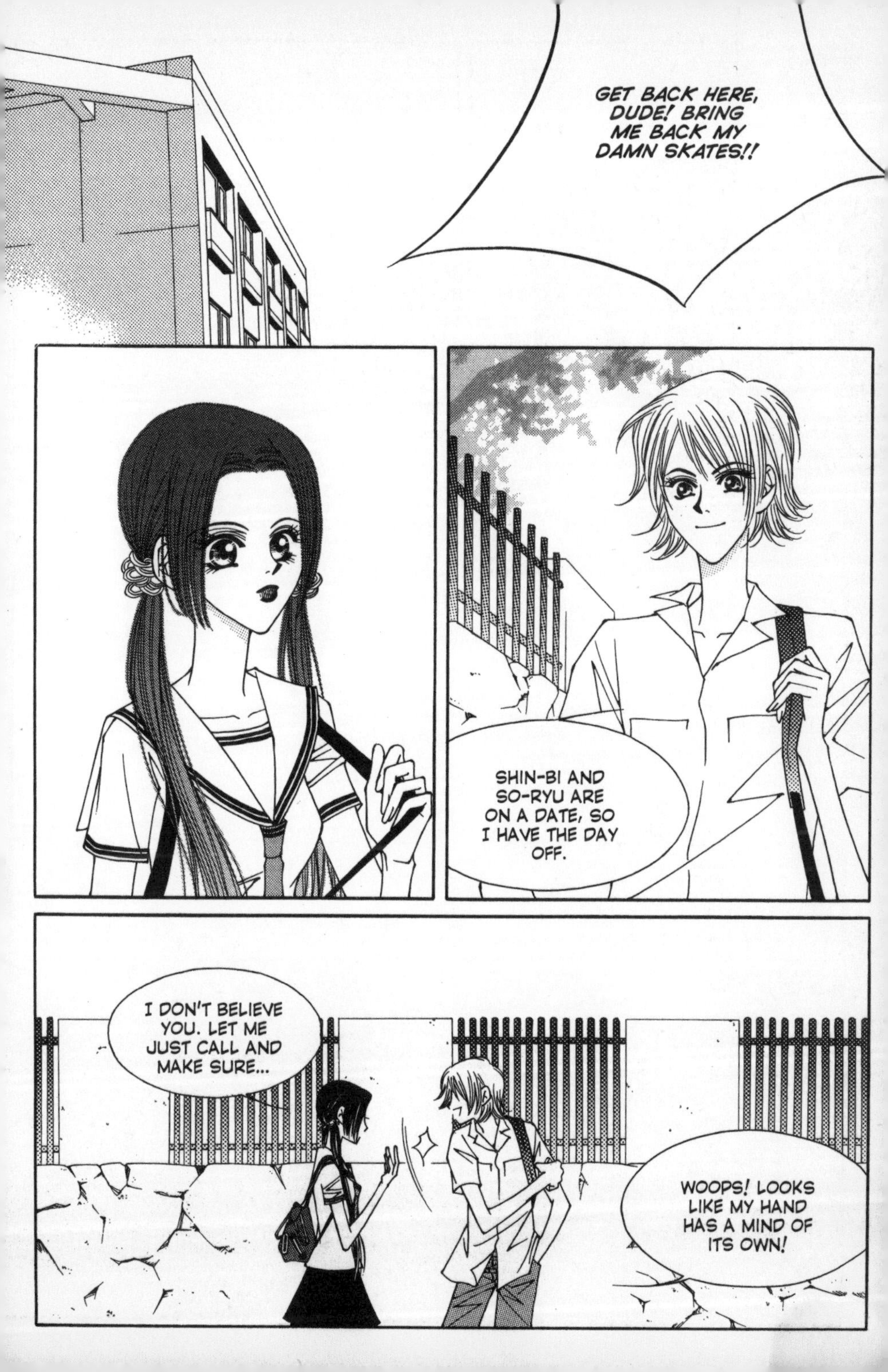
GET BACK HERE, DUDE! BRING ME BACK MY DAMN SKATES!!
SHIN-BI AND SO-RYU ARE ON A DATE, SO I HAVE THE DAY OFF.
I DON'T BELIEVE YOU. LET ME JUST CALL AND MAKE SURE...
WOOPS! LOOKS LIKE MY HAND HAS A MIND OF ITS OWN!

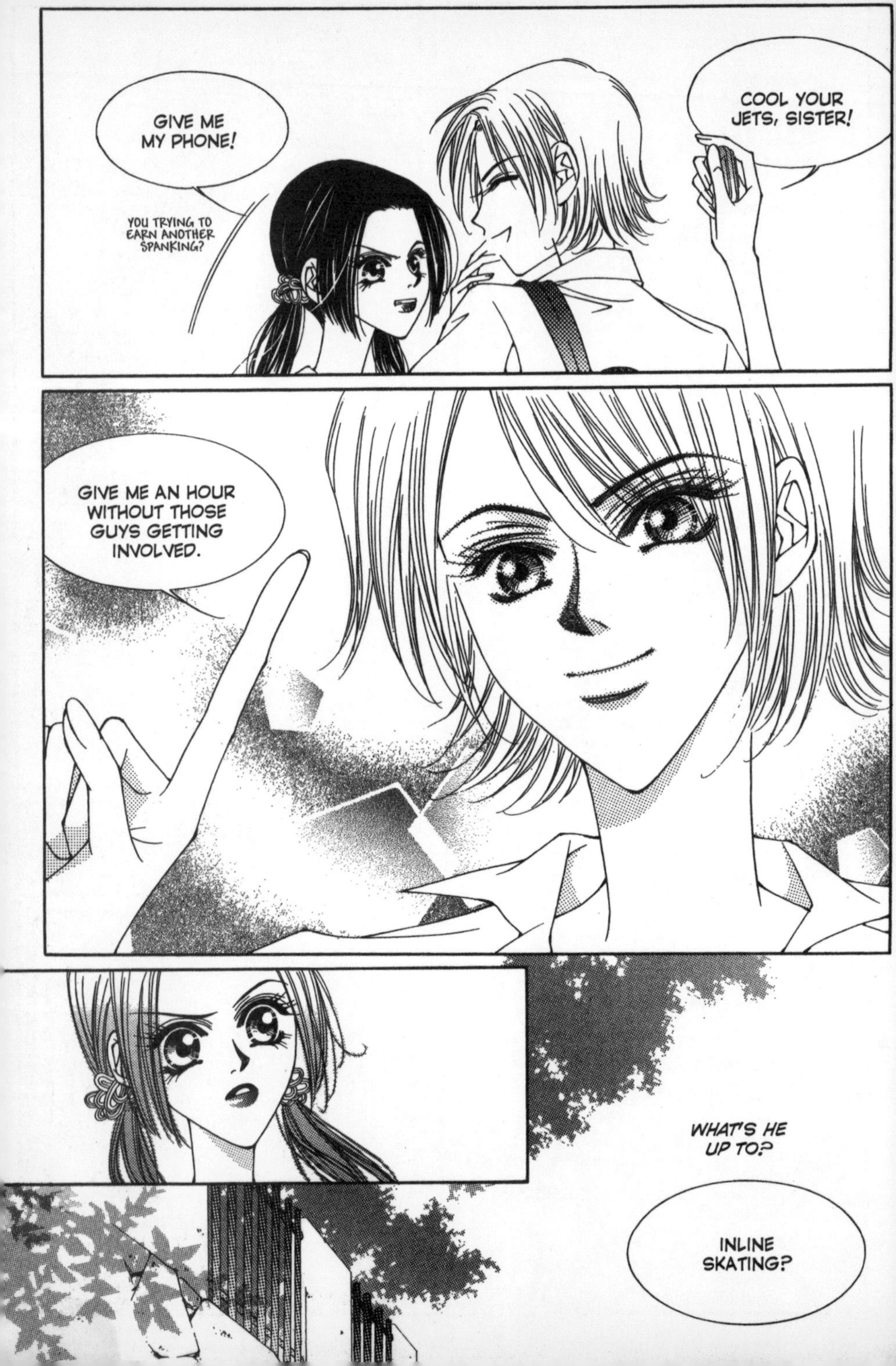
GIVE ME MY PHONE!
YOU TRYING TO EARN ANOTHER SPANKING?
COOL YOUR JETS, SISTER!
GIVE ME AN HOUR WITHOUT THOSE GUYS GETTING INVOLVED.
WHAT'S HE UP TO?
INLINE SKATING?

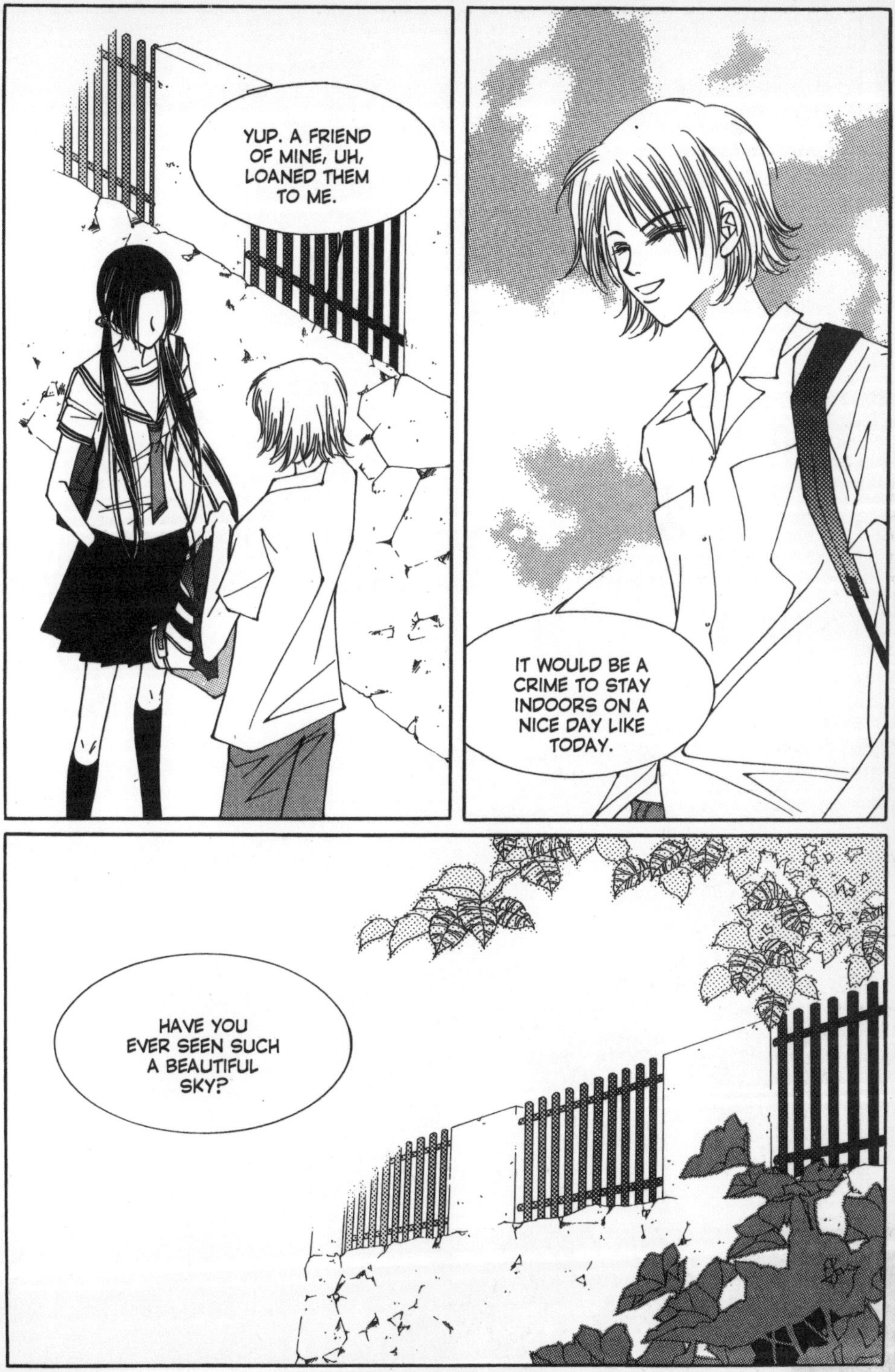
YUP. A FRIEND OF MINE, UH, LOANED THEM TO ME.
IT WOULD BE A CRIME TO STAY INDOORS ON A NICE DAY LIKE TODAY.
HAVE YOU EVER SEEN SUCH A BEAUTIFUL SKY?

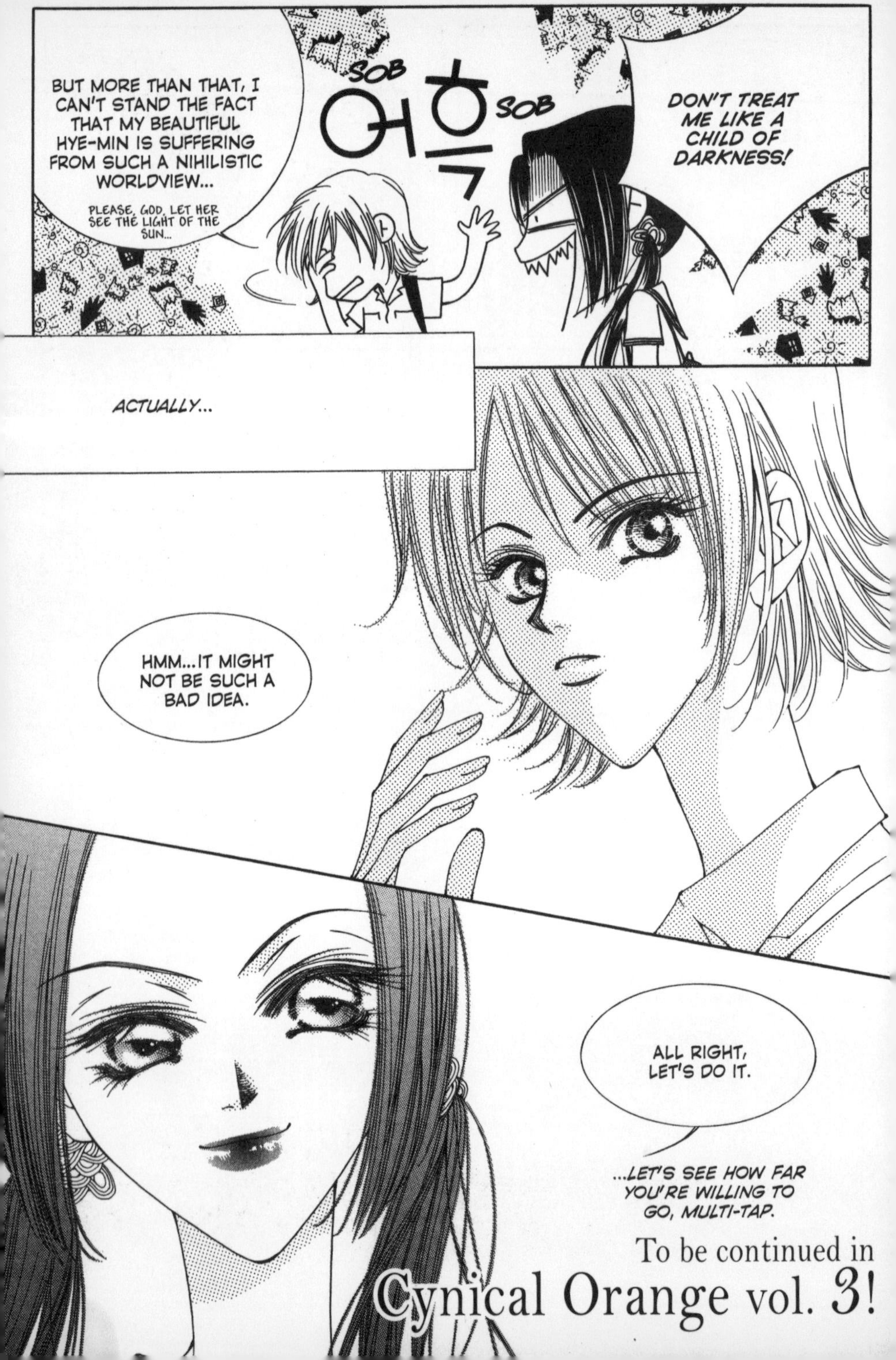
BUT MORE THAN THAT, I CAN'T STAND THE FACT THAT MY BEAUTIFUL HYE-MIN IS SUFFERING FROM SUCH A NIHILISTIC WORLDVIEW...
PLEASE, GOD, LET HER SEE THE LIGHT OF THE SUN...
SOB
SOB
DON'T TREAT ME LIKE A CHILD OF DARKNESS!
ACTUALLY...
HMM...IT MIGHT NOT BE SUCH A BAD IDEA.
ALL RIGHT, LET'S DO IT.
...LET'S SEE HOW FAR YOU'RE WILLING TO GO, MULTI-TAP.
To be continued in
Cynical Orange vol. 3!

BORA? IS THAT A NEW CHARACTER? SHE LOOKS LIKE A NICE GIRL.
I GUESS YOU ARE CAPABLE OF DRAWING A KIND FACE AFTER ALL.
YEAH. SHE LOOKS LIKE SHE HAS A WARM HEART.
I CAN DRAW NICE STUFF WHEN I SET MY MIND TO IT.
BUT WHEN IS SHE GOING TO SHOW HER TRUE FACE?
YOUR CHARACTERS ARE NEVER THE WAY THEY APPEAR TO BE!!
SHE'S HIDING SOMETHING FOR SURE!
MWA-
HA-HA
WHY, OH WHY...?

=BONUS TRACK=

THE TRUTH IS OUT THERE.

SHIN-BI OH

- BIRTHDAY: JULY 10 (CANCER)
- BLOOD TYPE: A
- HEIGHT: 182CM
- WEIGHT: 68KG
- CHARACTERISTIC: HIS APPEARANCE DENOTES THE SIDE-EFFECTS OF MODERN MEDICINE. (HIS HAIR IS NATURALLY WHITE DUE TO PARENTAL DRUG ABUSE.)

AS FAR AS THIS CHARACTER IS CONCERNED, I'M GIVING MYSELF FREE REIN. THIS MAKES IT A LOT MORE FUN FOR ME, AS AN ARTIST, TO DRAW HIM...BUT WILL IT CONFUSE MY READERS? SHIN-BI'S APPEARANCE IS INSPIRED BY SALIERI FROM THE MOVIE AMADEUS. (REALLY?) I MADE HIS HAIR WHITE BASED ON MY FRIEND'S EXPERIENCE, SO PLEASE DON'T ASK ME HOW POSSIBLE IT MIGHT BE. (EVEN THOUGH IT IS...)

DRESS FEATURE:
FRENCH COSTUME OF 1760S THIS IS MY FAVORITE STYLE IN THE ENTIRE HISTORY OF MALE ATTIRE. ELEGANT AND REFINED, IT LOOKS GOOD ON ANYONE, YOUNG OR OLD, STICK THIN OR POT-BELLIED. THE EMBROIDERY IS UNREALISTIC, AND IT'S DECORATED WITH LACEWORK MADE POPULAR BY THE MARQUISE DE POMPADOUR! GREAT JOB, ROCOCO!

SO-RYU HEO

•BIRTHDAY: OCTOBER 3 (LIBRA)
•BLOOD TYPE: O
•HEIGHT: 158CM
•WEIGHT: 47KG
•CHARACTERISTIC: AN ULTRA-POWERFUL KILLING MACHINE RESIDES WITHIN HER. IT'S POWERED BY ALCOHOL. ONCE ACTIVATED, SHE LOSES ALL ABILITY FOR RATIONAL THOUGHT.

MY ORIGINAL INTENT WAS TO CREATE A CUTE, PETITE GIRL, BUT SOMEHOW SHE TURNED INTO A TRULY VIOLENT FEMALE. EVEN HER NAME, SO-RYU, IS TAKEN FROM SO-RYUKEN, A MIGHTY SKILL FROM <STREET FIGHTER>!

DRESS FEATURE:
CRINOLIN STYLE OF EARLY 1860S
A LAYERED SKIRT WITH A TRULY AMAZING CIRCUMFERENCE. THE BELL-SHAPE IS UPHELD BY SEVERAL METAL HOOPS UNDERNEATH. WEARING THIS SKIRT CAN LITERALLY COST YOUR LIFE. IT MAKES ESCAPING FROM FIRE EXTREMELY DIFFICULT.

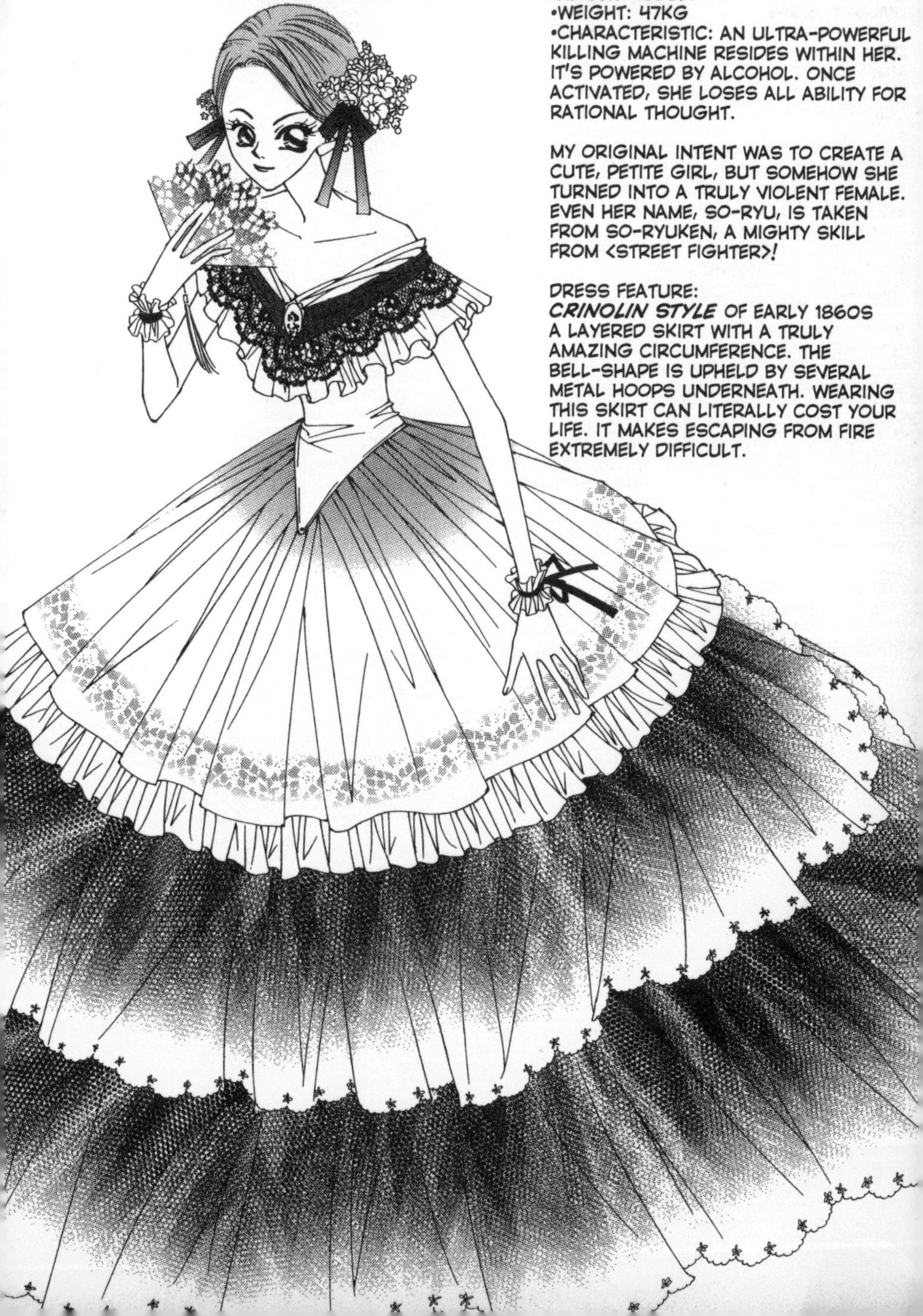

THE FIRST DREAM OF THE NEW YEAR

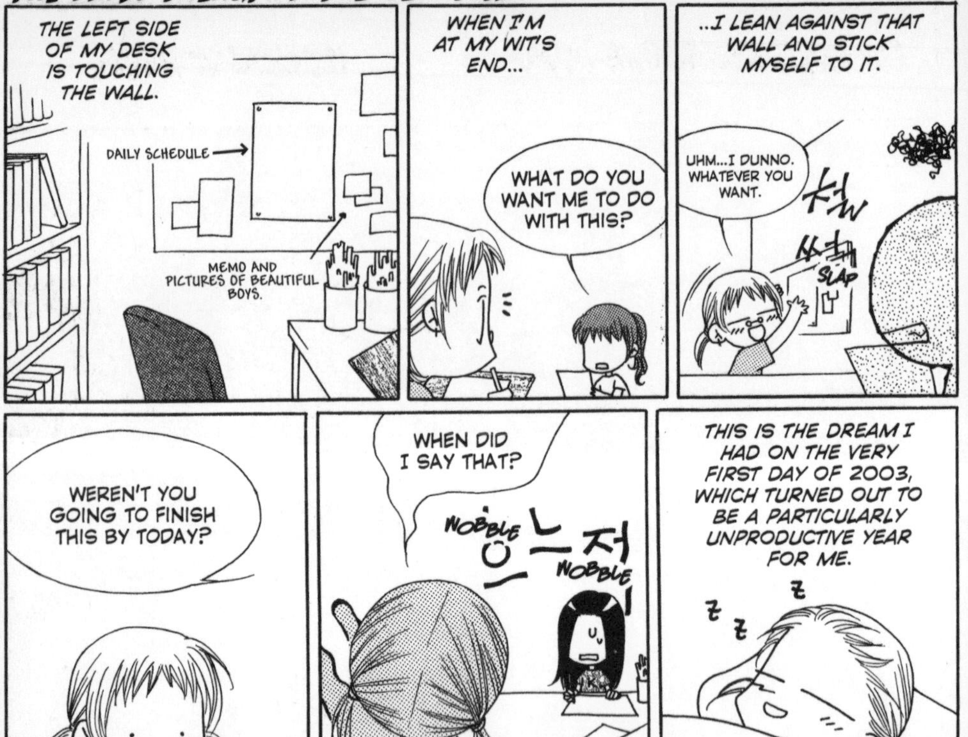
THE LEFT SIDE OF MY DESK IS TOUCHING THE WALL.
DAILY SCHEDULE
MEMO AND PICTURES OF BEAUTIFUL BOYS.
WHEN I'M AT MY WIT'S END...
WHAT DO YOU WANT ME TO DO WITH THIS?
...I LEAN AGAINST THAT WALL AND STICK MYSELF TO IT.
UHM...I DUNNO. WHATEVER YOU WANT.
SLAP
WEREN'T YOU GOING TO FINISH THIS BY TODAY?
WHEN DID I SAY THAT?
WOBBLE
WOBBLE
THIS IS THE DREAM I HAD ON THE VERY FIRST DAY OF 2003, WHICH TURNED OUT TO BE A PARTICULARLY UNPRODUCTIVE YEAR FOR ME.
Z
Z
Z
DON'T YOU HAVE TO TURN IT IN BY TONIGHT? DO YOU THINK YOU CAN MAKE IT?
BEATS ME.
STICK
SHUK
SHUK
SHUK

WHAT IS THE MEANING OF THIS DREAM?

1. YOU MIGHT GET STABBED BY SOMEONE YOU TRUSTED.
2. BLOOD IS AN AUSPICIOUS SIGN, SO IT'S A GOOD OMEN.
3. EITHER OF ONE OF MY FRIENDS OR BOTH OF THEM ARE PLOTTING TO KILL ME.

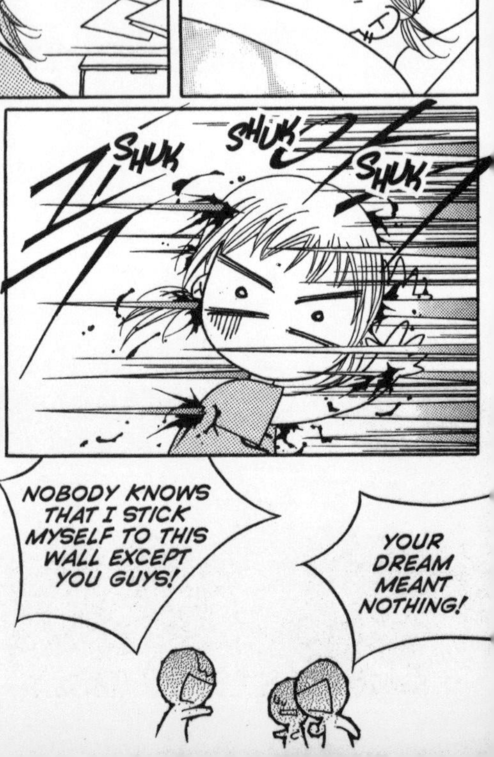
NOBODY KNOWS THAT I STICK MYSELF TO THIS WALL EXCEPT YOU GUYS!
YOUR DREAM MEANT NOTHING!

FORMULA SSANGMUN-DONG

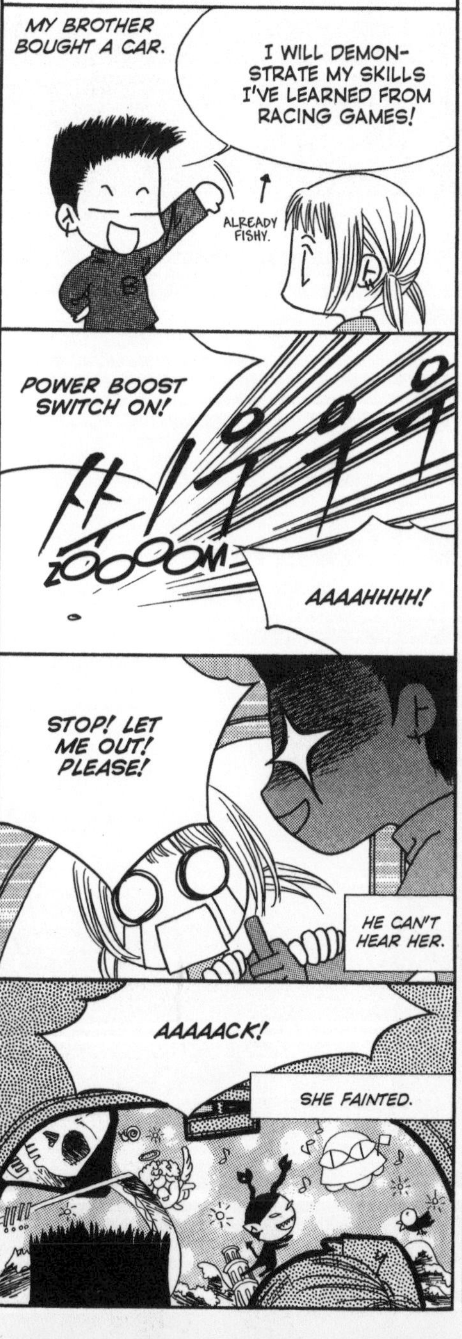

MY BROTHER BOUGHT A CAR.
I WILL DEMON-STRATE MY SKILLS I'VE LEARNED FROM RACING GAMES!
ALREADY FISHY.
POWER BOOST SWITCH ON!
ZOOOOOM
AAAAHHHH!
STOP! LET ME OUT! PLEASE!
HE CAN'T HEAR HER.
AAAAACK!
SHE FAINTED.

IRON-MASK RACER

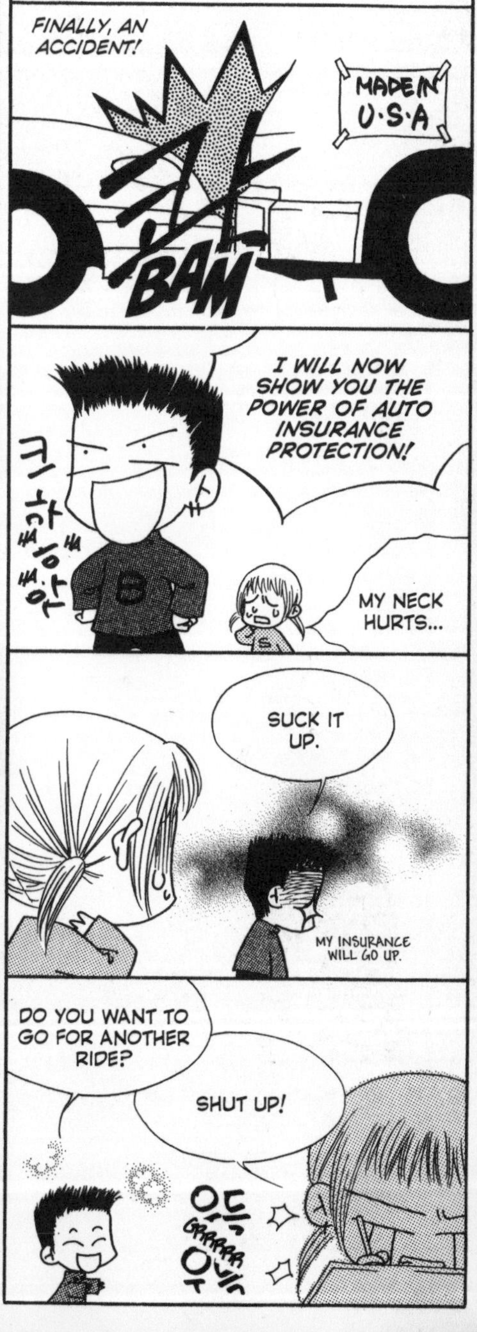

FINALLY, AN ACCIDENT!
MADE IN U·S·A
BAM
I WILL NOW SHOW YOU THE POWER OF AUTO INSURANCE PROTECTION!
HA HA HA HA
MY NECK HURTS...
SUCK IT UP.
MY INSURANCE WILL GO UP.
DO YOU WANT TO GO FOR ANOTHER RIDE?
SHUT UP!
GRRRRR

CHOCOLAT

vol.3

JiSang Shin·Geo

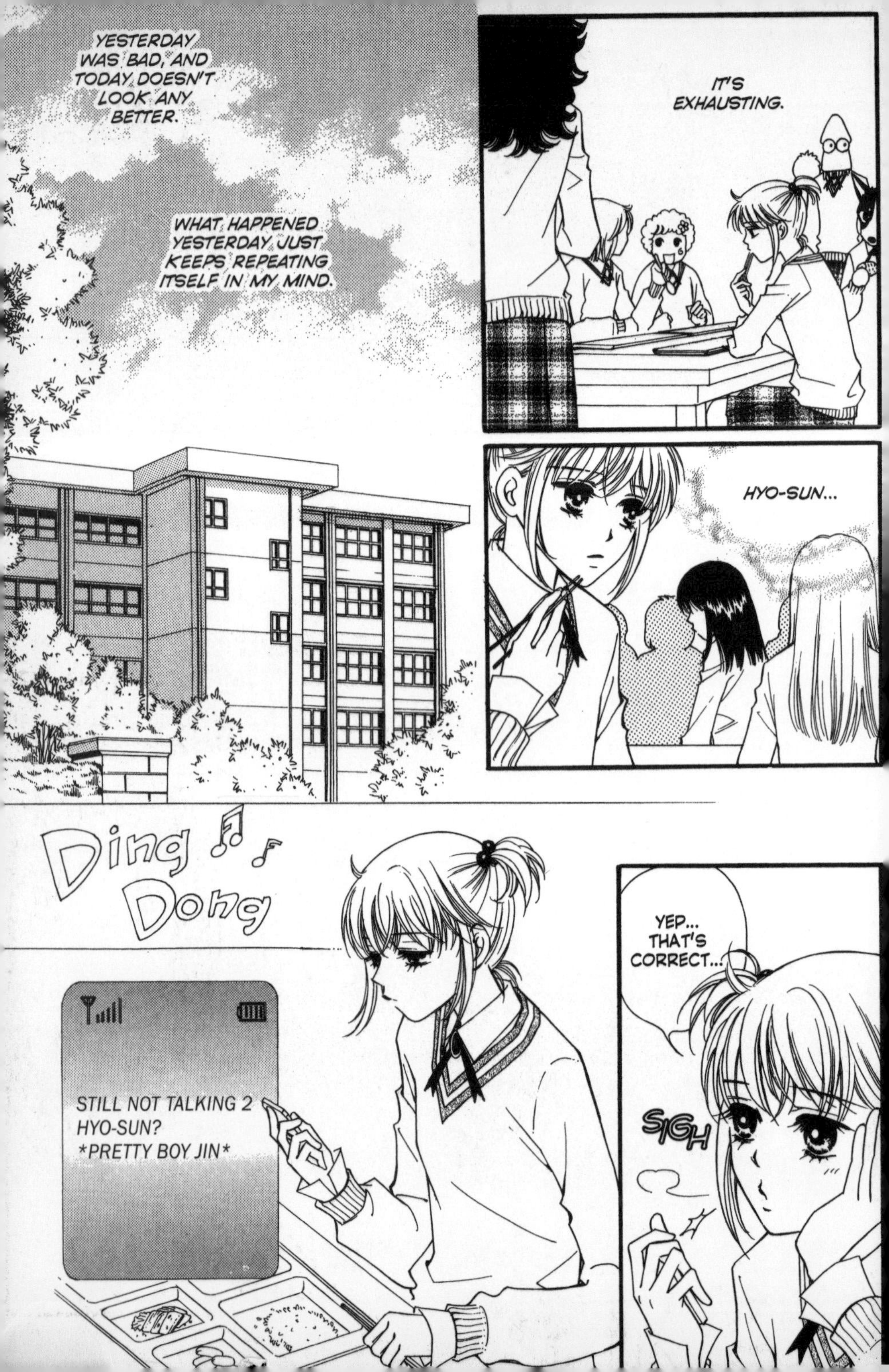
YESTERDAY WAS BAD, AND TODAY DOESN'T LOOK ANY BETTER.
WHAT HAPPENED YESTERDAY JUST KEEPS REPEATING ITSELF IN MY MIND.
IT'S EXHAUSTING.
HYO-SUN...
Ding Dong
STILL NOT TALKING 2 HYO-SUN? *PRETTY BOY JIN*
YEP... THAT'S CORRECT...
SIGH

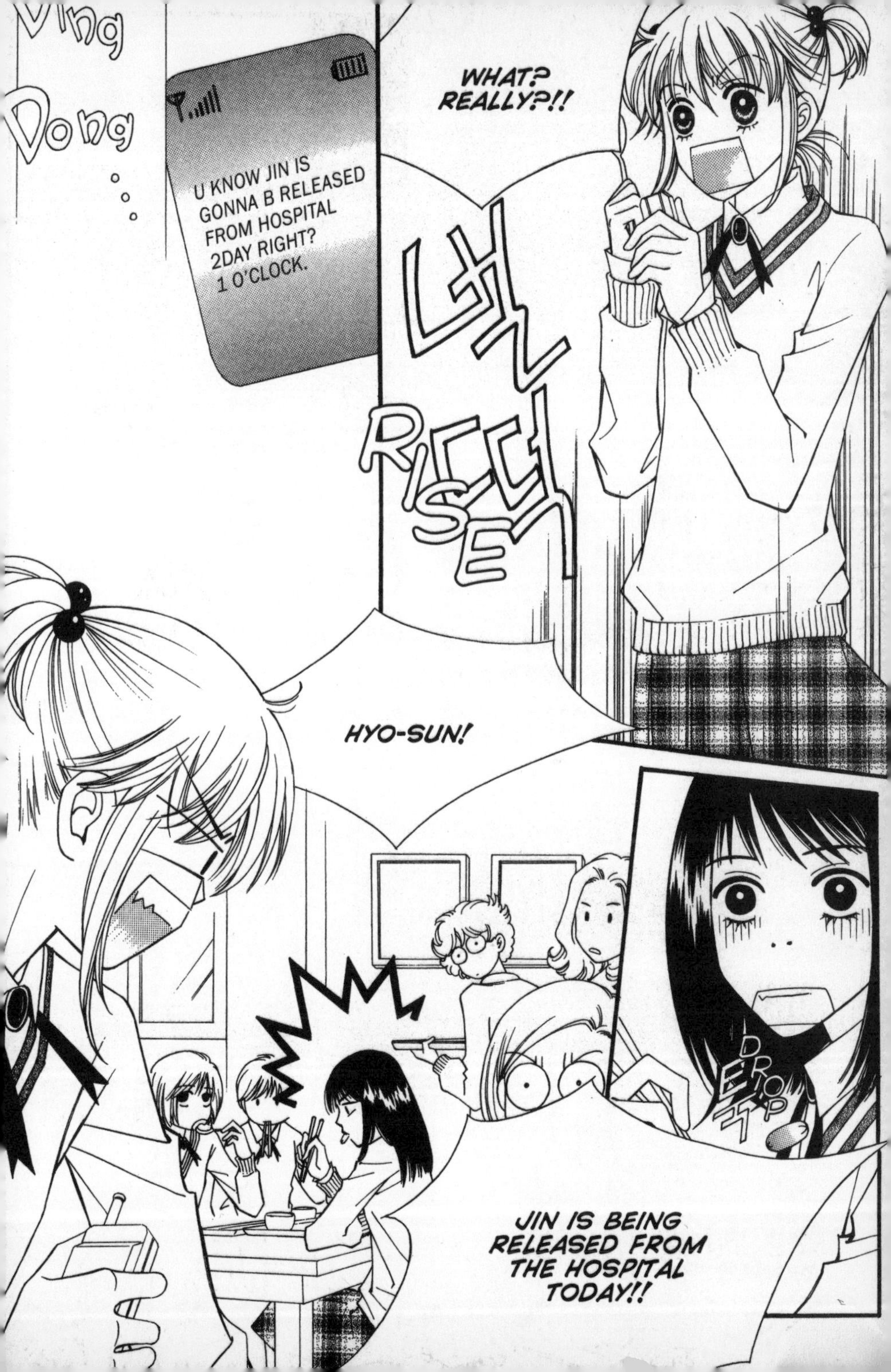
Dong
U KNOW JIN IS GONNA B RELEASED FROM HOSPITAL 2DAY RIGHT? 1 O'CLOCK.
WHAT? REALLY?!!
RISE
HYO-SUN!
JIN IS BEING RELEASED FROM THE HOSPITAL TODAY!!
DROP

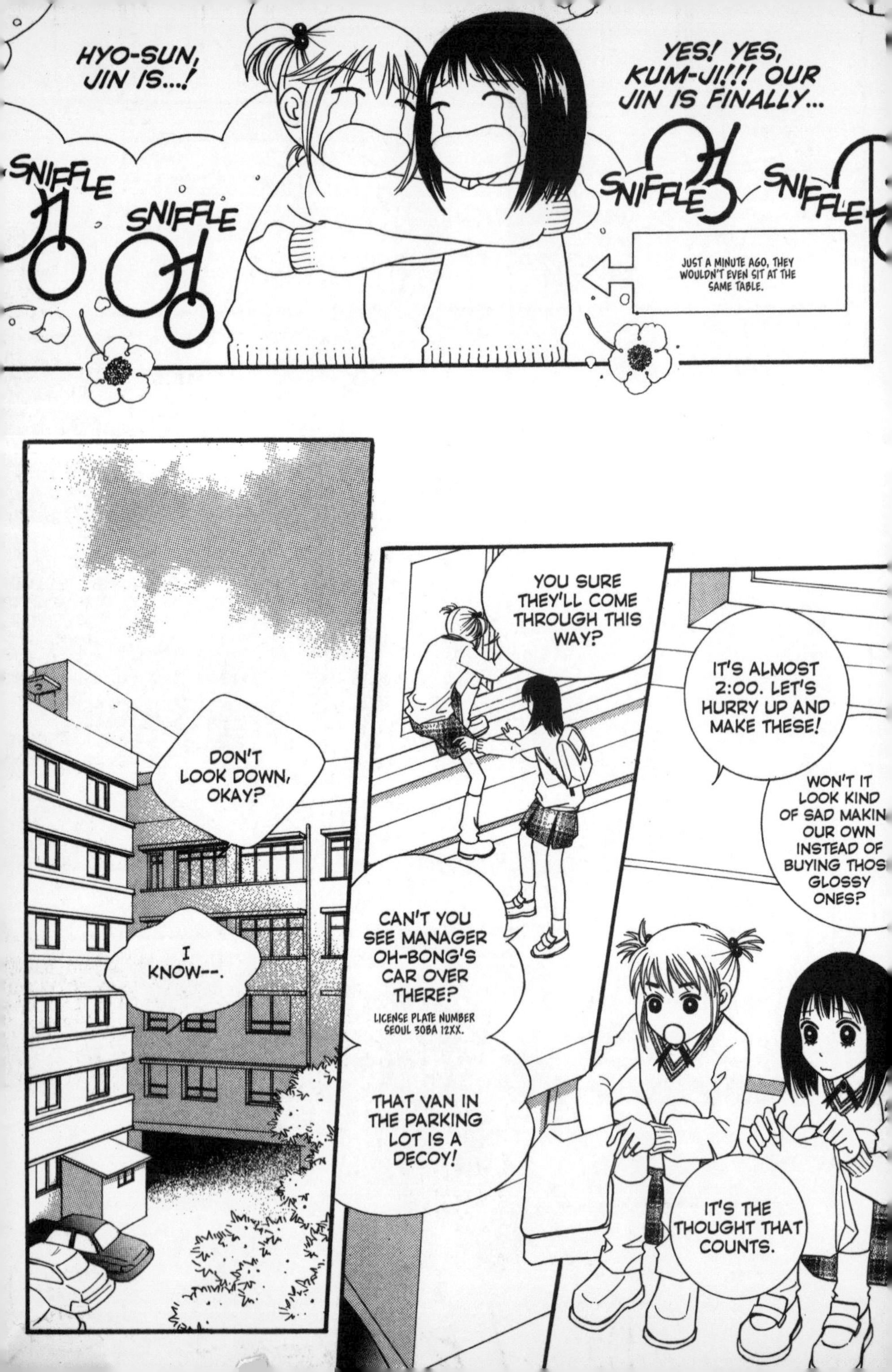
HYO-SUN, JIN IS...!
YES! YES, KUM-JI!!! OUR JIN IS FINALLY...
SNIFFLE
SNIFFLE
SNIFFLE
SNIFFLE
JUST A MINUTE AGO, THEY WOULDN'T EVEN SIT AT THE SAME TABLE.
DON'T LOOK DOWN, OKAY?
I KNOW--.
YOU SURE THEY'LL COME THROUGH THIS WAY?
CAN'T YOU SEE MANAGER OH-BONG'S CAR OVER THERE?
LICENSE PLATE NUMBER SEOUL 30BA 12XX.
THAT VAN IN THE PARKING LOT IS A DECOY!
IT'S ALMOST 2:00. LET'S HURRY UP AND MAKE THESE!
WON'T IT LOOK KIND OF SAD MAKIN OUR OWN INSTEAD OF BUYING THOS GLOSSY ONES?
IT'S THE THOUGHT THAT COUNTS.

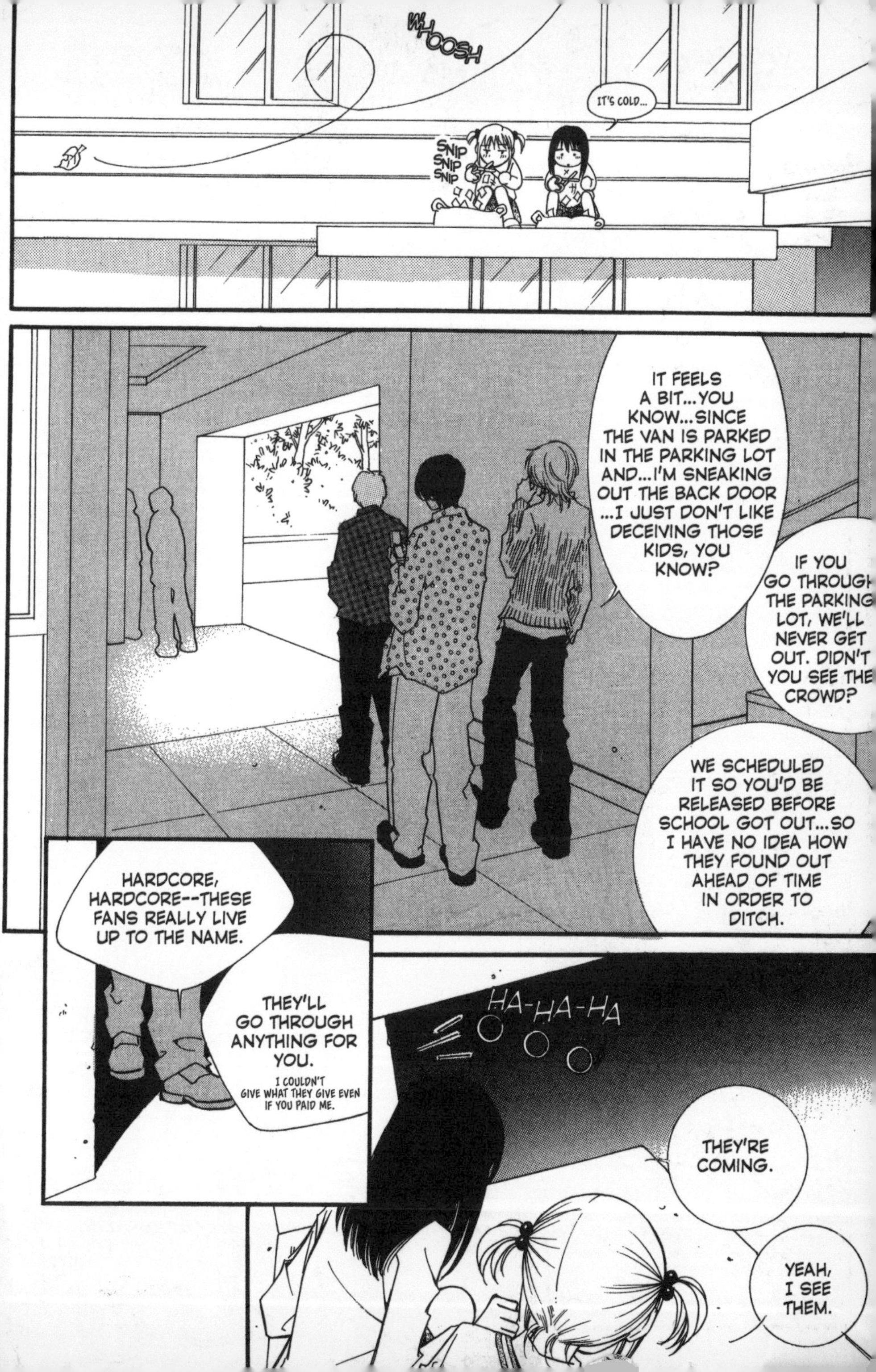
WHOOSH
SNIP SNIP SNIP
IT'S COLD...
IT FEELS A BIT...YOU KNOW...SINCE THE VAN IS PARKED IN THE PARKING LOT AND...I'M SNEAKING OUT THE BACK DOOR ...I JUST DON'T LIKE DECEIVING THOSE KIDS, YOU KNOW?
IF YOU GO THROUGH THE PARKING LOT, WE'LL NEVER GET OUT. DIDN'T YOU SEE THE CROWD?
WE SCHEDULED IT SO YOU'D BE RELEASED BEFORE SCHOOL GOT OUT...SO I HAVE NO IDEA HOW THEY FOUND OUT AHEAD OF TIME IN ORDER TO DITCH.
HARDCORE, HARDCORE--THESE FANS REALLY LIVE UP TO THE NAME.
THEY'LL GO THROUGH ANYTHING FOR YOU.
I COULDN'T GIVE WHAT THEY GIVE EVEN IF YOU PAID ME.
HA-HA-HA
THEY'RE COMING.
YEAH, I SEE THEM.

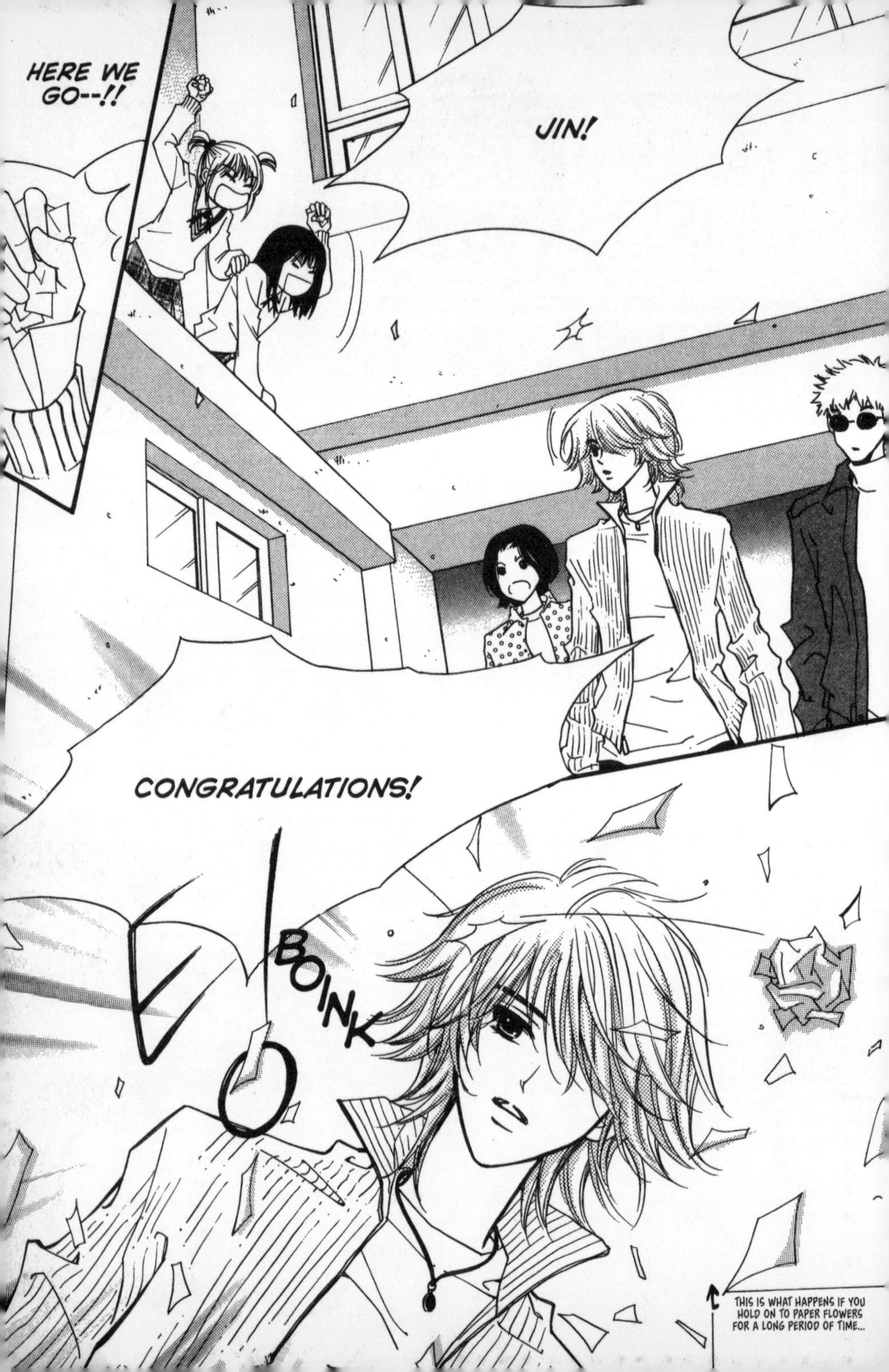
HERE WE GO--!!
JIN!
CONGRATULATIONS!
BOINK
THIS IS WHAT HAPPENS IF YOU HOLD ON TO PAPER FLOWERS FOR A LONG PERIOD OF TIME...

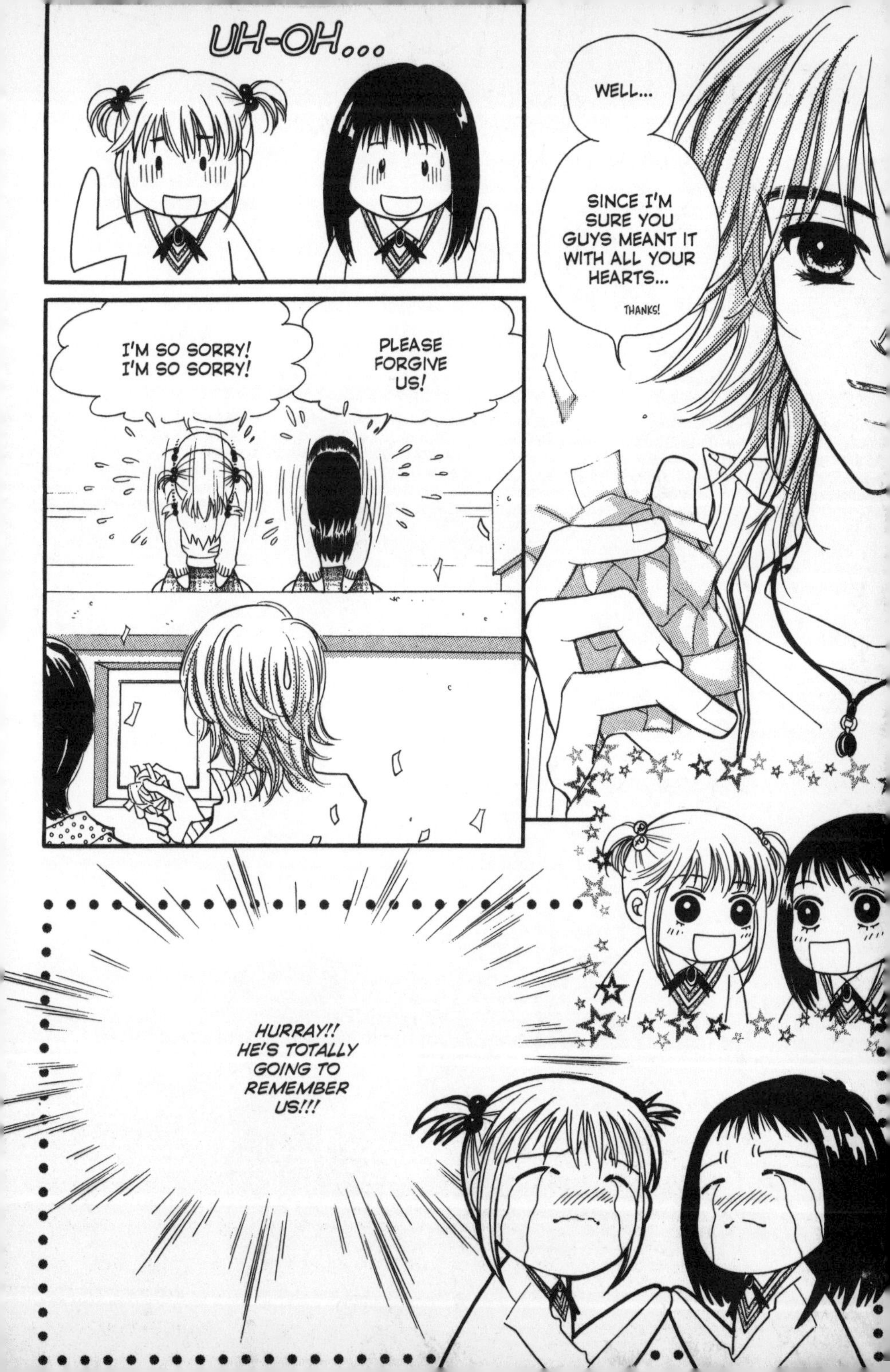
UH-OH...
I'M SO SORRY! I'M SO SORRY!
PLEASE FORGIVE US!
WELL...
SINCE I'M SURE YOU GUYS MEANT IT WITH ALL YOUR HEARTS...
THANKS!
HURRAY!! HE'S TOTALLY GOING TO REMEMBER US!!!

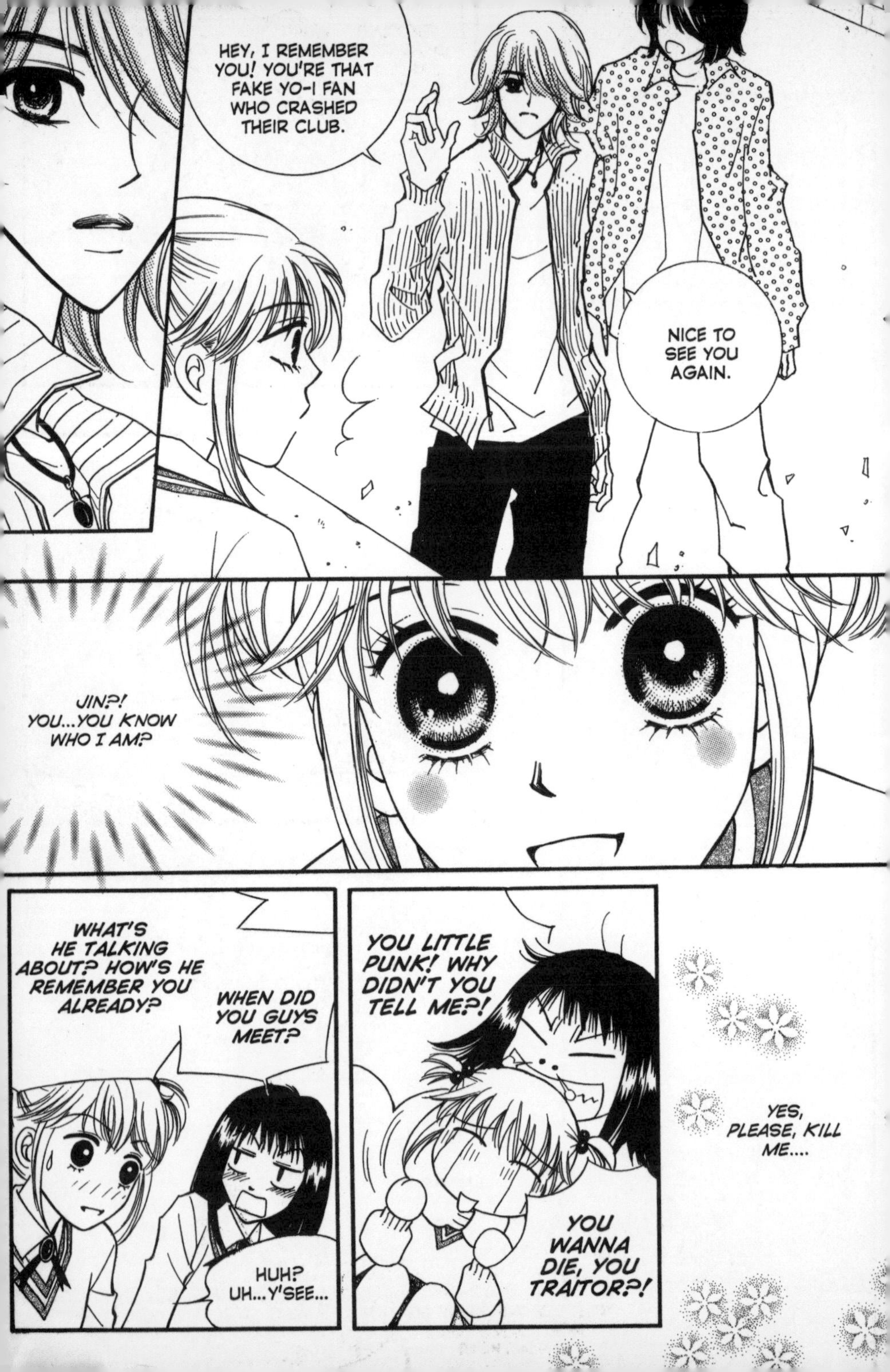
HEY, I REMEMBER YOU! YOU'RE THAT FAKE YO-I FAN WHO CRASHED THEIR CLUB.
NICE TO SEE YOU AGAIN.
JIN?! YOU...YOU KNOW WHO I AM?
WHAT'S HE TALKING ABOUT? HOW'S HE REMEMBER YOU ALREADY?
WHEN DID YOU GUYS MEET?
HUH? UH...Y'SEE...
YOU LITTLE PUNK! WHY DIDN'T YOU TELL ME?!
YOU WANNA DIE, YOU TRAITOR?!
YES, PLEASE, KILL ME....

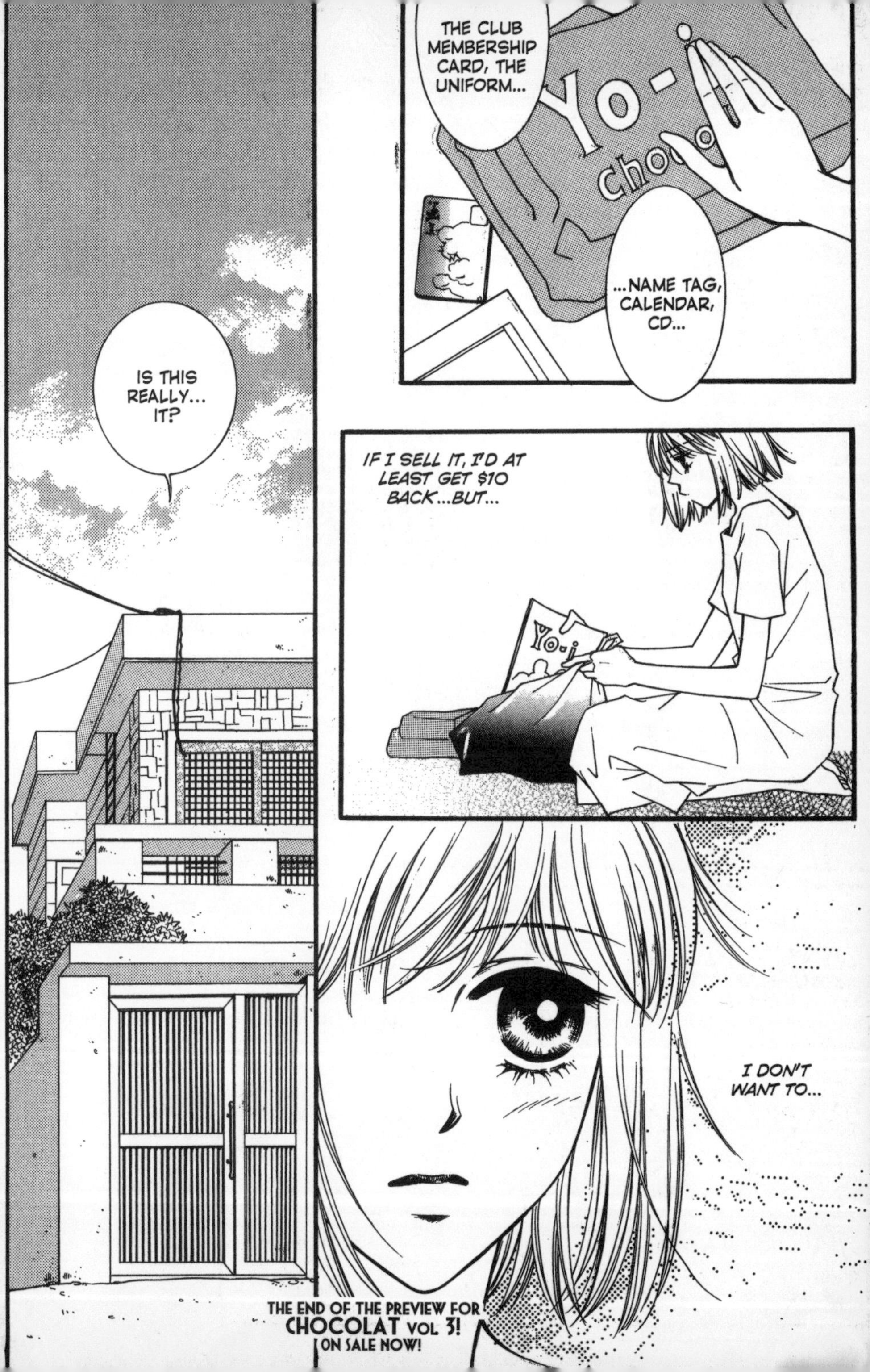
IS THIS REALLY... IT?
THE CLUB MEMBERSHIP CARD, THE UNIFORM...
...NAME TAG, CALENDAR, CD...
IF I SELL IT, I'D AT LEAST GET $10 BACK...BUT...
I DON'T WANT TO...
THE END OF THE PREVIEW FOR CHOCOLAT VOL 3! ON SALE NOW!

Danbi Original

Cynical Orange vol.2

Story and art by JiUn Yun

Translation SukHee Ryu
English Adaptation Jamie S. Rich
Touch-up and Lettering Terri Delgado · Marshall Dillon
Graphic Design EunKyung Kim

ICE Kunion

English Adaptation Editor HyeYoung Im · J. Torres
Managing Editor Marshall Dillon
Marketing Manager Erik Ko
Senior Editor JuYoun Lee
Editorial Director MoonJung Kim
Managing Director Jackie Lee
Publisher and C.E.O. JaeKook Chun

Cynical Orange © 2005 JiUn Yun
First published in Korea in 2002 by SEOUL CULTURAL PUBLISHERS, Inc.
English text translation rights arranged by SEOUL CULTURAL PUBLISHERS, Inc.
English text © 2005 ICE KUNION

All rights reserved. The events and characters presented in this book are entirely fictional.
Any similarity to persons living or dead is purely coincidental. No portion of this book may be
reproduced by any means (digital or print) without written permission from Sigongsa, except
for the purposes of review.

Published by ICE Kunion
SIGONGSA 2F Yeil Bldg. 1619-4, Seocho-dong, Seocho-gu, Seoul, 137-878, Korea

ISBN : 89-527-4478-0

First printing, August 2006
10 9 8 7 6 5 4 3 2 1
Printed in Canada

www.ICEkunion.com/www.koreanmanhwa.com